CUFFS AND COMMITMENT

FAIRLAKE

ROMEO ALEXANDER

ROMEO ALEXANDER

Editing by Jo Bird
Beta Reading by Melissa R

TREVOR

With a sigh, I leaned back, rubbing my eyes. The words on the screen were starting to blur, and I had to look at my phone to see I'd been dealing with a combination of reports and emails for almost three hours.

As a rookie, I'd told myself that if I'd known just how much paperwork being a cop involved, I'd have chosen a different career. I told myself the same thing when I became Chief. But I hadn't learned, and I swore it grew with every passing year, despite things going digital. Sometimes I thought I should have stuck with the Army, but there were reasons I'd left that life behind.

My eyes were drawn to the lower right-hand drawer of my desk, but I resisted the urge to open it. Getting lost in the past was a surefire way to find myself drifting through old memories and lingering feelings instead of getting things done. Along with the growing paperwork, I swore getting older just brought more things to think about and regrets to obsess over.

"Ugh," I grunted, pushing myself up from my desk and walking over to the glass cabinet tucked in the corner. One advantage to being chief was it was perfectly acceptable to have a bottle or three of liquor nearby. You never knew when the Fire Chief or the Mayor would show up, or God forbid, some other government figure.

Pulling the stopper from my favorite brandy, I poured myself a small measure. Despite enjoying the occasional glass, I wasn't fond of drinking a lot. Sometimes I thought it was just the idea of the alcohol that was enough, and it was a good brandy.

It was a quiet day. I hadn't heard a phone ring in the precinct for over an hour. The same couldn't be said about my computer or phone alerts, but at least the officers under my command were having a peaceful day.

Not that things happened a lot in Fairlake. Sure, small towns nestled in the Rockies weren't without their troubles, and Fairlake was no exception. Quiet and peaceful as it was for the most part, you still had angry drunks starting fights. And the town wasn't without its bullies and abusers, people who liked taking their anger out on their spouse or children. There was the occasional break-in, accidental gun firing, and things that happened when people got stupid ideas in their heads.

Fairlake had always been a quiet place to live, safer than many others, but things had been a little tense lately. And there was the unsettling rumor that some meth manufacturers were inching back into the woods outside town. I couldn't say whether they had moved back in full force, but there were troubling signs. Reports of strangers in the woods were more frequent, and there was an unsettling uptick of break-ins and vandalism at the edges of town.

With a grimace, I poured myself another measure of brandy before dropping into my seat and opening the bottom drawer despite my decision not to. I stared at the worn frame holding the old picture. I was barely eighteen, my black hair without a trace of the white apparent as I crept into my late forties. The lines on my forehead wouldn't appear for another decade or so, and my face had thinned, giving me the nearly square jaw that only made me seem harder than I liked sometimes.

Beside me, Troy was as bright and cheerful as ever as our arms wrapped around each other's shoulders. We were both squinting, but even nearly three decades later, I could remember the exact shade of blue his eyes had been and how they always crinkled when he'd laughed or smiled, which was most of the time. We were smiling in the picture, which I didn't do as often lately. We were both so excited to leave Fairlake behind, joining the Corps, and eager to see what the world had to offer us outside this little town.

Now I was back here, planted for life, while Troy was planted six feet under, in the box his grieving parents had chosen for him only a few years after the picture had been taken.

I was spared little more than a sour twist of my stomach by a soft knock at my office door. Setting the glass behind the screen to conceal it, I cleared my throat. "Enter."

Expecting one of my officers, I raised a brow when Fire Chief Borton walked in instead. "Aaron, what brings you around these parts? And please tell me you aren't here over something Bennett did. He's been contained all day and behaving himself...for once."

Borton chuckled at the mention of easily the most infamous and well-liked of my officers. "Your little troublemaker hasn't been seen. I came to wish you a happy birthday and see if you'll change your mind about doing something about it."

"I told you I'd celebrate my birthday when I officially went 'over the hill.' And we agreed that's fifty, so you're four years too soon," I told him dryly, picking up my glass and taking a sip. I didn't want my officers to see me drinking in the office, but Aaron couldn't judge me when I knew he kept a couple of bottles of his own in his office. "So, no."

"Aren't you getting too old to be prissy about your birthday?"

"You're getting to be an old hen, Borton. Peck peck peck, all the time."

Aaron chuckled again, which told me he was in one of his good moods. That was probably because, as he'd reported, Bennett had not been over to the station today, usually under the guise of visiting a couple of his firefighters and finding trouble somewhere along the way. It might have also had something to do with the fact that there was little trouble under either of his roofs, except that he had two teenagers at home. Still, his mood wasn't usually so playful, even if it was manifesting as an excuse to harass me.

"What has you so happy?" I asked, raising a brow. "Please tell me you didn't go behind my back to plan something. I'd hate to end our friendship by murder."

"Murder," he snorted. "As if you'd get rid of me that easily."

"Okay," I said, setting my glass down and leaning forward, gently closing the drawer I'd accidentally left open. "Then—?"

"Do you remember that little case I asked you to nudge open last year?" Borton asked, no longer bothering to conceal how pleased he was.

I thought about it for a moment and then grunted. "The one with that firefighter of yours...Julian."

"That's the one."

Technically it had been a favor between professionals, but Borton and I were friends as much as we were coworkers. When he'd explained his suspicions of a not-so-subtle cover-up that had screwed over his newest firefighter and wondered if I could help add a little pressure, I'd been willing. Not just because we were friends, I knew he would never ask me to stir up a political pot for nothing. Aaron had good instincts, and I'd always thought he'd potentially missed out on a career as a cop.

"Did you hear any news?" I asked.

"Bones is under investigation, and the asshole who started the whole thing is apparently on unpaid leave," Borton said with a smile. "It only took a year for them to get off their asses."

"The reminder passed my desk a couple of months ago," I said, steepling my fingers under my chin. "I called Police Chief Durkins and brought it up again. He assured me the matter was being looked into, but from his tone, I didn't think so. Probably worried that Fire Chief Bones might try to bring him down with him."

"I should've known you'd interfere," Aaron said, grinning. "Alright, so how'd you get the fire under his ass?"

"Casually mentioned that I'm on pretty good terms with Mayor Collins, the governor's favorite brother-in-law," I said with a smirk. "Durkins is a hardheaded moron, but he can find enough brain cells floating around in that thick skull of his to make sense of two plus two. If he didn't investigate, someone else was going to. At least this way, they could work together to save their asses and take out the lowest rung on the ladder."

Aaron walked over to the cabinet, rummaging around for the whiskey I kept in case he or Collins popped in for a visit. "Didn't think to mention this to me?"

"My grandfather liked to tell me that when you had ducks, chickens, and geese running around, it was better to wait till the egg hatched before telling what color the chick would be," I said, taking a sip.

"I'm no expert, but there should be a big difference between the size of a goose egg and a chicken egg."

"And there's a big difference between thinking my words made Durkins get his head out of his ass and knowing they did."

Aaron chuckled, finally taking a seat on the other side of my desk. "It's nice to have a few good friends in your pocket."

"Oh yeah, this is why I got into this job, the politics," I said dryly.

He eyed me over the rim of his glass. "Weren't you in intelligence or something in the service?"

"Something like that," I said, rolling my eyes. "And I wish everyone would quit getting these weird ideas about that. Wasn't like I was a spy."

"No, but you talk a bit when you're drunk. You certainly had to do your fair share of outmaneuvering people."

"Also did a lot of trying not to get shot," I said.

Despite the consensus that the wars in the Middle East had only been Desert Storm and then a decade later in Afghanistan, there had been more than enough action on the ground in the intervening years. Most of it was 'peacekeeping' and the occasional operation that was either admitted to or denied, but it was still enough for some to see action. Some, like myself, were 'lucky' enough to have made it through. Others, like Troy, had been unlucky, and their last sights had been of that sun-baked hell hole.

Being morose didn't exactly do a lot to deter him. "Right. Well, don't pretend as if you don't enjoy sticking them on the hook and watching them squirm."

That much I couldn't deny. Fire Chief Bones had been told that one of his own had been sleeping with an underage girl, and rather than do his due diligence, he had shoved it under the rug, taken the whistleblower, and pushed him onto Borton. Admittedly, Julian was doing a lot better in Fairlake, especially since he was apparently dating one of Aaron's other firefighters. Still, he had roped Durkins into the affair, and they'd both broken the law.

That was bad enough, but the idea they had abused their positions to avoid...what? Rocking the boat? Potentially looking bad as the ones in charge? It wasn't Bones' job to make sure his people obeyed the law. People would do what they were going to do, right or wrong. It had still been his job to take the accusation seriously and investigate it, and it had been Durkins' job to ensure the law had been upheld.

"I'm not a fan of the way I had to do it," I admitted, tapping one finger on the back of my other hand. "But if that's the way to get things moving like they're supposed to, sure, I get some pleasure in that."

Ends justifying means was a slippery slope that even the noblest people could find themselves slipping down. I wasn't a fan of underhanded methods to ensure things were done properly and hadn't been since my time in the Corps. I wasn't naive, though. Sometimes the only way to make sure things were done was underhanded methods. That didn't mean I would rely on them, but the tools were always there if necessity came knocking.

"You're over there wondering if it was a good thing or not," Aaron said, raising a brow.

"If it was necessary or not," I corrected, picking up my glass. "That it resulted in a good thing is beside the point."

Not that it was necessarily a complete win. Putting pressure on the neighboring town of Fovel could easily come back and bite us. Bones would probably come through just fine and let things go once the dust settled, but Durkins? The man was an idiot, but he had a long memory and more than a little bit of cunning. His pride was the worst part of him, and I knew I had pricked it by stepping into his territory. I strongly suspected I wouldn't get much help from him in the next year or two, even if I needed it.

I had good men and women working for me, but they couldn't be everywhere or do everything. Neither Fovel nor Fairlake were large enough to have plenty of officers on standby if something particularly messy cropped up. Hell, it had only been a few months since there'd been a violent kidnapping and car chase. The victim, a local by the name of Devin Mitchell, had been lucky his kidnapper, an up-and-coming drug 'kingpin' out of Denver, had been thwarted. If the car had reached the woods, I would have needed to pull resources from Fovel. Something Durkins couldn't deny me, but he could drag his heels in a way that wouldn't have drawn attention. Just that little hindrance could have been enough to make the difference between ending everything right and not. It hadn't come to that, but with the alarming rise in issues on the borders of Fairlake, that could be a problem soon.

"You worry too much about that shit," Borton said with a shake of his head. "You did a good thing."

"I made a good thing happen through ways that might not be all that good," I corrected, feeling an old argument coming. "Sometimes the way a thing goes down matters more than how it ends up."

"You did something you felt you had to do to make the right things happen for the right reasons."

"Plenty of awful things have been done for the right reasons. Road to hell and all."

Borton sighed. "You get way too hung up on this stuff."

"I could say you don't get hung up on it enough," I pointed out.

If anything, the disagreement was comfortable in its familiarity. It wasn't the first time we disagreed on how to handle something, and it wouldn't be the last. I knew, in this case, it was a simple matter for him. One of his own had been harmed, and he wanted to see that wrong righted. He could be just as firm and gruff with his firefighters as I was with my officers, but there wasn't a soul alive who didn't acknowledge that he cared a great deal about his team.

He would, with little hesitation and probably little regret, cause a great deal of harm to someone who hurt the people he cared about. It was, as he'd confessed to me once after a few too many after-hours drinks in my office, the number one reason he had become a firefighter instead of a cop. He wanted to do his part to help this town but didn't want to put himself in a position where he would do something he couldn't take back.

I understood his position all too well, but I still had a responsibility to the community and the law, not just my officers. No matter how much I might want to, there was no way to justify going too far outside the law to get something done. This latest act toed the line a little but was still allowed.

"If you throw the word 'duty' at me, I might just forget my promise and set up a surprise birthday party for you anyway," Aaron warned me.

I finally chuckled. "Why should I have to? You already know what I'm going to say. It spares me having to repeat myself."

He sighed, brow creasing at a soft thump from the doorway, followed by distressed beeping. "What the hell was that?"

My features smoothed as I repressed a sigh. "A Roomba."

"A Roomba?" he asked, twisting in his chair to stare at my open doorway.

It had not been my idea, and in fact, I'd been against the entire thing from the beginning. My 'innocent' officers could all pretend otherwise, but I knew full well who the ringleader behind the little automated vacuum's arrival at the precinct had been. I would give Bennett credit, he'd managed to pull off a convincing act of innocence, but I'd worked with him for too long to believe it.

"Not my idea," I said.

"What's...on its head?" Aaron asked.

I finally gave in to temptation and looked between the chairs as the device whirred its way to the center of the office with remarkable precision. Perched atop was the strangest sight, a disc with what appeared to be small tubes pushed into it at an angle, though a few tubes were more upright than others. Right above those was a small, plastic object. It took me a moment before I realized it was a flower bud of some sort.

"It's..." I began, blinking when a flame appeared in the center of the flower. We both watched as it spread, and a high-pitched song began to play as the bud opened up. Each petal was adorned with a candle as the flaming flower spun, still shrilly touting happy birthday. "Bennett."

We both jerked back when four of the tubes let loose a pop, sending colorful confetti in four different directions. I finally sighed when some drifted to land in my glass. Plucking it out, I took another drink as the remaining four tubes gave another loud pop, sending more colorful paper in every direction. As I'd noticed before, some of the tubes hadn't been set correctly, and some of the paper landed on the Roomba...and the burning candle.

"Your office is on fire," Aaron informed me helpfully as he noticed the pieces begin to catch, scorching the top of the device.

"Thank you, Fire Chief Borton, for noticing," I said dryly, picking my head up. "Livington!"

"He's already left," I heard a voice pipe up, Jesse, Bennett's partner.

"Fine, then you can explain that this little stunt set his electronic pet on fire," I called back.

A familiar voice yelped. "Not Fredrick!"

"What the fuck is a Fredrick?" Aaron asked in bewilderment, and I had to wonder why the man was bothering to question anything.

To my horror, Bennett appeared in the doorway, wide-eyed and wielding a fire extinguisher. I stood up as he pulled the pin. "Livington, don't you—"

Aaron didn't bother, diving out of the chair as a wide foam arc sprayed with a hiss of compressed air. I closed my eyes as the foam hit the device, splattering in every direction, including onto my desk. For a moment, there was only the faint whirring of the device as it turned back and forth, trying to discover a surface with its sensors. I reached up, wiping specks of foam from my jaw, and bowed my head to glare at Bennett.

Behind him was the rest of the precinct, staring into the office with wide eyes and twisting mouths. They were waiting for the inevitable explosion but were desperately trying not to laugh at the sight.

"Livington," I growled as he knelt on the ground to wipe foam from the device. "You have precisely ten seconds to explain before you find my foot lodged so deep even your boyfriend won't be able to pull it out."

"He would be really disappointed," Bennett informed me. "He's pretty fond of—"

"Livington!"

"Right. Sex life, not fit for public consumption, I remember."

"Explain!"

"He wasn't supposed to catch fire," Bennett explained as he picked the beeping device off the floor.

Sighing, I rubbed my brow. "How the hell did you even

manage to get it to stop at that exact spot? It's a *vacuum,* for God's sake!"

"I mean, if you know what you're doing, you can make anything do just about anything you want," he said, and I narrowed my eyes. Bennett Livington didn't give a direct or overly detailed response unless he was trying to conceal something.

"You mean you had someone do something to its programming," I said. Unlike Aaron, I hadn't fought the wave of technology that was bound to catch up to us eventually. That didn't mean I liked it or used it more than I had to, which meant I didn't know a damned thing about programming. But I knew anyone with the knowledge could do it with the right equipment. "Who?"

Bennett's eyes widened. "Why would I put someone else in the line of fire?"

"Because the more chaos you can cause, the happier you are," I growled at him, turning my attention to Aaron, who was still standing near the shelves. "Since Isaiah and Julian are the only two on your team who are friends with this degenerate—"

"That's homophobic, Chief," Bennett interrupted.

I turned my gaze on him. "When I have you fired and locked up for arson, it won't be because you take it up the ass, Livington. Aaron?"

Borton shook his head. "Isaiah can work a smartphone, and Julian deals with stuff, but like, circuit boards and all that shit from what Isaiah tells me. Julian doesn't get the software stuff. Too much like people. What? Don't give me that look. It's what Isaiah told me, word for word."

"He speaks the truth," Bennett said with a shrug. "I like Julian, but he's kinda weird with people."

"And you're just fucking weird," I snapped, glaring at the group behind them. It only took me a moment to find the one person doing their best to appear as nonchalant as possible. "Ritz!"

Richard Ritz tried to cringe behind his partner, the woman rolling her eyes. "Yes, Chief?"

"You're one of the people in this precinct who went to college."

"Uh...yes, Chief."

"And the only one who went for computer science."

"Y-yes."

"And I bet if I opened up your file, I'd find that you're still pretty good with some of those languages for computers," I said.

"Might be," he said, even though we both knew he was cornered and helpless.

I glared at him. "What'd he offer you to help him pull this little stunt off?"

He mumbled something, and I snapped. "Louder, so I can hear you."

"A bottle of that wine my girlfriend likes and any six shifts I need covered," he finally said, thumping his head against his partner's shoulder.

"Judas!" Bennett barked, looking horrified at Richard.

"And you?" I asked Annie, who looked less than impressed by her partner's behavior.

"If I knew anything, I wouldn't say," she told me, meeting my eyes coolly. Not that I was surprised in the slightest, she was one of the few officers in the precinct who didn't seem bothered by my usual attitude. Sadly the frontrunner of that little race was Bennett, who was also the leader in being the biggest pain my ass. She didn't cause trouble and didn't try to stop it either, but at least I knew she wouldn't involve herself in any nonsense.

"Fine, everyone but Ritz and Livington, back to work or I'll start thinking of ways to make you suffer with them," I growled, scattering the accumulated group. I wasn't an idiot, I knew the entire lot would end up laughing about the whole ordeal out of earshot.

"Aaron," I said, glancing at the fire chief. "You were meaning to scrub out a couple of your store rooms, weren't you? Pretty sure you used the word 'vile' the last time you brought it up."

His eyes widened, sensing where my thoughts were going. "Yeah, but I'm not—"

"Good," I interrupted before he could finish his protest. "Ritz, you'll be having a couple of extra shifts this week to go over there and help our good people at the firehouse by cleaning out those rooms to Chief Borton's liking. You'll keep having those extra shifts until the place is immaculate, and no, you can't force those on anyone else."

Richard sagged. "Yes, Chief."

"Good, and you," I said, turning on Bennett. "First, you're going to clean this mess up and the rest of my office, except for my desk. You leave that alone. And then, you remember our archive room?"

"Filled with files in neat little rows," Bennett said slowly and, if I wasn't mistaken, with a small hope that I was about to grind to dust.

"No, the old one."

"The one filled with boxes...and dust."

"That's the one. You're going to spend your extra shifts cleaning and organizing it."

"But, but, my allergies! Dust will drive me crazy!"

"Good, you'll know how I feel on a weekly basis," I growled, swiping my desk clean. "At least you can take a Claritin and call it a day."

Bennett's shoulders slumped before he looked up, smiling. "Happy Birthday?"

"Get out," I growled at him, calling after his retreating

back, "And we're not using our funds to replace that stupid machine if you broke it!"

I heard a groan from the hallway but no argument, which told me I'd got my point across. With a sigh, I looked over my desk, opening the middle drawer to get the wipes to clean it. "You wouldn't know that's a full-grown man."

"If memory serves, you were the one who recommended him for the station back when he was job shadowing. Oh wait, it was you he was shadowing," Aaron reminded me. "You can't tell me you didn't know what he was like back then."

"Yeah, I knew," I said, tossing the wipe away with a huff. "But maybe I held out, hoping he'd grow up."

"Didn't you have that old archive cleaned up a year or two ago?"

"Two. The room's clean, but that doesn't mean the work isn't going to be dull as hell. Maybe it'll give him time to think."

Or give him time to come up with something worse than a singing Roomba.

With a disgusted sigh, I grabbed my phone from the desk and headed for the door. "I'll walk you back to your station."

"Leaving early?" Aaron asked in mock surprise. "Could it be that Chief Price is getting lazy in his old age?"

"It's my birthday, as everyone keeps reminding me," I growled. "I get one early day a year."

"Sure," he said, following me out so I could close my office door behind me.

"You know where to find me if you need me," I barked at the room of officers, every one of them trying to hide their smirks. "And if anyone else gets any bright ideas, don't."

I reached the front desk to find Ira sitting in her usual position behind it. She had been working the desk before I left for the Corps, and the way she was headed, she probably would up until the day she died. No one was sure how old she was, and there was an odd timelessness to her no matter how old she physically got. Her red hair had faded and was now streaks of intermingling gray and silver, though it was as long and thick as ever. More lines on her face appeared and disappeared seemingly at her whim, and she had seen and known more than anyone in the precinct.

"Leaving early?" she asked, tucking away her book and not even bothering to jiggle the mouse to pretend she was doing any work.

"No good reason for me to hang around," I told her as she took the glasses off the bridge of her nose and let them dangle to her chest from the gold chain around her neck. "Shouldn't you be heading home yourself?"

"You know I go home when I go home," she chuckled, leaning back in her seat. "City pays me all the same."

"Fine, but if you end up leaving late, have one of the overnight idiots take you home," I said, jabbing a finger at her. "I mean it."

"My eyes are as sharp as they ever were," she said, her fingers stealing to the cover of her book. "Except for reading now and then."

"Nathan told on you years ago. You don't have shit for night vision," I told her, arching a brow.

Her late husband's name brought a laugh to her lips. "He was always such a busybody...and a snitch. Fine, if it's too late, I'll have Bennett take me, as I'm sure you'll have him here for a while yet."

"Thank you for reminding me," I grunted, calling back into the main room. "Ritz, Livington! Those shifts start now, so settle in for a long night. Ritz, I want you at the fire station in twenty, ready to get to work!"

I heard affirmation from both of them, neither sounding very happy.

"Oh, I remember when this place wasn't nearly as entertaining as it is nowadays," Ira said with a wistful sigh.

"Not the word I'd use for it," I told her with a snort.

"Speaking of," she said, pulling a box from under her desk. "Here you go. Some of those chocolates I know you're so fond of."

"I said no fuss over my birthday," I grumbled as I itched to reach out and take the box. Her daughter-in-law was a genius when it came to making chocolates, and I'd yet to find anything as good as she made.

"If I wanted to make a fuss, I would have slapped a singing flower on top," she told me, her eyes glinting.

I snatched the box up. "Looks like everyone was in on that little stunt. It's nice to know I can keep order in my own house."

"Happy Birthday, Trevor," she said with a chuckle, picking up her book.

I rolled my eyes, then hesitated. "Get the idiots here something to eat and not pizza."

"Anything in mind?"

"Sandwiches?"

"Hmm, I'll call Grant down at the bakery to make up some of those divine loaves and call over to Greene's to see if they can get Annie to deliver some of that deli meat and cheese, a few odds and ends to go on it."

"You're going to gossip with that pink-haired woman at the bakery, you mean," I said with a sigh.

"It's lavender now."

"Of course it is."

Ira glanced at Aaron. "Get him out of here, would you? Otherwise, he'll second guess himself and skip out on the only early day he's taken in three years."

"Yes, ma'am," Aaron said, grabbing me by the arm. "Let's go."

"Traitor," I told him, tucking the box into the front of my shirt.

"Ira says jump, I do, then wonder how high she wants me to go," he chuckled. "I need to get a few supplies together for Ritz to get cleaning anyway."

"It's not a toxic dump, is it?" I asked, wary of what I was throwing Richard into.

"No," he snorted. "Sandwiches. God, you're something sometimes, Trevor."

"What the hell is wrong with sandwiches?"

"Nothing," he said as we walked down the sidewalk. Most of the municipal buildings were near one another in what was essentially the center of town. From there, the next 'layer' of the city was primarily businesses. Everywhere else was residential, though the homes tended to be nicer on the eastern and northern sides of the city and the worst dotted around the south. "Speaking of nothing, I noticed you weren't all that upset about that birthday Roomba."

"I gave them extra duties that had nothing to do with the job," I reminded him dryly.

"Yeah, but there was a lot less shouting, and it'll take them, what, an extra shift or two to clean up? Pretty light for almost setting your office on fire," Aaron said, stopping at the entrance to the fire station. I heard laughter echoing from somewhere in the building, watching a river of soapy water leaking from the truck bay.

I knew what he was aiming for and eyed him warily. Along with all the rough talk and overbearing protectiveness, there was a man with a sharp eye and a shrewd mind. It didn't help that we'd been working in tandem for years, and he was the only real friend I had in the town.

"That was the first stupid thing he's done in a couple of months," I said quietly, glancing toward the open bay door where I could hear repeated slapping sounds. "Like, really stupid."

"Really?" Borton asked, his brow shooting up.

"Shooting that drug dealer took the wind out of his sails for a bit," I said. The call had been necessary, and after the investigation that happened anytime an officer discharged their gun, he had been found innocent of any wrongdoing. Still, that had been the first time Bennett had ever taken a life, and he hadn't gone untouched. The first few weeks of him being quiet hadn't been too worrying, but after a month, I realized he hadn't aggravated me.

As much as the man drove me nuts, there was no denying he was a good officer and a good man. He was always the first on my list regarding officers doing anything with the community for good public relations. He was great with kids, knew how to get a laugh, and could make just about anyone feel good about themselves.

"So you'll take a minor fire in your office if it means he's back to himself?" Borton asked with a snort. "Alright, that makes sense."

"And you were willing to ask me to pull strings you couldn't to help one of your own," I pointed out.

"Yeah, but at least that doesn't involve a fire in my office or any other bullshit."

I raised a brow, glancing at the open bay door. "Right, no bullshit. So you tell me why it doesn't sound like they're in there washing the truck and more like they're screwing around."

His mouth opened and then closed as he turned, marching over to the door. Once more, his mouth opened. "What are you idiots doing?"

"Uhhh," came a voice I recognized as one of the strange twins that worked for him. "Wet t-shirt contest and sponge fight?"

"Put that fucking hose down, Larry," Borton snapped. "Whose idea was this?"

"Isaiah said he wanted to see Julian all wet!"

"Hey!" I heard the protest. "I said I wanted to see it after you sprayed me. You started it!"

"Just because you're horny for your boyfriend all the time doesn't mean you have to blame me!"

I rolled my eyes when I heard what was probably supposed to be a war cry, followed by a yelp from Larry as two wet bodies slammed into one another. Deciding I didn't want to stick my nose in whatever was going on in there, I turned back toward the parking lot to find my car. Bennett was already there, throwing out a large bag while he chatted on the phone.

"Livington," I snapped, realizing he was probably calling his boyfriend to tell him he'd be late.

Bennett turned around. "Uh, yeah, Chief?"

"You supposed to have that kid of yours this weekend?"

"Um, not really my kid but—"

"Your boyfriend's kid...the boyfriend you're living with and helping raise the kid with."

"Uh, yeah. Supposed to come over tomorrow and stay with us for a few days."

I huffed, unlocking my car. "Leave here by ten, and you're going to start those extra shifts on Monday, got it?"

He perked up. "You got it, Chief!"

"Dumbass," I muttered, knowing he could hear me as I slid into the car, wondering why that simple insult made him laugh so hard as he walked away. I usually didn't call him that, but I felt it was well-earned.

I watched him go after turning on the car and shook my head as he disappeared, his voice echoing out of the back hallway before the door closed. I didn't know the story between him and his boyfriend, except that the guy, Adam, had been Bennett's best friend since they were kids and apparently had been straight. Now they were living together, raising Adam's son part-time, splitting it with Adam's ex-wife, who had come to live in town a year before. It made sense that Bennett's love and family life were as weird as the rest of him, but he seemed happy.

I stirred at a buzz from my phone, rolling my eyes at the email reminding me money had been pulled from my account. I wished I could claim that Alice had purposefully set the dates for the alimony payments so they would always fall on my birthday. She had certainly been bitter enough by the time our marriage had rotted away to reveal the hollow core that had been there for far too long.

Pulling out of the parking lot, I reflected for the millionth time that I couldn't blame her for her bitterness. She had seen the end of our marriage long before I knew the ground had given way under our feet. She tried her best to save us, but there was always something in the way, namely me.

There was always something pulling me away. Fairlake was quiet, but that didn't mean I didn't have a job to do and a duty to follow through on. Looking back, I could see all too clearly how my passion and dedication to our marriage had been overshadowed by the passion and dedication I had for the job. Nights alone for her stopped being something she had to deal with being married to a cop and became something she expected as she was eclipsed by a job.

I pulled into the driveway of the small house we'd bought when I was a regular officer, staring up at it before turning off the engine. We'd once planned to have kids, knowing we'd have to expand to a bigger house one day if we wanted more than one. The talk of kids started to wane when there seemed to be so little time for them in our lives, and now I knew she had busied herself, filling the silence of her empty marriage.

Opening the front door, I stopped in the entryway to remove my shoes before stepping onto the hardwood of the living room. There was a large leather couch under the equally large front window. The couch went mostly unused compared to the plush armchair at the far end of the living room facing the TV on the wall. Shelves on each side of the TV were filled with pictures and a few odds and ends, but otherwise, the room was undecorated.

I crossed the hallway into the dining room, which had seating for four, but was only ever used by one. Even then, I typically ate in the living room or my office. Opening the freezer, I pulled a bottle of vodka out and began to pour myself a drink. I'd never been fond of vodka, but Alice had turned me onto it through cocktails.

In truth, this house had been more hers than mine, and it had once been filled to the brim with every aspect of her. She had been gone for years, going to live with her sister in Omaha and taking all the life out of the house. Her vibrance and color had made me fall in love with her in the first place, as well as the gentleness that had wilted in the coldness of our marriage. She hadn't found her strength and voice until it came time to call for the divorce, and by then, it had been too late for either of us to appreciate it.

Taking my drink, I walked back toward my office. It had once been her craft and hobby room but now contained only a narrow bookshelf crammed with books I hadn't touched in years and a cluttered desk.

In truth, I didn't miss our marriage. She was a good woman, but after she'd left, I realized I had never truly believed in the two of us. When it came down to the two 'loves' of my life, my love for my job and duty had been stronger than my love for her. For all the bad that could be said about me, and there was plenty, including how far I'd let things go between her and me, I threw myself into the things I cared about.

In her absence, I had seen how much my life had become cycles, a constant circle that moved endlessly but never went anywhere. When you pierced that circle, there was little substance at its core, only a few things I had left. A car accident had taken my mother while I was deployed, unexpected cancer had taken my father ten years before, and I was left an only child. I had Aaron as a friend, but he had his own life to deal with, a family he was devoted to, hell, two families. Besides my job, I had a house filled with ghosts of my past and little to savor.

Picking my head up, I eyed the small plaster statue of Jesus on my desk, a thin chain draped around it. Picking it up, the dog tags jingled as I brought them close. Troy's parents had kept so much of his but had given me his tags, a way for me to have a piece of the Marine he had been, for the Marine they had known was his best friend.

Best friend. Right. God, sometimes I wondered just how those God-fearing folk would have felt if they'd known the truth.

"It's going to be twenty-five years," I told the tags, watching them catch the light, as clean and shiny as if they were freshly made. "Twenty-five years since I got that letter from your mom. Twenty-four years since I came to find you in that stupid graveyard."

I could still hear his snort right before he'd tease me for being the sentimental bastard I'd always accused him of being.

My throat tightened. "I miss you."

ETHAN

"Holy fuck, that is the tiniest little podunk town," I said with a laugh, leaning forward as the car exited the forest bringing the town into view.

My sister sighed. "Don't call it podunk. And you were the one who wanted to come here for a while."

"Yeah, I also said I wasn't going to live in the middle of Hicksville too," I said, squirming away when Bri swatted at me.

"Don't be an ass!"

"But how else can I drive you crazy?"

"You aren't required to drive me crazy."

"As the younger brother, it is my solemn, God-given duty to drive you crazy any chance I get," I told her, holding one hand out before me like I was taking a serious pledge.

"No, that's just one of your hobbies," she said, eyeing me. "You can always stay somewhere else. I'm sure Mom and Dad would take you in."

I snorted. We both knew I'd last approximately one week with our parents before they or I committed a felony. It wasn't that I was the black sheep of the family, but I wasn't exactly favored. Admittedly, teenage me hadn't made their lives as parents easy, but I didn't think any parent should expect their kids to be 'easy' like Bri had been. You rolled the dice when you had kids and then dealt with whatever Lady Luck gave you.

She glanced at me again, something she had been doing since picking me up from Denver airport. I knew full well she was trying to gauge if I was as 'alright' as I'd told her I was. I pretended I didn't notice her constant glances, which made it a lot easier for her to continue to put off asking me any questions I didn't want to deal with yet.

"I'm still a little surprised you asked," Bri finally said as she slowed down near town. "You always stayed in nice big places."

"I stayed with you and Adam when you were in Boston a couple of times," I reminded her.

"Our place was nice, and Boston is big."

"Okay, touché."

I knew what she was asking, though, and I considered whether this was one of those questions I wanted to answer. There was a host of them I wanted to avoid like the plague for a while, if not completely. There were plenty of things about my life that my sister didn't know, and I had no intention of ever having her discover them.

"You ever feel like your life is just repeating itself?" I asked as the car came to a stop at a light. I stared out the window, watching a trio of kids racing down the sidewalk toward some unknown destination. "Like, sure, it feels like you're moving, but it's really just old ground?"

"Need I point out my failed marriage?" she asked with a snort.

"Is that how marriages fail?" I wondered. Relationships had never come easy to me, though I'd tried now and then. Turned out most, if not all, people weren't ready to deal with a boyfriend who was gone for weeks in some far-flung part of the globe, potentially putting themselves in danger because they didn't know how to leave well enough alone. I sympathized with people trying to date while on active duty.

Hmm, maybe I should have tried dating a service member.

"My marriage failed for a lot of reasons," she said with a sigh that held more weight than a simple exhale of air.

"So, it wasn't running in a bunch of circles?"

"We were both running in circles, but at some point we started running in different circles. I was climbing the corporate ladder, he was expanding his business. I was trying to get prestige, he was expanding his brand. At some point, we stopped thinking about each other and started doing our own thing without realizing it. By the time I realized, I was pissed, and he was disinterested."

"One pissed and one not caring," I winced. "That's an ugly combination."

"And that combination is what destroyed what was left," she said, turning onto a side street. "He picked up, came back here, and I came after him when I thought there was still a chance."

I eyed her carefully. "Yeah, so uh, how's that part working out?"

"You mean, how am I dealing with the fact that my ex-husband is now dating his best friend, a guy, and seems to be more in love with him than he ever was with me?"

"I'll take that as not dealing very well."

"I'm dealing," she said softly, loosening her grip on the wheel. "I came back out of desperation, not because I thought Adam and I had a chance. It doesn't bother me that he's bi, and it's not like he was cheating on me."

"Uh, so they waited to do their thing after the papers

were signed?" I wondered, realizing there was a lot more to this story than I originally thought.

"We weren't divorced, but we weren't together anymore," she said, snorting. "He moved out of our apartment, moved back here, and we didn't talk for months. We weren't together. He didn't cheat."

"Alright, that seems to be all the hard stuff taken care of," I said, raising a brow. "So, what's the real problem?"

"I'm trying to make peace with the realization that he never loved me like he clearly loves Bennett. And the fact that I always wondered about that back when we were married and came here for the holidays a couple of times."

"Damn, even back then?" I asked with a low whistle.

"Not like...it wasn't something I could prove, and I don't even think it was romantic, not for Adam anyway. But they loved each other even then. If they weren't together, I'd call it brotherly," she said with a chuckle. "But they were close, and it always made me feel awkward. So now I get to see the man I loved more in love with someone else than he ever was with me, and the fact that I was right."

I shot her a sympathetic look. "Sorry, I, uh, probably shouldn't have asked."

"It's fine," she said, then shrugged when she saw my doubtful expression. "Do you know who I get to talk to this about? A shrink. I don't really have friends here, not yet. Things are much better between Adam and me, and he's as amazing as I always knew he'd be with our son. And before you ask, yes, I like Bennett. I always have. But it's not like I can talk to them about this. They'd just feel like shit, I'd feel like shit, and I'm tired of everyone feeling like shit."

"So, what? You get to feel like shit, and they get to be happy?" I asked with a scowl. "That's a stupid way to live."

She pulled into a driveway, stopping and turning to me. "Ethan, I need you to dial back on the protective brother act.

27

It's not anyone's fault that they get to be happy right now while I'm still trying to get my feet steady on the ground, alright? So don't be a dick to them."

Her voice was even, if a little sharp, but the fire in her eyes told me that as much as she'd gained control of her temper, it wasn't completely gone. Not that either of us could really talk, hot heads ran in the family, and sharp tongues were usually a close second.

"I'm not going to be a dick, but that doesn't mean I can't admit it's shitty that you get to feel like dirt while they don't," I told her, bringing up the stubbornness that was in third place.

"I'm not going to be unhappy forever, but I'm not going to begrudge them the chance to be happy for the rest of their lives," she said, narrowing her eyes. "Plus, it's not like I'm some sad bitch, drifting around my house in a gown, wailing about my lover having left me for a cute man."

"Cute?" I asked, brow shooting up.

"A little annoying but, yes, cute," she said with a sudden laugh.

"Is it better or worse that the person he's with is good-looking?"

"My replacement better be as hot or hotter than me, as well as being a better match, or I'm going to be offended," she said with a smirk.

It sounded enough like something I would say that I couldn't help but laugh. In little ways, it was nice to be reminded that no matter how different she and I could be, especially in how we'd chosen to lead our lives, there was still a common core we shared.

"I've got a place of my own," she said, looking at the narrow house before us. "Which is good enough for now. I've opened my own office in Fairlake, and I've got clients coming in and making me money. *And*, I have a date next

Friday. So my life isn't exactly what I want, but I'm finding a way to make a new one, and I think I might like it."

The sheer earnestness of her explanation took me aback. I'd known my sister had been struggling and had the crib notes version of the entire thing. It had been more than a little shocking that she'd decided to move to this little town in the middle of Colorado with seemingly no net to catch her. Especially when she would be surrounded by living reminders of the life she left.

Yet here she was, not quite a year into reinventing her life, and she was doing well. Sure, she wasn't exactly on top of the world, but she wasn't stuck either. Her wheels had found traction, and she was starting to blaze out of the rut. It meant starting over and rebuilding a damaged structure, but she was doing it without any real bitterness or fear.

I opened my mouth to tell her that and how strong she was to work this hard. "So, is it safe for you to tell me how good Adam was in bed?"

She blinked before swatting me across the chest. "Get out of my car."

"How big his dick is?"

"Keep going, and you're going to end up sleeping in the garage."

I laughed, even though I knew she was only half-joking. Shoving open the door, I wasted no time as she opened the trunk for me. There were only a couple of, albeit large, bags to pull out. Honestly, it was a lot more than I was used to traveling with, and it had been kind of fun to cram more clothes than usual into the larger bags along with all the stuff I'd normally use for work. I didn't know how long I would stay with Bri, so I packed as much as possible without loading everything.

Truth was, I hadn't planned to come to Fairlake in the first place.

* * *

My BREATH WAS PULLED *from my lips, yanked into the wind, disappearing into the New York City landscape.*

It wasn't the highest point in New York City, but you could see enough to appreciate it lit up at night. The traffic was just far enough away that you could pretend it was background noise instead of impatient people threatening each other over the roar of their honks.

Glancing over my shoulder, I peered back into the apartment at a faint noise. Nothing shifted except the curtains, and I told my heart to calm down. We were in New York City, among the masses, where my name might be known, but no one knew I was there. I wasn't in some shit hole hovel in the middle of Eastern Europe, hiding away while I crammed together as much information as possible on the trafficking rings that operated, sometimes openly, in the area.

The entire exposé had been sensational, and there were still news outlets talking about it while others were peeling it apart to use themselves. My bank account was filling up rapidly, and the name Ethan Crane was on people's lips. Some in praise, and some wondering how they might drag me away into a nice quiet part of the country where they could really tell me what they thought about my work.

And me? I felt nothing.

Oh, the work had been fantastic. Well, my work had been fantastic. The source material left me with one more sickening thing to add to the monument of humanity's sins against itself I had accrued over the years. My research had been impeccable, and my writing had seamlessly stitched it together. All in all, it was probably the best work I'd ever done, and maybe it would be enough to show the world that ugliness should never be hidden and that we needed to deal with the dark crimes committed all around us.

The apartment was paid up for six months, but I might not be there that long. Sometimes I was back in the country for that long, and other times I'd be gone in a few months. It all depended on what new story called to me.

Except...they'd stopped calling to me for a while. Even this most recent, my prime piece of work, had simply been something I had felt needed to be done. There was no drive to expose, no need to educate, or burning passion to show the world what it fought so hard to avoid. Just a quiet sense of obligation that was enough to tug me along, and even then, I was left to go through the motions.

The motions. The thought was enough to make me laugh bitterly. How do you 'go through the motions' when those motions constantly put you in danger of an ugly death or something worse? Leaning over the edge of the balcony, I could lean far enough and crane my head up so I couldn't see the balcony I held onto anymore. Instead, there was just the city spread out before me, and I didn't feel a twinge of fear or panic.

Was this my life now? Going through the motions even when they brought me to the edge of destruction?

What would happen if I let go, allowing gravity to do what it had done since the beginning of this dismal rock flying through space? Would I feel something wake up inside me? Would fear grip my heart as I realized I was doomed to a messy death somewhere on the street below? Or would I feel a sense of relief that, Christ, it was all over with, there was nothing and no one, and I could—

A cheery jingle broke through my thoughts, startling me enough to jerk back and whirl around. My phone was lit up on the mattress as the song continued. Frowning, I stepped in to see it was, in fact, the last person I expected to call and the only one I would answer.

"Hey, Bri," I said.

"Hey," she said cautiously. "What's that noise?"

"The wind," I said, closing the balcony door behind me. "Sorry, didn't realize it was that loud."

"No, it's fine, just—"

There was enough silence on the line that I grew worried. "Hey, are you okay?"

"You know, I was going to ask you that," she said, clearing her throat.

"Sorry," I said, feeling relief drown out the worry. "I should have called you when I got back to the States. I just...with everything, I got caught up."

"I figured, but that's not...I just..." She cleared her throat again. "Anyway, do you have time to talk? Or are you too busy being Mr. Famous?"

"Infamous more like," I said, earning a chuckle from her.

"I really shouldn't be laughing. Christ, Ethan, what the fuck were you thinking going out there? Do you have any idea what those people would do to you?" she snapped.

I laughed. "Well, did you read it? I'm pretty sure I went into detail about how they handled people. I wouldn't recommend asking for pictures though, not if you've got a weak heart, are pregnant, or ate a heavy lunch."

"Yeah, um, about that,"

"Oh boy. I'm in for a ride, aren't I?"

"A lot's happened since we last talked."

God, that had been, what? Almost seven months? Shit. I really was a terrible brother sometimes.

"I got time," I said, glancing at the balcony. "And I might have an idea I want to pass by you, but you go first."

* * *

I HAD THOUGHT it was the perfect time for me to spend time with my sister. She had gone through so much while I was away and would need help. Before I'd left the States, I'd known she and Adam were having a hard time and talking about divorce. However, I hadn't expected to find out everything else that happened after that.

It turned out she didn't need me either.

"Earth to Ethan," she called from the other side of the car.

I jerked, turning to face her. "Oh, shit, zoned out for a while there."

"I noticed," she said dryly. "Please tell me you weren't getting some idea for another one of your reports."

"No," I snorted, shouldering one of my bags. "You know, you never told me what made you call me at four in the morning on a Wednesday."

She looked surprised at the question. "It's going to sound really stupid."

"You can't sound any more stupid than half the shit I've heard from people already," I assured her, suddenly curious about what could make my ever-put-together sister look so uncertain.

"I just," she began, then cut off, frowning toward the road. "Now, what the hell is he doing here?"

I turned to see a shiny new truck rolling up, stepping out of the way as it pulled into the driveway. Bri tossed her hair over her shoulder as the window rolled down, and Adam's familiar face peered out, smiling softly down at her.

"Hey," he said, the rumble of his voice gentle. Then he looked up. "Hey there, Ethan, it's been a while. You're looking good."

"That has *so* much more meaning nowadays," I said with a smirk.

Truth be told, I was looking like a hot mess. I'd barely slept the night before, and the time it took to get to Denver certainly hadn't helped. My dirty blond hair was falling around my face in thick clumps, and I was sure the green of my eyes was probably lost under circles of black. Bri had been polite so far, but I hadn't been eating the best the past few months, and I'd lost a lot of weight. I wasn't unhealthy looking, but I was skinnier than before and paler too. My face was already narrow, and with the weight loss, it was probably gaunt.

Bri let out a heavy sigh, but Adam's brow only rose slightly. "I see you've been brought up to date on a few things."

"I swear," Bri said, shooting me a dirty look, "I don't know who this man is. I couldn't get him to leave my car."

"Maybe have some *cute* cop come and arrest me then," I told her, smirking as she shot me a look that, if possible, would have imploded me on the spot.

Adam chuckled. "I see you're still...you."

"A pain in the ass who doesn't know when to quit?" Bri suggested.

"Language," Adam chided gently.

Bri's dark expression disappeared immediately, and without hesitation, she stepped to the rear door to open it. There, sat in a plush car seat, was a wriggling ball of flesh that flailed chubby arms at her. She made soft noises as she unhooked the child, propping him on her hip immediately to run a hand through wisps of pitch-black hair, but the bright eyes he'd surely got from my sister.

"Wow," I said. "You guys went and had a baby, and a pretty one at that. Congrats on the, uh, genes?"

Bri rolled her eyes. "Forgive Ethan. He sees a baby and has a complete meltdown in the center of his brain."

"I'm pretty sure I did the same thing for the first few weeks," Adam said.

"You did it because you had Dad Panic and were terrified you were going to break him," Bri said, adjusting the baby, who was now trying to grab her earrings. She barely paid attention to his hands but blocked each grab with unerring precision. "Ethan sees a baby and is convinced they're going to puke all over him, give him a new deadly strain of disease, and then proceed to eat his face."

"That's...a lot," Adam said, clearly unsure how to handle this new 'information.'

"I do not," I said, rolling my eyes.

"Not a fan of kids," Adam amended for my sister, watching me carefully. I hadn't known Adam very well, but he had always been extremely serious. There was patience and care in the way he moved and talked, something I was sure came in handy with his carpentry work. Personally, I'd always found it a little unnerving to be around, like he knew something about me I didn't want him to know but was keeping it to himself.

"They're fine," I lied, flopping a hand at him as best I could while holding onto the bag strap. "Just not my thing."

"At all," Bri said, holding up a free hand to make a scissor motion where Adam could see.

"Oh," he said in understanding.

"Not a fan of me having any," I corrected for her, wishing she wasn't holding my nephew so I could throw something at her.

"Put one of those bags down and hold your nephew," she said, walking toward me.

My eyes widened. "Bri, c'mon, it's been a long trip! I just wanna...oh, fuck."

I had no choice but to drop my bags, and I was glad my electronics were wrapped as I fumbled to take the kid all but shoved into my hands by my smirking sister.

"Language," she said, turning to Adam. "What're you doing here? You've got him for the whole weekend while I get Ethan settled in."

"Hi," I told the baby, trying not to hold him too far out, but not quite sure what I was supposed to do with him. To my horror, he grinned, and a thin dollop of drool formed at the corner of his mouth, threatening to run down his chin. "And that's gross."

Colin found that extremely funny.

"Had some free time coming back from my parents," Adam explained. "Figured you'd be back by now, and you wouldn't say no to saying hi to him while I said hi to Ethan."

"True, but I figured you and Bennett would be wrapped up in parent time," she said, glancing at me. "God's sake, Ethan, it's a baby, not a bomb. Quit holding him like that."

"He's leaking," I explained, staring at the baby, who was now beginning to kick his legs, jiggling in my grasp.

"He's a baby. They do that. How would you like it if someone held you like that?"

"What the hell am I supposed to do?"

"Put him on your hip," Adam called out. "And Bennett isn't getting out until ten."

"God," I grumbled to Colin, working him around to my hip and curling an arm under his padded butt. The result was drool on my shirt, but that was better than on my skin. Big green eyes peered back at me as he reached to poke and grip my face. "Ow, hey! What are those, nails or talons?"

"I thought you said he was getting out at six," Bri said.

"He apparently decided to wish his Chief a happy birthday."

"Not the eye," I hissed, trying to get Colin's finger away from my squishy parts but not wanting to hurt or startle him. "Dude, c'mon. Is there any way I can convince you that just having a staring contest is perfectly fine?"

Apparently not.

Bri sighed. "From anyone else that would be a normal and sweet gesture. What did this 'birthday wishing' involve?"

"I caught 'Roomba' 'confetti' and 'fire' and decided it was best not to have him repeat the story while his chief was in earshot," Adam said, chuckling heavily.

"You know, when Chase called Bennett a dumbass and a

menace, I thought he was exaggerating, but clearly, he was not," Bri said with a shake of her head.

"Chase has his own way of explaining things," Adam said, glancing up as Colin tried to shove his fingers between my lips.

"Speaking of, how's Chase doing? I keep meaning to ask," Bri continued, still not looking my way.

"Alright, you," I said, wrapping my lips over my teeth and using them to gently grab his groping fingers. "How about that?"

From the squeal, Colin thought that was the most delightful thing to have ever happened to him, which meant my plan was backfiring on me as he reached out again.

"He's...dealing," Adam said with a sigh. "Bennett's a little worried. I guess it's been almost a week since Chase heard from Devin."

"Well, from what I know, he won't have to wait forever," Bri said, finally glancing over her shoulder.

"Bennett likes to remind him that just because you have to wait a while doesn't mean you have to wait forever."

"He's speaking from personal experience on that one, huh?"

"Bri?"

"Don't, Adam, seriously. It was supposed to be a joke."

"It didn't sound like one."

"Well, one day it will, I promise."

"Your mommy and daddy have soooooo many issues," I told Colin, who leaned back as I made exaggerated expressions at him, lips curled into a smile. "And guess what? They're going to be the ones raising you! And people wonder why I'm not having kids of my own. Yeah, I know!"

Colin was delighted, while my sister looked less so, and Adam just shook his head. At the very least, I had convinced

Colin to stop spearing my face with his finger daggers, so I counted that as a win.

"He still thinks he's witty," Adam said with a chuckle.

"He has his moments," Bri said, extracting Colin from me. "Come here, sweetheart, let Mommy say goodbye before she commits felony murder! Yes!"

"Please don't talk about fratricide in front of me," Adam told her as she tucked Colin back into his car seat. "I'm dating a cop and would be obligated to report it or risk jail time and sleeping on the couch. Wait until I'm out of earshot."

"I wouldn't dream of making you an accessory before the fact," Bri said, reaching up to poke him on the forehead. "Now, get home while I get Ethan settled in. And tell your mother I'll still be dropping by on Sunday for our bridge game."

"She'd expect nothing less," Adam chuckled, the truck making a heavy noise as he began to back out of the driveway. "Take care, Ethan, because I know you won't behave."

"Well, he's...different," I noted as I watched the truck make its way down the street. I couldn't put my finger on what was so different about Adam, at least not in words. I had always thought of him as a pretty steady person, but he'd somehow managed to find an even greater store of solidness inside him.

"He's...something, anyway, c'mon," she said, heading toward the front door again. "It's a good thing I thought to have Adam do some tweaks in the basement for me, otherwise I'd be throwing your ass on the couch."

When I'd presented the idea of coming to stay with her for a while, I hadn't thought about whether or not there would be space for me to crash. "Uh, I mean, if there's no room, you should have said something."

"No, there's room. Adam had to tear a few things down

and put better stuff in its place, like walls. Someone came in for the wiring and stuff he listed, and I didn't really listen when he rattled it off." She chuckled.

"I see not much has changed in that regard, then," I said, remembering how much my sister's eyes threatened to glaze over whenever Adam talked about his work.

"Eh," she bumped the door open with her hip. "It's not that I don't care that he's enjoying himself. I just...am not fit to understand what the hell he's talking about half the time. I used to tell myself I should study up on a few things to keep up a little, but...that never happened."

Silently, I followed her into the house, finding we were standing in a living room stuffed with furniture, toys, and shelves of books. It was a straight shot through an open archway into a dining room, followed by another archway into a kitchen. I could see a small hallway on the other side of the living room, where a faint light spilled from another room.

"Basement door is at the back," she told me. "Bathroom's over there in the hallway. I keep the light on so I can see at night, but keep the door closed because Colin has learned about the toilet and is absolutely fascinated by it."

"The flushing or the water?"

"Both."

"Just wait until he remembers scissors can be used for cutting hair and gives it a shot himself."

"I was five, Ethan."

"And I'm sure Mom still has the picture of your attempts at being a stylist. I'm pretty sure you could have taken a weed whacker to it, and the result would have been the same."

She slapped her hand over a panel, bringing the lights in the living and dining rooms on in a flash. "And I'm sure we can all remember the time a certain someone thought they could fly if they were wearing a Superman costume."

"Hey, at least your hair grew back. My arm still aches when it gets too cold."

She pointed toward the hallway. "Colin's room is on the right. Try not to have too many parties when he's around."

"Oh yeah, that's me, constantly throwing ragers."

"No one says ragers."

"Orgies."

"And no more of that talk around him either. The little shit is a sponge, and he's already making good progress toward talking. The last thing I need is to have his first word be fuck. And since that used to be one of your favorite words."

"Look," I said, following her into the kitchen. "It's not my favorite word. But sometimes no word works for a situation quite as well as fuck."

"This from the man who can write pages and pages of horrible things without using it once," she said, flipping on a light to reveal a clean kitchen lined almost entirely by counters and appliances. The only free spots were a small table beside a window and a closed door in one wall.

"Probably because I wouldn't get too much attention if I did that," I chuckled. "Or, well, not the kind of attention I want."

It was funny how you could describe or show, in graphic detail, the most horrifying abuse and torture committed on another person, but swearing was still considered going too far. It got doubly funny how squeamish people could be about perfectly normal displays of sex. You could detail the elements of sex trafficking, and people gobbled it up, but those same people would squirm if a little too much skin was shown in a movie and relegated books that did the same to a tiny niche in the market.

Sometimes I wondered what that said about the human

race, and sometimes I chose not to dig too deeply for fear of what I'd uncover on top of what I'd already discovered.

"Yes, fame, accolade, and a shit ton of money," she said with a snort, opening the door to reveal stairs. "Mom and Dad are still having a hard time figuring out how you made a 'poor' choice into a success."

"Probably because they lacked the imagination to realize there was plenty of opportunity in what I said."

"You described it as traveling and showing what you found," she said with a snort, descending to a landing and turning to take another, longer flight of stairs. "Watch these steps. I think they were designed as some weird trap for the unwary."

"And would you look at that? I managed to make money and a name for myself doing just that," I proclaimed sarcastically as I followed her. Whoever had designed the stairs had, in fact, either hated people or was one of the worst carpenters. They were slightly too tall and narrow to take without feeling like you were going to fall forward and crash to the stone floor below. "They had as much faith as they have imagination."

"You know they only wanted what was best for you."

"They wanted what they thought was safe. That's not the same thing."

"It is to them."

I forced myself to keep my lips pressed together, refusing to dig up this old argument with someone new. My parents had *never* approved of anything I'd done, and that went double for my career. Even when presented as investigative journalism, they had balked at the idea of me operating independently rather than through a known network. They wanted something that was 'safe' and reliable, something guaranteed to make consistent money and provide benefits.

"Not all of us can be accountants and lawyers," I said once we reached the bottom.

"I'm pretty sure you could have been anything you wanted, and it would have made them happy," she pointed out, opening the door in front of us. "But you always had to pick the harder option."

"I chose what I thought was best for myself," I said, already feeling tired.

"I know," she chuckled, flipping on the light. The room was larger than I expected, and I peered around to see bare, clean walls, a tiled floor, and a dome light in the center, casting a healthy glow. There was a small TV and loveseat shoved into one corner, a tall armoire, and a bed opposite. It was nothing fancy, but it was more than enough for me to be comfortable. "It's what I've always appreciated about you...envied too."

"You?" I asked in surprise. "You were the golden child, the one with the best grades, got the dream job, the dream everything. Mom and Dad always wished I'd 'grow up' and start being like you."

"Yeah, they weren't happy when I told them growing up wasn't one of your problems. They keep holding out for a version of you that's never going to exist," she said, stepping into the room and looking up toward the half windows on the upper wall. "You still keep late hours?"

"I'm out of work. I can sleep whenever I want."

"I think I still have some blackout curtains lying around somewhere. I'll dig them out and we can hang them over the windows in case you start pulling some late nights."

"Sure. You really told them that?"

She turned, and for the first time, I could see concern in Bri's eyes. "Yes, Ethan, I did. Don't get me wrong, sometimes I wish you didn't make things so hard, but they're just as much to blame. And sometimes I wish you were better at taking care of yourself."

I blinked and then chuckled. "If I wasn't good at that, I'd probably be dead right now."

Or far, far worse.

"That's what I mean," she sighed, shaking her head. "You never really think things all the way through. You just kinda...do them. You're not stupid, and you've got plenty of sense. And I'm sure by now, you've learned all sorts of things to keep your skinny butt alive. But you've always just been so...I don't know. You've always been able to take care of yourself, to make your life work for you, but sometimes I wish you had something a little more solid in your life."

"Solid?" I asked, raising a brow.

She looked around the room. "Look at my life, all these things I have to keep me grounded...keep me sane. I've got a career I can always count on, I've got a steady home again, I've got Colin, and believe it or not, I think I'm going to have to start putting Adam and Bennett in that same category. But you...what do you have that grounds you, Ethan? I mean, really."

"Last I checked, I do plenty with my job."

"Yeah, you do. You've always done things. You do and do, but you throw yourself into all these different projects, all these different...missions. Then you come back, hang around on a month-to-month lease. You might visit family, but you don't have anyone you can call a friend, and I'd be surprised if your relationships last longer than a few months."

"This is starting to sound dangerously close to a Mom and Dad speech."

"Absolutely not," she said with a laugh, tossing her hair over her shoulder. "I'm just saying it would be nice to see you have something other than your work to keep you going. I just want you to have a life outside of the 'truth.'"

"And just how long have you been making up this little speech in your head?" I asked her with a wry smile.

"I refuse to answer that question," Bri chuckled. "Now, get settled in, and before you crash after your long day, I'm going to go heat something up so I can feed you."

"For my not skinny ass? Because it's a pretty good ass, I've been told that."

"I'm sure you have," she said dryly. "But you aren't hearing it from me. I might not be able to make you fat, but at least I can try to put some meat on those bones."

"*Now* you sound like Nana," I snorted.

"Well, that's a lot better than the alternatives," she said, stopping as she passed to kiss me on the cheek. "And, welcome to Fairlake. Maybe you can find something interesting here to occupy yourself while you do whatever it was you came to do in the first place."

"One can only hope," I said, watching her go, closing the door softly behind her.

I stood there for a while, peering at a room utterly devoid of any real life or color, which seemed fitting for me to crash in for a bit. At that cheerful thought, I dropped my bags onto the bed and began pulling out what I needed. There was, of course, the toiletry bag, assorted hygiene products, and hair clippers which I planned on using when I didn't feel halfway toward being a zombie.

The rest of the essentials involved my laptop for writing and whatever else I needed the internet for, and the Switch I gamed on when I had spare moments and needed to occupy my mind. The battered, leather-bound notebook came out next, which I laid carefully on the table beside the loveseat. The notebook had been replaced several times, but the cover was always applied to the new one. It had been a gift, handed to me with a notebook already in it, from a young girl while

I'd been in South Africa, writing my first exposé on the violence erupting in the region.

"Keep it," she had told me in a thick accent. "To write about you."

"Me?" I'd asked with a chuckle. "I'm not here to write about me."

"About you. To keep your heart," she said, pressing the notebook against my chest with a smile. It had been dark brown, thick, and extremely well-made. I learned later that her family ran a farm a few miles from where I'd been. I had no idea what caused this stranger, a girl of maybe fourteen, to give me something when the leather could have been used to support her family. Still, I kept it and occasionally jotted down my thoughts.

Three weeks later, I found her on the side of the road, face slack, eyes lifeless, and dust covering her skin. Just another victim of the very thing I'd come here to try to explain to the world. I had helped deliver her body to her family's farm, a family still hopeful they would see their child despite an entire night having passed since she'd left for town.

I never forgot her mother's wails and kept that cover with me wherever I went. In it went all the things I didn't put in my exposés, the thoughts and feelings that arose as I went through my investigations and digging. There is where I put my heart, as instructed by a girl who had every right to touch more lives than mine if she'd been given the time.

Untying the leather string, I opened the notebook to a random rambling in pencil, scribbled in a slower hand than the other scribbles on the page.

SOMETIMES I LAY OUTSIDE *and stare up, and it feels like I might float free from all this shit. But it's this shit that keeps me here, and*

I can't help but wonder if that's all there ever will be. I used to think I was unchained and free to live my life, but now I wonder if, instead, I'm just unmoored, tossed about in a sea. A sea of shit and sick. Seems like the only way out is to sink to the bottom and drown in it.

I REMEMBERED that night and what had led to that depressing passage. Before the images could bubble up in my thoughts, I pushed the memory away and kept it silent.

"Not to rush you," Bri's voice called down the stairs. "But food's almost ready."

"Coming," I called back, closing the notebook and retying the cord around it.

The whole point of coming here was to get away from what I'd written in that brief entry, or at least attempt to before I lost my mind from the sheer peace and quiet this town seemed filled with. I wasn't sure how that was going to work, but it was a lot better than continuing to feel like the rising tide of shit and sick was slowly eroding my sanity.

And hell, maybe Bri was right. Maybe there was something here to hold my interest. Stranger things had happened.

TREVOR

The ache in my head was growing steadily, and no matter how much I rubbed my temples, it wouldn't leave me in peace as I looked over the reports. It was only Tuesday, but I was ready for the weekend to start. Not that it mattered since I usually worked weekends, but it was the thought that counted.

"You're sure about this?" I asked Jane, peering over the reports.

"That's what they gave us," she said, looking uneasy.

I'd known there would be issues with Durkins after my little 'stunt,' but I hadn't expected them to come so soon. If anything, I'd expected the issue would be something he'd want to stay on top of before it spiraled out of control for all of us. Drug dealers were a fact of life, even in small towns like Fairlake or Fovel, and you had to learn to accept them to a certain degree.

Hell, before marijuana had been legalized in the state, I was content to ignore most of the dealers unless they were bringing in too much. As harmless as the drug was considered, people who brought in more than they could sell to a small clientele were trouble waiting to happen. Either they were setting up a mini-empire, or someone else would come sniffing around to see what was going on. But the ones throwing out dime bags here and there? Well, unless it was to a minor, we had bigger fish to fry than a few stoners.

Durkins didn't always have the same attitude, which made his 'reports' from Fovel all the more frustrating. This wasn't pot I was worried about, it was meth, of all things. I'd been sent the information and seen the official reports from various agencies. I knew how much damage meth could do if it was allowed to spread through a community. That wasn't even covering the potential hazards of having manufacturers on your doorstep. They were as nasty and territorial as gangs in the cities and generally got away with things if they chose their spots right.

"That bastard," I muttered, pushing the file away. "That miserable, petty, vindictive bastard. The least he could do is choose something that isn't going to screw over decent people."

I knew those bastards were camped in the forest and starting to accumulate. The problem was, they were a lot smarter than the ones we'd chased out a few years before and the time before that. Apparently, they had learned from their predecessor's mistakes and were keeping a low profile. That didn't change the reports of more strangers than usual being seen in the forest and camping there. And it didn't change the fact that we still had more missing hikers and campers in the past year than we'd had in a while.

"Bad weather and animals," Durkins had passed it off as in his report from Fovel. "City idiots who think they can make it out here because it's pretty."

The man's opinion was worth as much as his morals, and both spit on the badge he stuck on his flabby chest. I knew he was deliberately underreporting on his end, or at least in his summary, while keeping Fovel's real reports to himself. I suspected he had fewer reports than I did and probably believed the problem was closer to Fairlake than Fovel, which meant far less trouble for him, especially if he didn't help to nip it in the bud before it blossomed into a full-scale problem.

"Chief?" Jane asked, looking wary.

"Have you ever considered a career in politics?" I asked her, glaring down at the paperwork.

"Ugh," she grunted, wrinkling her nose. "I think I'd rather shovel shit on some Kansas farm like my brother."

"That's actually a decent comparison," I snorted. "If that's the case, and you ever find yourself being offered my position in the future, don't take it. Because the shit you'll be shoveling will come from the people, the politicians, and every other municipal asshole."

"Me?" she asked with a laugh, but I could see she was startled by the idea.

"Yes, you," I grunted, shoving the folder aside so I didn't have to see it anymore.

"Not really what I pictured for my future."

"As a choice or a possibility?"

"Both?"

"And here I was going to offer you my job so I could go into early retirement," I said with grim disappointment.

"Ask Bennett," she said with a snort.

"Him?"

"Yeah, why not? He believes in the job, he's good at it, and people like him."

All things I had noticed as well, but I wasn't sure it was the sort of responsibility I wanted to place on his shoulders. Jane wasn't tougher than Bennett, but she was...grimmer. There was a sturdiness to her that gave her a better chance of dealing with the crap that came with the position. I was sure

Bennett could manage it, but he would lose some of the brightness that endeared him so much to other people.

"I guess I'll have to wait a couple of decades and decide which of you idiots I want to suffer the most," I said with a shrug.

Bad weather and animals, my ass. Chief Durkins and I both knew that was absolute bullshit. The weather had been relatively mild for the past few years, save for a nasty blizzard that knocked out the power a couple of years ago. By all reports from the DNR, there have been fewer wildlife incidents lately and a steady decline for the past decade.

"Is there anything we can do?" she asked.

"You personally? No, just keep doing your jobs," I said, then hesitated. "If you can sniff around and see if anyone has noticed anything else happening on the edge of town, that'd be great. Especially if they've noticed strangers who are a little...off."

"You realize in this town you're going to get a lot of reports of strangers, right?"

"You and your partner are smart enough to sort through the bullshit for things worth paying attention to."

"Sure, Chief, we can do that," she said, watching me curiously.

"Good, thank you for bringing me this," I said, even if it had done nothing to make me feel better.

Nodding, she turned and left my office, leaving me in an even worse mood than before. I had no way to prove my suspicions about what Durkins was up to or that my worries about what was happening at our borders were valid either. My only plan for the moment was to gather as much information as possible and hope something worthwhile was dug up.

The problem with wait-and-see was that often problems weren't noticed until they were teetering on disasters. If the manufacturers managed to get a strong enough foothold in the forest, the nightmare that would come crashing onto my lap would be huge. The blowback for my 'ineptitude' would be bad enough, especially when people like Durkins would inevitably feed it. The bastard would happily ride the wave and try to make it bigger to take me out, and I could only shudder to think what sort of outsider they would bring in to take my place.

The worst was the damage it would cause to Fairlake and its people. It would open the town up to a whole host of problems, and that wasn't even counting the number of dangerous and violent people making the meth and those guarding it. Users would flow in, dealers in the town might start selling it, and new dealers would crop up. All in all, I was staring down a barrel at the possibility that my quiet little town could get a lot less quiet and a lot more dangerous.

I had to think of something to get around this because my gut told me a storm was brewing, whether we were ready for it or not.

I flinched at the buzz of my phone and sighed, leaning forward to press the button. "Yes, Ira?"

"We have Mayor Collins and a...reporter here. Both want to speak to you," she told him, her voice giving nothing away.

"Reporter? From where?"

"I think you should probably ask him yourself."

"Fine, I'll be right there."

Just what I needed, a reporter of all things. A small newspaper reported news for the county, and a two-man team sent out a weekly newsletter covering the town's news. They always made appointments, however, so I was always ready for them to show up and ask questions. Anytime a reporter showed up unexpectedly, it was from out of town, and it almost always meant trouble for whoever they were interviewing.

Either this was a stroke of rare genius on Durkins' part to apply more pressure to me before word managed to get out, or someone else had already done some digging and wanted to find out more, or this was a coincidence because someone upstairs wanted to screw with me. Whatever the reason, I pushed away from my desk with a grimace, fully prepared to deal with whatever stupid shit was waiting for me.

The officers were all doing their own thing, and I thanked whoever was screwing with me that Bennett seemed preoccupied with his computer. I hoped it was work-related, but I'd accept a game of solitaire, whatever kept him occupied. The whole town might know he was hell on wheels when he got a bright idea in that goofy head of his, but I didn't need outsiders knowing that as well.

"I'm telling you," a strange voice piped up as I neared the front. "If you think this series gets interesting, you should look into the Fairy Tails series."

"That would be the one where tails is spelled like a tail and not a story, right?" Ira asked.

"Exactly," the new voice said, and I could imagine it accompanied by a smirk. "It's ten times as spicy, though I wouldn't let your boss see you reading it."

"A little more spice in my diet couldn't hurt," Ira chuckled.

"Hopefully not too much," I said, announcing myself. "The last time you ate something too spicy, you wouldn't let Horowitz live it down for two weeks."

Ira shot me a knowing look because we both knew full well we were not talking about food. Mayor Collins stood a couple of yards from the front desk, looking bemused but beaming when he saw me. The man was built more like a linebacker gone to seed than a politician, a product of his time working in a steel mill north of Fairlake before becoming mayor. His arms and chest were still thickly built, but his middle grew a little more every year.

"Trevor," he greeted pleasantly in his deep rumble that sounded like it came from the depths of the earth.

"Fred," I greeted in return, looking at the other visitor.

The stranger was about average height, and his build was proportionate. The sides of his hair looked recently shorn, leaving the top, which was blond at the tips and darkened naturally as it reached his skull, to flop around his face. There was a stud in his ear, silver with a green gem twinkling in it. When he turned to face me, I saw an angular face with just enough jaw to keep his chin from looking sharp. There was a scar cutting through his left brow, curling up around his forehead. There were dark rings around his eyes, but the eyes themselves were bright, and not just green. They flashed with evaluation, curiosity, and something else.

"Trevor, huh?" he asked, pushing up from the desk to hold his hand out. "You can call me Ethan."

"Chief Price while I'm on duty," I told him, taking in his swagger and the way his smile came just a little too confidently to his lips. He struck me as someone still young enough to know arrogance but old enough to have the experience to fuel it. "Is there something I can do for you, Mr.—?"

"Crane, Ethan Crane," he said, and even having barely met him, I could hear the amusement in his voice. "But you don't have to be that formal."

"I keep things professional while on duty," I said, immediately sensing him trying to shift the conversation in his favor.

"Well, maybe I'll just have to find you off-duty one of these days," he said, clearly amused. I knew what he was trying to do, and he knew I wasn't allowing it...and found it funny.

I didn't think he and I were destined to get along.

"Is there something I can do for you, Mr. Crane?" I asked again before he could continue.

"Actually, I just wanted to have a conversation," Ethan said, eyes roaming the precinct. "Poke around, get a feel for things."

My eyes shifted to Fred, the question clear. The mayor chuckled. "Mr. Crane here caught me while I was doing my rounds and had a few questions about Fairlake. I didn't see the harm in letting him meet some of the movers and shakers in town."

"I even got to meet the local grocery store owner," Ethan said with another amused smirk. "Greene's Market, I can't decide if it's a cliché or be amazed the store is considered a focal point of the town."

"He's not used to small towns," Mayor Collins explained as if that somehow did away with the borderline sneering comment. "So he's amazed about all sorts of things."

"Greene's Market has been in business since 1891. Named because the wood of the original building had a green color, and the original owner wasn't aware of how to spell 'Green.' But apparently, he had a head for business since it's stayed open for over one hundred and thirty years," Ethan recited. "It's stayed in the family the entire time, and the owners are known for their extreme and donating to good causes. They do a lot for the town, and I expect, being the only large convenience store around, they get a lot back."

Fred's brow quirked. "Well, that's a fine memory you've got there from our conversation an hour ago. Don't remember mentioning donations, though."

Ethan drew his phone from his pocket, giving it a wiggle. "Amazing the things you can pick up from the internet."

"There...those reports shouldn't be public," Fred said, looking disturbed.

I crossed my arms over my chest. "Mr. Crane found the online newsletters. Mr. Canticle was given an award last year for the donations he and his family made to the children's ward over in Fovel."

From the look on his face, our illustrious mayor hadn't known the local newsletter had gone digital. I was regarded as stubborn about using technology, and even I knew that... two years ago.

"Heya, Chief, I got a...Ethan?" Bennett piped up from behind me, voice shifting from lighthearted to curious. "What're you doing here?"

"Being given an impromptu tour of the town," Ethan said with a shrug.

I turned, raising a brow. "You two know each other?"

"That's a very complicated question to answer," Bennett said slowly.

"Pretty sure it just requires a yes or no."

"Yes, we know each other."

"And how's that?"

"And there's why it's complicated because I knew that question was coming."

I glanced over to silently ask the same question of Ethan, who gazed back at me with an amused expression that gave absolutely nothing away. I wasn't sure how someone could manage both, and I frowned when his scarred brow twitched as if daring me to keep pushing.

"Well?" I asked, taking the silent dare and glancing between them.

Was this some ex of Bennett's? It wasn't like him to act awkward about knowing someone. I watched him glance nervously between everyone, licking his bottom lip as if fighting the words. I wouldn't have thought Bennett could feel awkward or embarrassed.

Ethan snorted, shaking his head at Bennett. "I'm Bri's younger brother."

The name rattled around in my memory, and I glanced at Bennett, who sighed. "Adam's ex-wife."

Well, that explained why the name sounded familiar. I'd probably heard it a few times. And as strange as it was to witness—and a little funny—it at least explained why Bennett was acting so oddly. "So, you're acquainted with your boyfriend's former brother-in-law?"

"Briefly," Bennett muttered. "Met him for the first time this weekend when we dropped Colin off with Bri."

"You know, from what I've been told, you're supposed to be immune to being shy or bashful," Ethan said, looking at Bennett. "And here I am, seeing firsthand that's not true."

Bennett huffed. "You're enjoying this, aren't you?"

"I am," Ethan said, and I frowned at him. It was one thing for me to get amusement out of watching Bennett shuffle about awkwardly, but I didn't like this stranger doing it. Especially when it looked like he was getting a little *too* much enjoyment out of it.

The Mayor cleared his throat. "Well, I suppose you wouldn't object to a little tour?"

"I'm not a tour guide," I told him, arching my brow.

"Well, of course not, but I'm sure Bennett could do it," he replied, and I could see he was avoiding meeting my eyes.

Fairlake wasn't a popular tourist attraction, but we saw our fair share of strangers. That included people like Ethan, who knew someone in town. I couldn't recall a time when our mayor had decided they were eligible for a guided tour. What exactly about this cocky man had provoked Fred to start acting like a personal guide?

"Bennett is working," I told him slowly, staring him down. Thankfully, I didn't hear any argument from Bennett, even though we both knew he wasn't busy with anything that couldn't wait. He might have sensed something was going on, which I wouldn't put past him, the man came off like an idiot without two brain cells to rub together, but he was more observant than people gave him credit for. That, or he didn't want to be the one to give the tour.

My suspicions about Fred were confirmed when he reached up to adjust his tie unnecessarily. He only did it when he was nervous, and now I was even more irritated and intrigued about what had led to him taking time out of his day to show a stranger around town.

"Oh, I haven't a thing to do," Ira said, surprising me as she pushed up from her desk. "I suppose I should give you a little tour."

"Well, that's kind of you," Fred said, beaming at her and probably glad for the opportunity not to have to meet my gaze any longer.

I arched a brow at her in curiosity, but she only smiled, completely unfazed by everything as usual. Ira was usually quite content to stay at the front desk, pretending she was working when in reality, she was reading her spicy romance novels. Getting her to leave the desk for anything other than necessities was a chore.

"Oh, don't think you're getting out of coming along," Ira told Fred, looking at him over the top of her glasses. "I wanted to ask after that new girlfriend of yours."

I smirked as I watched Fred's face twitch, and he realized why Ira was so willing to play tour guide. Though as I watched her eyes drift to Ethan and saw a happy gleam, I realized there was more to it than just small-town nosiness. I suspected that while I wasn't pleased at this intruder, Ira was, at the very least, intrigued, if not delighted.

"Excellent," Ethan said, the sly look on his face disappearing as he offered her an arm. "Then I'll let you lead the way and trust your judgment."

"You think I don't know a bullshitter when I see one?" she asked him wryly.

"Does that mean I should stop?" he asked.

"Goodness no," she chuckled, looping her arm through his. "Let's go this way. Come along, Fred."

The only pleasure I was going to get from this was the defeated expression on the man's face as he followed after the chatting duo, shoulders slumped. One good thing was I could hear their progress as Ira began to explain the rooms and, if I heard right, some of the history of the building as well.

I turned to Bennett, who was looking conflicted. "Tell me why your boyfriend's brother-in-law is skulking around the station."

Bennett frowned. "Boyfriend's *former* brother-in-law."

"Is that really important right now?"

"Considering I want to slap a ring on Adam's hand one of these days, yeah, that distinction is pretty important."

That gave me pause. "You've...not even been dating for two years."

"I won't expose myself by saying the exact number of days we've been dating, but that's beside the point."

"Huh. It's that serious?"

In another surprising turn of events, Bennett's eyes lit up with an expression I'd never seen on his face before. Not that I hadn't seen him happy, that was his default state, but this wasn't his usual style. There was a warmth I wasn't used to seeing, something almost shy about the way he smiled. "Yeah, yeah, it is."

"Right," I grunted, not sure what I'd just managed to step in. I didn't exactly go out of my way to know the status of my officers' personal lives, at least not their romantic ones. I didn't have to, people gossiped enough that I learned things against my will, and so I'd known things between Bennett and Adam were serious, I just hadn't realized marriage was already a possibility. "I'll hold off on any congratulations until we see if he's insane enough to agree to spend his life with you."

Bennett's familiar grin returned. "Thanks a lot, Chief. I can always count on you to boost my morale."

"Uh-huh," I grunted, crossing my arms over my chest. "Still doesn't tell me why he's here."

"I have no clue," Bennett said, eyes widening. "I only got to talk to him a bit on Sunday. I mean, he seemed alright, just—"

"Just what?"

"I don't know. I got a weird feeling about him."

"Yes, so did I. Particularly the part where I found out he was a reporter and was asking for me."

"For you?" he asked, cocking his head. "Well, that's...huh."

I narrowed my eyes. "You are not improving my bad feelings on the subject. What paper does he work for? Why would he be here asking about me? This is Fairlake, for God's sake. What in the fresh hell could be interesting to him?"

"Doesn't work for a paper. At least that's what Adam told me," Bennett said with a shrug. "I guess he's independent. Does these long stints of, like, investigating places and things, then writes a bunch of stuff on it. Then turns around and sells it to papers and news...places."

If I thought Bennett might have answers that made me feel better, I was sorely disappointed. "What kind of investigations?"

"Uhhh, I didn't ask, and Adam didn't go into details. Just said he looks into illegal stuff. Finds stuff people wouldn't want him to talk about and then goes and talks about it. Pictures, interviews, the works."

Great, just what I needed. In the middle of an ego battle with another police chief, quietly trying to ascertain just how bad the meth manufacturing problem was, there was now a cocky reporter here to boot. It would have been too easy to dismiss my reaction as knee-jerk. I had never pretended to be comfortable with nosy people, especially reporters. Didn't help that his attitude, in those few minutes, had already managed to rub me in the wrong way.

"I'm guessing from the look on your face you're not a fan," Bennett said with a laugh. "If I'd known he was going to go poking around, I would have warned you. Adam says he's always been...difficult. Adam seems to like him just fine, but he's always been a handful, according to Bri. Never knew how to sit still."

We both jumped when we heard a chuckle echo from somewhere behind Bennett. "I've heard that phrase enough times to know when I'm being spoken about."

Ethan appeared, and my eyes narrowed when I realized he was alone. "Where are Ira and Fred?"

"She decided it was the prime moment to corner him in the break room and ask about his new girlfriend," Ethan said, sipping from a Styrofoam cup. "He doesn't seem all that keen to answer her questions, but she's, uh, quite talented at getting what she wants, isn't she?"

"Oh, if Ira wants to know something, she'll take down any obstacle in her way," Bennett said with a chuckle. "Doesn't matter if she has to bribe, blackmail, or bully her way in, she'll get what she wants."

"Ah, now there's a woman after my own heart," Ethan said with a sigh.

"I'm not sure if Ira would be flattered or give you *that* look for suggesting anything, uh, what's her word for it? Untoward? Yeah, untoward."

"It doesn't have to be untoward. Just a nice dinner, a few good glasses of...hmm, she strikes me as a whiskey drinker."

I arched a brow. "And how would you know anything about that?"

"You get a sense for these sorts of things," he said, apparently trying for mysterious and landing firmly on irritating. "Bennett's a beer man, but that's like saying ducks like water."

Bennett snorted. "Not that hard to figure out. I'm a simple man."

I eyed him. "You said it, not me."

Bennett stuck his tongue out. "Guess the Chief."

"Leave me out of—"

"Tequila."

I stopped short, blinking as Bennett chuckled. "Guess you're not that good."

"Oh yeah?" Ethan said, sounding unbothered by Bennett's revelation.

"I've been in his office enough times to know it's brandy and *maybe* bourbon if it's been a rough week."

Ethan looked me over, and I frowned at him, which only made him smile. "Nah, he's got tequila written all over him. Now, the part I'm stuck on. Is it when he's had a *really* bad week, or is it when he wants to have a good week?"

Bennett shook his head. "I've never seen him drink anything else."

"There's a keyword in there that you're not latching onto."

"I don't have to see it to know. Shit, tequila is right up there with beer for one of the most identifiable smells."

Ethan smirked, glancing back at me. "And what do you have to say?"

"I think if you're done with your guided tour, then you should probably continue with the rest of the town," I said, glad I sounded bored. I had no idea what told him I was into tequila, but his accuracy was unnerving. "We still have jobs to do."

Bennett snorted. "And with that not-so-subtle hint, I

should probably get back to my desk. Try not to antagonize him too much, please, I still have half a shift ahead of me, and he's already grouchy enough on a good day."

"Livingston," I growled.

"Already going," he said, waving at me as he disappeared down the hallway.

Ethan's eyes followed Bennett out of the room long enough that I cleared my throat roughly. His attention snapped back to me, and he grinned once more. "Don't worry."

"Just so long as you aren't getting any ideas," I warned him, instincts telling me I was on the right track...in a way. "I don't care if your tastes run into blond idiots and older, wiser women."

"Even if I *was* interested in Bennett, a whole line of people would happily skin me alive if I let the thought linger for more than a moment," he informed me with a snort. "Don't mistake me, he's definitely good-looking, but I don't steal other people's toys."

"Delightful," I grunted, not at all relieved to hear Bennett referred to as a toy.

His eyes appraised me, and it was then, now he was closer, and the sunlight was streaming through the doors, hitting his face, that I saw flecks of yellow in his eyes. "Hmmm, which branch?"

I squinted. "Excuse me?"

"Which branch of the military? You've got the whole," he waved over me with his free hand, "former military vibe to you."

"If you want to conduct an interview, talk to Ira, and we'll see what we can arrange," I told him curtly. Of course, the chances of me allowing that in my schedule were somewhere between zero and none. I was quickly beginning to under-stand why some considered him difficult. His flippancy irritated me, yet he still managed to charm the normally immune Ira and rope Fred into this little venture. On top of all that, he was irritatingly and disconcertingly perceptive. "And the same can be said of my officers."

"Covering all your bases," he said with a hum.

"We don't need anyone coming in and trying to stir up trouble," I told him.

"And I'd do that?"

"I don't know what you'd do. You're a stranger to me."

He chuckled. "Small town mentality?"

"Something of the sort," I told him stiffly. Most of the town's xenophobic attitudes were kept to a minimum and were dying out with each successive generation. That didn't change the fact that we did see ourselves as a community and weren't fond of people coming in from outside and causing trouble. That went even more so for me, especially when my instincts were telling me, amongst other things, that trouble was already lurking close to town as it was.

If he was bothered by the idea, Ethan didn't show it as he brushed past me toward the front doors, stopping to stare outside. "Truth be told, I've never been in anything resembling a small town...not for pleasure anyway."

"Perhaps you should try it," I told him. "Instead of keeping yourself busy, busy yourself with relaxing."

"Never been very good at that," he chuckled, draining the cup and tossing it into a nearby trash can. "I suppose it wouldn't hurt to try, but somehow, I get the feeling that isn't going to happen. I'm sure my sister's right. I'll find something to entertain me."

I gritted my teeth and chose to say nothing, sensing that pushing things further would only get even more of his interest. He hadn't affirmed or denied it, but I suspected he was on the lookout for something to occupy his time, and I didn't want to give him a potential target. If anything, I hoped he'd quickly lose interest in whatever potential he thought Fairlake had and go somewhere else.

"Leaving so soon?" Ira piped up, bustling back with a smug expression on her face. By the look on Fred's face, she had a reason to be smug.

"Figured I'd get a bit of air," he said. "It feels stuffy in here without you around to keep me company."

"Oh pfft, flatterer," she chuckled, taking her place behind the desk again. "You be sure not to make yourself scarce. This old woman could use a bit more flattery every now and again."

"I wouldn't want to disappoint," Ethan said. "And thank you for the conversation today, Mayor Collins. Apologies for getting you snagged. I didn't realize how dangerous my company would be."

Somehow I thought the only one who believed that parting shot was Fred from the grateful, if forgiving, smile he gave Ethan before the younger man disappeared. I raised a brow, and he cleared his throat, muttering something about needing to deal with a few things before the afternoon was over and followed after Ethan.

"Get everything you needed?" I asked dryly as Ira pulled her book out, not even bothering to pretend to work. Not that I was going to reprimand or fire her, and we both knew it.

"As if he could keep something like that from me," she chuckled. "I knew that boy when he wandered around my neighborhood, finger up his nose and thumb up his ass."

"I really hope that's not literal," I said, wrinkling my nose.

"Well, the thumb part isn't," she said with a chuckle. "Don't think I don't remember seeing you around here too, Trevor."

"Me? I was a good kid. Behaved myself."

"You were until you met Troy Prince," she chuckled, and I

felt an ugly swooping feeling in my stomach. "Oh, that boy couldn't sit still to save his life and couldn't stay out of trouble either. Then you went and became bosom buddies, and he taught you how to have a little fun. Honestly, if I think about it, he reminds me a little—"

"I really don't want to know the end of that sentence," I told her bluntly.

It was an unusual display of rudeness on my part, and her eyes flickered above the top of her book to settle on mine. People in town around my age and older rarely brought up Troy around me. It felt stupid at times to still be sensitive to the reminder of the man everyone had known was bonded to the hip with me growing up, but...I didn't want to deal with it. They could all reminisce without me, and even after years, no one had tried to push it.

I could see Ira was tempted to push it, and I frowned at her. Worse, I saw the moment she relented, and it looked a lot more like pity than acceptance as she turned her eyes back to her book.

"Thank you," I said, glancing out the window and huffing when I saw Ethan still standing outside as he stared up at the precinct. "And you made a new friend."

I didn't bother to react to her chuckle. "You sound like a disapproving father."

I looked at her, utterly unimpressed. "I have no intention of even glancing in the direction of whatever...flirtations the two of you shared."

"Oh, he is dangerous, I'll give him that," she said with a pleased laugh. "But I'm pretty sure he wasn't the least bit interested in me. Even if he was, I'm long past the point of being enamored with tow-headed troublemakers with a nice smile."

She tucked the book in front of her face, and I knew she was already sinking back into the story, not bothering to acknowledge anyone else around her. I left her there to return to my office and my pondering.

I didn't know about her assessment of his smile, but my instincts told me she was right about something. Ethan was certainly dangerous. In just a few minutes, my gut told me trouble would follow him as long as he remained in town. I didn't think there was a way for me to shorten his stay, but at the very least, I hoped he found something that caught his interest before he wandered off into the world again.

And yet somehow I didn't think I would be as lucky as never to see him again.

ETHAN

"Kid, you and I are going to fight," I informed the chubby demon in front of me.

Colin grinned, showing mostly gum but a few tiny teeth as well. My threat meant absolutely nothing to him as he took my wireless mouse and once more tried shoving it in his mouth. It was a little too big for his drool-filled maw, however, but apparently, he was going to give it his best shot. The whole time, he stared back at me with his big eyes as if daring me to follow through on my threat.

"Alright, fine, maybe not fight, but I'm not going to be happy," I told him, knowing that readjusting your firm stance was a sign of weakness. I wasn't sure if babies could detect that sort of fear, but Colin certainly could because he continued to look pleased with himself.

What had possessed me to try to do research in the living room undisturbed? I had slept till almost two and, after getting something to eat, settled down to do some digging around. I had barely an hour to myself before Bri and a wiggling Colin burst through the door.

"Someone decided that puking *down* Mommy's shirt

rather than on it was the better option," she announced as she dropped a large diaper bag and a suitcase onto the chair. "Do you think you can handle watching him while I take a quick shower? Or would that be too much for your poor brain?"

"I'm capable of watching a baby for what, fifteen minutes, without either of us getting injured or killed," I informed her with a snort.

"Alright," she said, and while I could respect her not bothering to hide her doubt, I still scowled. "Shout if you need anything."

I waited until I heard the door shut before raising an eyebrow at Colin, who was on his feet, holding onto the corner of the coffee table. "She honestly thinks something catastrophic will happen if I watch you for fifteen minutes. I've survived death squads trying to kill me, street gangs hunting me, and a bombing raid. You think she'd have some faith."

Which is precisely when Colin decided to teeter on his legs, reaching out and grabbing hold of the cloth runner on the coffee table. Since a plastic plant and my cup of coffee were the only things on the table, there was nothing keeping him up. Down he went, with the crash and clatter of my cup and the plastic flower pot, to the floor as my nephew tipped out of sight.

I shot up, leaning over to see him sitting on the floor, the runner in his hands as he fiddled with it. "Right, good start. Well done."

"What was that?" I heard from the bathroom.

"I threw him out the window because he sneezed on me!" I shouted back.

After that, I decided the best course of action was to drop him between my legs on the couch and hope I could continue what I was doing. It took approximately thirty seconds before I learned that babies were much like drunks, prone to breaking things and requiring something to occupy their attention, or they'd find an inconvenient way to occupy themselves, which was how I found my wireless mouse becoming his new chew toy.

"I'm really hoping your mom has some nice antibacterial wipes in that overstuffed bag of yours," I informed him. Colin gurgled around the mouse, making it click as he continued nibbling. "That's not a teething ring."

Seeing he didn't care in the slightest what I had to say, I gently reached around him to tug the device from his mouth. The thing probably wasn't sanitary to begin with, and if it was, it definitely wasn't now. I was careful not to pull too hard, but I was quickly learning just how much of a death grip babies had when they were determined to keep hold of something.

"Thank you," I told him softly as I finally got it away, curling my nose at the saliva coating the front of it. "Ah, yes, *thank you*."

Which was when I felt his chest hitch and his body quiver. Frowning, I set the mouse on the table to look at his face, only to be alarmed at the sheer amount of scrunching.

"Oh, don't do that," I said, eyes widening. "Absolutely do not do th—"

I shuddered as the cry burst out of him with more force than lungs that size should be capable of. Wincing, I immediately placed him on my knee, bouncing as I tried to quiet him.

"Oh, c'mon dude, don't do this to me," I moaned, wincing as he found a new pitch.

Bri appeared, wrapped in a bathrobe, her hair around her neck. "Well, that's not a very happy sound."

"I'm not the one making it!" I protested.

"Thank God for that," she muttered before bending down to take Colin off my leg. "What'd you do?"

"I wouldn't let him chew on my mouse," I said, gesturing to the spit-soaked device. "And then he started the shrieking."

"I thought that might be your 'I was told no when I really want to' scream," Bri told Colin, chuckling as she dug through the bag. She pulled out a colorful ring and handed it to him. "Here, sweetheart."

The screaming stopped immediately as Colin shoved the ring into his mouth while I watched in disbelief. "Seriously? Just...he has different cries?"

"He's got hungry noises, diaper is full noises, noises he makes when he's denied something he wants, all sorts."

"And you can...tell the difference?"

"If you're around long enough, you'll pick them up."

"You sure that's not, like, a mom superpower?"

"If it is, then I'll have to inform Adam that he is, in fact, a mother."

"Okay, fine, maybe it's just a parent superpower," I grunted.

"Maybe," she said, sitting in the chair and pulling Colin into her lap. "I think if you're around it long enough, you start to pick up on things."

"I'll take your word for it," I said, turning my attention back to my computer. The mouse was a loss for the moment, and I stuck to using the trackpad and the touch screen, copying part of the article into a document before opening up a new search window.

"I'm terrified to ask," Bri said, her tone cautious. "But you've been pecking away at that computer for over a week now. Just what have you been doing?"

"What? I'm not allowed to spend time on the computer?" I asked, reaching for my coffee and realizing it had been dumped. With a grimace, I went to fetch a towel from the kitchen. The problem with getting caught up in research was I could get easily sucked into it and forget the most mundane things like, say, picking up a mess your tiny nephew made while you were in charge of keeping an eye on him. It was honestly a miracle Bri hadn't said anything, but she was pretty occupied with her now cooing son.

"You spent the weekend relaxing, went out to see the town once, and then spent the week after that on your computer," she reminded me as I returned to mop up the mess, pretending I didn't see the knowing expression on her face.

"Good detective work," I chuckled, wrapping the towel around the puddle's attempt to spread further. "Fine, I've been digging around the town's history."

"Fairlake?" she asked in surprise.

"No, some other podunk town in the middle of Colorado."

"You know, no matter how often you try to force it, you're never going to make that much sarcasm attractive."

"A good thing I have several other things going for me in that department."

"Save for humility."

"Why be humble when you can be pretty?" I asked with a wink, gathering the towel to rinse in the sink.

Her derisive snort carried through the house. "At the risk of making your ego even larger, I like the haircut, by the way. I meant to say something days ago."

"Thanks, thought about dyeing it, but figured I'd give someone around here a heart attack," I said, wringing the towel out until the water ran clear.

"You're aware that even in Fairlake, it's the twenty-first century and not the fifties, right? You can color your hair. The woman at the bakery colors hers all the time, and no one thinks twice about it."

I knew that, and I'd been tempted after I'd cut and washed it. It was something I'd always enjoyed doing growing up, and after a few rough beginnings, I'd gotten quite good at it. The last time had been two years before, and I'd shaved it all off before I'd flown out to the heart of Mexico to do some digging up and down the coast to track cartel activity. Vibrant purple hair was all well and good when you were safely in the city and wanted to stand out, but not so much when trying to draw as little attention as possible to stay alive.

I didn't know what stopped me, any more than I knew why I decided to put my old piercings back in after getting to New York City. I'd go to my grave before admitting it, but my parents had been right about a few things. Sometimes even I didn't know why I did the things I did. Sometimes it just felt right, so I went with it.

"So, what made you decide to research Fairlake?" she called, pulling me out of my reverie. "I got the feeling you weren't all that interested in the town."

She was absolutely right because there wasn't much about the town that drew me. True, there was an allure to a small quiet town of close-knit people, but I thought that was true for many people who'd known nothing but urban sprawl growing up. I couldn't picture settling down and living in a place like Fairlake and still reserved my opinion on whether or not my sister had lost her mind moving somewhere like this.

Still, it seemed fair to give the place a chance and see what kind of stories there were. Even I knew a place like Fairlake had to have its share of interesting stories. Of course, interesting could range anywhere from an interesting family tree to unsolved murders.

Both of which Fairlake had.

"I never said I wasn't interested," I called back, opening

the freezer, pulling out the tequila to mix with orange and pineapple juice, and adding ice. "There were some things worth seeing."

"Oh yeah? Bennett told me you stopped by the police station."

Boy, I knew the stereotype for nosy neighbors in small towns had to be based in *some* fact, but I was beginning to suspect it was less stereotype and more way of life in Fairlake. Then again, if I really wanted to do some digging because people were far larger treasure troves of information than any curated articles could be, that could be to my advantage.

"Well, the mayor decided to stop by and see if I might find something to my liking," I told her as I returned with my glass.

Her gaze flickered to the drink, but other than a faint shadow over her brow, she gave no reaction to my cocktail. "I like how you'd only been in the town a few days and ran into the mayor. I've only ever seen him in passing

"Guy looks like an ex-boxer," I snorted, sitting on the couch again.

"So, find anything to your liking at the police station?" she asked, now bouncing Colin on her knee.

"Would have been nice to know the local police chief is fucking daddy material," I said with a snort.

"Language," she hissed, glaring down at Colin.

"Freaking daddy material, then."

She snorted. "Somehow I don't think that's much better. And I'm torn. I wonder if you should never say that around Bennett or if you should, but only if you promise to make sure I'm around to see the look on his face."

"So, like what, does he have daddy issues and somehow attached himself to his boss in some maladaptive coping mechanism?" I wondered.

"I...no? What? Stop reading psychology textbooks, they're rotting your brain."

I laughed. "I'm joking."

"His relationship with his parents is great," she said with a shake of her head. "But from what I've heard, most of the officers at the precinct have a sort of parent, child relationship with him. Or at least, that's how Adam made it sound. I don't think Bennett's ever admitted that to anyone."

"Lovely," I snorted. "But seriously, have you seen the guy?"

"Can't say that I have, actually."

"Oof," I grunted, giving a little shimmy of my shoulders.

"I really do not want you to say whatever is going on in your head right now," she told me with a frown.

"Oh, you're no fun."

"Well, I don't want you to tell me right now. Wait till someone is down for his nap."

I smirked. "Alright, there's the Bri I know."

It hadn't been all that long ago that I could call her up and have a friendly chat about someone good-looking. Neither of us ever pretended it was anything but shallow, meaningless conversation, but we had done it ever since I'd told her I was bi when I was still a teenager. Hell, we'd even gossiped about Adam when they'd first started seeing one another, and sometimes I wondered what he'd think if he found out just how much I knew about his more...personal bits.

"All I know from Bennett is the guy can be pretty terrifying," Bri said, finally setting Colin down now he was interested in something on the floor.

"Oh, I could see that," I said with a chuckle. "He's a pretty imposing guy. Tall, still keeps himself in shape, and has this look about him, like he's ready to kick someone's ass at the drop of a hat."

"Aaa," Colin piped up from the floor, drawing our attention.

"Oh, shi...no," I sputtered at the kid's attempt at speech.

"Aaaa," he sputtered again, this time gripping what looked like a plush apple with a smiling face printed on it.

"Yes, Colin," Bri said with obvious relief. "Apple."

I grinned sheepishly as she frowned. "Honestly, Ethan."

"Sorry," I said, still abashed. "I don't mean to, it just happens."

She sighed. "I know controlling your mouth has never been one of your strong suits, but could you try?"

"I am," I huffed, wondering how I would learn to control my mouth because, as she'd said, it had never been my greatest skill...unless my life was in danger. Considering how scandalized she looked, it might just be if I continued. "In my defense, I'm not used to controlling what comes out of my mouth...or dealing with kids."

"You can't honestly tell me you've never been around kids the whole time you were working," she said with a frown.

I raised my brow. "Did you, uh, read what I wrote?"

"Skimmed," she admitted, cheeks coloring. "It was, uh...well, that wasn't the easiest thing for a new mother to read."

"Well," I said, unable to keep the sourness out of my voice. "Then, hopefully, you read enough to know when I dealt with kids, they had worse things to worry about than picking up a few curse words from me."

Triumph flashed through me when I saw her wince in shame, turning her eyes to look down at her son as he fumbled about on the floor. People took for granted the kind of world they lived in or the things they believed to be a given. For all our troubles and tribulations growing up, neither of us had experienced even a drop of what some of the people I'd seen had gone through. Thousands of kids in the world wished their greatest problem was whether or not they could shove a wireless mouse in their mouth or if their uncle was a little too free with foul language.

On cue, Colin dropped onto his cushioned butt, soft ring still clenched between his lips as he gazed up at me. It was a little unsettling to see my sister's eyes staring at me from within his innocent face as he suddenly gave a short laugh and waved his hands when our eyes met.

Triumph curled up and died as my own shame took its place, burying it rapidly. It wasn't my sister's fault she lived in a world where she and her son were relatively safe, so her greatest concerns seemed petty to me. It wasn't Colin's fault he was lucky, born to two blood parents who would raise him lovingly and protect him fiercely and was gaining a third parent who would probably do just the same.

"Look," I said slowly, shaking my head as Colin watched everything I did. "I'll try harder. I'm sure I can think of something that'll get me to behave myself, some trick or...I don't know, something."

Bri flashed me a grateful smile. "Maybe we could pull out a swear jar."

"Yeah, kinda thinking financial loss isn't going to be a big motivator for me," I said with a snort.

"I keep forgetting you're rolling in it," she said, bending down to prevent her son from stuffing the runner from the table into his mouth.

"Yeah, well, I wonder why," I said, bending forward to look at my screen.

Bri occupied herself wrestling with her son's death grip on the runner, distracting her from the conversation, for which I was grateful. The money I made from my writing was substantial. After one of my articles had exploded in popularity around the news outlets, there had been a huge uptick in demand for what I wrote. Which meant I could spend more time on investigations, more time writing, and in the end, have a lot more money than I knew what to do with. Now I had major outlets wanting everything I wrote for a substantial fee and smaller publishers buying rights to chunks of it for a decent amount of money.

It wasn't something I liked to talk about, let alone advertise. I did my best to keep just how much money I made a secret from everyone except my lawyer and personal accountant. I needed the money to continue working and to allow myself to do more good with it, but the sheer amount after a few years growth was staggering and unnerving. Anonymously donating to worthy causes always felt lackluster, but I did it anyway, along with the occasional attempt to fund housing and medicine.

Even then, it still felt odd profiting from my work when it was based on other people's suffering. The guilt never really went away, so I tried to assuage it by spending the extra money I didn't save on helping as best I could, then burying the rest of my discomfort under everything else in my life. It might pop up now and again, but at least I could keep it from haunting my everyday life.

"You never told me specifically what you were looking into," Bri said, finally winning her battle, much to her son's annoyance.

"I told you, the town."

"That's vague."

"Well, I started with its basic history. When it was established, the first names to pop up in the record as landowners. Most of the oldest families are gone, but there is one left in Fairlake."

"Old family?"

"Well, one member. The rest of them all moved north a handful of years ago. It's that, uh, cute firefighter friend of Bennett's, Isaiah."

Bri chuckled. "Is there anyone in this town you're not going to show interest in?"

"Your ex-husband and his new boyfriend will take a top spot on the list."

"And we all thank you for your gracious and difficult sacrifice in these trying times," she said dryly.

I raised a brow. "Do you want me to tell you the worst mayor they've had? He got hung by a mob back in 1902 for, well, small ears and all. Let's just say he was a little too interested in some of the single ladies in town and thought he could take what he wanted."

"Charming."

"Well, there was the noose."

"Not saying it wasn't deserved, but that doesn't exactly make the story more charming."

"Best one technically was the wife of the mayor at the time. He died during a series of fires that were going on after a long, nasty drought. She took over, got the town together, saved plenty of lives, housed a bunch of people, and gave hell to government aid administrators digging their heels in. The Elizabeth T. Ripscom library near the town hall is named after her."

"I...alright, I'll take your word for it."

"And that doesn't even cover the past few decades. Shit, there was a murder almost in the heart of the city about a decade ago. By all accounts, the guy was a piece of shit who probably murdered his wife, though that's not really talked about much. Still, gunned down in broad daylight and no witnesses? C'mon, that's one hell of a piece."

"Don't you dare," Bri said with a sharpness that drew my head up.

"Uh," I cocked my head. "Am I missing something here?"

"Devin Mitchell," she said softly.

I checked my notes. "The son. Records put him in Denver."

"We're...not sure where he is at the moment," she said slowly, glancing toward the front window. "But from what I've heard, he's doing pretty good and is set to return."

I blinked, squinting after a moment. "Spill."

"There's nothing to tell you. His old friend, Chase, went to get him from Denver last year, and he lived with him for a while, getting clean and back on his feet."

"Clean?"

"You heard me."

"And now he's AWOL?"

"No, he's...doing something he feels he needs to do."

I remembered her talking to Adam about Chase the week before, and some of the puzzle pieces clicked into place. "He went back out into the world and left Chase."

She frowned. "Leave the story alone, Ethan. I mean it. Devin doesn't need to come back to Fairlake after everything he's been through and find you writing some story about his monster of a father. Trust me, everyone in this town knew who he was, what kind of bastard he was, and Devin most of all. Find something else to pick at, please."

"How do you know all this?"

"Because Bennett is close to Chase, and Bennett slipped some things to me so I would understand. I'm tied into Bennett's life a lot more with him being a third parent, so he wanted me to be aware. I don't know everything, not even close, but I know enough to ask you as a personal favor, to leave this one alone."

The old, familiar urge to rebel against being told what I could or couldn't do rose in me, poking at the back of my tongue, just begging to be released. With a sigh, I swallowed it back down and nodded to show her that I would. It had been interesting to use it as a jumping point for an idea I'd had, but I didn't want to start my time here by ostracizing the only family I had left who didn't treat me like a problem.

There was bound to be plenty in this town to sink my teeth into. It was my firm belief that no matter how small or quiet a place was, there were always plenty of skeletons in the closet.

"From only a week's worth of digging, it sounds like you've got plenty to work with," Bri said, pushing up to her feet. "You could write a book on the history of Fairlake."

The idea *had* crossed my mind, but just as it had then, my nose wrinkled at the thought. I wasn't interested in chronicling the history of a small town I had no emotional connection with. Even writing something interesting or scandalous about it was only a way to keep me occupied while adjusting to my impromptu vacation. A week was not nearly long enough to feel normal again.

And normal was what I was positively surrounded by since I'd arrived in Fairlake. Everywhere I looked, people were going about their daily lives, shopping, taking their kids to and from school, and kids running around and playing. Even at home, I watched Bri go through the routine of being a parent, positively glowing even when stressed or frustrated. It seemed like wherever I looked, there were happy, fulfilled people who had found something to latch onto.

The realization was more bitter than I thought it would be.

"I'm sure I'll find something," I told her instead of immediately shooting down her idea. I had the feeling she was worried about me and was only trying to help, and I didn't want her to feel like I wasn't at least trying to take in her ideas. "There's bound to be something that can grab my attention for more than five minutes."

"This from the man who just spent a week straight

pulling up a whole goddamn history on the town," she said with a snort, bending down to scoop Colin off the floor.

"Language," I chided, smirking when her eyes widened, falling to Colin's face warily.

"Right, point made," she said slowly, relaxing when Colin looked content with the ring in his mouth.

"I was just looking for an excuse to give you shi...uh, trouble," I managed, huffing when she laughed at my admittedly feeble attempt to correct my language.

"There's hope for you yet," she said, turning to walk back toward what I assumed was her bedroom. "Maybe you could write about the police, firefighters, and paramedics? You like writing about action stuff, so why not write about the people who see the most action in town?"

"I'm not sure what kind of action I'm going to see trying to write about small-town police and firefighters," I muttered.

"Well, from the sounds of it, you want plenty of action from the police chief."

"Not quite the same thing."

The idea was amusing, if only because I was sure Chief Price would sooner kick my ass than do anything remotely fun with it. It had been fun to poke a little at him, even as I tried to pick up on things about him.

And well, I hadn't seen a ring on his finger either. There were several reasons a man his age might not be married, though I found it difficult to believe a man with his looks and reputation wouldn't have a string of people lined up to try to settle down with him.

God, this was asking for trouble, and that alone was enough to settle it for me.

I plucked my phone from the table, doing a quick search before tapping the call button next to the result. It buzzed a few times in my ear before a familiar voice piped up.

"Well, hello, Ira, I'm not sure if you remember me, but this is Ethan," I stopped as I heard her warm reply, smiling. "Alright, you do remember me then. Nice to know I made an impression. So, I was wondering if you could fit in an interview with your chief? Yep, the very same...hmmm, well, that's a little off for my schedule. Is there, perchance, something I could do for you to hurry that along a little?"

I waited. We both knew this was a bribe but a relatively harmless one. It would all come down to just how dedicated she was to her—

I grinned. "I think I might be able to swing by and grab a few things from the bakery just for you."

Oh, this could be fun.

Whistling to myself, I walked along the sidewalk and jogged up the stairs to the station. I smiled when I spotted Ira behind the desk, her nose buried in a book as it had been the last time. I wasn't surprised to see it was an entirely different one, despite the thickness. Something told me she was a speedy reader.

She glanced up, her eyes crinkling at the corner as she held up a finger. I patiently waited as she finished whatever sentence or paragraph she was on before sliding a bookmark between the pages and setting it aside. She looked pleased as she eyed the box of baked goods in my hand, the same order I had promised her a few days before on the phone to get an interview with the police chief earlier than two weeks from now.

"As promised," I said, sliding the box onto the desk and nudging it toward her. "Two chocolate banana muffins, two cherry garcia muffins, and it turns out they did indeed have the lavender muffins as well."

"Oh! I wasn't going to hold my breath on those," Ira said, obviously pleased. "I honestly thought lavender was the strangest thing to put into *any* food. But the owner himself came out to give me one for free when he premiered them, and I haven't been able to give them up. Honestly, the man is a genius, and our town is so much better for having him."

My encounter with the owner, Grant, had been much less noteworthy. I'd glimpsed him when he came out to deliver a basket of cookies to the woman manning the front counter. The two couldn't have been more opposite if they'd tried. Everything, from her hair, clothes, and personality, had been bright and colorful, while he'd been far more subdued and reserved. The look in his eye had been almost feverish as he greeted me in the politest tone imaginable before disappearing into the back.

"He struck me as a busy man," I told her as she dragged the box to the side. "And he certainly had quite the selection."

"Oh, I know. I don't know how he manages it. Ever since he became popular on the internet, he's been swamped with orders from everywhere."

"The internet?"

"Oh, one of those social media sites. I don't bother to keep track of them. I only have Facebook to keep up with my kids and grandkids."

I chuckled. "Fair enough. Probably Instagram, that tends to be the one where creators get a lot more attention."

"Creators, huh?" she said thoughtfully, tapping the edge of the desk. "Well, I suppose that's certainly a word for it, isn't it? And he certainly does create, I'll give him that. But at least he's getting the recognition he deserves, though I do wish the poor man would get some help in that kitchen of his. He's going to work himself to death if he keeps trying to keep up with the hype."

I didn't want to tell her the hype would most likely die

out before it became a long-term problem. As much as the internet helped to get some people the attention they wouldn't have normally gotten before the advent of the internet and smartphones, it didn't tend to stick. I was sure he would eventually see a drop in demand for his product and return to more or less normal, albeit with a handful more local regulars.

"So, just how much trouble will you be in for bumping me up the queue?" I asked lightly as I eyed the cover of the book she'd been reading. To my amusement, she'd picked up the series I recommended and was already working her way through what appeared to be the third book. Apparently, the kinky spice that ran through that series was not something she was adverse to.

"Oh, honey, I'm *never* in trouble. If I want to bump around his schedule, I can bump around his schedule. If he didn't want that, he'd do it himself like all the other chiefs before him instead of paying me."

"Just how many have you worked for?"

"Enough," she said, eyes glittering with amusement. "And that's dangerously close to asking how old I am."

"I could just look it up and find out for myself," I said with a laugh.

"Then you do that," she chuckled. "But I will say it's quite an experience, looking after a man I once saw wandering around in a diaper. He grew up to be a good man and a good chief, though, so I'm not complaining."

"Well, I wouldn't expect you to complain," I said with a chuckle. "He does seem to respect you a great deal."

"He respects everyone who works in this building, even down to our nighttime janitor, Phil. He doesn't take any bull, but at the same time, doesn't give any in return. He can seem a little rough around the edges, and he's been called intimidating more than once, but he would never do anything to harm someone under his command," she said, looking me over. "And I hope whatever interview you're planning, you're not also planning on bringing any trouble into his life."

"I'm not sure if I should be offended you think I'm going to be trouble," I admitted to her.

"Oh, sweetheart, you look like trouble, you sound like trouble, and I'd bet my job that you've been a handful since the moment your momma gave birth to you."

"Well, it's hard to argue with the truth."

I heard heavy footsteps coming our way and turned to see Chief Price barreling around the corner, a scowl on his face. "Ira, is my two o'clock here yet or—"

He stopped short the moment he spotted me, and I was impressed his scowl somehow found a way to deepen. No matter what Ira said, he definitely looked like someone who'd be happy to kick my ass and chew hers out for allowing me in.

"Is this my two o'clock?" he asked calmly. His eyes were locked on mine, and I didn't miss the way they swept over me as I leaned against the counter. His brow furrowed further, clearly impressed with my choice of casual clothes. I hadn't thought it necessary to get dressed up...and I didn't have anything formal with me anyway.

Well, it was either my clothes or my presence. Hard to pick which one.

"Well, it's not two anymore, but yes," she said lightly, opening the box to pull out a muffin.

"I thought my two o'clock was Fred."

"He rescheduled to tomorrow for lunch with you."

His eyes fell on the box, and I couldn't help the snort when I saw his face shift, lips parting slightly before frowning again. I didn't bat an eye when he turned his annoyed glance on me, only changing my smile into one a little more innocent. I couldn't prove it, but I was sure he'd put things together and realized Ira was, in fact, amenable to being bribed for the right price.

"Right," he grunted, finally looking up at me again. "Then I guess you should follow me so I can keep up with my schedule."

From the sound Ira made, I was guessing his schedule wasn't demanding, but instead of prodding him further before I'd even talked to him, I smiled benignly and followed him into the hallway. I noted how crisp and clean his uniform was and couldn't avoid spotting that his pants hugged an ass and thighs that would have been the envy of anyone half his age. There was the faintest hint of the bottom of a tattoo on his thick arm, though the rest appeared free of anything save muscle and a thin layer of dark hair.

Well, I might not get anything worth writing from the interview, but at least I'd enjoy watching the interviewee. I pushed the thought to the back of my mind as we passed through the main room, where I earned a few curious glances from the officers on duty, including a bewildered Bennett. I waved to him before disappearing into the back office and braced myself.

Showtime.

TREVOR

Almost sure the sound of my teeth grinding together could be heard. I made a conscious decision to unclench my jaw as we walked between the desks in the main room. There was a slight stir as everyone saw what was a stranger to most of them, and I could feel Bennett's eyes following our paths. Thankfully, no one said anything as I led Ethan toward my office, stopping just inside the door for him to enter before closing it behind us.

I wasn't sure what precisely had happened, but I knew damn well Fred hadn't rescheduled of his own accord. He had someone who dealt with his schedule just as I did, and I knew Stephen didn't veer from the mayor's predetermined schedule unless someone interfered. And, of course, anyone who had worked with Ira for years knew she was an interfering busybody with no shame when it came to getting what she wanted.

"Muffins?" I inquired, keeping my voice neutral as I fought the urge to walk to my liquor cabinet. I had a feeling I'd need to keep my senses dealing with Ethan.

I wasn't surprised to hear him laugh. "Those were indeed muffins."

I fought the urge to flex my fingers, taking a seat behind my desk, unsurprised to see he'd already taken one of the seats on the other side. Either he didn't care about protocol or niceties, or he was deliberately spitting in the face of them to try to mess with me. I didn't know which was worse, though a close runner-up was the realization that either way, it was getting on my nerves.

"Let's try not to get off on the wrong foot," I said evenly, opening the fridge under my desk and pulling out a bottle of water for myself instead of what I really wanted. "There's no point in denying that you managed to bribe her. I'm more surprised that her price was so low. Water?"

"Sure," he said, making himself comfortable. "I've found that everyone has their price. It's just a case of whether or not you can afford it that matters."

"I'd say a willingness to bribe someone is what matters," I said, handing another bottle of water to him. "It begs the question, what else are you willing to do?"

"I'm willing to do a lot of things," Ethan said, cracking open the bottle. It was said with a wry twist of his lips and a tone that made it almost suggestive. "Are you curious about what I'm willing to do? It's quite a list."

Alright, so it was definitely suggestive. I wanted to say it was just him attempting to tease me, taunting me with the questionable things he was willing to do to get what he wanted. On the other hand, some part of me was suddenly aware of the way his throat bobbed when he took a few deep drinks of water and the curve of his neck when he tilted his head to watch me.

I cleared my throat, leaning back in my seat. "It is usually a good idea to know what people are willing to get up to.

You've already proven you're willing to bribe someone to get information."

"Oh," he snorted. "Well, that conversation is not nearly as much fun."

I watched him briefly, covering the pause by taking a drink. I had the distinct feeling I knew how a rabbit felt when a fox was steadily appraising them. There was no doubt in my mind that if I played along with his way of handling conversations, I would find myself tripped up and giving him exactly what he wanted. That alone was irritating, but the sheer confidence with how Ethan held himself was just as annoying because he knew full well what he was capable of doing.

It was a shame really. In any other context I would have found someone as perceptive, insightful, persistent, and intelligent as him interesting. Not only that, but I would have enjoyed the sight of him a lot more. I wasn't so irritated with him that I was blind to his physical charms. The way he slouched slightly told me he was longer in the torso than someone his height, offset by broad shoulders. His shirt sat low enough to see the line of his collarbone, and the definition there told me he was no slouch in the physical department.

His facial features were a little too pointed on their own, but the whole was greater than the sum of its parts. What might have made him seem a little sharp-edged or pointed instead worked together to give him an appealing elf-like appearance. That alone wouldn't have been enough, but the way his lips and brow moved, and even the scar through the one brow, gave him a playful, mischievous quality. I could see how other people found him charming and attractive.

Which added to the potential danger because I'd bet my salary he was fully versed in utilizing each and every tool at his disposal.

"Penny for your thoughts?" he asked, cocking his head.

"In this economy, I'll have to bump you up to fifty cents, or perhaps even a dollar after taxes," I told him.

"Oh, you *do* have a sense of humor," he said, sounding pleased. "That's good to know."

"Don't get too comfortable with it," I told him, setting my bottle aside and leaning forward to rest my arms on my desk. "Now, let's get to why you decided to bribe your way into talking to me."

If anything, the question amused him, though I couldn't see what was so funny about it. "Well, when it comes to the people in this town, you were the one everyone said I should talk to."

"Me?" I asked, raising a doubtful brow. "I'll admit, that strikes me as unlikely."

From the flash of confusion on his face, my sudden politeness was throwing him off. "Well, not *just* you. Of course, there are other people, but you came up quite often."

That sounded more accurate, but I wouldn't acknowledge it aloud. I wasn't comfortable with the idea of people in the town considering me an important figure. True, I was the police chief, one of the few figures of authority, but I was perfectly content to lead my team of officers and leave it at that. I knew other people disagreed with me, but thankfully they didn't push it.

"Fine," I said slowly. "Then again, let's start with what it is you're looking for."

"An interview."

"Yes, I gathered as much. However, what kind of interview are you trying to get here?"

"I've been researching the town itself," Ethan said with a shrug, setting his closed bottle onto the empty chair beside him. "And I found myself interested, so I'm here to find out more."

"Is this a personal interview or a professional one?" I asked, trying not to sound wary. The last thing I needed was to give him a reason to think I wanted him to drop the subject as quickly as possible.

His eyes glittered as he smirked. "If this was a personal interview, it would be over a nice dinner, maybe a few drinks at the bar."

I was pretty sure only years of practicing self-control was what kept me from reacting to his statement with more than just a slight raise of my brow. "That doesn't sound like an interview."

"Oh, sure it is, but the type I reserve for good-looking men and women."

It was smooth, I'd have to give him that much. "I'm old enough to be your father."

"True, but you're not my father, which means finding you attractive is neither weird nor illegal," he said with a chuckle, resting his arms beside him.

I was hard-pressed to figure out if he was flirting with me to mess with me or genuinely hitting on me. The first I could handle easily because I didn't think I was vain enough to be flattered to the point of stupidity simply because a good-looking man was hitting on me. The problem was, a feeling deep in my gut told me he was not, in fact, taking me for a ride or not *just* taking me for a ride.

"Then perhaps you should have started with that opener, and I would have saved us both a great deal of time," I said, ready to end this conversation as soon as possible.

"Because you'd prefer it that way? I don't mind," he said with a chuckle. "Can't be anywhere too fancy, though. I don't have a suit with me."

"You're assuming I'm interested," I said, leaping toward the first obvious counterargument to this strange game he was playing. "Bold strategy."

"I notice you're not exactly saying you're not interested while looking like you're very interested."

"I take it back. That's not boldness, that's arrogance."

"One man's arrogance is another man's confidence. So, dinner?"

"Absolutely not," I said, a little too fast for my own taste.

Despite my original intent, he had already taken me off balance and caught me in a vulnerable position. I needed to drag the conversation back to why he was here so I could figure out if he was, as my gut believed, going to be a problem. That and the sooner we moved away from this subject, the sooner I could stop wondering if the hair on the rest of his body was the same blond as the tips on his head or the roots.

"Ah well," he said with a sigh, seeming genuinely disappointed. "Then I suppose we'll have to settle for a professional interview, won't we?"

I clicked my tongue. "For the record, I meant whether you were interviewing me as a police chief and officer or as Trevor Price."

"I know what you meant, but if I could get a date as well as an interview, then well...call me greedy."

"I can think of a few things to call you," I growled, feeling my annoyance grow. Worse, part of me was charmed by that statement. It had seemed completely genuine, which only irritated me further. "Is this sort of thing supposed to endear me to the idea of letting you interview me? Because currently, it's making me wonder if I might have a couple of hours free instead."

He chuckled, clasping his fingers under his chin. "I'm having a hard time deciding if you're a great deal of fun or one of the least fun people I've met."

"You're not here for fun," I reminded him.

"So you claim," he chuckled, then spread his hands out.

"But I think you severely underestimate just how much I enjoy my work."

"You're not doing much to change my original assumption," I told him, quickly losing patience with the conversation. I wondered if he was just here to mess with me rather than actually do anything productive. If that was the case, then at least I could relax and treat him as an annoyance.

"Oh, you mean the assumption that I'm just here to start trouble for you when you're already busy?" he asked, his eyes alight with a new look that only added to my discomfort.

"I could do without further complications, yes."

"No offense, but what could possibly keep you so busy? The crime rate in Fairlake is, even by small-town standards, quite low."

"And you would know this how?"

"It's not difficult to look up statistics in this day and age."

"The wonderful age of the internet," I said wryly.

He chuckled. "It makes things easier and faster, that's true, and yes, it does give access to things you might not have had before, but that's not always the case. Statistics and reports can be requested by anyone, they just have to send a nice letter. Admittedly, you'd have to march to their office if you wanted it quickly, but I'm in no rush to get it by snail mail."

I raised a brow. "Why would you need them to send you a copy if you already have what you need?"

"Because I like a hard copy, and sometimes there are discrepancies between what's online and what's on paper," he said, watching me. His smile hadn't changed, but I had the distinct feeling he was watching for something specific. "A bit like how there's often a difference between what's stated and what's real. Whether in official reports or the words from people's lips."

Just when I thought I could relax and 'enjoy' being antagonized, alarm bells went off in my head. He was still trying to get a rise out of me, but I felt greater purpose behind this verbal thrust than the ones before.

"Is that why you decided to go into your field of work?" I asked him, staring back as blankly as I could manage. "To dig for the truth?"

"Reality," he said in a tone I took as a correction.

"Interesting clarification," I said slowly, rolling the idea around my head and finding it pretentious. There was little if any, difference between the two ideas, and I dismissed it as him trying to complicate a simple issue. "So I take it you've been doing some digging."

"Not really digging," he said with a shrug. "But I've been doing my research. I won't bore you with the details. It's quite an interesting town, especially recently."

"I wait with bated breath to find out what you consider interesting," I said dryly, giving in to the temptation to be a little snappy.

He chuckled. "Probably a lot more than you."

"Somehow I feel like you're interested in far too much and all the wrong things."

Ethan grinned. "And from what I've seen and learned, you probably find too little interesting."

"Oh, I see," I said with a snort. "Is this where you evaluate me? I thought this was an interview."

"It is, but if I can, I try to ensure I have a good idea who I'm dealing with before I interview them. Now this is the part where you get huffy and tell me I don't know the first thing about you."

He didn't, but I hadn't planned on pointing that out. This wasn't some daytime soap opera. "And this is where you pretend I said that, and go on to show me just what you know about me, amazing me with your investigative prowess."

A normal person would have been irritated by the apparent dismissive condescension, but I wasn't surprised to see that he was not normal and laughed. In that, at least, he reminded me of Bennett, who also enjoyed a bit of back and forth, even when he knew I was irritated. The difference was Bennett was more like a husky that couldn't help causing trouble but was inevitably friendly and playful. Ethan, however, reminded me of a large cat playing with its food before devouring it.

"There's not really a lot about you that can be said," he said with a shrug, and whether he meant it that way or not, I felt the sting of his words. "You've lived a fairly peaceful life as far as I can tell. Of course, I'm only looking at the surface and what can be determined as fact. I'm sure there's more to Police Chief Trevor Price."

"Am I supposed to fill in the gaps for you?"

"There's not many gaps, at least on the surface. Born in Fovel, raised in Fairlake. Joined the Marines at eighteen and, from what I could see, was set to have a solid and possibly illustrious career if your medals and promotions are any indication. I'm sure you saw some...interesting things during Desert Storm, utter cluster fuck that it was."

"Cluster fuck?" I asked wryly, not that I disagreed with him, but getting him to talk and give more information was a lot easier than balking at his words.

He snorted. "You have Marines on the ground for two reasons, to fuck up shit or deal with already fucked up shit. You don't put people through what's considered the toughest training in the military then leave them to light guard duty."

It wasn't so much his tone, which was still light, but his words that eased the tightening of my nerves. For all his irreverence and flippancy, he seemed to have some respect for what he was talking about.

"And then," he said, cocking his head. "Despite a budding

long-term career, you left the service, came back here, and settled down. There was about a year, nearly two, before you joined the police force. By all accounts, clean record, a handful of commendations, married at twenty-nine, and then divorced eleven years later, approximately two years after your promotion to chief of police."

It was bizarre and almost insulting to have my entire life and career summed up in a few sentences. "What? Didn't want to bring up buying my first house? Perhaps when my parents died? Don't want to inquire how my marriage failed?"

"I mean, unless something was missing from the divorce paperwork, that's not an uncommon story," he said, leaning back and looking bored. "C'mon, workaholic husband, neglected wife? That's not exactly groundbreaking."

Finally, he had managed to find a tender spot, and I scowled at him. "Right, well, unless we want to talk about your relationships, I suggest we get to the interview part of this. And while you're at it, leave my personal life out of it."

"Now, where's the fun in that?" he snorted. "The personal is what makes the person who they are. It doesn't matter if they hide behind a title or not."

It would have been insightful if it wasn't for the obvious jab behind it. The problem remained, however, I still wasn't sure what his angle was, which I suspected was the entire point of this conversation. In fact, I didn't think he was here for an interview at all, and my previous suspicions were voicing themselves in my head.

"As fun as this verbal banter has been," I said in a voice that left no doubt about how little fun it had been for me. "I have other things to worry about today. You may not think I'm busy, but your assumptions about my job are not my concern."

Ethan cocked his head. "Just what is it you think I'm trying to do?"

"Probably the same thing you've done every time you decide to sit down and write something. And probably what you've done several times, start trouble."

"Oh? Is this where you reveal what you know about me?"

"Doing a bit of digging when you have law enforcement databases at your disposal isn't difficult. You had quite an interesting sheet growing up."

Ethan rolled his eyes. "Oh, God. What stuck out to you? Intoxicated minor? The DWI? The breaking and entering? The shoplifting?"

"We can't forget the resisting arrest."

Ethan chuckled. "They gave me that because I outran three of their doughnut-scarfing wastes of a badge. They had to drag out a fucking canine unit to chase me up a tree so they could finally catch me."

"And what reason would you have to run?" I asked.

"I was breaking the law," he said with a shrug. "That's what happens when you're underage at a party with drugs and alcohol, and the cops break down the door. And if you've already got a few charges under your belt, well—"

"Yes, and this seems to weigh on you," I said with a shake of my head.

Ethan shrugged. "If I was bothered about breaking the law, I probably would have gone into law. You'll notice I haven't."

I would call him cocky...again, but he didn't seem bothered one way or the other about his previous offenses. So I was dealing with someone who didn't care about law, himself, and morality. "And yet you tell someone whose job and duty it is to uphold those laws."

"Are we about to have a morality discussion? I normally require drinks before I dive into that tricky topic."

"I don't think morality should be that difficult a discussion."

"And that's precisely why I'm not going to have it with you," he snickered. "That attitude is the quickest way to tell me I need to veer away from the topic."

I sensed another judgment. "Fine, are we finally going to talk about why you're here? Or are you going to continue to waste our time with this ridiculous conversation?"

"Sure, want to tell me what's keeping you so busy? You've insisted you are while avoiding discussing it."

"Last I checked, any ongoing investigations aren't public knowledge unless I say so."

"So, there is an ongoing investigation. Curious as to what could possibly be going on in this sleepy little town. Another murder? Attempted kidnapping?"

And just like that, I realized I'd managed to trip myself up and offer him precisely what he'd been looking for. The only comfort, cold and small as it was, was that my instincts had been accurate again.

"Enough," I said, putting my hands on my desk to stand and glare down at him. "If all you're going to do is antagonize me and try to dig up trouble to slap your writing on the internet, then we have nothing to say to one another."

"Sounds to me like you have plenty to say," Ethan said, leaning forward in his seat. "You're awfully defensive all of a sudden."

I was, and I hated that he so easily detected it. "I wouldn't call it sudden. You've been goading me from the moment you came in here, and I have no interest in continuing to be prodded."

"Funny how it coincided with my curiosity over a current investigation."

"I'm done with your attempts at being clever," I told him abruptly, motioning toward the door. "Next time you want an interview for one of your drama pieces, find someone who has time for it...and the desire to be smeared across the internet."

He stood slowly, the smile gone from his face. "If you're going to put yourself on the same level as the other people I've investigated, then I'd say you deserve to be smeared."

"Yes, drum up some more sensationalist headlines to make money off of," I told him with a wave. I had browsed through a few of the titles and comments on some of his pieces. From the looks of it, he was merciless, not afraid to shock people to get attention, and had no shame. "But do it somewhere else. This town doesn't need your crap."

Ethan snorted. "If I thought you'd actually read what I wrote, I might take offense. But fine, if you're going to get all growly and start stomping your foot, I'll go. I'm sure I can find out whatever I want, but thanks for the interview."

"Is that what you're calling this?" I asked with a snort.

"I mean, I don't know about you, but I certainly got a feel for you and how you go about things," he said with a cock of his head. "Now, if only I could find out what has you so testy. Is that just your personality or does the fact that I'm...well, me, make you nervous?"

Whatever previous thoughts I had about him being attractive had died, and any charm he might have was gone as far as I was concerned. "Out. And if I see you here again, you'll be escorted out."

He stopped, twisting around to grab his bottle of water. The absolute traitor that was my brain happened to notice that the casualness of his jeans didn't stop them from hugging his ass. It wasn't the world's most impressive ass, but it was certainly enough to draw my attention.

Before I could yank my eyes away, I noticed the telltale puckered signs of a scar on his lower back. I saw it too late, and he stood up, his shirt falling over it. It had looked jagged and hooked around his side, but where it had come from, I didn't know.

At the door, he turned around. "So, just for the record? Is that a no on dinner and drinks?"

Jesus Christ, what was his problem?

"Out," I barked, scowling when he laughed and left me alone.

Before I could do more than grumble and wonder what I could do to head this potential problem off at the pass, Bennett appeared in the doorway. I sighed, leaning back in my seat and rubbing my brow. "Livington, unless whatever you have to say is an emergency, leave me the hell alone. And if you did something, again, then clean it up. Don't tell me about it, and don't do it again."

"Wow," Bennett said with a chuckle. "That's a pretty good summary, but you'll be happy to know I didn't do anything wrong...I think."

"Comforting," I grunted, opening my desk drawer to pull out a bottle of pills and dump a few in my hand.

"I take it you and Ethan didn't enjoy yourselves," Bennett said, watching me pop the pills into my mouth and chase them with a swallow of water.

"I can't imagine where you got *that* idea," I grumbled. "Do you need something?"

"Kinda was wondering what he was here for."

"You and I both."

"Oh...you don't know? Then what—"

"He attempted to goad me, provoke me, tease some sort of drama out of me to post on the net," I summarized for him, giving in to temptation and going for the liquor cabinet. "And then hit on me...multiple times."

"He hit on you?"

"I'll pretend you didn't mean to insult me with the sound of surprise."

Bennett laughed. "No, I mean, I guess I shouldn't be surprised. Adam told me Ethan tended to be a handful and wasn't afraid to hit on someone."

"Yes, his attempts at charming me for whatever information he was looking for were thankfully unsuccessful," I grunted, pouring a glass. "He will have to leave here empty-handed and disappointed."

"What if he wasn't trying to charm you?" Bennett asked curiously.

I paused, frowning. "What?"

"I mean, what if he was actually hitting on you?"

I narrowed my eyes. "Why would I welcome something like that?"

Bennett snorted. "I don't know, Chief, what could you possibly get from someone intelligent, funny, and good-looking hitting on you?"

"You're aware I have an ex-wife, right?"

"Yeah, so does my boyfriend. Didn't stop him from getting together with someone intelligent, funny, and—"

"Spare me," I sighed, waving him off.

"I already know you bat for both teams, Chief, and hell, if maybe having a cute guy hit on you makes you happy, then go for it," Bennett said with all the brightness of the damn sun.

"What about my expression right now tells you I enjoyed even one second of that?" I asked, narrowing my eyes for emphasis.

"You *are* looking a little red in the face," he said, watching me closely.

"I'm annoyed," I said, sitting again.

"Right, well, can't say I didn't try," Bennett chuckled.

"Your attempts to get me to pursue something with one of the most irritating men I've ever had the displeasure of meeting is duly noted. I'm considering if there's a way to take disciplinary action based on that."

"Hey," he grunted, holding up a placating hand. "I just figured it was worth a shot. Never seen you try anything with anyone else in town. I wondered if maybe some new blood might help."

"And this new obsession with my love life is coming from where?"

Bennett's eyes widened in what could have been inno-cence, but I saw the way his gaze shifted away at the last second. "It's not an obsession. I just wondered, is all."

"I don't believe you," I told him candidly, wondering what sort of scheme was playing out in his head.

He sighed heavily. "Sure, sure, I know. I'm always suspect number one."

"I can't help but wonder why," I said with all the sarcasm I could manage. "Now get out, I've had enough difficult men in my office today, and you're not easy on my eyes."

Bennett hesitated. "But, uh, Ethan was?"

I realized what I'd said and scowled. "As in, I'm tired of looking at you all the time. Now get out of here before I find something else for you to scrub down!"

Which is exactly how I'd meant it...though on second thoughts, I had to admit it was true the other way too. If there was one thing I hated, it was how traitorous one's brain and body could be. Ethan had driven me absolutely bonkers, and now I had to keep a close eye on him to make sure he wasn't starting trouble while I wasn't looking, but that didn't detract from his looks.

Which was precisely how things should *not* go, especially when you considered yourself a practical person as I did. Honestly, I should probably wait a few days and then probe Bennett for information to see how long Ethan was planning to stay in town. Maybe I could find a way to accelerate whatever timetable he had, and he could go be someone else's problem.

Bennett stopped at the door. "Oh, uh, about something you said earlier—"

He let the words drift, obviously waiting to see if I would allow him to speak. It was unusually gracious of Bennett, who was usually prone to doing whatever he wanted, no matter how irritating he was. "What?"

"About him causing drama."

"That is what I said, yes, and his behavior in this office didn't prove any different."

Bennett chewed his bottom lip thoughtfully. "Did you, uh, see the stuff he's written?"

"Yes, the sensation pieces. Made to hit all the right emotional buttons and milk every drop of outrage and shock from the audience. The perfect way to draw readers and income," I said, glancing at my computer.

"You skimmed," Bennett said, his tone a statement rather than an accusation.

"I have better things to do than go through everything he's ever written," I huffed. "Good lord, the last one took up pages on my screen."

"Um," he said and then shrugged. "Screw it. Chief? Read the articles. Like, actually read them."

Staring at him, I wondered where this was coming from and why he was so serious. "Is there a reason I should take that advice rather than ignore you as usual?"

That made him smile. "Because I don't think you have any idea what's actually going on with his work. Don't get me wrong. He probably was being a shit in here. I don't know much about him, but from what I've seen and heard, that's on brand. But if you read his work, you might...well, just read it."

Bennett wasn't normally one for sticking his nose in my business, at least not to the point of insisting I do something.

His tone told me he was deadly serious, and I wondered what he'd read that made him look so somber.

"You ask me, I think he's got a lot more going on in that head of his than he pretends," Bennett said as an afterthought before disappearing.

Right, as if I didn't have enough on my plate. The mayor was getting skittish after the rumors had finally reached his ears, and I still needed to placate him while trying to figure out how to deal with the situation before it got out of control. The information Jane and Richard had dug up in the past couple of weeks unsettled me. They all but confirmed what I'd known before, but only that the meth manufacturing was happening, not specifically where and to what degree.

My resources weren't set up to deal with a more thorough investigation, and I couldn't exactly send a handful of my own men stomping through the woods. Problem was there were no significant leads, and I couldn't go knocking people's doors down. I needed a game plan without alerting everyone about how bad the situation could get.

And now Bennett wanted me to read some little...brat's drama reports?

Bennett's expression floated back into my thoughts, and I couldn't recall seeing him that serious without a good reason. I had always taken the advice and opinions of my officers before, though that was generally work-related.

Grunting, I brought up Ethan's latest article. It was, just as I'd told Bennett, pages and pages, and the website wanted me to pay for the privilege of reading the entire thing. After debating with myself, I decided to give the free trial a shot, jotting down a reminder to cancel it before it expired.

"Slavery of the Flesh," I read the title aloud and then the subtitle. "And how our sins are still punishing the innocent."

It was precisely the kind of sensationalist crap I expected

and had made me roll my eyes when I first glimpsed the article's title. I wasn't surprised that it started with a dramatic personal story as he recounted entering a 'smoky and sour smelling' brothel upon arriving in an unnamed town.

Continuing to read, I saw he enjoyed using particular descriptions to draw attention to the filth and squander he encountered, showing not only the young age but poor health and treatment of the brothel workers. I had to give him that much, he knew how to write, and he knew how to leave you feeling sickened in just a few paragraphs.

A far less personal account followed, detailing what could and did happen in the trade. Pausing, I scrolled ahead to see not only pictures he'd taken himself but graphs and charts as well. The entire thing came off as a mix between a hit piece and an eerily compelling statement of facts.

Grunting, I leaned back in my seat, took a sip from my glass and resumed where I'd left off, feeling the small presence of an idea blossoming in my head.

ETHAN

A week after my less-than-stellar attempt to get Chief Price to talk to me, I wondered if there was anything in town worth being interested in. I'd been sure there was something worth discovering, considering how the man reacted. If he had remained stony-faced and irritated, I would have thought he just disliked me. After several minutes with him, however, I began to suspect that I *unnerved* him. Generally, the only reason cops were unsettled by the presence of a reporter was because they had something to hide.

It wasn't until after that first week that I happened to overhear Bennett on his phone when he and Adam came to pick Colin up for a few days. I only caught a couple of phrases, but it was clear it was serious, and he sounded worried. I'd caught only 'manufacturing' and 'woods' but it was all I needed.

I didn't give any indication I'd heard anything but quickly went back to my notes when I knew no one was paying attention. There had been an issue with drug manufacturing several years before. The public reports were pretty sparse on details of how long the drug dealers had been operating in the area and just how much of a foothold they had.

It didn't surprise me. It struck me that the town's leaders were doing their best to keep the information as quiet as possible, not to worry the townsfolk. They had assured everyone the issue had been dealt with, and the forest was clear of unsavory types. I had to dig across different sources to guess that the operation had been there for a couple of years before it was dealt with and had required more than just Fairlake's police force.

There was more to this.

I didn't realize how engrossed I was until Bri tapped me on the shoulder. Blinking, I looked up from the screen and realized my eyes itched.

"What're you obsessing over?"

"Obsessing?" I asked and then looked over. "You're all dolled up, I see."

"I told you I had another date with Rob," she said, still watching me.

"Right, right. The guy you totally didn't expect would be a good date, but then he went and showed you a night of stars and wine," I said with a snort.

"It was a nighttime picnic, don't be a dick."

"I'm not being a dick. Honestly, he managed to improvise on the fly after your restaurant plans fell through. And managed to make you feel special in the process. That's not something I'm going to mock."

"Mmm," she hummed. "By the way, you still haven't answered my question?"

"What?" I asked.

"You managed to talk to me about Rob and my date but didn't actually distract me. You're going to have to try that shit on someone who doesn't know your tricks," she warned me.

I snorted. "Now, Bri, you don't know *all* of them. I've certainly developed a few more in our time apart."

"You're still trying to dance around the subject."

I thought I might be able to get out while she finished getting ready, but the click of her heels on the hardwood behind me told me that wasn't the case. Instead, I heard her heels hit the wood of the small front porch.

"You're not starting anything you shouldn't, right?"

"That hurts my feelings, Bri."

"Sure it does," she snorted. "Because I totally haven't noticed how you weren't doing a lot of work after you went to talk to Chief Price, and now suddenly you're zoned out on your computer like the world doesn't exist?"

"I was fully aware of the world."

"No you weren't. You might have learned a few more tricks over the years, but you've still got a lot of the same habits. You were like that as a kid, a teen, and you're going to be like that for the rest of your life. If something gets your attention, you home in on it with all the focus you can muster, and everything else around you fades away."

Well, I couldn't deny that, but I wouldn't give her credit just because she had the advantage of being my sister and watched me grow up. "I might have found something worth looking into. I don't like to count a chicken before it's hatched, though, so don't ask."

"Oh, I'm going to ask," she said with a snort. "Because I know just what sort of thing attracts your attention. It's usually something that's going to piss people off and get your ass in trouble."

"Your opinions on my work are so touching," I told her dryly.

She crossed her arms over her chest. "Am I wrong?"

No, she wasn't. I did tend to find myself falling from one scrape into the next. I had no doubt there were still plenty of people in the world who would happily see my dead body thrown into a ditch or pay someone else to do it. Then again, even as a kid, I'd always had a knack for finding trouble, and yeah, sometimes I went out of my way to seek it.

"Yeah, I guess not," I said with a shrug. Right or not, I hoped she saw me as more than just the teenage trouble-maker I had been. I thought I'd done quite well, taking my impulses and habits from my younger years and turning them into a productive, helpful outlet. "I guess you and Chief Price can start an 'Ethan is trouble, better give him shit' club."

"Good lord, are you feeling sorry for yourself?" she asked, sounding surprised.

"More like irritated."

"Because I'm concerned?"

I sighed and shook my head. "Forget it. It's not a big deal."

"Kind of sounds like a big deal," she said slowly.

"It would just be nice not to have someone I care about constantly thinking I always go out of my way to cause trouble," I said with a shrug. "But there's not a lot I can say against that, so why even bother in the first place? When it comes down to it, you're right. I attract and am attracted to trouble. Yes, it's irritating, but also, yes, that's reality. Two true statements."

"You know, if I thought you actually were trouble, I wouldn't let you stay here," she said.

"Well, it's kind of hard to find trouble in a place like this, so it would have been a safe bet."

"With you around? Please, you could find trouble in a monastery."

The thought made me wrinkle my nose. "Cheery thought."

Particularly because on my last trip, I actually *had* found trouble in a monastery, or rather what had once been a monastery. Plenty of old buildings in Europe were ruins people paid little attention to or historical sites they used. In this case, a brothel wasn't particular about the age of its workers or interested in their wellbeing.

Which wasn't uncommon in brothels around the world. Most workers were taken from their former lives and thrust into a new hell they couldn't have dreamed of. As for the owners, what was the point of treating their workers well? If someone got beat up or died, there were always more coming from the traffickers. A factory line of replacements, each one as innocent and heartbreaking as the one before.

The reminder turned my stomach, and I faced my sister. "Don't you have better things to do than bug me? Your hair's a mess. What's Rob going to think?"

"My hair is perfectly fine," she said, even as she slid a hand self-consciously through it. "You're evading...again."

"If you want me to come right out and say I don't want to talk about it, well, here's coming right out and saying I don't want to talk about it," I said with a vague gesture of my hand. "I didn't come here to go over my drama and trauma."

Alarm shot through me at the look on her face, an almost exact replica of the one I'd seen a few weeks ago when I first arrived. It was the face of a woman deeply concerned for a whole host of reasons and trying to find the courage to say them aloud. Good God, my sister wanted to have a heart-to-heart, which caused me more panic than when a local gang had broken down the flimsy door of the hovel I'd been staying in a few months before.

My attention latched onto a car coming up the road. "See? You wasted all that time trying to bullshit with me, and now Rob's here. You really should have better time management skills."

"I'm picking him up this time," she said with a shake of her head.

"Oh," I grunted, my stomach dropping as I realized that

unless I fled or outright denied her, Bri was working up the courage.

To our surprise, the car slowed as it neared the house, which is when I finally noticed the bubble lights now that it was no longer in the direct setting sun. "Bennett?"

"He's not working tonight," she said slowly as the car pulled into the driveway and came to a stop. She glanced at me. "So, do I need to say it?"

"I did nothing," I answered honestly because I hadn't done anything that would require a police visit. "I know pot's legal here, but coke is too, right? I mean, if I was moving some through the town for a little—"

"Not funny," she said.

"I'm glad someone else shares my opinion on that," said a deep, familiar voice, and I realized the car window was open.

"Hello, Chief Price," I said slowly, walking around so I could see him without blinding myself in the sun. "What in the fresh hell are you doing here?"

"He didn't mean the cocaine comment," Bri called from the porch.

"She doesn't know that," I told him with a smirk. "She's just really hoping it isn't true."

"Ethan Carter Crane!" Bri snapped, fists going to her hips. "Quit antagonizing the police chief!"

"What's he going to do, arrest me for being a shit? That's still legal," I called back to her.

"You know what? Screw it," she huffed, waving at us before turning around. "Arrest him. Plant drugs on him and then arrest him. I don't care. I have a date tonight, and I'll see about posting bail in the morning."

"And that's how you win an argument with my sister," I told him with a smirk. He had sat silently throughout the entire exchange. Finally, he turned off the engine which had my curiosity piqued even further.

"I'm not sure how I feel, seeing you're apparently like this with everyone," he finally said in his slow way. The only time I'd heard his speech speed up was when he'd been frustrated with me and sent me out of his office. Otherwise, his words came out in low, measured syllables as though he had no reason to hurry.

"Don't get me wrong, I absolutely meant the dinner and a drink comment, but don't think you're unique because I gave you hell," I told him, raising a brow.

"Was that supposed to make me feel better?"

"You strike me as someone who likes the truth, so there you go, take comfort in the truth."

"I thought it was about reality for you."

"They're not always mutually exclusive concepts."

His thick brow quirked, and I couldn't tell if it was amusement or curiosity on his part. He remained quiet, and I stepped back as he swung the car door open, sliding out smoothly. It was funny, he hadn't seemed quite as tall when I met him in the precinct, but now I realized the top of my head only came to his mouth.

Maybe it was just seeing him in full uniform, belt equipped with his tools and gun, or maybe it was being caught off guard by his arrival. Whatever the reason, I thought he looked not only taller but broader and stronger as the light of the sun bathed one side of his face, and his dark eyes took in my sister's house.

And because I couldn't help myself, I made sure he noticed me looking him over. "For the record, that dinner offer is still on the table."

The side of his face I could see tightened slightly as he glanced toward me. "That's not why I'm here."

"Yeah, generally speaking, when a good-looking guy in uniform shows up with handcuffs on his belt, it doesn't mean a good time for me."

He blinked slowly. "Generally?"

"Well, there's exceptions to every rule."

"I'm not that exception."

I chuckled. "I wasn't talking about you. Some people have interesting ideas about what it means to spend a weekend together, is all."

Whatever he might have had to say was lost as the sound of the front door brought us back to Bri. She marched down the steps leading toward the driveway, ever watchful.

"Well, he hasn't handcuffed you—"

"Shame," I interrupted.

"Which, hopefully," she continued, shooting me a dirty look, "means I don't have to worry about bail. If he gives you too much trouble, Chief Price, just handcuff him and leave him in the bushes, preferably in the backyard, so he doesn't clutter my lawn."

It was the first time I thought he might smile as he nodded. "I'll do my best."

"Have a good night with Rob," I said loudly, waving. "Make sure to use protection!"

"Or just taze him, whatever works best," she called, sliding into her car and starting it.

"Please don't taze me. That shit hurts," I said as she backed out.

"Why am I not surprised you know what it feels like to be tazed?" he asked warily.

"Actually, that one's not my fault. I just so happened to be in the line of fire for the guy they were trying to hit, but the cop had the aim of a Stormtrooper."

"That's...I'd have one of my people's ass for doing something so stupid."

"Yeah, well, I was told that accidents happen and when things are going on, to get out of the way. I mean, it was a busy street, and I didn't know what was going on until I was on the ground pissing myself, but sure."

He grunted. "Even when you're not the reason, you still find yourself in trouble."

"And now you sound like my sister," I snorted derisively. "So, are you going to share with me why you decided to show up here? Or were you planning on just brooding on the front lawn?"

"I'm not..." he cut himself off, shaking his head. "I'd like the chance to talk. And since your sister has left, I assume you're alone?"

"Good thing too. I can be noisy," I said.

He sighed. "Can you be serious for at least thirty seconds?"

"I'll try," I told him, waving him toward the house. "C'mon, you on duty?"

"No."

"Perfect."

His sigh made me laugh, but it actually wasn't meant to be a dirty comment. I wasn't kidding about being willing to take him to dinner and drinks, but somehow I didn't think he would take me seriously. I wasn't one to deny myself something nice when I could get it, and he was certainly nice to look at.

Well, and I suppose there was something commendable about his sheer determination to be as serious and humorless as possible. That and from what I'd seen, his career was just as respectable. Bennett lived partially in fear of the guy, but from what I'd heard, I wasn't the only one with a propensity for causing trouble, so that made sense.

He followed me in, and I didn't bother to check if he was scanning everything. Closing my laptop, I took it with me to the kitchen and set it on the counter.

"Are you planning to stay in Fairlake with your sister for

long?" he asked, his voice carrying through the house without him needing to raise it.

"Trying to get rid of me?" I snorted, reaching for a beer.

"I see you're back to being difficult."

I rolled my eyes. "That was a serious question. If you want to pretend like you weren't sweating bullets over my little interview, be my guest. I'm not beholden to such niceties."

"Interesting assessment," he grumbled, and I realized he'd entered the kitchen.

"Aw, you found something I said interesting, be still my heart," I said, opening the beer. "Now *that* was me being difficult. There's a subtle difference."

"Is there anything subtle about you?"

I screwed up my eyes in thought and then sighed. "Damn, was trying to think of a way to twist that into something dirty, but nah, not really."

To my surprise, he chuckled, the sound coming from deep in his chest. "I suppose it should be comforting that even you have your limits."

I knew he would eventually get around to whatever was on his mind if I gave him a chance. The problem with my angle when I met him in his office was I'd been too aggressive and yet evasive. Having thought about it, a more direct approach would have been far more effective.

In that brief conversation, I quickly realized he was a man who didn't tolerate nonsense, except for whatever Bennett put him through. He wasn't the greatest at speaking diplomatically, but what I had seen was passable for the average person. He exuded authority and used to having it respected by everyone around him.

He cleared his throat. "I read a few of your pieces."

Okay, not the sentence I was expecting, let alone the opener.

"Actually, read them, you mean," I said, cocking my head and taking another drink.

"Yes, and paid for the privilege as well," he said, sounding grumpy.

I chuckled. "You should have said something. I could have given you free copies of everything I've written."

"Well, the damage to my wallet has been done," he said, straightening slightly. "You were right before when you said I hadn't read them in full. Your work...surprised me. You might spend time painting a picture with your words, but you also lay down the raw facts to drive home the point. Your work isn't sensationalist garbage. I'm not sure what to call it, but I'm sorry for saying that. It was wrong and inaccurate."

I was surprised to hear those words from him until I considered what I'd managed to piece together about the man. I would bet an apology was not easily gained from Trevor Price, but I didn't think that was because of pride. He probably didn't consider it necessary to apologize unless he felt he was outright wrong.

"Oh, it's sensationalist," I said with a shrug. "You have to be able to create sensations in people in order to grab their attention. Then you use it to drive home the point of all the 'boring' and 'factual' stuff."

"I...suppose that's hard to argue with."

"In my experience, people like to think of themselves as logical, rational beings who get through life thinking things through, but we don't. We're squishy meat bags filled with hormones and emotions that dictate everything we do. If you want people to listen or pay attention, you go for their emotions and use them to keep them listening."

His brow rose slowly. "So, is that your 'reality'?"

"Close," I said, leaning against the counter and taking another drink. I didn't miss the way his gaze lingered a little lower than my eyes before snapping back up. "Now, you didn't come here to say you read my stuff and apologize. For the record, I completely appreciate the apology, but still—"

He cleared his throat. "Bennett informs me you've been feeling...restless and antsy. That you've been craving a project to keep yourself busy despite coming here to relax."

"Uh," I frowned. "How the hell would Bennett know that when he's talked to me all of...oh goddammit."

Trevor smirked. "Made the connection did you?"

"Ugh," I groaned, rubbing my face with my free hand. "My sister's been *gossiping* with her ex-husband's new boyfriend! God, and she acts like I'm a problem child."

"If you spend enough time around him, you'll find that Bennett is quite good at charming just about everyone."

"And apparently being a gossip."

"That is...almost three-quarters of this town, actually."

"See, that's where city living has an advantage. Nobody cares about you, but it also means they're not all up in your shit," I said with a laugh. "Christ, alright, fine. My sister's assessment of me is probably accurate, and I guess Bennett gets credit for passing it along. Is this your way of saying you have a project for me?"

"I might," he said slowly. "I did a little more digging about you."

"Oh boy, did you get the international arrest records?"

"The..." He stopped and stared at me. "The what?"

"Don't worry, just a few...things."

"That is not comforting in the slightest."

I drained the bottle, setting it down with a heavy thunk. "Look, when you make it your life's mission to dig into business, people in charge would prefer you didn't start digging into, you have to expect an arrest here and there."

"So, all of that was done in the name of your work?"

"Yeah. Well, most of it. The public indecency one was an

accident, and that assault charge I got in Prague was...not a big deal."

It very much had been a big deal and not something I was willing to get into. It had been a few months into the latest investigation, and I was not dealing with things too well. I'd drifted away to take a small break, ended up going on a drug and alcohol-fueled bender, and started a bar fight.

Or at least, that's what I'd been told had happened. I didn't remember much of it, which was probably for the best. What little I did remember was enough to last me a lifetime and earn a promise to myself that I wouldn't self-destruct in such an utterly stupid and impulsive way again.

"Don't worry about it," I told him more sharply than I meant to when his mouth opened again. "It's not up for discussion."

His mouth closed, and I couldn't read what was happening behind his eyes before he spoke again. "I wanted to discuss a potential business...arrangement."

I chuckled. "It would have sounded more natural if you'd said a job."

"I have a job for you if you're willing to take it. And if you're willing to do as I say."

"Mmm, that's tricky," I said, wagging a finger at him. "I do what I do because it allows me to handle things my own way. I'm not big on having a bunch of rules and a stupid bureaucratic system getting in my way."

"The rules are...negotiable, some of them."

"Ah, negotiating. Fine, sit down."

"What?"

"Sit," I repeated, reaching into the fridge and dragging the bottle of tequila out, grabbing two glasses, and slapping all three on the small table in the dining room.

"I'm...not drinking," he said.

"You are," I said, going back to the fridge, taking out the

containers of condiments and add-ons, slapping them on the counter, and getting the loaves of bread out of the basket. "I'll even make you a nice sandwich to help soak it up."

"None of this is necessary," he informed me, still standing in the kitchen.

I spread the mayo and began to layer fillings on the bread. "Hey, this is good bread. Got it from Grant's. And you know, with how he names things in that store, you'd think he'd have come up with something unique and weird for the bakery."

"He's... a mystery to most of the town."

"I'd think Police Chief Price would have a good idea of most of the people in a town this small."

"It's not *that* small, and you might as well call me Trevor."

I turned, walked in with a plate of sandwiches, and set them down between us. "Fine, Trevor it is."

He watched me warily as I poured us each a measure of tequila, it probably wasn't precisely a shot, but apparently, my sister didn't own any shot glasses. I slid one toward him, picking mine up and watching him expectantly. He glanced down, and though he didn't move, I could almost picture the internal sigh in his head before he reached out and took the glass.

"I'm not planning on getting drunk," he informed me.

"If you really think I'm going to sit here and try to get you drunk in some desperate attempt to take advantage of you," I said with a shake of my head, "then you have overestimated just how diabolical I am. I do have *some* morals."

"Yes, well, from what you've written, I can see there's a lot more to your morals than I originally gave you credit for," he told me softly.

I didn't bother to hide my surprise at the candid statement and gazed at him curiously. It almost made me wonder just how bad his original view of me had been, only to remind myself it was probably best I didn't know. I wasn't entirely sure what he'd seen in my work that changed his mind so radically. I always intended to inform people what was really going on and perhaps change their minds, but I hadn't meant it to be about my character.

"That doesn't mean I don't think you aren't capable of causing chaos when it suits you," he said, surprising me again with a small, amused smile.

"Funny, most people accuse me of stirring up trouble."

"Chaos usually means trouble for the people affected by it."

"Chaos is a natural part of existence. The only people worried too much about it are afraid of change."

"Order is a natural part of existence, so maybe they're not fond of losing stability."

I grinned, unable to help but enjoy myself a little. "Actually, most things are like electricity, they'll take the path of least resistance. That it sometimes happens to pick an ordered setup is just making things as easy as possible."

He smirked. "So you admit order is easier than chaos."

I laughed. "Not quite what I was aiming for, but I'll give you that one. I talked myself into a corner."

"Huh, I expected more of a fuss from you," he said.

"Then maybe you should stop trying to predict me," I said with a laugh. "You're clearly not very good at it."

He hummed. "People's behavior and reactions can be predicted fairly often. You just have to understand them enough."

It sounded like something I would have thought, though not said aloud. Human behavior was something I'd studied in school and in person because that was the best way to figure out how to get information from people and, in my work, keep me alive when necessary. It wasn't something I was keen to broadcast, however. It was human nature to become difficult when people thought they were being evaluated or manipulated.

In Trevor's case, however, I looked forward to whatever he learned about me.

"While you do that, how about we toast to whatever job you have for me?" I offered, holding my glass out.

I watched as he undid the belt around his waist and draped it over the back of an empty chair. My brow rose when he sat back down, reaching up to undo the top two buttons of his shirt before grabbing his drink.

Cocking his head, he held his glass out. "I need your help investigating the possibility that drug manufacturers are using the woods and perhaps part of the town for personal use. And I need it done without drawing too much attention. I don't want them alerted or the townspeople spooked."

My brow rose as I clinked our glasses together. "I wasn't expecting that. You have my attention. Let's talk."

TREVOR

For the next couple of hours, I gave Ethan as much information as possible. There were times, especially when I talked about what had happened the last time we had this little problem, when I suspected he was more knowledgeable than he was letting on. There was nothing in his reaction or his tone to indicate that. It was more gut instinct.

He listened intently, showing great interest in what I was saying, and even pulled a pad of paper from a drawer to jot down notes. Ethan wasn't afraid to ask questions, mainly to clarify a few points, but he didn't do it often. Most of the time he was content to let me go over the finer details while he listened raptly. A few times, he made encouraging comments or asked a leading question, but it encouraged me to speak even more.

In short, I realized, as a former intelligence officer and a police officer, that he would have made an excellent inter-rogator in another life.

It didn't hurt that he kept the drinks flowing, though he never went overboard during the conversation. It was a tactic I could never use in my professional life, but I suspected he'd probably used it more than once in the past. Drugs and alcohol were excellent lubricants for the road between people's brains and mouths. I still hadn't figured out whether he was doing it on purpose or out of habit.

"Which brings us back to the little detail about discretion," I said once I'd finished my information dump.

He chuckled, pouring us both another measure of tequila. "I'm pretty sure I already gathered you don't want people to figure out what I'm doing. And I'm also sure that if you're right about the manufacturers, which my gut tells me you are, then it's probably an even better idea they don't figure out what I'm doing. And as for the official paperwork, I sent it to you already. You'll find it in your inbox."

Well, that explained what he'd been doing on his phone earlier. "No offense, but I have to cover all of my bases."

"I think you mean cover your ass."

"Sometimes my ass and my bases are one and the same thing."

Ethan chuckled, draining his glass in one smooth gulp. "Don't worry, under all this, there's a professional who understands how the game is played."

I wasn't sure how I felt about it being called a game, but then again, I suppose I'd had the same thought when dealing with the politics of my position. The difference was I didn't usually treat it as a game, even though I knew others did. Then again, Ethan *was* apparently quite good at playing, as far as I could tell, so I had to imagine that if you were good at something, you could find enjoyment in it.

"Plus, if you look through the paperwork I sent you, you'll see I'm just as intent on covering my ass," he added with a chuckle.

My brow rose. "Should I be concerned?"

"Standard boilerplate liability and NDA shit," he said with a wave of his hand. "If I get my ass in trouble doing something I shouldn't, you aren't going to be held liable. If I get hurt in the line of duty, following the rules, you are responsible. I won't tell people without express permission from you, blah blah blah. All standard PI shit."

"I wouldn't know. I've never used one," I admitted. "But I'll look over everything to see what you mean."

"I'm sure you'll be browsing every inch of the page," he chuckled.

"And you just sign things without looking over them?" I asked, unsure if I should be unsurprised or horrified.

"Ah well, see, I did that at first and got screwed on the first thing I ever wrote," he said with a snort. "I was... unhappy about that and decided to start paying more attention. Then I realized I'm absolute garbage at reading legalese without help. Thank God I make enough money now to just thrust any new paperwork at my lawyer and make them tell me what's in it."

I closed my eyes, snorting. "Well, I suppose this is as good a time as any to admit that most of the paperwork I have to deal with goes through Ira first."

"Really?" Ethan asked though he sounded more curious than surprised. "Hmm, I knew she was sharp, but I didn't think you used her as your legalese translator."

"She's been doing her job longer than I've been an officer and almost longer than I've been alive," I said with a chuckle. I thought about pointing out she'd been doing it far longer than he'd been on this earth, but the thought drifted away before it could reach my lips. Maybe it was dealing with him for a couple of hours without any animosity, maybe it was reading what he had obviously written to share the experiences he'd had, or maybe it was the tequila. "She's got a lot of knowledge crammed into her head."

"Hmm, maybe I should have pumped her for information instead," Ethan snickered, wiggling his empty glass absently.

"You can still try," I told him mildly. "But only as long as I get to watch."

"Ah, a voyeur," he said with an air of knowledge and a wiggle of his eyebrows.

I sighed. "I'm not sure if I should be impressed that you managed to go this long without a single innuendo or insulted that you think sexual innuendos will somehow bother me."

"Well, they did bother you before," he pointed out.

"Because the entire meeting was done under the pretense of being professional," I said, cocking my head. "This is drinks at your sister's house."

"While we talked about business."

"And now you're talking about voyeurism."

"I could talk about other kinks."

"How gracious of you, but regrettably, I think I'll have to pass."

"Oh, fine," he said, but I could see the look in his eye and knew he wasn't quite done. "So, how about a question?"

"I have this strange feeling it won't be related to the work you've accepted but about something I'd rather not talk about," I said with a heavy sigh.

"Oh c'mon, think of it as employer and employee getting to know one another."

"I wasn't aware that was standard for this type of work."

"It's not, but there's not a lot that's really standard."

I leaned forward to pour myself some tequila, knowing I'd probably need it for whatever was about to come out of his mouth. That it was *excellent* tequila didn't hurt, either. "Fine, but I can refuse to answer."

"Like that wasn't an option from the start," he said with a roll of his eyes, holding out his empty glass. "Now, did you know you were bi because of a guy or a girl?"

"That's starting this little game of yours off with a mighty big assumption," I told him, pouring him a measure of tequila equal to mine. Neither of us was drunk, but I felt the floatiness of having had more than just the couple I'd promised myself.

"Yeah yeah yeah," he said quickly, waving me off. "Don't play hard to get. Either answer the question or refuse to."

"Is this new impatience because you're drunk or because you're that eager to know?"

"If you think this is me drunk, you really didn't do a lot of field sobriety tests when you were working the streets instead of a desk."

I had probably done more field sobriety tests than anything else in my career, but that wasn't the point. "I didn't assume a whole lot when I was younger. I dated a few girls at school, but it was another boy I'd grown up with that made me...aware I wasn't quite as straight as I believed."

"Ohhhh, the old childhood best friend stereotype," he chuckled. "Boy, does *that* sound familiar around here. This guy have a name?"

"Troy," I said. "Yes, we were best friends, and before you start plowing forward, yes, we were involved. Yes, I was in love with him, and no, he didn't break my heart. He died when both of us were stationed in the middle east. He was never given the chance to break my heart."

The smirk on Ethan's face flickered before finally fading as his brow furrowed. "I...well, alright, that came back to bite me in the ass *real* fast."

I was more surprised at myself than anything. Troy was a subject I didn't talk about, and when someone else brought him up, I was quick to change it. I had made peace with the loss as best as I could over the years, but that didn't mean I wanted to go back over old scars and poke at them. I knew Ethan hadn't meant anything by his questions, but I also didn't want him to keep pushing for more information.

"Yeah, sorry about that," he said with a grimace. "Probably should've checked before I started running my mouth."

"Don't be," I told him with a wave of my hand. "You had no way of knowing."

"Yeah, well, someone in my line of work should know there's always more to a story."

"And I'm pretty sure Troy would have kicked my ass if he saw the way I acted, and he'd be right."

Interest flickered to life in Ethan's eyes. "What was he like?"

"He was…" I began and then stopped, realizing what I was about to say, and gave a laugh.

Ethan's brow arched. "Did I miss a particularly funny joke?"

"No," I said with a shake of my head. "I was just going to say he was a lot like you. We always were a weird pair of friends to other people. I was always so serious and usually pretty quiet. But Troy? Troy didn't take a lot seriously unless he had to, and even then, he could find something funny. He was much better with people than I could ever dream of being, and he was pretty good at finding something interesting about others."

Ethan grunted. "Alright. I can see where you would see some similarities."

Something in his tone brought me up short, but as he tipped another measure of tequila into his glass, I decided to keep my question to myself. As I watched him slide the bottle toward me, I realized it was bitterness I'd heard.

"What about you?" I asked, hoping the topic was safe since he'd been the one to bring it up.

"Ah well, not really anything interesting to talk about," he said with a shrug. "Figured out I was into both pretty early on. Kind of hard not to realize you're bi when you sleep with a guy for a few months and then turn around and date his sister."

I blinked. "Uh...you did what?"

Ethan laughed. "It wasn't on purpose. I didn't know they were siblings. Well, half-siblings, same Dad, different Moms. She lived with her mom and occasionally went to stay with her dad, where he lived. It just so happened I was never around when they were in the same house."

"And the last name didn't tip you off?"

"Her mom insisted on her not sharing her dad's last name."

"Why?"

"Well, considering these are siblings that were only a couple of months apart in age—"

"Oh," I grunted. "Dad didn't know how to keep it in his pants then."

"Right on the nose," Ethan snorted. "And they had two different social circles, so they didn't spend much time together in school. God, seeing his face when he saw her and me spending time together is still ingrained in my memory. She didn't find out until after we broke up, and I'm told it was a meltdown."

"How'd she find out?"

"I told her when I broke up with her."

I sighed. "And why would you tell someone that? God, anyone would be weirded out by that."

He smirked. "Because of the reason I broke up with her?"

"Cheated?" I wondered.

"Nah, she was pissed that her brother was dating a guy, and she'd found out about it. I let her have about five minutes of saying some of the nastiest homophobic shit you can imagine before I ended it right there," Ethan said with a shrug. "And while she was gaping at me in disbelief, I told her I'd been sleeping with her brother before we started seeing one another. She didn't say anything, just walked away. She went home and freaked out on him, then tried to smear our reputations around the school."

"High school is something else," I said with a shake of my head.

"It really is," he chuckled. "It's alright. It backfired on her horribly. Everyone *loved* him, so they didn't give a shit that he was into dudes and hated her for being a bitch."

"And you?"

"People liked me, but I had the magical power of not giving a flaming fuck, so I just ignored it."

"Your superpower," I said with a small smile.

"I don't know about superpower, but it works more than people think. Even as a kid, when you show people they have no power over you, that you really couldn't care less about what they think, they lose all power over you," Ethan said with a smirk, pushing up to his feet.

"Liquor running through you?" I asked.

"Nope. I've been sitting here drinking and talking for so long I'm going to lose my mind," he said, turning to the kitchen.

I *could* have blamed the alcohol pushing through my system when my eyes followed his path out of the room, but that wouldn't have been fair. Even stone-cold sober and irritated with him, I admired his body. Now I was neither of those things, and I didn't resist watching him.

He turned around faster than I could react and cocked his head. "You want to come with me for some air?"

It was a bad idea, and I couldn't think of a good reason to deny him, so I pushed up from my chair. "Alright, fine."

He walked out of sight. "You won't be able to stare at my ass as well outside, but that's life for you."

I stopped, sighing heavily and following him. The small yard had lawn furniture, and Ethan plopped down on the swing against the fence. Seeing that he'd left space for me to sit beside him, I hesitated before following him.

His face glowed softly when he spoke. "You definitely were."

"What?" I asked.

"Checking out my ass," he chuckled.

I glanced at him. "Well, there's no point denying it when I've obviously been caught."

"Satisfy a curiosity of mine," he said. "Were you checking me out half as much as I was checking you out in your office?"

I sighed. "And I've been caught again."

"How long since you've been with someone? You were ogling a guy who was obviously driving you up a wall?"

"I see we've reached the point of the bottle where you hold back even less than usual."

Ethan laughed, the sound breaking the gentle quiet of the night. "And the point where you're being less stingy with information."

He had me there, and I had to smile. "Maybe it's just...seeing another side of you I didn't bother to notice before."

"I'm almost afraid to ask just what you saw."

"It was...I'm not sure how to even describe it. Reading your work, I expected it would just be...sensationalist, overblown, dramatic, money-grabbing, and a way to make yourself feel better about your life because 'oh look, I'm doing something.'"

"Wow, you managed to summarize some of the worst critiques of my work and professional life in a few sentences. You really don't mince words."

"That's what I expected, not what I saw."

"Okay, what *did* you see then?"

I looked up at the sky, watching the clouds slowly glide

across the blanket of stars. "You certainly know how to write in a way that has punch, but it wasn't sleazy. All the pretty writing in the world couldn't hide the fact that you had seen and directly experienced the horrors or that there are plenty of stories you never wrote."

I thought it was telling that Ethan didn't shift, squirm, or move in the slightest, simply sitting still beside me as he stared into the night. "There are...many."

I nodded, unsurprised. "And I saw someone who had willingly thrown themselves into those places, right in harm's way, to get the best understanding of what he was trying to study. And I don't just mean danger to your body but to your mind. More often than not, the worst things in the world aren't being shot at, but seeing just how evil people can be to one another."

"It's...just when you think you've seen it all, that you've reached the bottom of the barrel of human depravity, someone comes along and shows you a new layer. Or a new barrel. I don't know, I'm not good at metaphors." He laughed.

"Or how people just...become so used to it," I said, ignoring his attempt to lighten the mood. I didn't think I was too far off the mark in believing he used humor as a deflection, as much as I had my own methods of dealing. "It's amazing and horrifying just how adjusted people become. Both the victims and the people doing these terrible things."

"Yeah," he said softly. "And you're right. Most of the time, it's not the times I was shot at or even the time in Mexico when some guy took a machete to me. It's...other things. The things I've seen done to other people. Those are the things that keep me awake at night or find me when I'm asleep."

I had my fair share of memories that sat with me over the years, so I knew what he meant. "Is that where the scar on your back came from?"

"Yeah," he said. "I've got a couple of others, including the bullet wounds on my chest. I uh...don't take my shirt off around my family," he said, sounding nervous.

"They don't know?" I asked. "What you really do, that is."

"Oh, they know. They've read my stuff. But if you read a few of them, you might have noticed I never talked about what actually happened to me. None of my pieces mention the times people tried to hurt me and succeeded. My family already knows enough to scare the shit out of them. No point in adding to it by showing they have a good reason to be scared."

I nodded, understanding. "I never talked about what I saw or experienced when I came back either. My parents and friends...well, it was enough for them to know where I was and to hear the news on TV. They didn't need more worries on top of the ones they already had."

He glanced at me. "Did they...know about you and Troy?"

"No," I said softly. "As cliché as it might sound, that was a different time. We talked about making things official and out in the open when we were out of the Marines. But we never got the chance to decide one way or another. He died in an ambush a year before we both would have had the chance to get out. After that, I couldn't face staying in the Marines."

It was so strange, looking back on us at that age. We had been so determined to make something of ourselves, to prove we were capable. It had seemed like the perfect chance to do that and to be able to get out of Fairlake. With that experience and the GI Bill under our belts, we dreamed of starting a new life. We didn't have it all figured out, but at that age, we had convinced ourselves we would one day figure it out.

"What's that like?" Ethan asked.

I looked at him, startled. "Losing him?"

"God no," he snorted. "I've already managed to ruin our

fun with this conversation. I meant loving someone like that. You clearly still love him, so it must have been something when you two were together."

"We were still young," I said, watching him closely now. "At that age, love can come so quickly, and it's so strong. So, of course, it was great, but I can't tell you how it would have gone if things had been different."

"I wouldn't know. I've never been in love. At least, I don't think so."

"Really?"

"Really."

"You're...how old?"

"If I tell you that, you'll groan when you realize the age gap between us. I'm still banking on trying to get into your pants at some point, so I don't want to kill that."

The sudden shift back to his 'normal' self almost took me off guard. His ability to toss his own morose feelings to the side and settle back into his playful ways was disconcerting, but at the same time, I had to envy him for it. Even if it was a defense, I admired how easily he could shut off his thoughts and focus on something that brought him pleasure instead.

"In my pants," I repeated dryly. "These specific ones, or are you aiming for a different pair?"

"I mean, it's not so much the pants themselves as what's in them that matters."

"And how do you know what you find won't disappoint?"

He glanced at me, half of his face in shadow, the other in the moonlight. "Come on now, do you really think I'm going to be deterred that easily? I'm not going to be disappointed."

"Are you going to tell me how you know, or leave it a mystery like you did with knowing I was a tequila lover?"

"Ha, knew it," he crowed softly, leaning back in the swing and slouching. Whether he did it to get comfortable or because he knew my eyes would immediately dart to the inch of skin that showed itself as his shirt rode up, I didn't know. "And I knew that because something told me your tastes in booze weren't as cliché as someone might think."

"That...that's how you guessed?" I asked, unable to hide my surprise.

"Eh, something told me that despite what I was seeing, there was more beneath the surface," he said.

I snorted in disbelief. "So, a guess. And here I was, almost impressed."

"It's not that hard," he said with a shrug. "People aren't as hard to figure out as they'd like to believe. And yeah, there will always be outliers, but you can usually make some pretty good inferences based on a few things. First, you learn how to read people, and then you learn how to trick people into telling you more about themselves."

"So you're a grifter?" I asked with a laugh.

"A professional one," he said with a haughty sniff.

"Alright," I said, intrigued. "What else can you tell about me using your grifter skills?"

"You're a pragmatist with a sentimental streak a mile wide. You love order, not because of the control it gives you over other people, but because it helps you make sense of your life, gives you something you can measure."

"I'm pretty sure I already gave away my love of order."

"True, but that's where your sentimental streak comes in. You could have thrived in the Marines, but like you already said, you couldn't bring yourself to stay there after Troy. You came back to your hometown, settled in, and made yourself a part of the community. You've got a few things in your office that come from your past and are kept out in the open, don't think I didn't see that picture of your family. From what I've heard, you're *way* more tolerant of Bennett's shenanigans than you should be, and it's a poorly kept secret that you have your officer's backs with a loyalty that even a German Shepherd would envy."

My brow arched again. "All fair points, I suppose, though I wouldn't call much of that impressive. But if you tell anyone about Bennett, I might have to bury you in the woods."

He chuckled and, to my surprise, reached out and took hold of my hand, holding it up. "And while I don't think you do it now, you used to bite your nails as a nervous habit."

I stared at our hands, surprised to find his fingers rough with callouses as he brushed the tips over my trimmed nails. His hands were warmer than mine as they held onto my fingers with a firm grip that was controlled enough not to make me uncomfortable. To my surprise, I felt something stir in my stomach before it pooled into my groin.

Christ, I was getting hard from him holding my hands. What was I, a teenager again?

"You keep your nails ridiculously short," he explained, turning my hand to ensure my nails were in the moonlight. "Sure, you could just be someone who doesn't know how to trim their nails, but they're rounded perfectly, which means you know how to sand them. I'd bet a decent amount of money you were a nail-biter as a kid. Maybe even later."

"Another guess?" I asked, still feeling my groin stirring with our physical contact.

"An educated one. But even those can be wrong."

"Well, you've got me there. It's been years since I did it."

He smirked. "Like I said, you might not always be right, but more often than not, you're on top of things."

"A few statistics and a willingness to take a risk," I said, noting he hadn't withdrawn his hand from mine.

"You don't do what I do without being willing to take risks," he said.

In the few seconds of silence that followed, I watched as

his eyes slid to our hands. There were a few more heartbeats before I felt his grip on my fingers ease, and he drew his hand away. My heart jumped in my chest, and I reached out, taking hold of his hand before he could pull it back into his lap. It was done before I could wonder what I was doing, but even realizing that, I held onto his hand and stared at him.

"Something on your mind?" he asked softly, no trace of teasing or humor in his voice as he stared back at me.

It was the perfect moment to pull my hand away, mutter an apology, and try to ignore my embarrassment. The thing was, I knew the impulse hadn't come from just our conversation, which had managed to touch me in some undefinable way, or from the tequila that was warming me but not entirely taking my sense away, or even my desperation born from months and months of loneliness. It was all those things and the fact that Ethan wasn't the slightest bit shy of expressing interest in me and my desire for him specifically.

I wanted him, pure and simple.

I smiled knowingly. "You never told me why you wouldn't be disappointed."

His eyes crinkled at the corners as he leaned in. "Now, what do I get for telling you that?"

Snorting softly, I closed the distance between us, hesitating when we both tilted our heads in the same direction...then again. Huffing, I held my head still, scowling when he laughed and did the same. After a couple of heartbeats, he slowly tilted his head in the other direction, finally allowing us to close the distance.

Our lips met, and I felt him lean closer, his fingers twining around my hands and pushing them against my chest. I could taste the smallest trace of tequila on his tongue when it slid across my bottom lip before my mouth parted to let him in. With my free hand, I reached up to grab the back of his neck and pull him closer, deepening the kiss.

It was the first kiss I'd had in...God, I couldn't even remember how long it had been. A few years? Some dive bar a few hours from Fairlake, where I'd hoped to find companionship for the night, ended up drunk and having a strange woman who had straddled my lap shove her tongue down my throat. That kiss had been nothing compared to this one, which was trailing a brand of fire from my lips all the way down to my groin.

Ethan's free hand slid down my front, his fingers pressing against the fabric of my shirt just enough that I was sure he was inspecting my body through my clothes. I only had a moment of hesitation. While I was in better shape than most of my peers, I knew I probably didn't measure up to the men and women he'd been with.

If there were any complaints on his part, he kept them to himself as his fingers slid down to rest on my groin. A low grunt escaped me when I felt his fingers curl around the hard outline of my dick, squeezing it and stroking firmly through the thick fabric of my pants.

"And there's me being right again," he chuckled against my mouth.

Not that I was impressive in terms of size, but I didn't consider myself lacking either. "You never did tell me how you knew."

"Those pants don't exactly cover things up," he snorted, nipping gently at my bottom lip.

I snorted, following his lips before he could get too far away. "Then I suppose we should probably do something about it."

"Nice to see you know when to throw shyness out the window," he chuckled.

"I blame it on a certain bad influence."

"Funny, you're not the first person to say that."

"I wonder why."

It was only then I realized he'd already managed to undo the button and zipper of my uniform pants, and all without me noticing the smooth way his hands moved. It wasn't the time or place, but the way he distracted me while he fiddled with my pants reminded me of a pickpocket. That it meant he'd probably learned those skills was no surprise, but neither was it that he was using them in a sexual context.

But as I felt his hand slide under the waistband of my underwear, I decided we could address his criminal fingers later.

The brush of his fingers across the sensitive skin of my cock brought my breathing to a near shuddering stop as he slid them to the base, wrapping them around carefully to extract me from my clothes. The outside air was cool, but his skin burned hot as he stroked me slowly. I had to force myself to take a deep, slow breath as he continued to grip me, moving slowly as he bent forward to nip and lick at the base of my neck.

"Ethan," I said softly in warning.

"No marks," he snorted. "I know."

It wasn't what I wanted to say, but after I'd made sense of his words, I grunted in affirmation. The last thing I needed was lingering marks on my neck when I returned to the precinct. Even if most of the officers had the sense to keep their questions and opinions to themselves, I didn't need them whispering behind my back.

My attention snapped back to reality when Ethan slid off the swing. I watched, heart hammering, as he slid to his knees, his hand still wrapped around the base to pull my dick toward him. At this angle, the moonlight bathed his face, and I could see the eagerness in his features as he leaned forward. We had barely started, and I could already feel a tightening in my gut, signaling that I probably wouldn't last long.

"It's been...a while," I warned him.

His smirk sent another jolt of arousal to my groin. "I wasn't exactly intent on a marathon session."

What he *was* intent on became immediately obvious, and I watched his lips wrap around me. My eyes fluttered at the wet warmth surrounding the head of my cock, and my body tensed at the sensation. I was almost amused at how slowly he worked his mouth down my shaft, jerking in surprised pleasure when his tongue massaged the underside of the head.

Without thinking, I ran my hand through his hair, gripping tight when he reached the base and began flexing his throat muscles to draw out a low groan of pleasure from me. Ethan pulled away quickly as I felt his throat muscles spasm, probably in protest of what he was doing. Gag reflex or no, it didn't stop him from sliding down once again.

There was no doubt in my mind Ethan was thoroughly enjoying himself as he began to work up a rhythm now he'd managed to lube me up, steadily building speed. His enthusiasm was intoxicating as he sank to the root once more, only to let out a deep groan that reverberated up the length of my dick. I couldn't help but let out a helpless noise as he resumed bobbing, his hand jerking me off as he worked his lips.

My earlier prediction was quickly becoming a reality as I felt the muscles in my legs tighten, my gut filling with warmth and anticipation. Despite the breathless state he was leaving me in, I managed to gasp out what I hoped was a sufficient warning. I wasn't surprised when Ethan didn't hesitate. If anything, there was a renewed enthusiasm for what he was doing, as if desperate.

Not caring that one of the neighbors, even at this hour, could be outside, I groaned loudly as my orgasm erupted. Pleasure rocketed through me, reverberating as I felt my cock jerk in Ethan's mouth. In turn, he bowed forward,

139

running his tongue rapidly on the underside of the head and bringing out another jerk of pleasure as I poured into his mouth. Ethan was as enthusiastic as he had been before, and I could only watch helplessly as he held me in his mouth until every last drop had been swallowed.

Only when he drew away before I grew too sensitive did I realize what his other hand had been doing. Hand pumping his own dick, he stood up, and before I could understand what he was doing, he turned and slid onto my lap, sitting down carefully so he could lean back against my chest. I was still lightheaded from my orgasm, but I didn't waste any time reaching around, nudging his hand out of the way, and taking him in my own.

He was impossibly hard in my hand, throbbing with each beat of his heart as I began to jerk him off, trying to replicate the way he'd been doing it himself a moment before. He stiffened against me, pushing into my grip, which I considered a good sign. His breathing shook, and I could feel his legs flexing as he thrust into my hand. Unlike me, he leaked profusely the more he was aroused, making the movement of my hand even smoother.

Despite my orgasm only seconds before, I found myself obsessed with the quiet sounds slipping from his lips. I didn't know if he was mindful of being outside and the risk of being overheard or if he was always so quiet. The guttural groans and sharp grunts of pleasure coming from him were still intoxicating, and I wondered what he would sound like while I was inside him or him inside me.

"Trevor," he grunted, nearly growling my name as his hips twitched.

As he had done with me earlier, I maintained my pace, holding onto his hip with my other hand to keep him steady. All I needed was for him to sit there and not worry about falling off my lap as I jerked him off.

I felt the moment his orgasm rose as his body went wire tight, pressing against me as his hips finally stopped thrusting and simply shuddered. Warmth pooled over my hand and arm as he shot hard, groaning heavily as his orgasm finally overtook him. His head fell back onto my shoulder as he pressed hard into my hand and breathed deeply before the strength in his body disappeared as quickly as strings on a puppet being cut.

His breathing was still ragged as he leaned back, comfortable and boneless. I continued holding him against me, letting go of his softening dick to let him have some peace. I didn't measure how long it took before he stirred to life, pushing himself forward with a chuckle.

"Well, that was fun," he snickered, standing up and pulling his pants back up.

"Before, I would've questioned your idea of fun, but I think we've finally found something we can agree on," I said softly, trying to adjust my pants without getting anything on them.

"Oh, hold on a sec," he grunted as he watched me and disappeared into the house for a few seconds before reappearing with a paper towel. "This would probably help."

"Could have saved us the trouble and the waste if you had just let me swallow it," I told him wryly before accepting the paper towel.

"True, but I wanted to feel your body while I got off," he said with a shrug. "It's a pretty damn good body."

I snorted, balling up the paper in my hand once I was clean. "Thanks. You have to work twice as hard for half the results at my age."

"Yeah, you're positively ancient," he said with enough sarcasm I was surprised it didn't physically manifest around us.

"You wait," I told him, pushing off the swing slowly to

arch my back and stretch the muscles that had tried their best to bunch up while I was sitting down. "You'll see."

"If I'm lucky enough to make it that long," he chuckled. "With my lifestyle, I'm not exactly destined for a long life."

"I've known plenty of people who thought the same, and they're still around and kicking," I told him. "Me being one of them."

"You? Mr. Cautious?"

"Even the cautious can find themselves dead when they least expect it."

"Do they find themselves dead if they're dead?"

"I'm...not having a theological discussion right now."

Ethan laughed, and even now, without being aroused, I enjoyed the sound. "That's fair. They're not exactly my favorite discussions anyway."

Silence settled between us, not uncomfortable but not exactly easy either. I was suddenly aware of what we'd just done and wondered if either of us had made the smartest decision. I wasn't bothered that he was probably close to twenty years my junior, both of us were adults and could make our own decisions. Hell, with what Ethan had seen in his life, he probably counted as nearly my age, if not older. Even if he didn't act like it, I'd bet good money the things he'd seen and experienced had aged him considerably.

"You should probably get moving. I'm sure it's past your bedtime," he said finally, shooting me a knowing smirk. "I'd offer for you to stay, but I get the feeling you won't."

"And why's that?" I asked, pretending I didn't feel my heart jump at the thought.

"Because if people see your car sitting in the driveway come morning, the whole town is going to start talking," he said, arching a brow.

I grimaced at the thought. "There is that."

The last thing I needed was everyone to have confirmation I'd done more than drop by for a visit. And it wasn't just to spare the whispering. I had come here to bring Ethan on board for my investigation. It wouldn't help my cause if I was seen spending too much time with him if I wanted him to stay incognito.

"Or," Ethan drew out slowly. "You *could* stay here."

"You're supposed to be my secret ace in the hole. Being around you all the time won't exactly help," I reminded him. "Hard to do that if you're around all the time."

"True," he drew out, but the smile on his face told me he was already a step ahead of me. "But I mean, your car has been sitting out front for a good while now. And if you wanted to keep things quiet, a phone call would have done a lot better than showing up."

I opened my mouth only to realize I had absolutely nothing to say other than, "Well, fuck."

Ethan snorted. "But...there is an alternative solution."

"That being?" I asked, raising a brow.

"Your car already rolled up here. People are going to note that you've been here for a while. So why not let your car stay here so it's seen in the morning?"

"And why would I do that?"

"For the same reason you'll be seen with me at other times. Maybe I stop by to have a few minutes alone with you in your office, or I'm seen at your house. Maybe I'm even seen going out and about with you on your days off."

It only took a few seconds for me to realize his plan. "You want people to think we're together."

"Want has nothing to do with this," he shrugged. "But we already accidentally set the groundwork. Why not play it to the hilt? Unless you're worried people will be bothered by the idea of you fucking around with a guy."

"In this town? Probably not," I said with a shake of my head. "And it would give them something to gossip about.

Not the guy part, but the fact that you're clearly younger than me."

"Gossiping about what you and I are up to while we play it off as just friends is a hell of a lot better than them wondering why else you'd be spending time with me," he said, cocking his head.

I narrowed my eyes. "Is this just another excuse for you to get me to dinner?"

He snickered. "I already did that. And don't worry. I'm not trying to put a ring on it. Me and relationships have never worked out. I'm just taking advantage of what we already have, and if it means I get to do a little more with you in private, even better. Every job has its perks."

"God, I forgot I'm technically your employer."

"I'm freelance, so no corporate rules against fraterniza-tion. You're safe."

There might be some rules around it at the county or state level, but I didn't know for sure. In all fairness, I couldn't think of anyone wanting to put something like that on the books. And in truth, his logic made a great deal of sense. If people were talking about what they thought we were doing instead of looking too heavily into what we were actually doing, all the better.

And hell, I was only human. The opportunity to spend private time with this frustrating man was sorely tempting. Apparently, age didn't always bring wisdom, at least not when it came to good-looking guys with wicked smiles and an even sharper sense of humor.

"I'm going to regret this," I said with a heavy sigh. "But I'm not sharing a bed with you. The last thing I need is for you to decide to get hands-on when your sister is around."

Ethan rolled his eyes. "As if I couldn't get hands-on other-wise. But fine, I've got a pull-out in my room. I'll take that, and you take the bed."

"I don't—"

"Either that, or we're sharing a bed, and I can promise you I'm getting gropey."

I wasn't *quite* sure why I was reluctant to share a bed after I'd just had my dick in his mouth, but the idea made me draw back anyway. "Fine, I'll sleep in the bed. But I do have to work tomorrow."

"So leave early to get ready," he said with a shrug. "Your house is only a few blocks away."

"How do you—"

"Public records aren't exactly difficult to get your hands on."

"Right," I said, suddenly wondering if his constant need to have information was another way for him to feel in control of his life, much like his tendency to get reactions out of the people around him. "Fair point."

"Alright, let's go have a nightcap," he said, turning back toward the house. "And brace for giving the town reason to wag their tongues."

Again, I could only wonder just how much I would regret this decision.

ETHAN

When I woke up the next morning, I wasn't surprised to find Trevor gone. A little stiff from the less-than-comfortable pull-out bed, I stretched with a low groan before flopping over to fish my phone off the floor where I'd left it charging. When I looked at the time, I was even less surprised to find Trevor gone. The man had probably left almost three hours before to get ready for his shift.

Yawning, I rolled off the edge of the bed, scratching my stomach as I made my way up the stairs.

The smell of coffee was thick in the air when I entered the kitchen, so I took that to mean the half-full pot was reasonably fresh. Pleased I didn't have to wait for it to brew, I poured myself a tall cup, took a sip, and let out a sigh of relief.

A thump somewhere in the house drew my attention, and I smirked as I watched Bri walk in, her hair in a messy ponytail and still wearing her shirt from the night before. There was a bleariness to her features that wasn't usually there, even when she'd just woken up.

"Have a late night?" I asked, smirking when she jumped.

"When the fuck did you get there?" she barked, glaring at me.

"I take it from your colorful language that Colin isn't here," I said, arching a brow. "I'm guessing you and Rob had a great night then."

Her cheeks colored, but she didn't stop cleaning up the living room, which just involved adjusting the pillows and refolding the blankets. "It was...a nice night."

"Good," I said, raising my coffee cup in a gesture of cheers.

"I, uh, was expecting a lot more than that out of you."

"Oh, sorry."

"No, it's—"

"Is he a good lay?"

"Dammit, Ethan, that wasn't an invitation!"

"And that wasn't an answer."

She tossed a pillow haphazardly onto the couch. "We didn't...we spent the night together, but we didn't do more than kiss, alright?"

"So you slept with him in the most literal sense?" I asked, raising a brow.

She glared at me. "Yes. And if you have a smart-ass thing to say about that, keep it to yourself."

I held up my hands in surrender. "I wouldn't dream of it."

"Now that's a damn lie," she grumbled.

"Seriously, I'm glad you had a good night. I mean, sure, it's a little weird that you didn't at least get a grope in to make sure he could get more than an inch into—"

"Ethan."

I laughed. "So, he's good? Like, a good guy."

Her cheeks went pink again, but this time it was accompanied by a soft, wistful smile. "He is. At least so far. I won't make any hard judgments yet, but yeah."

"Good," I said, taking another drink.

Apparently, she decided the living room wasn't a complete disaster anymore, grabbed a mug of coffee from somewhere out of sight, and joined me in the kitchen. "We stayed up pretty late. I came back here to do a few things and ended up falling asleep on the couch."

"And if you didn't sleep with him, what the hell were you doing up so late?"

"Talking. You should be familiar with the concept considering you haven't stopped from the moment you learned how."

"Ouch," I said with a laugh. "I'm not going to deny it, but ouch."

She smirked. "That brings me to why I saw a certain familiar car leaving our driveway this morning."

Our. It was unconscious on her part, but little moments like that made me believe that for all her complaining about my habits and behavior, Bri wasn't all that annoyed by my presence.

"I guess he didn't make a great escape like he planned," I said with a chuckle. "Or, at least, that's what we want people to think."

She paused. "Uh...what?"

"He hired me to do some investigation for him, but he doesn't want people to know I'm digging on his behalf. That way, the wrong people aren't suspicious, and the right ones aren't worried." I told her, figuring it was easier to tell her the truth than have her constantly questioning what I was up to. At least this way, I could use the 'it's an official job' statement as a shield.

She hesitated. "Digging up what?"

"Now that I can't tell you," I told her. "Truth be told, I probably shouldn't have told you I was working for him, but that's probably not addressed in the NDA, so I'm probably safe."

Not that I thought Trevor would come after me in court for something as small as telling Bri, but people had surprised me in the past.

Her brow furrowed, and I could practically see the wheels spinning in her head as the sleepiness evaporated from her face. "Which means it's dangerous."

"First of all, danger isn't new to me," I reminded her. "And secondly, just because it's private doesn't mean it's dangerous."

It could become dangerous depending on where my investigations took me, but I wasn't going to stand around and make her worry.

Bri sighed heavily. "And now I'm feeling even less confident about this."

"C'mon, Bri," I said softly, stepping past her to grab my laptop and set it on the small dining room table, opening it up to begin jotting down ideas. "It's paying work, it's official work, and it's for the good of the town. Those are all reasons you shouldn't worry."

"Maybe," she said, refilling her cup before joining me at the table. "But I also know you're not one to take an easy job. I remember asking you if you would, years back, and you called it boring."

"Your little girlfriend wanted me to find out if her boyfriend was cheating on her," I said dryly. "Which is boring."

"But safer."

"Have you ever seen what happens when people get caught investigating cheaters? I can promise you, you wouldn't call that safer. People get stabbed over that shit."

She grimaced. "And Ted did end up trying to attack her when she broke up with him."

"Oh, well, shit," I grunted. "She alright?"

"She's fine. Got away by hitting him with a vase and

booking it into the parking lot, screaming her head off. I'm just annoyed that you made a good point."

"I make those a lot, yet everyone seems irritated about it. Why is it other people can make good points, and everyone just nods their heads and smiles, but if I do it, everyone's getting grumpy."

"Call it the Ethan Effect," she said dryly.

"True, it must be my charming personality."

"Right. Sure. Charm. We'll go with that."

I laughed, bringing up the map I'd made of Fairlake. I'd created color coding that could be applied and taken off with a click of a button. There was one for where crimes occurred the most, one for income levels, and one for residential buildings and businesses. Anything I wanted to know at a glance had been laid out in a few hours, well before Trevor had even shown up.

A couple of clicks showed me the south and north of town were the lowest-income areas, and I wasn't surprised to find those were also the places with the most criminal activity.

I wasn't surprised the south also shared a border with the forest Trevor mentioned. In fact, the crime rate had increased in the past year. Not enough to stick out on a graph, but certainly more than before, making it stand out to me.

"Interesting," I muttered, searching for any reports from the neighboring town of Fovel, which shared a border with the same woods.

"Are you even listening to me right now?" Bri asked sharply.

I looked up, eyes going wide. "Oh, uh, if I lied, would you believe me?"

"No."

"Right, then no, sorry."

"I was saying that I hope he's at least paying you well for this," she said, arching a brow.

"Oh, well, yeah. This is Trevor. He's going to be fair," I said, realizing we hadn't actually discussed the fee I would be charging. Considering I didn't use my credentials very often, I didn't have a set fee for anything. It had been done on a whim, and I used it partially as a way to give my work a sense of professionalism that my personality would otherwise detract from.

"He's Trevor now, huh?"

"Yeah, but you probably shouldn't get into the habit of saying it."

She rolled her eyes. "And before you go back into your zone...again, would you explain why he would want people to think he didn't manage to make an escape?"

"Because his whole point of hiring me was to do quiet digging. Kind of hard to do that if people already saw me with the police chief more than once. So...if he was here late and left early in the morning, but not so early the neighbors didn't notice..." I explained, drawing it out to see if she would connect the dots on her own.

She frowned. "I...are you pretending to date him?"

"Something like that."

"Do you even know how to pretend to date someone?"

"Wow, for having had such a good night, you're certainly extra bitchy this morning."

Bri laughed merrily, shooting me the finger. "Oh, you can dish it out but not take it?"

"I'm very sensitive," I told her, shoving my bottom lip out. "You hurt my feelings."

"Uh-huh," she said in a tone that left no doubt she didn't believe me.

I huffed. "I have dated before."

"I'm not going to dignify that with a response. We both know how well that's worked out for you in the past."

"Yeah," I said, shrugging. "My charming personality and stunning bedroom abilities are only good for drawing them in, not keeping them."

She arched a brow. "Don't get me wrong, you're right, at least about the personality. I'm not touching the sex part, no way in hell. But you've never shown an interest in someone before, at least nothing significant. It's always been people that, deep down, you knew weren't right for you."

"Didn't you already yell at me about bringing pop psychology into our conversations?"

"Think about it. There was the nun—"

"She wasn't a nun yet, just...going to be."

"And then there was the guy who told you how much he hated being away from his friends and family for long periods. Surprise, surprise, the same thing applied to the guy he was dating. The woman who hated drinking. And don't think I don't know you were sleeping with one of the Cartel people while you were down there."

My brow rose. "I'm surprised you know about that. And she wasn't Cartel. Her dad was."

"Ethan. I'm going to ignore how fucking dangerous it was for you to do that *while digging up dirt on the Cartel to show to the world*. And go right into how you knew that relationship was doomed from the moment you batted your eyes at her."

"Wait, why am I the one batting my eyes? Why can't she bat her eyes? Is this an independent woman thing? Do you make Rob bat his eyes at you instead?"

"My point is, you've repeatedly chosen people you know damn well you don't have a long-term possibility with."

"Right," I said bitterly, dropping my attempt at lightening the conversation. "Because my life allows having someone in it. That's not even taking into account that, as you and everyone else like to point out, I'm a pain in the ass."

"You are," she said. "Which, yes, makes you difficult to deal with sometimes. But if that was all there was to it, do you really think I'd have much to do with you?"

"Well, I'm your brother."

"Blood doesn't mean shit. Just look at how much you aren't around Mom and Dad. And Bennett's friend could tell you a few things about his boyfriend's family."

"Chase?"

"Well, Chase and Devin both, now I think about it. But I meant his friend Isaiah. I guess his boyfriend has an interesting family."

I narrowed my eyes. "Just how gay is this town?"

"Very," she said blandly. "And before you ask, yes, I've made sure Rob isn't gay, and no, he doesn't have a gay best friend."

"Some people would call that homophobic."

"Some people didn't have their formerly straight ex-husband get into a big gay, happy relationship either. I just need to make sure I'm not cursed."

I snorted, thinking she probably didn't have to worry about that much. "And for the record, we're not pretending we're dating. We're just going to spend enough time around one another to make people gossip. Just enough to make them think I'm only around him because he looks good in his uniform...which he does."

She shook her head. "I see you have your priorities straight."

"There's nothing straight about my priorities," I told her, enjoying the roll of her eyes.

"And how did you manage to get him on board with this idea?" she asked, raising a brow.

"Easy. I made it make sense to him in a simple and logical

way," I said with a shrug. "In case you haven't forgotten, I'm pretty good with people when I want to be. Plus, he wants it to succeed, so offering something that helped with that was perfect to convince him."

"Simple and logical," she repeated, sounding unimpressed. "Congrats, you figured out how to use logic to convince someone who's obviously logical. Next you'll tell me the same thing works on me."

"Nope," I said, wondering where I should start digging around. There were a few decent ideas at first glance, but I could at least put 'check the forest' lower on the priority list. "You're swayed by emotions. You just use your professional, self-controlled exterior as a defense to hide that."

Not that I thought Trevor was much better, but he was less obvious. Little moments hinted at a great well of emotion inside the man, buried under the several layers he'd built. My argument had worked not just because it made sense, giving him a ready-made excuse to accept it at face value, but because I suspected he *wanted* to accept the idea.

I still wasn't sure what to make of that. I could understand wanting more alone time with me if his enthusiasm last night had been any indication. The guy was clearly deprived of a lot of things, in my opinion, and not just sexual contact. It was interesting that he'd been the one to shoot down the idea of him staying the night, even before I'd presented it. He'd struck me as the sort to get a little attached after having sex with someone, but then again, people could still surprise me.

I wasn't surprised to see Bri look less than thrilled. "Oh really?"

"Really," I assured her. "And don't ask me to explain it."

"Why?"

"Because, like most people, you'd be really unhappy to hear things that go against what you believe about yourself.

And before you get mad at the idea, I'm not saying I'm any different."

I could tell she wanted to continue but gave an annoyed huff. "Fine, so you two are going to pretend to play kissy face for everyone? That's the plan?"

"More or less, though I think it's going to be more than kissy face."

"Why do you think that?"

"Well, considering I already had his dick in my mouth."

She choked on her drink, spraying it over the table so badly I drew my laptop away instinctively out of fear. "You *what?*"

"I said what I said," I told her, checking the back of the laptop to clean up any stray coffee spray.

"Yeah, I heard that. But *what?*"

"Why are you so surprised?"

She took a moment to consider before shrugging. "I guess I never thought he was...you know."

"Into dick."

"That."

"He's a special boy, just like me."

"A slut?"

It was my turn to snort my coffee, though I made less of a mess as I threw a chair cushion at her. "Bi, you bitch."

She laughed, setting the cushion on the table after catching it. "Fine, I didn't expect him to be bi. How the hell did you figure it out? And why the hell were you blowing him?"

"I figured it out because I'm good like that," I told her with a smirk. In truth, it had been a lot of things all adding up. The explanation would have taken far too long, and I still had plans for the rest of my day. "And as for why I was blowing him, have you taken a look at the man?"

Her eyes drifted upward as she thought about it. "True, he does look good."

"Especially in that uniform."

"Does he look even better naked?"

"We, uh, didn't get to the part where the clothes came off. Fun fact about dicks, you don't need to be naked to access them."

"Yes, thank you for that absolutely fascinating insight into how dicks work. I would have never known."

"There's an awful joke I could make right now, but because I love you, I'll keep it to myself," I said.

She narrowed her eyes. "Or the fact that you're currently living under my roof is keeping your tongue in check. It's nice to know there's *something* that can do it. And don't think I don't know it wasn't about the fact that Adam and I didn't work out."

"Perish the thought," I said loftily, closing the laptop and standing up.

"You might be a decent liar in other circumstances, but you're not a good one right now," she said, watching me closely. "What are you doing?"

"I'm going to do the job I was hired to do," I told her. "Right after a shower and a change of clothes."

"Do you need the car?" she asked.

"Nah," I said with a wave of my hand. "I can manage on my own two feet. Plus, it's better to have your own mental map of an area, and what better way than to do it on your feet?"

That wouldn't stop me from having access to the map on my computer now I had it in the cloud service I used. Still, if I was going to stick around town for a while, which I might, considering I was now gainfully employed, getting my hands on a car of my own wouldn't be a bad idea.

"And you're sure this isn't dangerous?" she called after me as I made my way toward the bathroom.

"Not currently," I called back, knowing full well that wouldn't keep her off my case.

"What the hell does *that* mean?"

"It means what it means."

"Ethan!"

"You worry too much," I said, closing the bathroom door before she could confront me.

"I'm serious!" she yelled through the door, and I flipped on the water to drown out her voice.

"And I'm seriously naked," I said, stripping off my clothes just in case she decided to call my bluff. At least if she saw me naked, she had no one to blame but herself for entering after being warned.

"Goddammit," I heard her hiss, followed by her heavy footsteps, signaling she was not happy with me.

I, however, had a day to plan and an investigation to dig into.

As much as I had wanted to check out the south of the town, I decided to take a walk to the north first to get a feel for the area. It wasn't one of the places I wanted to focus on, but unsavory types had a way of connecting with one another whether or not they were on opposite sides of town. At the very least it would allow me to see part of the town without attracting attention immediately.

Not that I was going to draw attention right away. While I was fond of dressing with a little flair when I wasn't in the field, I figured looking 'pretty' would draw too much attention. I wore a plain shirt with a faded Metallica logo, torn jeans, and boots that had seen plenty of action over the years. Nothing about my appearance would draw attention, including my hair, which I let fall to one side in an untouched mess, and I replaced the nice piercings in my ears with something simpler.

It was probably overkill, but I hadn't survived this long in places where I wasn't welcome without being a little paranoid. No matter what my sister and friends might think, I was perpetually worrying about my own safety. Sure, my quick wits managed to get me out of tough scrapes more than once, but as I'm sure someone like Trevor would tell me, an ounce of prevention was worth a pound of cure.

After an hour walking around the area, not a lot caught my interest. Most of it was just lower-income housing, a rundown apartment complex, and a trailer park I didn't dare walk into yet. A trailer park in a small town like Fairlake could either be even more aware of outsiders or the one place where people learned to mind their own business. I didn't want to find out which the hard way.

Having seen my fair share, I decided to stop at a little store on the corner near some rougher-looking houses. The storefront had probably once looked like a nice brick building, but time and neglect had stripped the white paint and showed that the 'bricks' were just a veneer, now crumbling away from the concrete walls. A single bulb sat above the door, still lit despite the afternoon sunlight and buzzing as I approached.

The inside was no better. Grabbing myself a drink and something to snack on, I made my way to the front and set everything down.

"Anything to drink?" the guy behind the counter asked, glancing at the liquor behind him. All of which, I noticed, were in a small room lined with bulletproof glass.

"Actually, yeah," I said after a moment's thought, realizing

I could use something. "Just a pint, cheapest whiskey you have."

"Sure," he said, turning around to grab it and adding it to the total.

Pulling out my wallet, I slid a twenty and a five across the counter. "So, this is probably a stupid question in a town like this, but is there anything fun worth doing around here?"

The guy behind the counter shrugged, his expression that of a man who'd seen plenty at the store and expected very little out of people. "Not really. Not unless you're looking to get into trouble."

"Pfft," I snorted. "What's wrong with that?"

"I guess that depends on the trouble you're willing to get into," he said, handing me my change and staring at me.

"I guess that depends on the trouble you're willing to point me toward," I said, still smiling.

"I get plenty of that in here as it is," he grunted. "If you want trouble, go find it somewhere else. Plenty of that to be found up at Pheasant Run."

I don't think he could have more plainly told me to get the hell out of his store. At the very least, I now knew my original theory had been right. The trailer park probably was where I wanted to end up going.

Sure, desperation led to desperate measures, but not everyone was involved in drugs and violence. Far too many found themselves in their position because of circumstances outside their control or just plain bad luck.

With a grunt, I pushed the thought out of my mind and turned to leave, glancing over to see one other person in the store bent over to peer at something in the coolers. There was something slightly off about the guy, but from the distance and angle, I couldn't quite put my finger on it. Considering it didn't ring any alarm bells, I pushed it aside and headed out.

Once there, I opened the whiskey, wrinkling my nose at the smell. Whiskey rarely smelled good to me, but this particularly foul bottle managed to smell of stale smoke and paint thinner. Grimacing, I set my palm over the bottle's mouth and soaked it with the liquor to pat on my clothes and neck. With that done, I took a deep breath and a large swallow of the liquor, swishing it around my mouth and swallowing it down to make sure it was on my breath for a while.

My throat clenched at the god-awful taste, somehow worse than the home-brewed liquors I'd had over the years. Fighting back my gag reflex, I cracked open the other drink and took a big gulp. There wasn't much I could do about the aftertaste from the liquor, and I shoved the pint into the back of my jeans in case I needed a refresher.

With that done, I turned to walk away. Only to stop short when faced with what had to be one of the biggest men I'd ever seen. Not only was he tall, but he was built like a human tank. I had to crane my neck to peer up into his face, which was heavily furrowed as he stared down at me. Normally, I'd find the idea of a huge redhead bearing down on me arousing, but under the circumstances, I jerked back in surprise.

"Jesus, hello," I snapped, stepping away from him.

"Why did you do that?" he asked.

"What? I'm not allowed to have a drink?" I asked, scrambling to get my senses working. "Still allowed to do that, last I checked."

"Yeah," he grunted. "But you didn't just drink it."

"I guess I didn't," I said, wondering if I could use confusion to my advantage and keep him off balance.

"You put it on yourself."

"Yeah, and?"

"Why?"

"Why do you care?"

The question stumped him as he stared at me like he'd just caught me using cheap whiskey as cologne. Honestly, I didn't know how he'd even gotten out of the store without me hearing him. I didn't know what it was about big guys, but they were either the loudest people or so quiet you'd swear they'd had ninja training.

"Maybe I like the smell," I finally said as he continued to stare at me long enough that I was beginning to feel uncomfortable.

To my surprise, he smirked at me. "Not that brand. Not unless you're *really* desperate."

I couldn't help but laugh. "Well, shit. I guess I didn't have all the details worked out."

"Yeah," he said. "But why?"

"Ask me no questions, and I'll tell you no lies," I told him. "You caught me out, but that doesn't mean I have to spill the beans."

"Sure," he said with a shrug.

"So, does the man with investigative skills have a name?" I asked, wondering if I could pump him for more information before I swam into deeper waters.

"Julian," he said.

"Right," I said, wondering if he was always this verbose or just like that for my benefit. "Well, Julian, you can call me Ethan."

His brow furrowed again. "Ethan?"

"That...yes, that's my name."

"Bennett knows you."

I blinked, a light flickering in my brain, and I immediately recognized the name. "Oh. You're Isaiah's—"

"Yeah," he said, far faster than before, and I noticed how his eyes darted around. "I am."

I squinted, lowering my voice. "Is this a thing where you're not like...out?"

He glanced down at his feet, and despite his size, I was struck by the impression that I was talking to a chastised little boy. "Working on it. Just...not around here. It's better with people I know."

I couldn't relate to his problem but didn't think it was right to bring that up. Coming out for me had been a simple and relatively smooth process when I was younger. There had been a few nasty comments, but I wasn't surprised, considering I had them pegged as shitheads long before they knew I was into guys. My family hadn't been fazed, although my mother had spent some time wringing her hands over how the world would treat me.

Bri had been there for that particular worry-filled rant and had snorted, piping up, "Mom, I think you should be more worried about how *he's* going to treat the world."

Honestly, sometimes I couldn't decide if having siblings was a blessing or a curse.

"Well, if it makes you feel any better, I won't go around telling everyone," I told him.

I meant it as a joke, but I watched as the tension in his shoulders eased. "Okay."

I wasn't often taken aback by another person's way of speaking, but Julian somehow managed it. "I uh...no offense, but you're not one for talking, are you?"

"Not...really," he said, shrugging his broad shoulders. "I'm not good at it. I'm getting better, though."

After a moment of silence, I thought I understood something. "But I'd bet your...Isaiah is probably more of a talker, isn't he?"

"Yeah," he said with an almost sheepish smile.

God save me. If he wasn't taken, I probably would have been smitten on the spot. "Ahh, well, that makes sense. Balance has been restored to the universe."

I wasn't surprised to see him shrug again, which seemed

to be a large part of his communication. I was beginning to wonder if some secret code would allow me to translate not so much what he was saying but what he wasn't saying. Maybe with some one-on-one time and the help of a few drinks, I might be able to break it down. But that idle bit of intrigue on my part could wait until another time.

"So," I said after several moments of silence. "You live around here then?"

"Used to," he said, pointing toward the run-down apartment building about a block from the store. "Before Isaiah."

"Ah, cohabitation," I said with a smile. "Better place?"

"Definitely."

I imagined it wouldn't take a whole lot. The building looked like it hadn't seen proper maintenance for a decade. "Yeah, I can...imagine."

"Yeah," he said once more, and I wondered if he had any more words in his vocabulary or if he was running out.

"Okay, so if you don't live here anymore, why keep coming around?"

He looked back toward the store. "I like to come here. They were always nice to me."

"Ohhh, supporting your local business then."

"Sure."

I took a moment to debate whether or not the new idea I had was a good one. I was sure Trevor would probably say having a plan was better than doing whatever felt best at the time. Then again, I was probably giving the man too little credit. I didn't think it was possible to run a whole precinct and make it to chief of police without learning to listen to your gut at least a bit.

"So, I have some questions you might be able to answer since you're from this neighborhood," I said slowly. "But, before I ask, I need you to promise you won't go around telling people I was asking."

If he was surprised or curious, he didn't show it. "Okay. I...don't know what good I'll be. I didn't get out much."

I chuckled. "See, that I believe, but considering you called me out on what you saw, I guess you noticed a lot more than people gave you credit for."

For the second time, he smiled, though it wasn't nearly as warm as when he'd thought of Isaiah earlier. "Okay, what?"

"Well, believe it or not, I'm looking for drugs."

"Why?"

"Not for...trust me, it's not for personal use. And before you ask 'why' again, I'm not allowed to tell you."

It was the truth...mostly. I could theoretically tell Julian what I was up to if I was going to treat him as a confidential informant, something I'd made sure to put into the paperwork I sent to Trevor last night. As a matter of fact, the entire document was filled with loopholes that allowed me to do quite a lot of things. I wouldn't be surprised if I received the documents back with some revisions thrown in when he finally had it looked over.

"And I don't mean pot either," I added in a quiet voice, sure no one was around except the woman with two bags limping down the sidewalk on the other side of the street. "Harder stuff."

His brow furrowed. "Well, I know there's some stuff in Pheasant Run. My old neighbor used to get it from some guy named Rod."

"Rod," I repeated with amusement. "Alright, you know where he lives?"

"No, but she always told me if I wanted 'good stuff,' I should go see him and say Tina sent me."

"Tina," I repeated, excitement launching through me.

"Yeah, her name was Kelly, though," he said in a doubtful tone. "She told me he thinks it's clever."

"Well, that's the kind of cleverness you can expect from

small-time dealers," I said with a smirk. "Did you ever see him?"

"Yeah," he said. "He's...your height, black hair, has a tattoo on his neck."

"Of?"

"I don't know," he said and then smiled softly. "Kind of looked like a sperm."

"A sperm?"

"Yeah. The head, with a tail that...swooped up and then down?"

"Wait," I said, opening up my phone and tapping something into the search engine before showing him the picture. "Like that?"

"Yeah."

"That's a zodiac sign, Leo."

"Oh. That's what Isaiah is."

"Not all lions are as noble as your boy," I chuckled, tucking my phone away. "Anything else you noticed?"

"Twitchy, talked fast, and really pushy."

Well, that fit. The smartest thing a dealer could do was avoid their own product, but dealers weren't always known for their intelligence. Which meant I was dealing with someone who could either be really difficult to deal with or easy, depending on his particular brand of twitchy.

"Smokes...both things," Julian said after a moment. "Always smelled like a skunk and had a cigarette in his hands all the time. Newports."

"Wow, you got a good look at him if you know the brand," I noted with a chuckle.

"I know the smell," he said quietly. "My dad used to smoke them."

There was...a lot in those few words that I didn't think I would ever be able to parse. Clearly, he had a story of his own to tell, but just from how he acted, the subject was probably off-limits to the world. I wouldn't say it to this man who was a stranger to me, but I hoped he'd at least confided in his boyfriend, even if he wouldn't tell the world. Hell, what was the point of being in a committed relationship with someone if you didn't share the weight of your burdens with them?

"That's all I remember," he said, peering down at me. "You're not going to get into trouble, are you?"

Seriously? Was there something about my vibe that only the people of Fairlake seemed to be able to detect? Was this somehow connected to how absurdly gay the whole town seemed? Christ, I should have been investigating that in my free time instead of drug pushers.

"Well, here's hoping I don't," I said with a snort. "I'm certainly not trying to find any trouble."

"Well...okay," he said, and strangely enough, I actually believed he was settled on the matter. "Anything else?"

"Nope," I said brightly, pleased with the information. At the very least, it gave me a much stronger starting point than I'd had ten minutes before. "Just, you know, like I said, keep this between you and me. Let's just say I'm doing something I don't want gossiped about."

"Is it illegal?" he asked.

"No," I said seriously. "In fact, it's the complete opposite."

"Okay," he said with a shrug. "Then I'll be quiet."

"Somehow I think that won't be too hard for you," I said with a smirk.

"Yeah," he said, grinning this time. "I should go. Isaiah's expecting me, and if I'm late for dinner—"

"You'll be up a certain creek and no paddle in sight," I finished for him.

"A little," he said, ducking his head. "Be safe, Ethan. That place isn't very good."

"I figured as much," I told him. "And I might not look it, but I'm pretty good at taking care of myself."

He wrinkled his nose with a sniff. "You'll fit in. Be careful."

It was the only time I'd ever considered someone insinuating I stank to be a compliment. "You bet."

Julian walked away, and I felt my phone buzz in my pocket. After ensuring the man was done talking to me, I pulled it out, not recognizing the number. The area code was one I knew, having been in Fairlake for a few weeks, and the fact that it said it was coming from the police station was a dead giveaway.

"Please tell me you're sitting at your desk, in your uniform, frowning, looking impossibly manly and sexy at the same time," I said once I answered the call.

Trevor sighed heavily. "Did you know I typically make calls using the speaker? I almost did with this one, but I thought, 'No, that's a bad idea.' So, thank you for proving my suspicion correct."

"Ahh, well, you know me, I don't like to disappoint," I chuckled. "And...are you?"

"I am at my desk, which means I'm in my uniform. And because of this conversation, I'm frowning."

"And the manly and sexy part?"

"I'm not answering that."

I smirked. "You're no fun. Aren't you at least going to ask what I'm wearing?"

"Seeing as it's you, that answer could very well be nothing."

"Would you want it to be nothing?"

"I can't see how that answer would do me any good."

I glanced around, tracking a car pulling away from the trailer park. "It would certainly be something fun for you to think about until the next time you see me."

"It doesn't matter what I say, does it? You're just going to keep on this topic."

"Are you saying you *don't* want to see me naked?"

There was a heavy pause before he spoke again. "That isn't what I called about."

"I mean, if you don't want to see—"

"If I answer the question, will you let me tell you why I called?"

"Sure, but only if you answer honestly."

There was another pause, and he spoke quietly. "Seeing you naked ranks quite high in the things I would like to see."

"Mmm, I might just be willing to grant that desire," I chuckled.

"You're a terrible influence."

"Yeah, but let's not pretend you're not enjoying the idea that you might see me naked soon."

"Fine, we won't pretend. We'll acknowledge it as fact, and *then* we're going to move on to business."

"I can do that," I said with a snort. "So, what's up? Read through the paperwork."

"Ira did, although looking at it myself, I noticed you didn't go overboard on the legal terminology."

"Nah, I had Bart draw it up so it could make sense to people."

"Bart?"

"My lawyer," I told him, watching another vehicle, a truck this time, pull into the park. "Good man. A bit pretentious, but good."

"Ah, I think that's just lawyers in general, even the good ones."

"Don't let my sister hear you say that. She prides herself on being 'down to earth' and 'accessible' to her clients."

"Isn't she a real estate lawyer?"

"That she is."

"Well, you'd hope they're the more approachable types."

I could feel the restless energy growing as I watched the

traffic in and out of the park. "So, you had a reason for calling?"

"Just to tell you I've signed everything and sent it back to you."

That managed to draw my attention back to the conversation. "Really? No issues?"

His chuckle was rich and smooth in my ear. "Surprised? Why? Because you decided to add in several clauses and exceptions to all the rules and guidelines you slapped in there?"

"Uh, yeah, actually," I admitted. "I kind of expected a stronger 'do things by the book' reaction."

"If you were one of my officers, I would hold you to that standard. We have to hold ourselves high, otherwise, people wouldn't look to us when they need help," he told me, sounding more like he believed it and less like it was rehearsed. "But you aren't one of my officers. You're an independent contractor, who I just so happen to know knows how to get results."

"Because of what you read," I said, raising a brow.

"Exactly. No one gets the kind of results you do, in the places you do, and coming out in one piece by following the rules," he said, and I could almost imagine him shrugging those strong shoulders of his. "So long as you aren't doing anything illegal or hurting anyone, I see no point in restricting how you operate. If I want something that does fancy tricks, I'll get a dog, not a cat."

"Pretty sure cats can do tricks," I told him with a smirk.

"Well, then maybe I'll get to see what other tricks you have," he said, and I'd swear there was a hint of promise in his voice. If there was, I was all for whatever he had in mind. "What are you doing?"

"Working," I told him, returning to reality and looking around.

"I...the paperwork wasn't done."

"No, but I figured you'd sign. Better to get a head start on everything."

"Should I ask precisely what you're doing, or will you be you about it?"

I chuckled. "I'll be me about it. But I promise, after I've done some digging, I'll come find you and give you a report."

"And just how long will that take?" he asked.

"A good question, and one I can't answer at this point and time."

"Somehow, I figured that would be your answer."

"You did say you wanted me to operate in my own way," I reminded him.

"That I did," and I could hear the smile in his voice.

"Trevor Price, I do believe you're becoming fond of my eccentricities," I told him with a laugh.

"Perhaps. Just do me one favor?"

"What's that?"

"Be sure to check in every now and then so I know you're still alive," he said. "I know you're a professional and more than capable of taking care of yourself. Still, it would ease my mind considering I'm the one who put you on this path."

"That's...a little dramatic," I told him.

He snorted softly. "Just keep me updated on whether or not I need to start searching ditches for your body, alright?"

"I can do that," I told him with a smile. The request didn't bother me much. Maybe because he prefaced it by acknowledging I *could* take care of myself. It was nice to have someone worry about my well-being without treating me as incompetent or foolish.

"Good," he grunted, suddenly sounding awkward. "I suppose I'll see you when I see you?"

"Don't worry, it won't be too long," I said, still smiling. "I know you'd waste away without seeing me."

"I'm counting the days," he said, sounding exasperated.

I laughed. "I'll see you soon, Trevor."

"I'll hold you to that."

Still smiling, I tucked the phone away and turned back toward the trailer park, mentally preparing myself for what was to come. It wasn't surprising that I was excited to have something to sink my teeth into. I had never been very good at sitting still when there were things to do. What was surprising was I found myself looking forward to the downtime, when I could look Trevor in the face and tell him what I learned.

And well, maybe just to see his face and hear his voice.

TREVOR

Taking a sip of coffee, I winced at the sudden burn and pulled it away, slopping some on my desk and the papers. Cursing, I carefully set the mug aside and grabbed some tissues to dab up the worst. It was probably a good thing all reports were digitally stored.

Having cleaned up as best I could, I threw the wet tissue into the wastebasket and turned my attention back to the reports. There wasn't any good news in them, but nothing significant either. Jane had done her best, but people weren't talking that much to the police, which really wasn't a surprise. Still, there was enough to tell me there was a slight but still noticeable uptick in drug use in the town.

No dealers had been caught yet, but there were signs, especially with domestic and public disturbance calls. A few gossips in town were already talking about their neighbors. Not that anyone had anything concrete, as far as I could tell, just aimless rumors about people getting high.

"Everything and nothing," I muttered again, rubbing at my eyes. It had been a long week, and I thought I'd give myself the weekend to take some time to breathe.

No sooner had the thought left my mind than my computer lit up, signaling Ira was calling me from the front desk. I stared at it, contemplating ignoring it and going home. I had been in the office for nearly twelve hours and wasn't needed anymore. The night shift could handle things without my interference, and the idea of sitting in front of the TV with an ice-cold glass of beer or tea sounded perfect.

Yet, I'd no sooner ignore Ira than I would God if he descended to leave me a message and hit the button. "Yes, Ira?"

"You have a visitor," she quipped, sounding amused, which could either be a good or terrible sign.

"What?" I asked, frowning at my computer screen to see it was just past eight. "At this hour?"

A new, familiar voice piped up in the background. "Ask him if he's got his handcuffs on hand."

"Oh, Jesus Christ," I groaned. "Send him back before he says something I'm going to make him regret."

"Is he always that kinky on speakerphone?" Ethan asked Ira, and I sighed again as I heard her snickering before the line clicked off.

It had been almost a week since I'd last spoken to him, save for his at least once-a-day texts to inform me he was breathing and unharmed. A sense of excitement bubbled in my chest, shaking off the lethargy and apathy I'd been sinking into for the past couple of hours. Although, his presence made me want to be home even more, albeit for entirely different reasons.

Feeling like a skittish and slightly horny teenager, I turned to face the glass cabinet to make sure I hadn't managed to maul my appearance while sitting alone in my office. I knew this was probably the report I'd been promised, but that didn't mean I couldn't at least look presentable. And if he just happened to have other things on his mind, then so be it.

Thankfully I was standing behind my desk, taking a sip of coffee when he walked in, rather than preening myself. His eyes darted over me slowly, measuring my mood. I straightened my features when his eyes finally met mine, trying not to show how much I suddenly wanted to squirm under his scrutiny.

"You look like you've been at it for a while," he said.

I resisted the urge to check my hair, reminding myself it was too short to stick up after repeatedly running my hand over my scalp. "What makes you say that?"

He motioned in a circle around his eyes. "Red-rimmed and dry-looking. You've been staring at words for too long."

I let out a soft laugh, gesturing toward my desk. "As you can see, that's exactly what I've been doing. I never realized before that ninety percent of this job would be paperwork."

Ethan approached the desk, bending over to pluck the stained piece of paper up. I wanted to remind him that while I technically employed him, that didn't give him access to everything. The words faded as I found myself staring at the way his jeans hugged his ass as he snorted. "Looks like you've been finger painting with the paper instead."

"I forgot how hot fresh coffee is," I said, gesturing toward the still-steaming cup. "I should have stopped drinking it hours ago."

Something I'd been telling myself for almost twenty years, yet I always drank coffee late, no matter how early I had to get up the next day.

"Is this going in the archives?" Ethan asked with a chuckle. "I can't imagine this going in with the rest, but I've seen some really interesting stains on public files before, so maybe I can."

"There are more than our fair share of coffee-stained files

in the archives," I told him with a chuckle. "Though, that's about it."

Ethan held the paper up, looking it over thoughtfully. "You know, the first public record I ever looked at had stains on it. Except they were darker, and a few flakes were left that looked almost like rust."

"Blood?" I guessed, wondering how that could have happened and why it would have been put into the records with that sort of biohazard on it.

"I thought so too, which was strange since it was a report on the minutes of the school board," Ethan chuckled, then caught my confused expression. "I was supposed to be doing a report for school. Instead, we were all randomly assigned a job. In a fit of cosmic irony, considering my record, I got school board member. I was also told in no uncertain terms that if I didn't do the report, I would fail the class because it was a 'core credit.' God, I hated that teacher."

"What class would give you something like that?" I asked in bewilderment.

"Civics," he said in such a deadpan, unamused tone that I believed him instantly.

"Isn't that about government and taxes?"

"And apparently incredibly boring, self-important careers," Ethan said with a snort, then glanced back toward the door. "Were you heading out? I don't want to leave Ira alone for too long."

"Um...why?"

"Because I'm responsible for the wellbeing of another creature, and it probably doesn't count if I leave it with Ira for too long, even if she is thrilled to bits."

"For reasons that should be obvious, I just felt a horrible chill go down my spine followed by a terrible sense of foreboding," I said with a shake of my head.

"Ha ha," he enunciated sarcastically. "C'mon, I can finish the story in a minute, it's kinda funny."

Not sure what I was walking into, I left my mug on the desk and followed him, closing the office door behind me and locking it. Ethan hummed as I followed him toward the main lobby, where I could hear high-pitched squeaking and chattering.

"Still the way I left them," Ethan said in amusement as we entered the lobby.

I stopped as I spotted a carrier and then a chunky baby sitting on Ira's lap. It was then I realized the 'squeaking' was, in fact, Ira speaking to the child in baby talk, and the chattering had been giggles interrupted by knee bounces.

"That...is not a creature," I told Ethan, looking askance.

"He's a creature, alright." He snorted, reaching out. "My sister and Adam's creature. Adam sometimes takes him when he's working, but since he was doing roofing today and the babysitter couldn't make it, Bri asked me to watch him."

"Oh, now he's a him when he was an it only a few seconds ago," I said as Ethan took the baby from Ira.

"Trevor, shush," Ethan scolded as he shifted the baby to his hip, frowning down at him. "He'll hear you."

"You best behave yourself, Trevor Price," Ira warned, shooting me a look before waving at the baby.

"How did I end up the bad guy here?" I wondered aloud, knowing damn well it was the grinning troublemaker standing before me with a baby on his hip.

To add to my problems, a familiar blond head popped around the opposite corner, his eyes lighting up when he spotted us. "I *thought* I heard a familiar happy baby. Hi, Colin! Uncle Ethan got you today?"

"He says, as if he doesn't know where Colin is at all times of the day and night," Ethan said with a smirk.

"Shh, he doesn't need to know about my vast knowledge

until he's older," Bennett told him, grinning when Colin gave a happy exclamation at the sight of him. "Let him enjoy seeing me, and we can worry about everything else later."

I pointed at Bennett as he edged closer. "Think carefully whether you're going to be able to pull yourself away before you pick that baby up, Livington. You've still got three hours left on your shift."

Ethan nodded his head toward me. "And Trevor's my ride, so he's intent on getting out of here as soon as possible."

It was said so casually, but I didn't miss the way both Bennett and Ira peered at the two of us curiously. There was no reason to suspect it, but I did anyway. That had been an intentional 'slip' of the tongue on Ethan's part to seed the rumors further. In fact, of anyone at the precinct, Ira and Bennett were the two you'd want to know a rumor if you wanted it spread. I couldn't count the number of times I had busted Bennett sitting on the front desk, munching away on one of Ira's snacks while the two traded juicy details about other people.

"I can't help it," Bennett said, letting Colin take hold of his finger and wiggling it. "Dare I say it, he's cuter than his daddy."

"That's like saying a puppy is cuter than a person," I frowned. "You can't compare the two."

"You're wrapped tight around this kid's finger, aren't you?" Ethan asked in amusement.

"Probably," Bennett said easily.

"Probably for the best since you have his dad wrapped around yours," Ethan snorted. "There's a weird sense of balance to that."

"Adam is not..." Bennett began, only to be interrupted by three sounds of disbelief from the other adults in the room. He blinked, peering at us like we'd just insulted his mother's pies before letting out a huff. "Whatever."

"C'mon," Ethan said to me, nodding toward the door. "Let's get this one home so he can have some mommy-son time before bed. I'm already late getting back, and Bri's gonna string me up by my boy parts."

"Boy parts?" I asked, bemused by his word choice.

"Look, if this child learns a foul or dirty word from me, I won't have to worry about being dumped in a grave in some far-flung part of the world," Ethan told me grimly. "My sister will save them the trouble and dump my body in the woods."

"He's not kidding," Bennett said seriously.

"Noted," I grunted. "Can we go?"

"Do you have his car seat?" Bennett asked in an unnaturally worried voice.

"Everything is jammed into that stroller," Ethan said, gesturing toward the device sitting in the corner where I hadn't seen it. There did seem to be a lot crammed into the compartments and storage of the stroller.

"Your sister certainly doesn't spare him anything," I noted.

To my surprise, color rushed into Ethan's cheeks. "I, uh, didn't know what to bring with me. So I kind of crammed in everything I could fit when I took him out with me."

Bennett snickered. "A bit overkill, don't you think, Ethan?"

"Look, I changed my first diaper a week ago, alright? I don't know this shit," Ethan muttered and then winced, glancing down at Colin, who seemed thankfully more interested in Ethan's necklace than the conversation.

"Get to work," I told Bennett when I saw his mouth open again. It was clear Ethan didn't know the first thing about taking care of kids and didn't seem very comfortable talking about it. If I let Bennett keep going, the situation was bound to get more awkward, and seeing Ethan so out of sorts was weird.

"C'mon, you little goblin," he told Colin, swinging him around and setting him in the carrier. He took great care buckling Colin into the seat, checking the straps before hefting the carrier off the counter. "We're going to dump you off at your mom's so I can stop getting bodily fluids all over me."

"Cute," Ira said, loud enough to earn a disapproving glance from Ethan.

I wasn't going to say it, but I agreed with her. He was obviously out of his element, and I'd guess he usually wasn't too big on kids. Yet here he was, watching one anyway and going out of his way to ensure Colin was taken care of. At a guess, I'd say it was more nerves than anything that had him so skittish dealing with the baby.

"So, what was the rest of that story?" I asked him as we left the lobby with Ira waving at our backs.

"Hmm? Oh!" he laughed. "Well, I got curious why there'd be blood on it. Whoever did the minutes hadn't signed them, not even the date, and I wondered who was supposed to since it was among a bunch of random stuff. Got the name after asking a teacher."

We stopped at my car, and he waited until I unlocked the doors before opening the back door and pulling out the car seat. Immediately, I could see him staring at the flat brick-shaped object as if it were a bomb waiting to go off. Chuckling, I held my hand out. "Here, you get his carrier out of there, and I'll get that."

"Sure," he said in obvious relief. "See, I had names of the people on the board at the time, but I didn't dig through everything to find out when they were there. The teacher knew, though, and gave me the year the minutes were written. Didn't take me long to get the name and look up old newspapers. Turns out he guy was cheating on his wife, and she shot him while he was at home doing paperwork. He lived, but somehow that little piece of evidence was left on the report he forgot to sign and still filed."

I took the carrier from him. "Your own bit of investigative reporting?"

"Yeah," he grinned as I bent down to attach the carrier to the car seat. "My teacher was *not* happy and would have failed me, except the principal stepped in. I was thirteen, and that was when I knew what I wanted to do with my life."

"Just like that?" I wondered, making sure the carrier was secure and chuckling when Colin reached out to grab my ear and give it a playful tug.

"Hey, sometimes life looks you dead in the eyes and says, 'This is just for you. Take it or leave it.' I mean, I explored the possibility of other things, but this was what I fell in love with," he said as he watched me carefully extract my ear from Colin's grip. "You wouldn't think tiny fingers could hold on like that, but the kid's got a death grip."

"They usually do," I said. "It must have been nice knowing what you were going to do from such a young age."

Ethan chuckled, waiting until I opened the trunk before unloading the stroller and stuffing it back there. "Well, I suppose I had to get at least one freebie. Everything else I ever tried never really made me wanna commit to it."

"Like what?"

"Eh, chess club. Soccer. Boy scouts. Hell, even the journalism club."

"Really?"

"Yeah, well, the G-rated events of last weekend's football match in the school paper weren't exactly compelling."

Thinking of what he had devoted himself to writing and his first step in that direction, I had to laugh as I carefully closed the door. "That I can see."

"Still, they weren't a total waste. I learned to think things through from the chess club. Discovered I really like being physically active in soccer, just not in a team environment. And Boy Scouts taught me there were plenty of handy survival skills, urban and wilderness, which I looked up in my spare time and have had to use more than once," he said with a grin.

"Like a hummingbird," I mused, opening the driver's side door. "Going from one thing to the next, picking up useful things as you go."

"And with all the attention span of one too," he snickered.

"So," I said, sliding in behind the wheel. "My little hummingbird. Is this a social call on your part or a professional one?"

"Both," he said, glancing toward the backseat and handing over a few toys I hadn't noticed in his hands. From the quality of the gurgling coming from Colin, I guessed they were personal favorites. "But I'll wait to give you the overview after we get this little one back into his mother's arms. Considering I can feel my phone buzzing every five minutes or so, she's ready for him."

I turned the engine on, eyeing him. "And...just what kind of social visit?"

He glanced back at me, smirking. "How social do you want me to be?"

"That tells me plenty," I chuckled. "At least I'm prepared."

"Oh?" he said, sounding interested. "Well, you officially have my attention."

"I thought I might," I said with a grin, pulling out of the parking spot.

* * *

ON THE DRIVE from his sister's house to mine, he dropped a familiar name. "Rodney Flan. I'm aware of him."

"Pretty much figured you would be," he snorted,

stretching out in the passenger seat. "He's, uh, an interesting person, that's for sure."

"You spoke with him?"

"Spoke with him? Hell, I met him, hung out, and smoked with him."

My fingers tightened around the wheel. "Did you now?"

Ethan looked askance at me, his smile knowing. "Yes. Cigarettes and pot. Don't worry, I wasn't going to put anything harder into my system while trying to pump the guy for information. If you're right about all this, which, by the way, you are, then I don't want to be addled."

"And being high on pot counts as not being addled?" I wondered.

"It does when you pretend to inhale but don't," he snorted. "Act a little different. Rub your eyes when they're not paying attention so they're red. Not that it's all that necessary. People don't pay that much attention, especially when they're high."

"Unless it backfires into paranoia like it can with stimulants," I countered.

"Please," he scoffed. "Have a little faith in my capabilities."

"I have perfectly reasonable amounts of faith," I assured him, even though I still felt uneasy about the entire thing. My precinct didn't have an undercover department, and I preferred it that way. I'd done my fair share of that sort of work in the Marines, and I knew how stressful it could be for everyone involved and how much planning and resources went into it. "But you're operating alone, with minimal resources and even less support. I have good reason to be cautious."

"Cautious is fine, cautious is great at times, but being paranoid isn't any good," he warned me.

"I feel like this conversation is going in circles," I said with a sigh, pulling into my driveway.

"Then let's stop being circular. I want to judge the interior decor while I give you the lowdown," he said, waiting until the car was parked before getting out.

"Of course," I said with a snort, wondering what he was expecting inside. "Then continue."

"Well," He followed me up the porch as I unlocked the door, "you were right, they're definitely operating out of the forest. Rod made a few comments about it, not enough for you to take action on, but enough for me to do some digging. Which wasn't all that interesting."

"And why wouldn't that interest you when that's what I sent you after in the first place?" I asked, opening the door and standing back, knowing full well he would eventually push through to start nosing around.

"Because we already knew they were operating there," he said, toeing out of his shoes before walking into the living room to peer around curiously.

"We didn't *know*," I said, removing my shoes as he disappeared into the dining room and out of sight.

"Basically did," he called back, and I heard cabinets opening. "And confirming what we already knew is only half the fun...less than half, actually."

"This isn't supposed to be fun!"

"If you don't enjoy what you do, then what's the point of doing what you do?"

"I do my job because it needs to be done, and I believe in what I'm doing."

"Yes, yes, duty and obligation, along with a sense of honor, I get it," he called back, his voice growing closer. "But you can't tell me you don't at least get a sense of satisfaction from it."

I thought about it momentarily, only to feel my thoughts stall before halting when Ethan reappeared in the doorway without his shirt. Technically, the shirt was thrown over his shoulder, leaving the rest of his torso on full display. Despite being of average height, his torso stretched for miles, ending in a toned chest sprinkled with a fine layer of hair far lighter than the dark blond on his head. There was just enough definition to see lines in his stomach and, distractingly enough, on his hips, which were also on full display due to his low-hanging jeans.

"I do," I finally managed to get out as he tossed his shirt onto the arm of the couch and disappeared down the hallway, where I heard him open the bathroom door. "But that's not the same thing as fun."

"Yeah, yeah," he intoned to the sound of a closing door. "Door on the left?"

"Office," I called after him, unbuttoning the top of my shirt and slowly following him as the door opened.

"What I think you'll find interesting," he continued as I turned the corner to see him disappearing into the office, "is that it's obvious they're getting help."

That was enough to pull me away from the surging hormones. "What? Help how?"

"Rod made a couple of interesting comments," he continued, and I heard something hit the floor softly, followed by faint jingling, "that made it obvious someone other than the manufacturers have their hand in what's going on."

"Outside help."

"Unofficial official help."

A chill ran through me as I approached the office. "Dirty cops?"

"Might be, or it might be someone further up the food chain, or just some rich person without a care in the world," he said, sounding intrigued at the very idea. "But until I can dig a little more, I can't tell you which one it is."

I finally entered the office, finding his jeans on the floor and Ethan clad in only his socks and a well-fitting jockstrap.

That in itself would have been enough to catch and hold my attention, but he was bent over the desk, peering at the collection of things I kept there. His bare ass faced the door, perfectly framed by the thin straps pushed against the underside.

"So, you *are* a religious man," he said, fingers resting gently on the statue on my desk.

"More like I'm not opposed to the idea completely," I said, advancing and undoing my shirt all the way to the bottom. "My ex-wife was the believer. It was pretty much the only thing of hers that she left behind for some reason. She loved that damn thing."

I watched as his fingers curled under the dog tags dangling over the cross, turning the name toward him. His thumb brushed over the bottom of the tag for a moment before he gently set it back down. I waited for him to comment, but several seconds passed without a word. It wasn't until he turned his head to look over his shoulder and smirk at me that I realized how long the silence had stretched.

"Something the matter?" he asked as if it wasn't blatantly obvious what was distracting me.

"I'm waiting," I said, making sure he was still watching me as I undid the button of my jeans, then slid the zipper down, "for you to finish your professional report so I can personally thank you."

I was harder than I remember being in recent memory when he slowly turned around, sitting atop the desk with his legs spread comfortably. The front pouch of his jockstrap was straining from what clearly his own display of excitement. However, he was doing a much better job keeping it from his face than I was as he put himself on such blatant display.

"I'm going to dig a little more information out of him in

the next few days if I can," he said slowly, hands resting on his thighs, fingertips digging ever so slightly into his skin as if from pleasure. "At least that way, I might be able to get some better starting places than just knowing there's someone else lurking in the shadows."

"And just how much danger does this involve for you?" I asked, stepping close enough that I could stand between his legs.

"Hopefully not a whole lot," he said with a chuckle, reaching out to take hold of my shirt and push it off my shoulders so it dropped down my arms to the floor. "I can't keep sticking with Rod. He might not be aware of much outside his own little world, but all it takes is one tweaker to mention seeing me spending so much time with you, and I'll find myself in trouble. So I'll get what I can and go from there."

"I'm putting a lot of trust in this," I told him, leaning forward to rest my hands on his thighs, finding the skin warm and soft but the muscles underneath as firm as I thought.

"I'm not going to put you or your officers in a bad light," he told me, a shadow creeping over his features.

"I don't want *you* getting hurt in the process," I told him softly, slipping my hands up his legs until my fingers could push under the fabric of his jockstrap. The length of his cock was practically burning with heat as my fingertips brushed along it. "I know you're capable, but that isn't going to stop me from being concerned."

The shadow on his face disappeared, replaced by a small smile. "Aww, are you worried for me?"

"Yes," I said simply because there was no point in trying to hide the fact. "I don't want to see you get caught up in something and hurt because I brought you in."

"I let myself in," he told me, his expression softening. "You're not responsible for everything that happens."

It reminded me of what Troy always told me when we were younger, and I 'fretted' about whatever we were doing. "Life is always going to happen no matter what you do" was one, and "You can't be afraid of what you can't plan for that you stop doing shit." Honestly, he'd been a fount of that sort of 'wisdom' for as long as I'd known him, and no matter what happened, he was utterly irrepressible. I'd even bet that if he were able to come back from death, he'd still have that same attitude despite what happened to him.

"I'll keep that in mind," I told Ethan as I gripped the band of his jockstrap to slowly slide it aside, leaving it on but allowing his dick freedom. "Just so long as you remember you have backup if you need it, and you don't have to do this alone."

"What? It's fair for you to ask something difficult of me because I did of you?"

"Tit for tat."

He chuckled, pushing my pants so they dropped to my ankles, his cock jutting out before him as mine strained against my underwear. "Fine, but in the meantime, I'd like a little dick and ass instead."

"A good thing I thought ahead," I said, wrapping my hand around the base of his cock as I leaned forward.

"Oh? Someone thought they were getting laid?" he asked, sounding pleased by the prospect.

"Call it intuition," I chuckled, pressing our lips together.

The moment our mouths met, I felt his dick throb eagerly in my hand, taking me a little by surprise. Either the man was a closet romantic, or he really enjoyed kissing. I wasn't going to argue either way and used my other hand to push my underwear down. His little peepshow and slow tease were enough to have me hard, aching, and more than ready for whatever he had in mind.

I closed the distance between our bodies, pulling him to the very edge of the desk and thrusting forward so I could grip the two of us. One hand wrapped around our shafts, I used the other to pull on the back of his head as I parted our lips. Ethan groaned far more emphatically and louder than he had on the backyard swing where we'd fooled around, and I felt my stomach twist in anticipation of the pleasure.

"Goddamn do you feel good," he breathed against my lips, his fingers playing through my hair.

"Funny, I was going to say the same thing," I said with a chuckle.

"Hmm, then I guess one of us should do something about that before I come all over the both of us."

"Can do," I grunted, letting go of him and our dicks to hook my hands under his thighs and pick him up. I wasn't surprised to find he was heavier than his narrow frame suggested. Most of his body was tight muscle, making him quite dense, but not so much that I couldn't pick him up.

"Oh shit," he said with a laugh, leaning forward so he could wrap his arms around my neck to steady himself before securing his legs at my waist. "Make sure you don't pull anything."

Oh, *now* the age jokes were going to start coming?

I wrapped an arm around his waist to help steady him before reaching with the other to grab his hair and pull it to tilt his head back. "Worry about me pulling other things."

"Ooh, do you use that voice when you're giving orders to your officers? I hope so. I wanna remember moments like this when you're being all bossy with your guys and girls," he chuckled.

I blamed the sheer level of hormones in my body for why it didn't take me more than a second to realize that, yes, that would be fun. It wasn't like Ethan was under my command in a professional setting, and if being my usual self in charge at work was a way to have more things like this happen, then so be it.

I had to use both arms to carry him from the room, though thankfully, the bedroom was only a few yards away. As much as I was willing to use my strength to throw Ethan around a bit, it *had* been a while since I'd carried something of his weight for longer than a few seconds. The last thing I needed was to prove his joking concern about pulling something true just because I was letting the inner caveman get the best of me.

Dropping him on the bed, I let him bounce once before shoving my hand against his waist to keep him in place. Before he could do more than get out the first syllable of a question, I took him into my mouth. He gasped as his hands found the back of my neck, gripping tight while I slid his cock along my tongue and into my throat.

It had been a while, but like riding a bike, I had him lodged in my throat, feeling my muscles grip his head as he thrashed in pleasure. If his reaction wasn't enough, I could feel it every time his cock twitched as I ran my hands up his thighs and over his hips. And just as he had while we'd shared our moment on the swing, he never stopped leaking as I slid him over my tongue to my lips and brought him to the back of my throat again.

"Fuck," he hissed when I pulled off him. "Someone was holding back last time."

"Caught off guard," I corrected, stepping away long enough to grab a condom and the bottle of lube from the nearby drawer. Tossing both beside him, I reached down and, with a good grip, managed to roll him over. When I yanked his hips, Ethan didn't hesitate to push himself upright, so he was on all fours. When he reached to pull his jockstrap off, I swatted his hand away. "No, keep it on. You wanted to make a display of yourself, you're going to keep doing it."

"Ohhhhh, I'm going to have *such* a hard time differentiating between bossy you at work and bossy you in the bedroom," he said with a chuckle, spreading his legs further to make an even bigger show of himself.

I thought about pointing out that him having a hard time with me was the whole point, then decided it would sound cheesy and snatched up the condom instead. Once open, I used a small amount of the lube to make it easier to slide over my dick, which stayed harder than the last time I'd tried to sleep with someone else. With that detail out of the way, I trailed a slick finger up the crack of his ass before sliding it into the grip of his warmth.

Ethan let out a small sigh, whether impatience or anticipation, I couldn't tell. Either one I could understand, but as much as I wanted to get to the main show, not only did I not want to rush things and end up making this bad for both of us, but returning the favor of a bit of teasing was appealing.

"Don't you dare," I warned when I saw him reach to grab himself. "Matter of fact, tuck that thing away."

"That thing," he scoffed and yet, did precisely as I said and concealed his straining length under the thin fabric once more. It was soft material, but the pressure of straining against the pouch probably wasn't all that comfortable.

If it bothered him, it didn't show as the fabric continued to strain, and he groaned when I added a second finger, this time curling them inside him to press against the nerves I knew were making his heart beat harder. I watched him carefully, using my other hand to slowly stroke myself through the condom as he stayed on all fours. When I'd first seen him in my lobby, I would never have imagined him in this position, naked and ready for whatever I had to give him.

I had to admit, it was worth the frustration and the wait.

"You keep fiddling with my ass and I might end up finishing before you get to sticking your dick in me," he said with a chuckle. It was the strained tone of his voice and the way he bowed his head, however, that told me, despite his amusement, he was being genuine.

"Been depriving yourself?" I asked, adding a third finger and spreading them apart for good measure, only to hear the low groan rumble up from his throat.

Ethan let out a small, shaky laugh. "Believe it or not, researching and hanging around druggies all day to pump them for information doesn't give you much time to deal with things on your own."

I slid my fingers out of him. "So that's why you were so eager to strip as soon as you got through the door."

"I'll admit, being incredibly pent up certainly didn't help," he said, then glanced over his shoulder. I could practically feel the way his eyes slid over my body with clear hunger. "But c'mon, the very idea of you being exactly the way you are right now? No way in hell was I passing up the chance."

I laid a hand on his lower back, letting my fingers curl around his hip to hold him in place. Not that I thought he'd try to get away, but feeling his stomach muscles shift under my fingertips as I held him in place added an extra thrill. Which built when I placed the head of my cock at the entrance to his ass, knowing that in a few seconds it was going to be where my fingers had been.

"We'll talk about your taste in men after we're done," I told him, pushing forward and hoping all this waiting and teasing was worth it...for both of us.

Holding myself at the base, I increased the pressure, surprised at how easily I slipped inside with little effort and not much prep. Yet from the sound he made and the sudden sensation wrapping around the first inch of my dick, that was more to do with Ethan's skills rather than anything else. Even with the grip, I could feel him relax around me, allowing me to push another inch into him, feeling the grip tighten again.

It became a pattern. I would stop, only for him to relax and allow me to slide in further. After a minute or so, I found the last inch disappearing into him with only a low groan to show how much he was enjoying himself. Even through the condom, I could feel his heat radiating around my girth, gripping me in an alternating rhythm almost as good as if I were moving.

Yet staying still wasn't something I was content to do, and I gripped his hip tighter to ease my hips back. I had no idea where he'd picked up the ability to relax his grip around me to let me ease out, only to tighten just enough as I slid back in to make my knees shake, but it was impressive. Either he'd had more practice than I thought, or the next generation was learning tricks mine had never dreamed of at that age.

Not that I would let that stop me, and I was careful to pay attention to what angle worked to make his arms shake and his hips push back into me. Once I had that figured out, I simply had to spread my legs enough to give myself the right height and begin thrusting in earnest. The strangled cry that left Ethan's lips told me he was a fan of both the force and the position.

Without thinking, I reached out and took hold of the strap of the jock, yanking it back toward me as I thrust forward. It gave me enough leverage to pull his body tight against my hips, and if the sudden added tension of the jock's pouch on his cock was uncomfortable, the groan he gave certainly didn't tell me that. If anything, his head bowed forward as though he were losing the fight to stay upright while I buried myself inside him with a snap of my hips and a yank on the band.

Despite how long it had been since the last time I'd been with someone, I found it easy to get back into the flow of things. Sweat broke out on both of us, his back shining with a thin layer as the light from the hallway illuminated the room. I could feel my legs starting to burn slightly and a tightness in my chest, but I kept driving myself into him with an abandon I hadn't felt in years.

With my hand on his jockstrap giving me the leverage and grip I needed, I reached under him, freeing his straining cock from the prison. I didn't need to tell Ethan what that meant, as he wasted no time shoving his hand under him to wrap around his shaft. Apparently, he needed both arms to keep himself upright, and he unceremoniously toppled forward, faceplanting the bed with a groan as he began furiously stroking himself.

The result was that the grip around me became erratic and fierce, and I knew he was quickly approaching the end. I surged forward, taking advantage of his even more vulnerable position to hammer away at him, the sharp slap of our skin becoming as loud as our groans. Using one hand to hold his upper body against the bed, I thrust hard into him, putting the last of my strength into one last shove before my body finally gave in to the inevitable.

Bowing forward, I grunted as I heard him cry out, his muscles tightening around me. Even as I filled the condom while my dick pulsed inside him, his muscles bore down around me with a strength unlike anything before. His body pushed against mine as it shook, drawing out even more pleasure as my orgasm rocked through me, fed by knowing I was responsible for the noises coming from him.

After I carefully slid out of him, Ethan slumped onto his side with a low groan. His hair was sticking to his forehead, but a smile was plastered over his face as his chest heaved. "Well, alright. We can talk about my taste in men because, apparently, it's gotten a *lot* better since I came to Fairlake, holy shit."

I looked over the bed. "Where, uh, is the mess?"

He gave a shaky laugh. "I, uh, had the sense to shove my dick into the underwear before it happened. So don't worry, didn't mess your bedspread."

I snorted, walking over to the doorway to grab the towel off the back of the door and sit on the bed beside him. "Might as well strip so we can get you cleaned up."

"How gentlemanly," he said with a smirk but promptly flopped onto his back in order to struggle to kick his underwear off. "A guy could get used to this sort of treatment."

I shook my head when I saw how much mess he'd made of himself. "Okay, you really did put off taking care of yourself."

"Or maybe I'm just messy."

"Considering the way you leak—"

He snorted, eyes watching my hands as I wiped him down carefully. "I always get comments on that."

I glanced up. "Just how many partners have you had?"

His smirk reappeared. "Less than you'd think, more than most people would like."

"That's vague."

"It's also an answer."

Now I was sure he used his playful and irreverent attitude as a defense mechanism.

"Not that it matters to me," I added lightly, tossing the towel aside. "I'm just impressed with your skill."

"You know, you're supposed to flatter someone before you try to get them in bed," he told me wryly, sitting up to inspect himself.

"At least this way, you know I'm telling the truth."

"I would never have accused you of blowing smoke up my ass," he said with a chuckle, looking around. "Where are my pants?"

"In my office," I told him, realizing why he might be looking for them. "But there's no need for you to have them. You can sleep naked."

His brow raised. "Can I now?"

"Yes, in here, with me," I added unnecessarily.

"And here I thought you were insistent that we sleep separately."

"When we fooled around like a couple of high school kids having drinks for the first time, sure. But I just worked my butt off to get us both off. We deserve some comfort while we sleep," I said, surprised to feel a flutter in my gut. "Plus, why not enjoy the benefits of this little charade you've cooked up?"

"I wasn't aware literally sleeping with someone was a benefit," he said, a slight smirk on his face. I took it as a good sign since he wasn't trying as hard to seem dismissive.

"In case you haven't noticed, the bed is very comfortable," I pointed out, gesturing toward it.

Snorting, he allowed himself to fall onto his back and wiggled. "Yeah, now I'm not being distracted by being pounded into it, it is pretty comfortable."

"I'm so glad you approve," I said dryly, gesturing toward him. "Now get to a side of the bed so I can lay down too."

"And here I thought you were going to let me take up as much space as possible," he said airily, moving over to one side like a normal human being.

"Keep dreaming," I said, dropping onto the bed and adjusting the alarm clock next to it.

"Retro," he commented as I adjusted the dials on the old clock.

"Had this since I was a kid, and it still works perfectly," I told him. "And if you think it won't wake the dead, wait till it goes off."

"Boy, I look forward to that," he said, then glanced toward the hallway. "Please tell me you don't sleep with the light on."

"Don't need a night light?" I asked with a chuckle.

"I might have seen some fucked up shit, but that doesn't mean I can't sleep in the dark," he grunted at me, rummaging around to slide under the blankets and make himself comfortable.

"Noted," I said, picking up the remote beside the alarm clock and hitting the button to turn off the lights in the house.

"Huh, not so retro," his voice floated up from the sudden pitch blackness.

"I'm allowed to have new and old," I told him, also sliding under the blanket.

"There's a joke to be made there."

"And if it involves comparing us to the old and new, you'll end up sleeping on the floor."

His chuckle rose from the darkness, and the bed shifted as he moved. To my surprise, I felt his chest press against my back before his arm slid over my middle, curling to hold me close. "Fine, fine. I'll play nice tonight. It's the least I can do after the fantastic and much-needed sex."

"I'm so glad I've managed to find a way to make you play nice for a while."

"Feed me and fuck me. I'm a simple man."

I snorted, grabbing his forearm gently and holding it. "I'll keep that in mind."

"By the way, I didn't ask before, but, uh, do you bottom?"

I arched a brow. "I...yes, I do. Why?"

"Because I have a good idea what I want to do in the morning, is all," he chuckled, pressing his forehead against my back and sighing deeply. "Don't worry about it."

I couldn't help my smile as I felt him settle against my back, relaxing in a matter of seconds. Ethan's breathing deepened a little while afterward, and I was impressed. Being able to fall asleep at the drop of a hat was something I retained from my time in the military. Apparently, Ethan had managed to pick it up himself, and I wondered what other things about him I didn't know.

It was probably better I didn't wonder about him at all. There would, of course, come a time when he would leave Fairlake, going back out into the world to do what he did best. Laying there with him sleeping so comfortably against my back, his arm warm against my side, I understood why I hadn't wanted to sleep with him after our first bit of fooling around.

Despite how frustrating and confusing he could be, there was no denying I was attracted to him. It went well beyond physical, and I could already feel a vague sense of loss at the inevitable parting of ways. Maybe even last week, I'd known on some level and had tried to put some distance between us to prevent what would end up being an inevitable attraction toward him. There was no way to put it off if I was going to be spending so much time with him while he used our 'relationship' as a shield, however flimsy it might end up being.

Ultimately, the best I could do was enjoy what time I had and hope I didn't end up with a broken heart again.

ETHAN

"You know," I began as I watched Bennett sneaking up on Adam for what was probably the fifth time. He wasn't particularly good at it, and it was clear from the way Adam was standing that he knew Bennett was there. "I'm beginning to suspect there's something seriously wrong with them."

On the blanket spread out on the grass, Bri snorted. "You're only just now figuring that out?"

"It's been a slow understanding," I said, watching Adam twist at the last second and pull a yelping Bennett into a headlock. "Bet the sex is great, though."

"A facet of their relationship I do my best to pretend doesn't exist," she said, wrinkling her nose hard enough to raise her sunglasses. "And shouldn't you be worried about your own sex life? You and the sexy police chief have been 'dating' for a couple of weeks now, according to...just about everyone."

I snorted. "I'm allowed to wonder, just not wander."

In the past couple of weeks since spending that first night at Trevor's, it seemed like the entire town was abuzz with the news. Of course, everyone was doing their best to pretend they weren't talking about it. Based on that, I quickly realized you couldn't trust the vast majority of the population of Fairlake to keep a secret because they were absolute ass at doing so.

"Fine, wonder about someone else's sex life," she said, lounging back in the sunlight. "One that doesn't make me want to pour bleach into my brain."

I chuckled. "You gonna watch your gremlin or just wait until he finds a way to kill himself?"

"I am perfectly aware of him," she said casually. "And I'm also aware Bennett and Adam are keeping an eye on him, and you're watching him like a hawk, even if you're pretending otherwise."

I chose not to respond, knowing she was right but not wanting to give her the satisfaction of knowing I had no retort. The little goober was growing on me, and it *was* kind of fun to watch him tootle around in the grass as fast as his little legs could carry him, which was impressively fast at times. Bri was the last to be able to react, considering she was spread out on the blanket while I remained in a chair beside her.

Not that I blamed her for taking it easy. She was in full-blown Mom mode at all times of the day and night. However, with at least three other adults who could be responsible for Colin, she was willing to relax. Not that it stopped her from glancing at him frequently, but at least she wasn't jumping up at every little movement.

She seemed to be of the mindset that since we were in the center of town in the decently sized park near the town's municipal buildings, Colin was generally safe. While it was true others were nearby that they knew and trusted, such as Chase and his quiet, dark-haired boyfriend who'd shown up in town and had barely left his side, as well as the animated

Isaiah and the far more taciturn Julian who also hovered around his boyfriend.

Those were the people I could identify as a good chunk of the town milled about the park and the surrounding streets, car traffic cut off for the Fourth of July celebration they held every year. The celebration was what I expected. People standing around with cans of alcoholic and non-alcoholic drinks, picnics, and grills all cooking meat.

"So, how's work going?" she asked casually, and I rolled my eyes.

"It's going *fine,* thank you," I said, hoping my tone was warning enough. True, I couldn't exactly hang around the dealers and users now I was known as the police chief's boy toy, but that didn't stop me doing more digging. People would be amazed how much even tweakers were willing to keep their mouths shut if you offered them money on the sly to find things out for you.

Sure, giving information to someone who could be talking to the cops was a good way to find yourself without a source, but having money for drugs in the immediate future was far more appealing. There was, of course, the discomfort of knowing I was feeding their addiction, but whether or not I was helping them get more than usual wouldn't stop them using. At the very least, I hoped my work would eventually cut the supply chain and make it easier for them to get clean.

Well, that was the hope anyway, and faint hopes like that were what allowed me to do my work in the first place. I alone couldn't help the people I wrote about, but I could hope if I had to let the things around me happen, it would draw the attention of the rest of the world. It was an ugly reality of my life, and sometimes I wasn't sure how effective it was.

"Speaking of," she drew out, pulling her shades down enough to peer over the rims.

I followed her eyes and felt my heart beat harder as I spotted Trevor in the crowd headed our way. There was someone else with him, but it was easy to ignore the stranger, even if he did look pretty good in his cop uniform. Trevor, however, looked even better, filling it out perfectly enough to make me wonder if we could use the handcuffs jingling from his belt loop.

Again.

"Well, howdy stranger," I called to him when he was near enough to hear me, glad I didn't sound nearly as jittery as my heart felt.

"And here I thought I'd avoid finding trouble today. Hello, Ethan," he said, sounding as growly and grumbling as usual. The thing was, I'd become pretty good at reading beyond the stony, sometimes grumpy mask he kept on his face. There was a slight uplift in the way he spoke, and I could tell he was pleased to see me.

"Trouble is over there," I said, nodding toward Bennett, who was currently chasing Colin around an amused Adam.

"I can't tell if you mean your nephew or Bennett," Trevor said with a glance over his shoulder. "Which says a lot."

"It also says a lot that you only refer to him by his first name when he's not around," I pointed out, making Bri snort in amusement. "Who's this? Don't recall seeing him around the precinct before."

"Ian Reiner," the officer announced, flashing an admittedly charming smile in my direction. He was strikingly handsome, but nothing was more striking than his eyes. One half of one of his dark brown eyes was a brilliant blue. "Transferred over from one of the Denver precincts."

I gave a low whistle. "How the hell do you go from that to some Podunk town like this?"

Bri sighed heavily as Trevor shook his head. "Ethan, how many times do I have to—"

"Shush. Just sit there and be pretty," I told her with a wave of my hand.

I wasn't surprised when she shoved her sunglasses down to glare at me. "Excuse me?"

"Pretty sure that's Rob I see coming," I said, glancing toward the nearby crowd who were chatting as they grilled. It wasn't a lie. I could see his shaved head maneuvering through the crowd, taller than most of them except the likes of Julian and Adam.

"What?" she asked sharply, sitting up and adjusting her clothes while looking around wildly for him.

"And with her sufficiently distracted," I said wryly, glancing at the two men, "you can answer my polite and not at all offensive question."

Trevor rolled his eyes again, but I ignored him as Ian looked around before answering. "It was about time I left Denver, and I needed to be here to take care of my mother, who moved here a few years back."

I raised my brow. Well, that sounds like you're leaving out a few details."

"Which," Trevor interrupted as I saw a flash of discomfort on Ian's face, "is none of your business."

"You never let me have any fun," I told Trevor lightly, even as I noticed the look of relief ease onto Ian's face.

"I let you have plenty of fun," he said gruffly, and I had to smile at the implications.

"Do I get to have fun now?" I asked, arching a brow.

"Behave," he rumbled, and I continued to grin, knowing he was getting frustrated with me. The problem, at least for Trevor, was he found himself strangely aroused when I was driving him up a wall. I had met a few people like him before and enjoyed myself, mostly due to my personality. They were the easiest people on the planet for me to seduce.

With Trevor, though, it was something else entirely, and I

couldn't quite put words to it, Which was ironic considering my job. Yet for someone so clearly defined by others and himself, reliable and steady, he still managed to stump me at times.

It wasn't that he was a mystery to me, he was pretty predictable, which I found strangely satisfying. With others, while I respected their dedication to codes of behavior, I found them stifling and too rigid for my taste. Yet, for some reason, with Trevor, I found it endearing. If I didn't know better, I'd suspect I was getting boring and predictable as I got older.

Well, that was until I looked at him while he glared at me, trying to figure out a way to make me pay for being a little shit when we had more privacy. He wasn't particularly creative when it came to 'punishment,' but that never stopped it from being fun. Being manhandled, pinned, and treated roughly while he bossed me around wasn't exactly innovative, but he wouldn't hear me complain.

To my growing amusement, he jabbed a finger at me. "You, stop it."

"Stop what?" I asked innocently, taking a sip of beer.

"You know full well what," he growled, and I had to suppress the urge to shiver at the unspoken threat.

"Nope, not one clue," I continued, knowing I was making things worse.

Trevor's eyes narrowed, but before he could come back with a retort, we were interrupted by the joyful shout of, "E! E! E!"

I glanced at my nephew in Julian's arms as he and Isaiah walked over, the latter chuckling. "He tried to make a break for the street where they're setting off bottle rockets. Figured we should stop him."

"Good idea," I said, feeling my stomach twist uncomfortably at the realization that I'd been so distracted I hadn't noticed him. "And I see he's doing his best bat impersonation."

"No," Julian said as he held the squirming child with all the ease of someone who was part giant containing a small child.

"No?" I asked.

"Oh, there he is," Adam's voice rose from behind them. Although he sounded calm, his brow was furrowed. "I was wondering where he'd wandered off to."

"The street, or attempted to," I informed him.

Adam's frown deepened, and I'd swear I could see paternal panic in his eyes before he quashed it. "I guess it's good no cars are being let through today."

"He's fine," Isaiah said with a snort. "Pretty adventurous, though. If he didn't look a lot like you, I'd wonder if he was yours."

Adam smiled. "He gets that from his mother. It apparently runs in the family."

"I think he's talking about me," I whispered loudly to the rest of them.

"Who would have guessed?" Trevor said, flashing a smile at me.

"Where's your shadow?" Isaiah asked Adam, glancing around.

"No longer trying to sneak up on me now he's been distracted," Adam said with a smirk, checking over his shoulder. "Oh, here he comes."

Bennett appeared behind him with another guy in tow, and I wondered how integrated into this town I'd become since I vaguely recognized him. Much like the new cop in town, this one was pretty cute though I was smart enough not to say that aloud. He was also wearing a uniform, so I didn't have to guess that I'd seen him working as an EMT.

"No," the man said with a chuckle. "I don't care if I'm trained for that sort of thing."

"You're no fun," Bennett complained.

"Well, maybe if I'm not around, you'll think twice."

Adam shook his head. "You clearly don't know Bennett if you think consequences will deter him from making bad decisions."

"Aww, it's so sweet when you worry about me," Bennett said, batting his eyes at Adam.

"That's not what he said," Trevor pointed out.

"Yeah, but just like you, Chief, sometimes you have to read between the lines to find the message."

"Keep going, and you'll end up reading a lot of lines. In the archives again."

Bennett grinned and turned toward me. "Heya, Ethan, don't know if you've met, but this is —"

"Kyle," Ian spat out, the first words he'd spoken in a while, his voice laced with surprise.

Kyle straightened, finding the man on the other side of the group, his face going slack before hardening into an unreadable mask. "Ian? What are you doing here?"

Their tone of voice was enough to get everyone's attention, though I didn't think Ian was aware of it as he shifted uncomfortably. "I, uh, transferred here a couple of weeks ago. Chief price decided today was a good opportunity for me to get to know people."

"Right, that makes sense," Kyle said, his voice stiff enough I thought if someone gave it a good shove, it would shatter. Personally, I didn't think it made any sense to him, but I wasn't about to interrupt what was clearly an awkward reunion.

"Thought you left Fairlake for good," Ian said slowly.

"Yeah, I did for a bit. Came back when I—" Kyle stopped,

his eyes flashing. "Well, I came back. Kinda weird seeing you in Fairlake, of all places."

"Things are different and a little weird," Ian said quietly, and I couldn't tell if it was guilt or pain in his voice. This conversation was clearly one neither man wanted.

"Right," Kyle said stiffly, turning to give an equally hard smile to Bennett. "I'm going to check the first-aid tent, see if any teenagers have taken their fingers off with fireworks they're not supposed to have."

"Sure," Bennet said brightly, and I had to admire his ability to pretend he hadn't just witnessed something more awkward than watching my sister play it cool around Rob, oblivious to what was happening a few yards away. Then again, from the looks of her, she was too busy trying not to laugh too loudly at what the guy was saying to her, so I couldn't blame her. "And maybe it could give you time to re-think your decision."

"Yeah, helping teenagers who injure themselves doing something stupid is really going to convince me to help you when you're going something stupid," Kyle said with a shake of his head as he walked off.

"E!" Colin bellowed with renewed vigor, still locked in Julian's arms, though now he was squirming more than before.

"Well said," I chuckled, realizing Ian had disappeared without so much as a word, though I noticed he'd walked in the opposite direction to Kyle. "So does anyone—"

"Not a clue," Bennett interrupted, his smile gone, frowning in Kyle's direction. "I've never seen Kyle look so serious before. He's normally pretty laid back and happy."

"Even laid back, happy people can get upset. Sometimes enough to punch their best friend," Adam said, shooting a knowing smile at Bennett.

"Wow, whoever you're talking about has serious problems," Bennett said, smirking.

"Not anymore," Adam said, quirking his brow.

"Gross," Isaiah said with a roll of his eyes. "They're doing the thing again, Julian."

"I see," the big man grunted, though he was clearly less disturbed by it than his boyfriend.

"E! E!" Colin added, unhappy that his indecipherable demand was not being met.

"Release the tiny beast so he can get what he wants," Isaiah told Julian with a laugh. "Or he's just going to keep screaming. Demanding little thing."

"He's certainly not shy about asking for what he wants," Adam said proudly.

"Yeah," I said with a snort as Julian let Colin down, making sure the boy had his balance before finally releasing him. "That's something we can also blame on Bri."

"I wasn't going to say it," Adam chuckled. "I was going to think it, but I wasn't going to say it."

"Smart man," I said with a smirk as Colin looked around and immediately scooted over to me at a somewhat unbalanced pace. "Dude, what are you doing?"

Colin would have slammed face-first into my kneecap if I hadn't reached out to catch him. Colin gave me a mostly toothless grin as he peered up at me. "E! E!"

"Holy shit," Adam said quietly. "Is he—?"

I blinked down at Colin. "What?"

"He's trying to say your name," Bennett said with a laugh.

"He can't talk," I said, eyes going wide.

"E!" Colin practically shouted at me, and I had to laugh at the sheer frustration in his voice.

"Certainly sounds like the way his mother says my name," I snickered, setting my beer aside to bend down and pick Colin up, gazing into his face. "Seriously, dude?"

"E!" he proclaimed, slapping my forearms in excitement.

"Christ, I think he is trying to say my name," I said softly, feeling a squeeze in my chest as I stared at his chubby, happy face. "Why?"

"Because, like his mother, he has bad taste in men," I heard Bri's wry voice explain from behind me.

"I can't be offended because of how things turned out," Adam said with a chuckle. "But do you really think Rob wants to hear that?"

Her eyes widened as she turned to face the amused man, earning a round of laughter from all of us. In the midst of the teasing, Bri found herself the target of, I looked up to see Trevor watching me. His eyes twinkled as he watched me trying to keep the wriggling, excited Colin on my lap. Between the strange look on his face and Colin's even stranger excitement, I found myself feeling confused and more than a little awkward.

"What?" I asked him, confident the others were distracted enough not to pay me any attention.

"Maybe I'll tell you later," he said softly, reaching out to squeeze my shoulder.

For a moment I was tempted to protest, but then Colin slapped my arm again, and Trevor's hand never left my shoulder. So rather than say anything, I let the sudden warmth in my chest settle into place, and I began to understand why people enjoyed this quiet life in this quiet town.

* * *

IRA LOOKED up as I walked through the precinct doors, whistling softly. "Well, I wondered when I'd see that handsome face again."

"Ira, you just saw me," I told her with a laugh.

"Sweetheart, I saw you at the Fourth of July gathering,

that was almost two weeks ago," she chuckled, closing her book, one finger shoved between the pages to mark her spot. "Are you that bad at keeping track of time?"

"I can be," I admitted, though that was less to do with airheadedness and more to do with being so busy. I'd been forced to expand my investigation to Fovel and had spent most of my working time there. At least people didn't know me there like they were beginning to in Fairlake.

The well of information from my Fairlake informants had begun to dry up. Most people were growing close-lipped about what was going on, partially because they'd cottoned on that I could present a problem to their supplies, but I noted an aspect of fear as well. From what I'd been able to tell, the manufacturing was picking up. It made sense. We were coming into Summer when the weather was reliable.

I was doing my best to keep a low profile, but I was afraid I wouldn't have long before I had to do something more daring to get what I needed. Fovel was larger than Fairlake by small-town standards, but it was still pretty insular, especially with the criminal and addict population. The information was drying up, and I knew I'd have to get my boots on the ground to find out more.

Wasn't that going to thrill both my sister and Trevor?

"Look, a man gets preoccupied here and there," I told Ira, avoiding her question altogether.

"Yes, I'm sure," she said, peering at me over her glasses. "Here to bother Trevor?"

"Why would I be here other than to say hi to one of my favorite ladies?"

"Honey, I've been working here for decades. Do you think flattery is going to help you?"

I held up a paper bag. "And how about one of those muffins you love so much from Grant's?"

"I do accept bribes," she said with a smile. "Don't be surprised if he's...well, grouchy."

"Bennett?" I guessed, setting the bag on her desk.

"Politics," she said with a snort.

"Oh, God," I groaned, knowing that dealing with job politics always put Trevor in a foul mood. "Who this time?"

"Bartholomew Durkins," she said, opening the bag and smiling. "Police Chief—"

"Of Fovel," I finished with a smirk. I'd made it a point to know all the local players. By all accounts, he was a competent chief or, at least, not a complete disaster. It was interesting that I'd never been able to get an opinion about him as a person, though, which was either a good sign or a terrible one.

"Someone keeps up on current events."

"Someone likes to know what people piss Trevor off the most."

"I would joke and say you make a pretty good candidate for the top of the list."

"But you wouldn't want to hurt my feelings?"

She rolled her eyes. "But even the densest person can tell it's practically foreplay between you."

"See, moments like this? They're what make me wish Trevor was around to hear them," I chuckled. "Just so I could see the look on his face."

"Sour, like someone just shoved a lemon wedge in his mouth," she said with a smile. "Which I don't see quite as often anymore. I wonder who might be responsible for that?"

If she had been talking about anyone other than Trevor, I'd have thought they were quite a good actor for our deception. It was Trevor, however, and despite his previous work in Intel, the man wasn't deceptive or a natural-born actor. It also wasn't the first time someone had commented on the change in Trevor's behavior lately. Bennett being the most vocal.

I knew it was a sign this was probably more than just a convenient cover for my constant presence around Trevor, and I wasn't sure how to feel about it. On the one hand, it was nice to have someone like me. Sure, I could say it was the sex, but I didn't think someone became calmer simply because they were getting laid. Sure, it helped to ease the tension, but that wasn't enough.

On the other hand, it left me feeling confused and a little worried. The whole point of the deception was to give me some cover while I tried not to draw extra attention to myself, with the added bonus of us having someone to enjoy ourselves with. I wasn't exactly the kind of person someone tried to settle down with. My history proved that repeatedly. As much as I found comfort being around him, living quietly in Fairlake, I knew it couldn't last, and I didn't want to hurt Trevor because of it.

"Maybe you can improve his mood," Ira said, gesturing over her shoulder. "He's in his office. The door's closed, but go ahead and let yourself in. If he gives you trouble, tell him I gave you permission."

"I do like passing the buck," I told her with a wink. The main room was quiet as the few still left on the evening shift went about whatever they were doing. I wasn't surprised to find Ira was right. The door was still closed, and I let myself in.

Trevor's head jerked up from frowning down at his desk only to frown at me as I grinned, adjusting my shoulder bag before closing the door quietly behind me. I could see the irritation etched into his features as he listened to whoever was on the phone, and the tension in his shoulders could have held up a bridge.

"I understand that, Bart," Trevor said calmly between

clenched teeth as he waved dismissively at me. "But by all accounts, it *is* going to be both of our problems soon. You think it won't become yours if you just sit around and let me deal with it?"

"Ah," I said softly, careful not to make too much noise as I set my bag on his desk. That, of course, earned me another dirty look, which I ignored, flipping the bag open as I circled the desk.

Despite his clear annoyance and attempt to make me go somewhere else, Trevor's eyes tracked me as I grew closer. I could hear the other man on the line, though I couldn't understand the words. From what I could make out, he sounded smug, and that, more than anything, was probably the source of Trevor's bad mood.

Which was obvious from not only his face but his disheveled appearance. The top buttons of his shirt were undone, exposing his undershirt and some of his chest hair. His short hair was a mess like he'd been running his hands through it in frustration. I probably shouldn't have found it attractive, but even if it was because he was annoyed, it gave him a freshly fucked look.

Which gave me an idea as to how to help him feel better.

Trevor grunted when I took the back of his chair and twisted it slowly, making him face me. His brow furrowed as I stood looking him over while the voice on the line continued talking. Trevor shot me a look that was still annoyed but wondering what I was doing, his brow dipped even lower when I slowly slid to my knees.

His eyes widened as I inched closer, and he covered the mouthpiece to hiss at me, "Don't you dare!"

When he didn't do more, I reached forward, smirking when he gave another warning growl. He seemed to have forgotten I knew him well enough that unless he smacked my hands away, he wasn't interested in stopping me. I could see his eyes track my hands as they undid the buttons of his pants and slowly unzipped them. I reached into his underwear without hesitation, pulling out his half-hard cock.

Trevor gave another grunt. "Bart, there's a time and place for this political backbiting. Don't pretend you don't know what I'm talking about. They're in the woods between our towns for God's sake!"

I leaned forward, taking his cock between my lips and running my tongue back and forth on the underside. Trevor's body jerked at the sudden sensation, and he shot me a sharp look as he strained to listen to the conversation. Since he still hadn't tried to stop me and had grown hard in record time, I assumed I was doing exactly what I needed to.

"It's...it's a matter of public...safety," Trevor spat into the phone as I felt his legs tremble. That might have been because I was steadily working him into my throat, taking him as deep as possible to feel each throb of his shaft. Deep throating had never been my specialty, but having his dick in my throat was enough to drive Trevor crazy. "And this...circling around the bush is just giving more time for...no! This has nothing to do with...Christ, Bart, you think too much about your position and not what you're—"

That last interruption had been my fault as I began to bob in earnest, trying to take him as deep as possible every time. He was as big a fan of vigorous sex as I was, and that was true even for blowjobs. His free hand gripped the arm of the chair hard enough that his knuckles were growing white. I knew I was only making it worse when I let out a soft moan of appreciation as the taste of him finally leaked onto my tongue.

If the look on his face was any indication, I was about to be in trouble very soon.

That didn't stop me, however, and I bobbed my head, not worried if the messy noise of my mouth was heard over the phone. For his part, Trevor was pressing himself against the back of his chair, trying to focus on whatever the other chief was saying, but I didn't think he was succeeding. His breathing came in short bursts, and I wondered if that was from the exertion of keeping himself in control or because he was close.

"Fine," Trevor finally snapped. "I'll deal with this in my own way. Just bear this conversation in mind when you need help cleaning up a mess you made...again."

He slammed the phone down hard enough that it was a miracle the plastic didn't crack. Trevor pulled me off him, only to yank me up and kiss me fiercely. His fingers dug into my skull as he held me tight, groaning into the kiss as I felt his dick throb in my hand.

Before I could do more than chuckle, I was spun around and slammed onto the desk. Just enough of my waist hung over the edge for him to loop his hand around and undo my pants, roughly yanking my jeans and underwear off.

He leaned over and rooted through the bag, making me chuckle. "I guess someone knows what I was up to."

"Wasn't hard to guess when you stuck my dick in your mouth," he said, giving my ass a hard enough slap that I knew damn well there would be a red mark.

"Hey!" I protested, trying to squirm only to be held in place. "You looked like you needed a little loosening up."

"Hope you're loosened up," he growled as I heard the condom wrapper open.

The 'threat' was enough to send a shiver down my spine as I heard lube being applied hastily before I felt the cool touch of his covered dick press against me. I hadn't thought this through thoroughly, otherwise, I might have prepped in anticipation of the consequences of my actions. Not that I didn't think I could take it, but I knew I'd end up quite tender if I let it happen.

Any argument I might have had was halted immediately when I felt him press forward. Without prep, there was noticeable resistance between my body and his dick before I finally took a deep breath and willed my body to relax. Which worked right up until the thick head breached me, and my arms shot out to grab the edge of the desk in a mad scramble for something to hold onto. My forehead thumped the desktop as the burning radiated up my ass, and Trevor inched his way in.

It wasn't the most pleasant of entries I'd ever had, but at no point did I try to stop him. It burned like hell, but some part of me savored this sudden surge of power and control on his part. The same part that loved him manhandling or pinning me, the part who enjoyed it when he started barking orders. Even though it stung like a bitch, I savored the feeling of him filling me.

I could only be thankful that he took a moment to let me adjust after he'd sheathed himself fully inside me. Despite having been fucked by him several times, this was still the fullest I'd ever felt. I could only lay there, panting against the desk before groaning when I felt him pull almost completely out. There was still plenty of resistance when he pushed back inside my ass, but the burn was accompanied by the tingle of pleasure.

It was then I remembered we were in the police precinct, and the only thing preventing us from being discovered was a closed door that could be opened at any time. Hell, if we made enough noise, the door wouldn't be enough to block the sound. Just yards away, his officers were working, no idea their boss was currently balls deep inside me. The thought almost made me come right then and there.

Trevor wasn't done, however, and began thrusting into me in earnest. At the first slap of skin meeting skin, I felt him rummage about though I couldn't see what he was doing since I was pinned to the desk. I laughed softly when I felt what seemed to be a shirt draped over my ass, apparently meant to cushion any noise. My laugh choked when he thrust again, and this time there was no sound from our bodies meeting.

It lasted only a few seconds, but Trevor managed to fuck me so hard the desk started inching across the floor. It was the first time I'd ever felt an ache forming *while* we were having sex, but it mingled so well with the constant barrage of pleasure that I didn't mind in the slightest. If anything, I had to fight to stay quiet while he softly grunted behind me. I couldn't reach around to grab hold of myself, and my cock ached from the need to be released until I felt him unceremoniously pull out.

"What…" I began, only to be spun around onto my back. Something, a pen probably, dug into my back as he yanked the condom off, stroking himself furiously. I watched, enraptured, as his head tilted back and the first blast of cum landed on my shirt, the next across my cock. I didn't waste the opportunity, immediately grabbing myself and using what he'd given me as lube. It only took a few strokes, feeling the dull ache of his absence in my ass, before my orgasm leaped to the front.

I yelped when, just at the moment of release, he knocked my hand away and took me into his mouth and down his throat. Struggling to keep quiet, I grabbed the back of his head and thrust up as I came hard. My vision went murky as the pleasure rocketed through me, taking every thought as I poured into his throat. I barely remembered letting go of his head before flopping back onto the desk, chest heaving as I tried to figure out just what had happened.

"Fucking…fuck," I managed, clearly at my most eloquent.

"That's one way of putting it," Trevor said, falling back into his seat. His cock was still out, sitting half-hard against the bottom of the chair as he watched me intently. "Just what the hell was that about?"

"Wanting to give you head to lift your mood," I said with a chuckle, finally finding the strength to sit upright and tug at my underwear and pants. It was a struggle, but I managed it without removing myself from the desk. "And I'd say I managed one of those."

Trevor smirked, tucking himself back into his pants before pushing his chair closer so he sat between my legs. His dark eyes peered up at me, and I had the distinct feeling he was looking for something. "Or you were trying to get fucked."

I shifted uncomfortably on the desk. "Well, I definitely got that. Christ, just how annoyed were you?"

"Pretty annoyed," he said, reaching out to rest his hands on my thighs and squeeze. "Then you came along and allowed me to work it out of my system. I might have been a little too aggressive."

I blinked, alarmed to realize he took my complaints a little too seriously. "What? God, don't get me wrong, I'm going to be feeling that one for hours, but that's not me telling you never to do it again. It's honestly kind of a shame I couldn't take that more often because, phew, it was...yeah, that was something."

"Pretty sure I couldn't do that every time," he snorted, looking over me. "You're sure you're alright?"

I bent forward, hating this suddenly unsure and worried side of him. I kissed him softly, hoping that was enough to make me sound genuine. "If I need to have an ice pack later, I'll be sure to let you know. Otherwise? I'm going to need a minute before I can walk. Pretty sure you just screwed my hand-eye coordination right out of my body."

"That's gotta be a new one," he chuckled, squeezing my legs.

"Maybe we should check the record books and see if you won any money," I told him, running my hands through his hair.

"Let's not do that," he said with a roll of his eyes.

"I dunno, someone might pay good money for it."

"I believe you're looking for either a prostitute or a porn star."

"Mmm," I hummed, nuzzling the top of his head. "You'd be good at either, just in case you were looking for a different line of work."

"After the day I had, I might consider it, but if my job gets me benefits like these," he said, giving my legs another squeeze. "Maybe I'll find a way to ride it out."

I snorted. "I guess that's one way of looking at it."

He smiled, gently buttoning up my pants for me. "Coming home with me tonight?"

"I think I might be able to manage that," I said with a chuckle, even as I knew constantly hanging around one another was only making it easier for him to get attached.

Then again, considering the speed I'd answered, and the warm feeling in my chest, maybe he wasn't the only one feeling more than they should.

* * *

SOMETHING WAS WRONG.

I wasn't sure what, but something was going on with Trevor. The guy had been quiet from the moment I'd shown up and had occupied himself with numerous little projects, including fixing the kitchen sink, which was working perfectly as far as I could tell. He was acting like himself for the most part, but there was something subtly distant about his behavior that I couldn't put my finger on.

At first, I thought he was simply enjoying having another person around without the need to talk or be all over one another. In truth, we weren't a physically affectionate couple. Maybe the occasional brush of hands over the other's body or my legs in his lap while we read or watched TV. Mostly we were content simply to enjoy being in each other's presence.

This was different, though. He was still here since we were in the same house, but he never lingered long, and I could sense something was off, but I had no idea what. We hadn't argued in the past week. When I stayed over the night before, it had been normal.

Maybe it was just the night I'd had or, rather, the dreams that had disrupted my sleep. By now, I was accustomed to their occasional appearance and could cope if they made it hard to rest well. I knew the dreams might linger for a few days though it could have been a one-off. Either way, I could sense that they left me unnerved and more worried about things around me than usual.

Which meant if I wanted answers, I would have to hunt Trevor down and get a straight answer from him.

Bracing myself, I went inside and slowly made my way to the living room, where I could hear music playing softly. I found him sitting cross-legged on the couch, which made me smile. The man could make subtle, self-deprecating comments about his aging body all he wanted, but Trevor was stronger and in better shape than a few people half his age. My eyes tracked to the glass of what appeared to be liquor.

"Hey," I said, crossing my arms and leaning against the doorway to watch him.

"Yes?"

"Can we...not beat around the bush? Just say what's on your mind."

The smirk on his face was irritating and surprising. "Since when don't you want to beat around the bush?"

"If I wanted to deal with someone who beat around the bush, I'd...I don't know, actually," I said, frowning.

"Go to someone else?" he supplied.

That made me laugh. "See, that's kind of the problem. I don't have anyone I can do that with."

His brow rose slightly. "No?"

"Think about it," I said with a snort, wondering how I hadn't realized sooner. "Look at the people around me. I've got a lawyer and an agent. You may not have met them, but they're no-nonsense and as straightforward a it gets. That's why I retain them. My sister is no fucking different. Then there's you, right up there with the rest. I don't have a single person I can bullshit around in my life.

His mouth opened, closed, and then screwed up into an expression of thought as he set his glass on the table next to him. "I...never thought about that."

"Yeah, neither did I until just now," I said with a laugh. "Kind of weird, the things you don't realize are happening until...well, I'm not sure."

Trevor tilted his head slightly. "It's not like you to sound so unsure about things."

"Yeah, well," I said uncomfortably. "It's been known to happen."

"Are you still sure about what you're doing? For work."

I sighed, knowing this would come, but still unable to help the heavy feeling in my chest. "For the most part. There are moments when I wonder if I need to stop, and other times when I think I'm doing alright. It changes day to day."

"Moments like...when you have dreams?"

"We all dream Trevor."

"Most people's dreams don't involve a lot of moaning, groaning—"

"Well, maybe not the dreams *you're* having," I smirked. "And I'm not sure if I should be insulted that you aren't dreaming of me like that."

"And crying," he finished.

I looked away. "Yeah, well, when a dream is so beautiful, what can you do?"

"Is this where I pretend like I'm not concerned and let you get away with your little joke to avoid the seriousness, or do I finally get the chance to nail you to the wall on something?" he asked softly.

The instinct to take advantage of the easy joke rose and then died as his eyes burrowed into me. "I have the feeling I'm not really going to have a say."

At that, he smiled gently. "I've been dealing with you long enough to know nothing will stop you doing what you want. That's...part of the appeal of this thing we have going on."

"That I'm difficult?" I asked with a snort.

"That you're here with me because you want to be, not because you're obligated," he corrected.

It was my turn to raise my brow. "And since when is that? Pretty sure we set this up for a reason."

"And it doesn't require you to spend as much time with me as you do," he said, sipping his drink. "You don't have to be here when you're not with your sister and nephew or not out working. But you make time, more than is necessary, to keep the rumor mill spinning."

With a huff, I walked over and took his glass from him, downing what little was left. "Her name was Julie."

"Julie?" he asked confusion in his tone.

"That's what they called her at the brothel," I told him, glancing around to find the bottle of liquor sitting on the shelf and opening it to fill half the glass. "See, Eastern Europe or not, they get a lot of Western tourism, and they wanted her to have a name her customers could pronounce. She never told me her original name, no matter how often I saw her."

"You...visited her?" he asked. "At the brothel?"

"I visited a lot of them," I told him with a shrug. "I left out the details of how I got to talk to many of the women, but yeah, I paid to see them. Who knows what the people in charge thought about the hours I spent there, but they probably didn't care. Well, they might have if they knew I was talking to them, getting their stories for later use. Julie was...something else though, special."

"I...don't remember a Julie in your work," Trevor said, watching as I took a deep drink from the glass.

"She was supposed to be the biggest, most important part of it," I said softly, staring down into the dark liquor. "She was...willing to talk the most. The others would stop and start. Sometimes they'd just stop and never talk to me again. But her? Despite everything she'd been through, a fire in her refused to be smothered as long as she could help it. It took half a dozen visits before she finally started trusting me enough to talk, but she talked."

I could still see the room they put her in for customers, far nicer than the ratty little cell she described where she was kept when she wasn't on the clock. Even then, it stank of cheap cleaning products that didn't quite cover the smell of piss and mildew or flowery candles they lit that only added a sickening sweetness to the air. They made sure she was washed, her hair brushed and wore clean clothes, but they couldn't hide the bruises on her arms from the needles or the thinness of her body that went without food far too often.

And they could do nothing about the heat radiating from her gaze when she finally pulled back the curtain.

"Her father was a drunk and a mean one at that. He liked to gamble and whore, and he was fond of taking his fists to his wife and children. The only reason he got away with all that was because his wife was the family's breadwinner, right up until she died. Then, suddenly, he found himself with a mounting pile of debt and no way out," I said, taking another drink. "The only way he could take the edge off was to drink more, hit his children, and...well, Julie apparently looked like her mother."

It didn't take long for Trevor to connect the dots, his brow darkening. "He was raping her."

"Even before her mother died, before puberty," I said, hearing the disconnect in my voice but unable to stop it. "Worked out pretty well for him until the day she put a sewing needle through his eye. She told me her only regret was that she didn't shove it further into his skull, then maybe the rest wouldn't have happened."

She had said it with a laugh, full of bitterness and hate, but then she'd flashed me a smile that I could only call beautiful. It was then I was struck by just how powerful human beings could be, even when they'd gone through hell and back. Maybe if I got her out of the brothel, gave her a chance at a normal life, she could have been so much more than a slave for the worst impulses of other humans. There would always be that sharp, jagged edge to her, but that was better than withering away in the hell she was locked into.

"Daddy Dearest didn't like that very much," I told him with a snort. "Evil bastard or not, I can't blame him for being a little cranky about a sewing needle to the eye."

"No less than he deserved," Trevor said softly.

"So he got the wonderful idea of how to get rid of his little problem *and* earn himself a nice bit of cash to help with his debt."

"He sold her?"

"Why not? He'd been raping her for years, beating her and her siblings. What does a person like that care about selling someone?" Derision was thick in my voice, and I swirled the glass. "She was fourteen when he sold her. She was nineteen when I met her...and she was a week shy of twenty when she died."

"I...why?"

"Because of me."

The admission hung in the air as I stared at the glass. There had been a plot of land not too far from the brothel, hidden in the woods, where they dug a few holes and tossed in the unlucky women who died from neglect or rough treatment. I'd known about it and expected a horror show when I'd finally gone there in the dead of night to get pictures while it was empty of the living. I hadn't been surprised to see the truck with a few bodies in the back, cold and sightless in death.

I hadn't been expecting one of the unseeing gazes to seem familiar as I shuffled around the crudely dug holes, barely deep enough to bury a dog, let alone a human. When I turned to face the body that had nagged at me, it was the first time in years I had to restrain myself from crying out in horror. Julie's brown eyes, empty of the fire that had burned in them, stared up at me as her head dangled over the edge of the truck. A jagged gash on her throat, like some gruesome smile, told me just what kind of end she had met.

"I was...planning to get her out of there," I explained hoarsely before downing the rest of the drink and setting the glass beside the bottle. "Talked to her and set up a plan to get her out of that place and out of the whole damn country. People in the area worked to help people like her get to safe places where they could start a new life under a new name. Honestly, once they were free of being grabbed easily, they were generally safe. Who'd expend that much energy and money to get a simple whore?"

My bitterness was thick, and I finally looked up to meet Trevor's eyes. "I don't know if they found out what was going to happen or if she got impatient. Either way, she was dead before I could finalize everything. She died because I interfered, and I can still see her staring back at me. Sometimes it's with the eyes that made me want to help her in the first place, and sometimes it's the cold dead eyes that told me I'd failed her completely."

"Oh, Ethan," Trevor breathed, his face a perfect mask of agony and pity.

"So there ya go," I said with a laugh that sounded fragile even to my ears. "You wanted me to talk, right? Was that enough talking for you? Or am I going to have to do more? I could tell you about the ten-year-old boy I found in another brothel for 'special tastes.' Managed to get him out, I mean, he's always going to be fucked up and never be able to trust anyone ever again, but hey, he's safe, right?"

Even when you save people, they were never truly saved. I'd seen that for myself several times already. Pulled from hell, demons still followed you for the rest of your life, and nothing could save you from them.

Trevor stood without a word, and before I knew what he was doing, his arms closed around me, pulling me back into his chest. I squirmed against him. "Hey! C'mon, don't...I wasn't being serious. I'm done, alright?"

"I know," he said, his voice soft. "C'mon."

"Where are we going?" I asked, suddenly more tired than I could remember being. Whoever said unloading your burdens was supposed to be freeing was a dirty liar, and I had a few choice words for the idiots who pushed that.

He didn't speak as he gently led me to the couch, pulling me down onto the plush surface. Just the sheer comfort of the couch under me was enough to intensify the feeling of weariness. Without thinking, I stretched my legs out to get even more comfortable and found Trevor guiding my head into his lap.

"You don't have to talk anymore," he said, and I would swear there was so much more meaning in that sentence than what he was saying.

I opened my mouth to protest, feeling a little ridiculous until his hand landed in my hair, giving it a light tug before smoothing it out. The tension in my shoulders eased as he did it again, fingers curling into my hair and caressing my scalp. Everything I'd said and felt wasn't magically washed away in some revelation of comfort and freedom, but I could focus on his fingers as he petted me.

After a few minutes, I found myself dozing. It wasn't quite sleep but not quite wakefulness either. I hovered on the edge of both as I lay there, somehow managing to take the comfort he offered. The demons I'd thought about only minutes before had gone from a clamor to a soft whisper. They weren't gone, of course, but they didn't seem quite as important at that moment. For the first time in a long time, I didn't need to drown the voices with even more energy and noise.

There, with just Trevor, I managed to find a peace I never believed existed for me.

TREVOR

August was coming to a close, but that didn't stop people enjoying their summertime activities, including gathering in their backyards. That, of course, meant having someone to man the grill and hungry people milling around in conversation while they waited for the food. Not that there weren't plenty of other things to tide them over, cut vegetables, salads, including a dubious chicken salad and what Bennett had called fruit salad that just looked like different types of jello.

I was doing my best not to look as awkward as I felt while sitting near the fire pit, keeping out of everyone's way without separating myself completely. It wasn't the first time I'd been invited to a cookout, but it was the first time since I'd been married that I'd gone to one. Bowing out had been out of the question when Ethan had been the one to invite me.

Any attempts to explain that these things just weren't for me, that it would feel strange seeing Bennett outside work, and that these were his people and not mine were met with a raised brow and a smirk. That hadn't deterred me but apparently hadn't persuaded him, despite the good points I thought I made. Before I knew what was happening, Ethan was between my legs, then we ended up on the floor, and somehow, after all was said and done, I had agreed.

I was beginning to suspect he was capable of hypnotism or was actually a witch.

"Hey, Chief," Bennett called as he approached, a plate in hand. "Want some cake while you wait?"

"Me and sugar don't mix all that well. Icing out of the tub is asking for problems," I grunted.

He snorted. "Store-bought? C'mon, I made this myself."

My brow shot up. "You...bake?"

"Don't act so surprised. A guy can bake. Just look at Grant."

"I'm less concerned about gender roles and more terrified by the idea that you're allowed around an oven."

Dark hair and a face set in a scowl appeared beside Bennett, snatching the plate from him. "Believe it or not, he's pretty good at it and has only burned himself half a dozen times."

"Hey! Chase!" Bennett protested, reaching for the plate.

"Your boyfriend put me on sugar patrol," Chase growled, holding the plate away. "Because apparently, I'm responsible for your bad choices all of a sudden. Take it up with him."

"Or, I could take it up with *your* boyfriend, who is a worse sugar fiend than I'll ever be and will happily let me indulge. Plus, he can give you that face that makes you turn into a puddle on the ground," Bennett said triumphantly, disappearing into the crowd of people filling Bri's backyard.

"Are you really that wound around his finger?" I asked Chase, who scowled harder.

"No," he snapped. His scowl only deepened when I raised my brow doubtfully. "Goddammit."

I chuckled as he stomped off, only for Ethan to materialize and drop into the chair next to me. "You think he's going to give in to Bennett now or try to stop him?"

"Doesn't matter. Neither one is going to work," I said, taking a sip of my beer.

"Yeah, he's got it pretty bad from what I can tell," Ethan said, staring into the crowd. "Which is pretty easy to read. The guy always looks grouchy, but the moment he's around Devin, BOOM, instant softy."

"It's always been a little like that with them," I said, looking over to appreciate Ethan in the bright afternoon light. Despite being 'undercover' so often, he'd seen plenty of sunlight if the copper color of his skin was any indication. His hair had also lightened considerably and reminded me of the old stereotype of surfers being bronze skinned and golden-haired.

"Oh, familiar with them?" Ethan asked, curious about another person's story as usual. Sometimes I thought he couldn't help himself, as if some internal pull kept him in a constant state of nosiness.

"Both of them, though for different reasons," I explained with a chuckle. "Chase was an angry little shit when he was young, got himself into more than his fair share of scrapes. I got called because of him more than once."

"That was when you were just a regular old officer, right?"

"That I was. Some of the other officers thought he was nothing but trouble."

"But you didn't."

"Oh, he was trouble alright, just not nothing but," I amended, spying Chase's large form moving through the crowd after the loud-mouthed blond troublemaker. "And now he's living a quiet life, working hard at the auto shop, and shacking up with his best friend."

"Devin apparently has a story too," Ethan said, leaning closer.

"Yeah," I said softly, ensuring my voice didn't carry. "But it's...not a good one."

Ethan's brow rose. "How so?"

"Let's just say his father was as rotten as a person can be without walking around looking like a zombie," I grunted. "Drunk. Abusive. And while no one could prove it, plenty of people around here don't think his wife died in some ridiculous falling accident either."

Ethan's eager expression dimmed, growing serious. "Christ. Wait, was that the guy who got gunned down in the middle of town?"

"That's the one," I said grimly.

"And no one knew what happened?" he asked doubtfully.

I gave him a hollow smile. "Oh, I can bet you plenty of people saw exactly what happened, but they didn't *see* a thing? General understanding in Fairlake was that there was a man who needed to be killed."

"And you were okay with that?" Ethan asked, sounding surprised.

I had to chuckle. "Was I happy about someone getting shot practically under our noses, and no one wanted to help us? No, not really. It goes against the idea that we're upholding the law. But I figured out how to deal with it."

"How's that?"

"By remembering that sometimes justice and keeping the peace are more important than laws. Not often, rarely even, but sometimes those things aren't the same thing. And this town got a lot better with him out of the way."

Ethan's eyes twinkled in amusement. "Sometimes I think you say these things just to get into my pants."

"Yes, because me getting into your pants is a difficult and

arduous process," I teased him. "All I have to do is start barking orders to people, and you—"

"Bennett!" an annoyed voice cried above the crowd. "Bring me back my cake or so help me! Adam! Come get your man!"

"Not my turn to watch him," Adam called back, clearly unbothered by Isaiah's dismay.

Ethan raised a brow. "Alright, let's move down the social group, Isaiah and Julian?"

"Can't speak much for Julian. Transferred here sometime last year and kept to himself. Had some trouble at the last firehouse he was at, but that got settled when it was found he broke another firefighter's nose for a damn good reason. While he was here? Mostly peaceful, save for the call to his apartment last year over an assault."

"Ooh, who'd he assault?"

"No one. Isaiah punched the living daylights out of Julian's brother."

"No shit?"

"Yes, shit," I snorted. "Bennett took that call, but the brother mysteriously decided to drop the charge. After that, I have no idea what did or didn't happen or what led up to it."

"So, does Isaiah have a history of that?" Ethan asked, sounding intrigued as if he'd never considered Isaiah to be the violent type.

"No," I chuckled, taking another drink. "He's led a pretty quiet life. Had a rough patch there for a while when his family left Fairlake for greener pastures, I guess. The Enders were one of the town's founders, and he's the last one left in Fairlake, and since he's with Julian, probably the last one we're gonna see."

"Damn, he loves this town that much to stay?"

"Well, there is that," I said carefully.

"Family drama?"

"Only rumors to work on."

"Like?"

"Like the fact that they're none too happy their only son likes the company of other men in his bed."

"Oof," Ethan winced. "Alright, that's not fun."

"I've heard it's not a lot better for Julian either," I said with a frown. It was a shame, really. Despite how little I knew them personally, what I'd come to learn made me like them. Both were good firefighters and, by all accounts, good men. They struck me as people any family would be proud to call a member, but after doing my job for so long, I'd learned just how stupid some people could be.

Ethan thought about that for a moment. "So, any good dirt on Bennett or Adam?"

"Are you just working your way through all the people you know? Because there are better ways to spend the day," I told him wryly.

"Says you."

"Shouldn't you already know about them?"

"I know they were best friends, then Adam left to start his own life. Met Bri, they got married, that went to shit, and he came back here. Then he somehow discovers dick is awesome, which I mean, I can't blame him. It *is* pretty awesome."

I snorted. "I won't argue, but I won't say more and risk giving you material to use against me."

"And then Bri showed back up, things got awkward, and now Bennett and Adam are a couple, and my sister is dating a plumber from Fovel."

"Which means you know more than I do," I told him, reaching over to rest my hand on his back. "Because neither of them has a history I know about."

"Alright, what about Kyle and Ian? They were weird as hell back on the fourth."

"Kyle and his brother were close growing up, and little shits who liked to cause mischief, but nothing worth talking about. Ian? I don't have a clue, and before you ask, I have *no* idea what's gone on between them, and no, I'm not asking either of them," I told him with a hint of warning. "That's their business, and I'm not prying."

Ethan gave a dejected sigh, flopping back in his seat and watching the crowd. I could tell from the way his eyes were darting around that he was looking intently for Colin, trying to track the little boy's movements. As much as Ethan acted uncomfortable around the child, there was no denying he'd grown attached.

"Looks like he spotted you first," I said, eyeing the small child as he made his way over from the sandbox in one corner of the yard.

"What?" Ethan asked, immediately looking, and I felt his shoulders relax. "Oh, Colin?"

"Right, you weren't looking for him," I snorted, emptying the bottle of beer and setting it in the grass beside my chair.

Either Ethan decided he didn't want to argue, or Colin's presence distracted him enough to keep him from firing back. Either way, he twisted in his seat to scoop the boy up as Colin let out a squeal of joy followed by a shrill "E-tan!"

"E-than," Ethan repeated, emphasizing the syllable Colin couldn't get his tongue around just yet.

"E-tan!"

"E-than."

"Eeeeeee-TAN!"

Ethan winced at the piercing shriek. "Alright, close enough for now. Holy cow, kid, you're going to ruin someone's hearing with those lungs."

"Has Bri forgiven you for that being his first attempt at speaking yet?"

"No, I suspect he'll be graduating high school before that

happens. And if you ask me, Adam is more butthurt about it. But being mister stoic and all that, he won't admit it."

"Fathers can be touchy about things," I said, reaching over to shift Colin's leg so he was straddling Ethan's thigh more comfortably. "Might want to hope, for your sake, he learns how to ride a bike from Adam."

Ethan grimaced, closing his eyes as Colin began groping his face. "I'll leave that to him, don't worry. Dude! I need those eyeballs."

I watched as Ethan gently but firmly guided Colin away from the more sensitive parts of his face. Colin immediately decided to drop to his knees in Ethan's lap, and I laughed softly when Ethan instinctively shoved his hand over his crotch. Still grinning, Colin reached into the front pocket of his overalls and shoved something toward Ethan with a giggle.

"Yeah, that's a worm, little dude. How did you find that in a sandbox?" Ethan wondered, taking the worm gently and holding it up. "And how you managed not to squish it is a miracle. Those belong in the dirt, not in your pocket."

Colin's face scrunched up as Ethan dropped the worm into the grass. "E-tan!"

"God, you sound like your mother when you try to say my name like that," Ethan muttered. "You're lucky you're, like, a hundred times cuter than her."

"He gets that from his father," Bennett announced as he appeared, a smear of icing on his shirt. "Do you mind if I steal him? Bri's looking for him to make sure he eats something other than junk."

"Yeah, sure," Ethan said lightly, but I watched him grab Colin's sides, giving them a light squeeze and a smile before holding him out. "Go with Bennett."

"Ben Ben!" Colin exclaimed, squirming excitedly in Bennett's hands as he struggled to get a grip.

"Oh sure, he sounds excited when he talks about Bennett but sounds so freaking exasperated when he tries to say my name," Ethan said with a shake of his head.

"Freaking?" I wondered.

"If I said 'fucking' within earshot of him, Bri would have materialized out of nowhere to remind me I need to watch my language," he said in a low voice.

I chuckled, leaning over to kiss him on the temple without thinking. "Despite what you say, you're pretty good with this uncle role."

"I'm not sure if I should be offended or not," he said with a bashful smile.

"You do what you want," I told him, now suddenly confident, wrapping my arm around his shoulder and pulling him closer.

"So, you glad I brought you?" he asked, and I wondered if maybe he'd been worrying about that without finding the courage to say it aloud.

"You know, I thought I'd hate it," I admitted. "My family was never one for gatherings, and I always hated going to them with my ex-wife. But strangely enough, I'm enjoying myself."

"Sat over here all by yourself?"

"All groups need a few introverts who just...watch. It's been fun watching."

"Yeah," he said softly, smiling when laughter burst from somewhere in the group. "I feel the same, except for the watching part. I never thought 'family stuff' would be my thing, but this...I don't know. It's almost enough to make me change my opinion."

"Well, sit here and observe with me for a while," I offered.

He glanced at me knowingly before reaching over to rest a hand on my knee. "Sure, why not? We can observe together."

* * *

MUSIC FLOATED THROUGH THE HOUSE, from the kitchen to my office. For reasons I wasn't going to guess at, Ethan had decided to scrub my kitchen. It didn't seem all that long ago he'd told me how much he hated housework and had sworn up and down he'd never do it so long as he could afford to have others do it for him. Apparently, that had changed, and he'd shooed me out while he busied himself scrubbing surfaces.

Which left me with little to do but have a drink while reviewing the files on my computer. Ethan had been helpful enough to put all his notes into a document to use as I saw fit. Thankfully I also had his verbal reports, so I could make my own notes, ones I could actually make sense of.

He'd squeezed information from the people of Fairlake and had worn down most people in Fovel. His latest report contained a note of hope, however. Apparently, he'd contacted someone on the mayor of Fovel's staff who might have some information for him. They were due to meet in a few weeks when it was safer, whatever that meant.

Honestly, I was more relieved than worried at the news. Deep down, I suspected that if Ethan hadn't been able to dig up anything substantial through groundwork, he would have put himself in danger by going into the woods. I had also suspected he had a good idea where some of the manufacturers were operating but was keeping that to himself. There weren't gaps in his reports or notes, but knowing what I did about Ethan and the intricate web that was his thoughts, I believed there was plenty to read between the lines.

So if someone in the mayor's staff could know something about this was all I had to worry about as opposed to Ethan putting himself in harm's way, I would take it. It was a lead far better than my officers or I managed to get. Durkins was *still* being an absolute prick, stonewalling my repeated requests for aid, including intercepting a direct request to the mayor.

Either I would have to take direct action or hope Ethan dug something up soon. Winter would only make them draw back further while they waited out the bitter cold, making a search far more dangerous.

Sighing, I leaned back in my seat, rubbing my brow and wondering what to do. To wait would increase the risk of Ethan finding trouble, but pushing could send the entire group underground and get a full blast of political shit in the face, making my job several times harder. Neither was particularly appealing, and I let my arms hang on each side of the chair as I considered which evil was the lesser.

"Working hard or hardly working?" Ethan's wry voice asked, startling me.

"Jesus, Ethan," I barked, snapping my head toward him. "What the hell are you sneaking around for?"

"I'm not sneaking," he said innocently, even as his eyes twinkled in amusement. "Not my fault your hearing is going with age."

"Oh, don't you start," I growled. Our age difference rarely came up, and usually only when I was griping about some ache or emphasizing that he hadn't even hit thirty yet. Every once in a while, though, he liked to take a jab at my age, if only because it got a reaction.

He chuckled, moving closer. "Fine, you were distracted, and the music drowned me out."

That was true, but I knew it was more than that. It was a strange dichotomy, but if Ethan wasn't talking, he was so silent it was eerie. If it weren't for the fact that I knew better, I would have suspected he'd had formal training. In his case, however, I suspected his training had come from the school of hard knocks, and I was still trying to figure out what other things he could do.

"Finished being a housewife?" I asked, grinning when he gave me a dirty look.

"Your kitchen was filthy," he said with a dainty sniff. Which was par for the course, but I cocked my head at a strange tinkling of metal. "I've seen better kept kitchens in third-world hovels."

"Well, then let me be the first to thank you for your tireless toiling."

"Always avoid alliteration," he said in a dead voice.

I chuckled, pushing myself up from the desk. "Does that mean we're allowed to use the kitchen? Because it's nearly time for food."

"We might be able to once it airs out a little," he said, leaning in close.

I wasn't blind enough to miss that offer, and I moved closer, accepting the kiss. It was strange, but I hadn't noticed until recently how easily he kissed me. Before, he only kissed me when it was foreplay or after sex when he was probably at his most vulnerable. Yet in the past few weeks, the kissing had increased.

"Someone's being sweet," I said with a smile, savoring the fact.

"I have my moments of innocent attention-seeking," he said with a smile.

I had only a moment to register something sly in his smile before he moved faster than I could track. Before I could react, my hands were shoved behind my back, metal pressing against them. I grunted in surprise, trying to step away, only to be reminded that the wiry man was a lot stronger than he appeared. He held me close as I felt another metal ring close around the other wrist.

"Ethan, what the…" I sputtered, finally stumbling back

when he released me. My attempt to bring my arms forward met with resistance, and I heard a familiar rattle of metal and frowned at him. "Really? Surprise handcuffs?"

"Everyone likes surprises," he said with a chuckle.

"In my experience, that generally doesn't extend to being handcuffed without warning," I said, giving the cuffs another tug. "Jesus, are these *mine*? How did you get them? They're in my safe, my locked safe." Along with my sidearm and identification, something I'd never given Ethan access to because there'd been no reason.

"Your passcode is thirty-two, seventy-six, ninety-one, four," he listed off, looking at me like I was some grand project he'd just finished.

That brought me up short. "How...did you watch me?"

"Nah, that's too obvious, but I own the same brand of safe."

"So?"

"So, they use the same number pads. Which means the same pitch of beeps for the numbers."

I stared at him. "You...learned my passcode from hearing the beeps?"

For the first time, I was surprised at something he'd achieved. He looked uncomfortable. "Well, yeah. I mean, I wasn't trying to...well, okay. I was. I heard the beeping and couldn't help guessing what it was, then trying it out to see if I was right. I wasn't...it wasn't to get into your stuff."

"It was to prove you could solve the puzzle," I said in understanding.

"Yeah," he said, and I couldn't help but smile at his relief. Sometimes there were moments when I got to see a little more, like the part of him that would always be afraid of getting in trouble. The part that acknowledged he was mischievous and a bit of a troublemaker and felt ashamed enough that it bothered him at times.

"Well, at least if you ever need access to my gun, I now know you can get to it," I said, giving the cuffs another tug.

Honestly, this little show was probably one of the most impressive things I'd ever seen him do. Not only had he figured out my code from electronic beeps, but he'd physically overwhelmed me with speed and precision before I had a chance to react. It was the first time I saw just how he survived in dangerous places and not just his investigative skills.

"Thanks, I'm very proud of myself," he said brightly.

"I'm proud of you too," I said, then gave the cuffs another rattle. "Now, let me out of these."

"Oh, that's not happening," he said with a wicked grin. "You're stuck in those."

I narrowed my eyes. "Ethan?"

"Now, now, you don't get to be all bossy and in control while you're handcuffed and helpless," he said, slinking forward to stick his fingers into my waistband.

My brow rose as I felt his finger brush my skin, gently sliding through the trimmed hair of my groin. "Is this your attempt at seducing me? Jumping me with surprise bondage?"

"Well, I was thinking—"

"God save me."

"That I could handcuff you, drag you to the bedroom where I could suck you for a little while."

"Uh-huh," I said slowly, irritated that I could already feel my body responding. Honestly, being with him was like being in my twenties all over again, and I wondered whether the people who'd been my age when I'd been his were lying about sex drive dropping off as you got older. Either I wasn't quite at the age for that to happen, or Ethan just brought it out in me.

"And since a certain someone decided my ass needed to

be used and abused yesterday," he continued with a smirk. "I figured it was only fair I get to have my own fun with your ass."

Now I was definitely reacting, and considering his fingers were pressing against the base of my dick, I knew he could feel it. "Interesting theory. Just how willing are you to test it?"

"Quite," he said, undoing the string on my sleep pants and giving them a shove so they dropped to the floor. And there, for anyone to behold, was the evidence that my body was more than pleased by what he'd said. "Wow, and it looks like you just might be too!"

"You're such a shit," I said, unable to stop laughing.

"I've been told," he said, dropping to his knees smoothly and so quickly there was no doubt he was enjoying himself. I could say whatever I wanted about how much of a brat he could be, but there was no question about whether or not he wanted me.

The room was perfectly lit by the incoming sunlight, and I was helpless to do anything but watch as his lips parted and he took me into his mouth. While we agreed I was better at taking him deeper than he could me, he showed far more enthusiasm and skill than I ever had. The fact that his eyes glittered with amusement and arousal as he swirled his tongue around my sensitive head only added to the thought.

"God, Ethan," I groaned as I watched my cock disappear into his mouth. Honestly, no matter how great it felt, watching it happen in front of me was a different pleasure. My groans grew even worse when I saw the last inch of my shaft disappear just as his throat muscles worked feverishly around it. "Fucking hell, you're getting way too good at this."

He popped off me with a laugh. "Practice makes perfect."

"So they say," I said roughly as he put his mouth back on me and began to bob.

There was something unbelievably erotic about watching him, just as it was whenever he let me take complete control and 'use' him. This man lived life by his rules, didn't look to others for guidance, and generally balked at the idea of someone telling him what he was or wasn't going to do. Yet he gave himself over completely when the mood struck me, and the sheer amount of trust that came with that was positively intoxicating.

This though? This was Ethan at his brattiest, his most playful, teasing me as he worked me over. Every time I tried to regain control, he slapped a hand onto my hip and held it steady, preventing me from doing anything but standing completely stationary before he began all over again. It was equally infuriating and arousing, as I both hated and loved feeling out of control and just a little used.

Which, of course, meant he had to up the ante by sliding a spit-slick finger between my legs and into my ass. I jumped in surprise at the suddenness, but one finger wasn't enough to do much more than get my attention, especially with his thin digits, which was probably why he was able to add a second finger without much issue and just a bit of saliva. It only boosted the jolts of erotic pleasure flashing through me as I shuddered, barely able to stay standing.

"Fuck, Ethan!" I growled, trying hard not to buck my hips again and risk him stopping.

"That is the idea," he said, nuzzling my groin.

"Then fuck me already," I told him, leaving any tone of command out of my voice and falling back on what I hoped sounded like a reasonable request.

Chuckling, he stood up and stripped, leaving his clothes on the floor with my pants. Before I could say anything, he stepped back and walked toward the bedroom, leaving me to follow with my hands still cuffed behind my back and my dick swaying in front of me awkwardly. It was almost impressive how prepared he was by the time I caught up, his cock half-covered with a condom as he finished rolling it down with a little flourish.

"You had this all set-out and prepared, didn't you?" I asked flatly, nodding toward the bottle of lube and the empty condom wrapper.

"You could say that," he said lightly. "Now, how about you get on that bed, and I'll take care of our problems."

Sighing, I looked at the bed and realized there was no way to get comfortable if I didn't want to cramp my arms or face-plant on the bed. Shooting him a dirty look, I knelt on the floor at the end of the bed and bent over the mattress. Ethan wasted no time kneeling behind me to push what was clearly three fingers, now lubed up properly, into me.

"You have the power to say no at any time," he said, and I knew it was equal parts gentle reminder and playful taunt. He wanted to make sure I knew I could stop this if I was genuinely uncomfortable with it, but he also knew me well enough to know I wouldn't make him stop. Even if I grumbled and complained the whole time, there was no denying that I enjoyed this as much as he did.

"Ethan," I grunted in warning, only to let my head hit the mattress with a groan when I felt his fingers spread apart to stretch me further.

"You just can't help being demanding," he chuckled, pulling his fingers free and repositioning himself.

One hand came down on my shoulder to hold me steady before I felt the now warm slickness of his dick pushing against me. I grunted when the head breached me, my ass resisting for a moment before relaxing as another inch slid inside. Bottoming had never come easy for me, and I definitely wasn't as skilled at relaxing physically like Ethan was, and it showed the few times he'd chosen to top.

That didn't mean I didn't enjoy the feeling of him inside

me. He was only the second man I'd ever bottomed for, and he had yet to disappoint. He took his time entering me, reading my reactions before he continued or paused his movements.

"Oof," he muttered once I felt myself loosen up enough for him to move. "You and your death grip."

"No...narrating," I grunted as he eased back.

"Bossy," he said, and I didn't have to look to know he was grinning.

I knew better than to feed into his playful demeanor and waited until I felt him slide into me again. A hiss escaped me when I felt his fingers close around the handcuffs, forcing the metal to bite into my wrists as he pulled himself forward to bury himself with a snap of his hips. It was all I needed to know, playtime was officially over as far as Ethan was concerned.

He didn't waste time demonstrating why I enjoyed him taking his turn occasionally. In only a few thrusts he managed to find the right angle that sent stars exploding across my vision as I lay there helplessly, at his mercy as he began a steady, deep rhythm. I had to give him credit, if he had intended to find a way to force me to lay there and let him do the work, he'd succeeded with flying colors.

Certainly didn't hurt that with every thrust of his hips, he pulled me back against him with the cuffs. The slight bite of the metal was just enough to accent the pain, mingling with the feeling of my straining dick being forced against the smooth bedspread. Whether that was his goal from the beginning didn't matter much as I felt the pleasure roll through me, building until it was all I could focus on.

Ethan reached under me, his hand finding my shaft and stroking it in almost perfect synchronization with his thrusts. He had never been the most patient of people when it came to sex, and considering the state I was in, the best I could do was growl in protest. But considering he was enjoying his little power trip, I might as well not even bother. The intense cocktail of sensations flooding my body became a storm that crashed around me, drawing a cry from my lips as my head slumped forward onto the mattress.

I was vaguely aware of my dick, but Ethan's grip never stopped as he stroked every last drop from me. It was only as the intense roar of my orgasm left me that I became aware of the warmth dripping onto my back and his absence inside me before I realized what he'd done.

I let out a heavy sigh. "You always have to make a mess."

His chuckle, while unsurprising, was a balm. "And I always clean it up. Just think of yourself as a good doughnut, better glazed."

"That's awful, and so are you," I muttered as I knelt there. "But you can win points back by uncuffing me."

"Shame, I kind of like you like this."

"Ethan."

Without a word, I felt the handcuffs shift on my wrist before their grip loosened with the soft tinkle of metal. They slid down my side onto the bed as I brought my arms around gratefully, rubbing my wrists even though they were only a little red.

"I'm going to get a towel," he told me softly, and I could *just* hear his footsteps as they left the room.

I lay there, only my thoughts to occupy me before I realized I could smell something familiar. Looking up, I grabbed the nearby pillow and brought it to my face, taking a deep breath. It'd been a few days since I'd changed the bed, and the faint smell of Ethan's cologne still clung to the pillowcase. It was strangely subtle for a man who portrayed himself as anything but. Just the slightest hint of some rich woodiness, spice, and something else.

"Here," he said, surprising me with his presence and the

gentle brush of a soft towel against my back. "You planning on getting off the floor?"

"And here I thought you were supposedly fond of me on my knees and helpless."

Ethan draped himself along the bed in front of me, a slight smile on his face. "Yeah, but maybe you'd look better if you were on the bed with me instead."

It was one of those little things that told me he wasn't involved with me just because it had once been a convenient cover and got him a decent amount of good sex. Those times when it was clear he wanted something from me other than flirting and sex, where he might crave affection and comfort.

Plus, seeing him stretched out on my bed, completely naked, looking absolutely content and happy to see me *was* pretty hard to resist. So I inevitably crawled over the bed and dropped down in front of him, laying my head on his bare stomach and closing my eyes. It took only a few seconds before I felt his fingers in my hair, giving it a light tug as I felt his muscles relax under me.

And there again, another moment when he lapsed into complete silence as we lay together, simply basking in one another's presence. Just letting the moments pass us by without a care in the world.

It would be another week before I came to find out that this was merely the calm before the storm crashed down on us.

* * *

I SHOULD HAVE KNOWN something was wrong when I heard a crash from my home office. Frowning, I set the bag of coffee grounds down on the kitchen counter and turned toward the hallway. If Ethan were here, instead of off on his 'secret rendezvous' with whoever in the mayor's office was supposed to be supplying him information, he would have teased me for drinking coffee in the afternoon despite not being at the office today.

"Not so good for the ticker, all that caffeine," he'd tease, eyes sparkling in that way that made it hard not to smile.

"Maybe the one who still drinks coffee shouldn't worry about other people's potential heart problems," I'd remind him.

Maybe he'd use the opportunity to tease me about my age, or maybe he'd just watch me with a look that was both attentive and something else I'd never been able to define.

I brushed the thought away as I peered into the office carefully, years of professional training and caution making me slow to dismiss the odd noise. For a moment, all I could see was the clean room with a slightly cluttered desk, the curtain fluttering gently in the soft breeze coming from the window I'd opened earlier when Ethan had left.

Then I spotted the pieces of broken ceramic scattered all over the floor, with a twinkle of silvery metal in the middle. Groaning, I stepped into the room, wondering how the old cross had gotten from the back of my desk to the floor. The sound twisted into a hiss when I felt a jagged line of fire stab my foot, forcing me to step back and lean on the doorway to inspect it.

Finding a piece of ceramic jammed into the flesh, I yanked it out, huffing as I held it in the palm of my hand. Sighing, I returned to the kitchen to retrieve the broom and dustpan and wracked my brain to figure out how the cross could have ended up on the floor. It had sat peacefully on my desk for years, and I knew Ethan wouldn't have touched it.

My 'internal grumping,' as Ethan liked to call it, suddenly stopped at the knock at the front door. Frowning, I stopped sweeping and set everything aside to hobble out to the living room and peer through the glass at the top of the door. Even more confused at who was on the other side, I unlocked it.

"Bri?" I asked in confusion, looking around to see it was just her.

"Colin's with Bennett and Adam for the weekend," she said, probably guessing who I was looking for.

I blinked, realizing I should probably let her in, and stepped back, gesturing for her to come in. "I'm sure they're all happy about that."

"They'll probably have him for a few more days after that. It's hard to let him go, but it's downright impossible to keep them away from each other," she said with a chuckle. "My parents are still confused as hell about what's going on and why I didn't take Colin and return to Boston."

"And being a lawyer, you probably could have done all that and a lot more," I said as I closed the door.

"I'm in real estate, Chief Price, not family law."

"Coffee?" I asked her.

"God, I live off of the stuff, please."

"Sure," I said, walking past her. "And you don't sound upset or unhappy about living here."

"Oh, sometimes I am. I miss the fast-paced, demanding, and downright aggressive environment I had in the city. Sometimes the only way I felt like I was doing something was by sharpening my teeth on other people," she said, following behind slowly, undoubtedly looking around. "The thrill of the challenge, needing to feel the pressure in order to feel alive."

"Wow," I grunted, measuring the grounds into the filter. "There's a lot of things that run in your family, aren't there?"

She laughed, and at least *that* didn't sound like Ethan. "There's...some. They just come out differently. But, yes, we're both like that. He was always just—"

"The one to do it his way, by his rules, and not those other people use," I finished as I poured water into the coffee machine.

"Yeah, used to drive everyone in our lives crazy," she said, crossing her arms and leaning against the doorway to the kitchen.

"Not you?"

"Oh, God, definitely me. I was his big sister. Everyone thought I was supposed to have some influence on him because he looked up to me, and I understood him...for the most part."

"They apparently didn't understand that there isn't a person on the planet who could make Ethan do something he doesn't want to do."

"You know," she said, "quite a few people in his life have figured that out."

"Well, it's not difficult, even for someone as thick as me," I said with a smile.

"And up until just now, I thought I was the only person who ever said it quite the way you did."

"Uh, with an air of exasperation and resignation?" I asked, pulling two mugs out of the cupboard.

She smiled, one that spoke of the many things she knew and how much of it didn't give her pleasure. "I'm sure he's heard it said with plenty of exasperation and frustration. Coming from people who are fed up with him or too tired to keep up. Maybe it's because I see a lot of myself in him that I don't often feel that way, or why I can keep up. Maybe it's because he's my brother. Or maybe it's just...because. I've never thought about it too hard, there are too many things in this world that need a lot of thought."

"And your love for your brother isn't one of them," I concluded, pouring coffee into the mugs. I pushed the sugar bowl toward one and pulled the small milk container out of the fridge. "Especially because it sounds like you've seen a lot of people walk away from him with their hands thrown in the air."

"That I have," she said, adding a little sugar and milk to her cup, stirring it when I handed her a clean spoon. "And I always admired how easily he shrugged that sort of thing off. It always seemed like he was good at brushing it off every time someone did something that should have just...well, hurt like hell. I know he feels things, but he was always so good at keeping it to himself, seeming in control."

"He's got a pretty good talent for keeping things close to the chest and seeming like he's not holding anything back," I said.

Her eyes lifted from her cup to level with my gaze. "Do you ever feel like he's keeping more from you than he should? Do you think all those things kill him more than we'll ever know?"

I remembered the look on his face when he told me about the girl he'd met while working. His voice had been hollow, his eyes distant, unfocused, and the skin on his face was so drawn it could have been a mask. There was no question in my mind he had only been half there with me that night while the rest of his mind was somewhere in a rotting building, watching a woman he'd respected, cared for, be degraded until the point of her death.

"I think he keeps a lot more back than we think," I said slowly. "Whether that's because it's too much for him to talk about or because he worries about the people in his life depends on what he's hiding."

"I wish he didn't," she said softly. "Worry so much, I mean. We're all a lot tougher than he gives us credit for."

"I don't think it's about whether or not we can handle it," I said, trying to explain how I understood it without giving too much away about Ethan. "But...there are things he's seen or things he knows. Things he doesn't want other people to have to deal with. It's not about strength. It's about keeping the darkness out of the lives of people who bring brightness to his."

Bri drew back slightly, brows shooting up in an open display of surprise. "Wow. Just how much time have you been spending around my brother? That sounded like something he would write."

I gave her a rueful smile and a shrug. "It sounded like something he would say when I ran it through my head, and I have a feeling he'd agree with the message too."

"And it sounds like you understand my brother more than I do," she said with a strange, almost sad smile. "Or at least, he tells you more. Not too worried about the light you bring?"

"Or I don't bring it," I said, suddenly uncomfortable with the turn of the conversation.

"Is that humbleness or a lack of confidence?"

"You can say a lot of things about me, but lacking confidence isn't one of them."

"Maybe I should rephrase and instead say, a lack of confidence in your importance to my brother."

"That would be...closer to the truth."

She nodded, taking a sip of her coffee and looking down. Her eyes widened. "What...why is there blood on the floor?"

I looked down and winced, not realizing I'd created a gory trail of smeared blood from my injured foot through the house. "Ah, that. I was in the middle of cleaning something up when you showed up. Didn't think I'd be dragging blood all over the place."

She sighed, setting her cup aside. "Then let's get your foot looked at."

I smiled at her. "You're not going to pin me down to treat a wound that'll be fine just so you can finally get around to whatever you came here for."

"At least wrap it so you stop getting blood all over the place," she said, looking amused.

"You look like your brother when you do that," I said with a sigh, setting aside my cup.

"What?"

"Smile because you've been caught out, and you're still going to get what you wanted in the first place."

"Funny, Adam told Ethan that once but with the names reversed."

"And I'm sure Ethan thought that was particularly funny."

"Obviously."

It only took me a few minutes to clean my foot and wrap it. Emerging from the bathroom, I found Bri in my office, sweeping the pieces of ceramic into a dustpan. I watched as she gently set Troy's dog tags on the desk. She started when she saw me but quickly covered it up as she looked down at my foot.

"Sorry," she said, gesturing toward the ceramic pieces and the dog tags. "It was strange just standing around and doing nothing while there was a mess."

I looked down the hallway, seeing it gleam from a recent wash. "I could have managed, but thank you all the same."

"Was it important?" she asked, glancing at the ceramic pieces.

I frowned, squatting down to pick up a piece of it, a small white dove that had managed to get through the disaster without breaking. "Hard to say. It was my ex-wife's, never could figure out why she left it behind. Maybe some part of her still hoped it would give me peace, even when she was about as opposed to my peace as it got when she left."

"I know a little something about that," Bri said with a wistful smile. "It's difficult to sort through the good and bad memories at the end of a marriage. I'm still working through it."

"Takes time," I said, dropping the dove into the pile. It had only been a strange reluctance that made me hold onto it for so long, and now it was broken, I realized I felt no sense of loss or remorse. I would toss it into the trash without hesitation or doubt, though I still wondered why I held onto it for so long.

"And those?" she asked, glancing at the tags.

"Those...belonged to my best friend," I said slowly, then figured there was no harm in the truth. "And the only man I ever loved."

"I'm sorry to hear that. He must have been special for you to hold onto them for so long."

"He was, but I've found that grief is like a pushy and overly invasive family member who lives nearby. You might have established boundaries, but even then, they show up every once in a while unannounced to pester you. They always leave, though, and you can go on with your life."

Bri picked up the tags, looking them over thoughtfully. "How does that work, being so snagged by the past?"

"I'm not snagged by the past," I said with a frown. "Or by people who are gone from my life. Mementos and memories aren't the same as being unable to move on."

"So there's still room for the living in the present?"

"This can't be the reason you came here."

Her fingers lingered on the tags. "No, it's just a concern that bubbled up in my head, is all. Christ, I feel like ever since I was pregnant, I worry about things I never worried about before."

"Like Ethan?"

"I always worry about him. It just got worse, but maybe that's not just because being a mother made me realize how dangerous the world can be when you're responsible for more than just yourself."

"Then what?"

Her brow furrowed. "At a glance, Ethan asking to stay with me, in Fairlake of all places, was strange enough. He's never shown the slightest interest in things that are 'normal' or quiet, and this town is all those things. He always preferred to spend a couple of weeks with his family and then do his own thing. I always suspected he was off partying the whole time, but that was the way he did things."

"But not this time," I said, sensing the prompt but also that she was finally building to the point of her visit.

"No, not this time," she said, her expression shifting, and I remembered Ethan's far-off stare while regaling his story weeks ago. "When I called him, he sounded...odd."

"Odd, how?"

"It's hard to explain, not without someone knowing Ethan *and* having heard it themselves."

"I see."

She flashed a smile that faded almost instantly. "No, you don't, but that's because I'm bad at this. Leaving an impression with words is my brother's skill, not mine. The point is, something in his voice just...scared me. And I don't mean that normal, almost routine worry I get when I think about what he does and where he goes when working or even 'relaxing.' This was...something deep inside me was terrified when I heard his voice that night."

Even though Bri grew quiet, I could see the shadow of fear on her face. Even diminished with time and filtered through memory, I could guess the emotion she was trying to describe.

"When Troy died," I said, waiting until she looked up, her eyes focusing on me. "My mother was the one who had to call me to tell me. I was in the field where it was next to impossible to get ahold of people, even in emergencies. But on the way back to base, I was told I had a call from home waiting for me. I had...no reason to be concerned, but I remember it felt like someone jammed a blade of ice into my heart, and my stomach became one big knot."

She nodded. "I don't know why I felt that way, and knowing Ethan, I probably never will. But when he suggested coming here, I couldn't say yes fast enough. Normally I would have doubted his decision, wondered what he really had in mind, wondered how long he would stay, and so on, but it was instant. I wanted him here as soon as possible. I even tried to talk to him about that feeling when I got him here, but...I chickened out at the last moment. I told myself I would wait and see, watch how he did."

I leaned against the doorway. "He seems to have settled in just fine."

For the first time, she brightened when she chuckled. "That he has. Against all odds and logic, he's managed to enjoy himself here. He's been spending time with people he might call friends now and with his family. God knows watching him trying to figure out Colin has been hilarious, but against his will, I can see he loves that little boy and is trying to be what he thinks is a good uncle."

"He's better at it than he thinks," I said, smiling at the memory of Ethan patiently trying to show Colin how to stack a set of large hollow blocks. Every time it got to a certain height, Colin would shove it over with a cackle befitting a villain, only for them to do it all over again.

"I try not to point that out too much. It's good for Ethan to think he's struggling with something now and again," she chuckled. "The point is, he's been doing great. And a big part of that is you."

"I suppose I should be thankful I'm considered shiny and interesting enough to hold his interest this long," I said with a small smile.

She rolled her eyes. "Christ, I'm beginning to see why he's into you so much."

"I have the distinct feeling I've said the wrong thing."

"You're just...difficult."

"I'm not—"

She waved a hand, cutting me off. "Not the point. The point is, between you giving him this job to feed his constant need to be doing something, and this relationship you two have started has done the rest of the work."

"I wouldn't really call it—"

This time she cut me off with a sharp, unimpressed look. "It's certainly not just for shits and giggles. I can tell you that much. Maybe you two are being stupid enough not to call it what it is, but I've been watching...*both of you*. It was obvious earlier that it was getting to be more than just fun for you, and now I'm pretty damn sure he's been there for a while. I'm only just now seeing the signs."

"Uh...like?"

"My observant and sometimes paranoid brother will know what's going on with you. He'll have figured out your feelings well before I did, and yet he's still hanging around. Not only that, but it's clear he hasn't put any distance between you. And before you say something, there are ways to do that while still keeping up the illusion that you two are a thing which, for the record, he'd know that no one else is even gossiping about it anymore. Now they're gabbing about what your recruit and a certain EMT's history are."

I huffed, appreciating and disliking how well she'd hemmed me in. "If this is all good in your eyes, why are we having this discussion?"

"Because I want to be sure I'm right. And that you're fully prepared for—"

She trailed off, and I pushed away from the doorway, glancing over my shoulder when I heard my phone ringing in the kitchen. "Look, I know what...I know the possibilities, okay? I know Ethan might one day simply disappear, or that if we continue our...relationship, I'll have to deal with being without him for weeks at a time, maybe months."

"You two haven't talked about this yet, have you?" she asked, though her tone told me she already knew.

"I..." Stopping, I huffed when my phone started ringing again, and I walked away to grab it. "No, we haven't!"

"You're both ridiculous," she called after me. "And if I have to pin you both down to force it, I will."

"I see being a pain in the ass runs in the family too," I muttered, seeing Ethan's name on my caller ID and answering it. "Aren't you supposed to be schmoozing right now?"

"Listen to me," Ethan hissed in my ear, his voice low and deadly serious. "Where are you?"

"Home," I answered quickly, sensing that wasting time was a bad idea.

"I need you to get my sister and Colin somewhere safe."

"I can do that," I said, straightening and turning to find Bri had followed me. The expression on her face told me that whatever was on my face wasn't good. "Now explain."

"The meetup was a setup," he whispered to me. "That guy never showed up, but a bunch of shady guys did. Came right out of the woods where we were supposed to meet. Sucks for them that I wasn't exactly where they thought I'd be. Sucks for me that they caught sight of me pretty fast. I managed to get away after talking, but I don't have a good feeling about this one."

"Ethan—"

"Stop," he ordered, and despite everything, I realized he was utterly calm. "There's a good chance they're going to get me. I can hear a bunch of them all over. They know who I am. Which means they probably know who my family is, and I wouldn't put it past them to go after them. Get my sister and nephew somewhere safe."

257

"Ethan, tell me where you are," I insisted, my heart thundering.

"I'm sending what I can to you."

"Your location!"

His voice finally wavered. "And look, if this...goes the way it probably will, I'm sorry, and you were perfect. I should have said it sooner, but I've been thinking about ditching this relationship's 'fake' part and making it something real. Maybe real for the first time in my life."

"Say whatever you need to say when I fucking find you," I growled at him, ignoring Bri's growing fear.

"Sure," he said, and I could hear him smile. "But I...wait, I think...oh *shit*."

"Ethan?" I asked before I heard shuffling and scratching on the line. My breath stopped at a grunt, followed by what I thought was the phone hitting the ground and several more thumps that sounded too much like someone being struck. "Ethan!"

There was a crack, and the phone beeped in my ear. I pulled it away to see the call had ended, and then all I could hear was the pounding of the blood in my ears and Bri's sharp breaths.

"Trevor," she managed, snapping me out of my daze. "What's going on?"

Slamming back to reality, I unlocked my phone and scrolled for the number I needed. "Call Adam, Bennett, whoever is with Colin. Ensure Bennett knows Colin is potentially in danger and that you are safe with me. Tell him to bring Colin to the station."

"Trevor what—"

"Your brother is in trouble, and you might be as well. So let me do my job, you make sure your son is going to be safe!"

She whirled around to yank her phone out of her pocket

and dialed just as my phone rang. It rang twice before Ira answered. "Trevor, aren't you supposed to—"

"I need everyone who isn't on necessary duty ready to move soon," I told her sharply. "I'm bringing two people, an adult female and an infant male, into the station where I need someone to guard them. The rest need to be ready to suit up and move out. I'll give the details when I get there."

"Of course," she said, her tone shifting immediately. Bri was still talking rapidly on her phone and glancing at me. "Anything else?"

"Alert the people who need to be alerted," I said, walking past Bri into my bedroom and opening the closet door to reach my safe. The sound of the beeping keypad sent a small dart to my heart before I yanked it open to grab my sidearm. "And make sure everyone knows this isn't a drill or a joke. I want everyone ready. I should be there within fifteen minutes with the female. Officer Livington will be arriving in the same time frame with the infant."

"Understood."

I ended the call and found Bri standing in the doorway, the phone at her side. "I-I told Adam. He said he's never seen Bennett move so fast or look so...I was told to pass along the message that Bennett understands, and ETA is ten."

"Good," I said, putting my holster on. "We're leaving as well."

"Trevor, please tell me what's going on."

"I understand you're frightened and confused, but I need you to work with me. We need to leave now. I'll explain how your brother and I got him into this situation," I told her, carefully but firmly taking her by the arm to lead her toward the side door.

"He's in danger...again."

"Yes, but this time he's not alone. We will find him, and we will get him back safe. But in the meantime, I have to make sure you and Colin are somewhere safe as well, understood?"

She nodded numbly and let me lead her outside carefully. I watched the neighborhood like a hawk as I led her to my squad car, telling myself I was telling the truth. Whatever was happening, whatever state Ethan was in, I would get him back in one piece.

And God help whoever might prevent me from doing that.

ETHAN

My head was pounding when I woke up, but that wasn't a surprise. Even dazed and confused, I remembered seeing the butt of the gun flying toward my face before I felt an explosion of agony through my skull. If I'd been capable, I would have been thankful for the darkness that followed immediately, sparing me from the worst of the blow.

Now I was in an entirely different sort of trouble. Wherever I was, it had four walls, though it looked more like a shack made by someone half-drunk and with only the vaguest idea how to use their equipment. Even in the dim light coming through a makeshift 'window' made of scratched plastic, I could see where they'd made several attempts to screw the wooden floor down.

"Someone call OSHA," I muttered as I spied a few screws sticking out of the boards, begging for someone to trip over and end up with one through an unsuspecting foot. "Because I've got *so* many violations to report. These assholes are gonna be drowning in fees by the time they're done."

My laugh was shaky and bitter, but it helped clear my thoughts. Just enough to force me to take a deep breath and examine what kind of state I was in. Other than the headache and inevitable swelling on my head, I was more or less in one piece. My thoughts weren't any more muddled than I expected, so if I had a concussion, it wasn't that bad.

Unsurprisingly, despite the room being closed and probably guarded, I still found myself tied to a chair. My feet were unbound, but thin, strong cords were wrapped around my wrists and chest. A test of the chair told me they'd bolted it to the floor, not that I could have broken the metal chair anyway. All of that, along with the lack of blindfold or gag, told me my captors weren't worried about me getting free, let alone knowing where I was or being able to call for help.

"Confidence, that's either unsettling or really helpful," I muttered, looking around.

I took a moment to curse myself for my stupidity. My instincts had told me the meeting with the aide had sounded strange, especially when they'd changed the location to the road that ran through the woods between Fovel and Fairlake. If I'd been just a little less confident, I would have called Trevor and arranged some form of backup. But no, I had to tell myself I could handle whatever happened and that I'd been in plenty of scrapes before.

Admittedly, this wasn't my first time being kidnapped by people pissed off at me, but it was the first time it had ever happened due to my own carelessness. It wasn't like me to take a situation so lightly, especially when I knew dangerous people were involved. I should have suspected my investigation had drawn attention.

The best I could say was that I had prepared things so I could get all the information I'd gathered to Trevor with just the push of a button. I'd hoped to collate everything and make it a nice big chunk of easy-to-read information, but I'd taken too long. At least if this went even worse for me and a little too final for my taste, then he had plenty of information to put him on the right path. So at the very least, I'd done as much of the job as possible before things went to shit, and I was forced to shatter my phone. It wasn't a perfect fix, I hadn't been able to make sure it was broken beyond repair, but I'd done enough damage in the few seconds before they caught me to make it difficult to get anything useful from the device.

That was small potatoes compared to the relief I felt at managing to relay the danger to Trevor before I was caught. Now at least, I could face whatever was going to happen, knowing he and his officers would go out of their way to ensure Bri and Colin were safe. I wouldn't be surprised if they had Bennett himself watching over them. The guy was as goofy and happy as they came, but I would place at least half my savings on the idea that he was far more fearsome than he seemed.

Which only left me with my current dilemma and not a whole lot of options. Other than making what I hoped was an educated guess at being somewhere in the forest, I had no idea where I was. I didn't know how long I'd been out, so they could have taken me miles in any direction. Furthermore, while I could guess who my captors were, I didn't know anything else about them, not their numbers, suppliers, or even what they wanted from me.

In short, I was up the creek, and my dumb ass had left the paddle at home.

The admonishment had no sooner bubbled up in my mind before I heard a commotion outside. It wasn't much, just raised voices approaching. I only detected two voices, a male and a female, neither of which I could immediately identify. The woman sounded irritated, and the man sounded stressed, but I couldn't make out their words. They grew quieter as they approached wherever I was being kept, which made it impossible to hear.

"I'll deal with it," I finally heard the woman snap, her voice cutting through the thin wood of the walls. Her voice didn't rise much, but there was no doubt who was in charge from the natural authority in just those few words. "Now go huff and puff at someone who has time for you."

I heard an angry mutter from the man but little else until I heard a creak from the other side of the door, letting sunlight through the crack at the bottom. Footsteps, heavy and thick-soled, echoed through the room, and I heard her murmur to someone else. When another pair of footsteps, heavier than the first, strode away from the door, I knew my suspicions about a guard had been confirmed. There was another creak, presumably the entrance to the outside, before the door to the room I was in opened.

Sure enough, the woman walked in, and I couldn't help but feel my brow arch at the sight of her. Her dark hair was in a tight ponytail, tied with what appeared to be a strip of leather. The vest she wore over a dark green shirt was also leather, with stitching to mark its wear and tear. Her jeans were spattered with mud, and the hems were frayed as they rested over well-worn boots. A gun holster was on one hip, and a hunting knife on the other.

"So," I began as she stopped, looking me over warily with dark eyes that gave little away. "When did meth makers start looking like Ted Nugent's wet dream?"

Her eyes crinkled as if she wanted to smile before she scoffed slightly. "I guess that answers my first question."

"Well, kind of figured you probably had questions. But you know, while we're on the topic, what did I answer?"

"Whether or not you were going to try playing dumb."

That made me chuckle. "Well, truth be told, if I thought that ploy would work, I definitely would have gone with it. But that only works on stupid people."

She crossed her arms over her chest, displaying the well-corded muscle in her forearms. "The next question is whether you're being smart or if you think you're manipulating me."

That confirmed my initial hunch that she was smarter than her rough appearance might lead someone to believe. When it came to criminals, especially in the modern day, they weren't necessarily sexist about how they ran things. It varied worldwide, but for the most part, if a woman proved herself a capable leader, criminals didn't care who wore the crown. Of course, it was also my experience that crime 'lords' of the fairer sex proved themselves by being tougher, smarter, or more vicious than the men. Usually, it was some combination of the three, and I needed to figure out what else she was besides intelligent and probably tough.

I was *really* hoping vicious wasn't included too.

"Manipulating someone requires you to have at least something you know about them that can be tweaked," I told her with a shrug. "All I know about you is that you're intelligent, scary looking, and probably in charge of the drug-making operation around here. Two of those three things would be incredibly attractive to me if it weren't for the third."

Her brow shot up. "Seriously? Seduction?"

"I'm not trying to seduce you," I said in a scandalized tone. "I'm a taken man, thank you very much."

"And yet you're trying to say something about me is attractive."

"Look, taken or not, I can still appreciate *the idea* of a badass woman with brains, alright? Doesn't mean I'm going to do anything about it...or want to for that matter."

Her brow rose. "I'm not sure what's more concerning, your taste in women or you in general."

"It probably won't surprise you to find out that I've been told that quite a lot," I said with a chuckle.

"You're right. That wouldn't surprise me," she said, walking over to the window and leaning on the wall next to it. The wall gave an ominous groan that would have sent me scuttling away as fast as possible so it didn't collapse, but she didn't seem the least bit concerned. "I'm going to see just how smart you are, Ethan."

"Oh, we're on first names, then? Kind of helps if I know yours," I said. "Unless you're going for mystery as a form of intimidation."

"Something tells me intimidation isn't going to work on you that easily."

"It's just my natural resilience. I can't help it."

"Right," she said, and I'd swear I saw her lips twitch in a near smile. "Ava."

"Which, if I remember, is supposed to mean life," I said, not bothering to hide the raw irony from my voice.

"Oh yeah? What's yours mean?"

"Strength."

"Huh, is that funny to you too?"

"Should it be?"

And there was the first flash of anger since she'd walked through the door. Apparently, while she enjoyed my little quips and playfulness, she wasn't fond of me turning questions back around on her. That was a potentially useful piece of information I would keep in mind.

I harbored zero delusions that I would somehow manage to talk my way out of whatever she had in store for me. There was no way she was planning on letting me get out of this building alive, let alone in one piece. Yet the longer I kept her talking and maybe even made myself amusing enough, the more time I bought. Whether that was for me to figure out how to get my ass out of the fire or before I was found in time, I wasn't quite sure yet. I was pretty sure my best bet would be to focus on the first plan, as that was one I could influence rather than waiting on several unknown factors that would result in my rescue.

I just had to keep calm, keep my wits about me, and watch for any weaknesses I could exploit.

"I've never found my name all that funny," I said, keeping my voice neutral and watching as the annoyance disappeared.

"You think quite highly of yourself, don't you?" she asked quietly.

"Would you believe me if I said no? I really don't."

"Is that so?"

"Don't get me wrong, I know where my skills and talents lie, and I have a good estimation of what I'm capable of."

"That's not the same thing."

"Oh, you wanted the personal stuff? Well, then still no, I don't think all that highly of myself. I know I'm good-looking, know how to make people laugh, and how to mess with some people. But that doesn't really make me think I'm this fantastic person."

"So, a bad one?"

I eyed her curiously. "Life isn't broken down into good people and bad people. I'm just a person. Sometimes I'm a hot mess, and sometimes I've got my shit together."

Was this some attempt to disarm me, to make me so caught up in myself that I was unnerved and vulnerable to mental attack? If that was the case, she severely underestimated how much time I'd spent knowing what she was asking about. I was all too familiar with my weaknesses and vices. She wasn't going to unnerve me that easily.

"Not to interrupt an interesting conversation," I said slowly. "But is there a point to this line of questioning? Because this feels like a conversation we should be having in a smoky room with a couple of drinks between us. Not that I'm opposed to that. You can supply the drinks—."

"You're cute, but you're not *that* cute," she said with a flash of a smile that did nothing to make me feel better. In fact, I was reminded of the animal shows I watched when I was younger and one episode in particular about apes. Turned out, a smiling ape was the last thing you wanted to see in front of you because it was their way of showing you their deadly fangs and hint at their willingness to use them.

"It says a lot about me that that's not the first time someone calling me cute didn't make me feel good," I said, no less comforted when her dangerous smile became a vaguely amused smirk.

"You have led a pretty interesting life," she said, now watching me closely.

"Ah, a fan or Google?"

"The second, and maybe a little of the first afterward."

Right, so that meant she not only knew my name but also my professional history. "Well, I'll always appreciate a new reader, even if that's a strange thing to say about you in particular."

"What I find interesting," she said, leaning forward slightly. "Is the question of whether or not you're even half as skilled as your writing makes you out to be."

"I don't recall bragging much about what I can or can't do," I said because, quite frankly, I never included anything in my writing that detailed things I specifically did unless it was relevant. It was all too easy to fall into the trap of talking yourself up rather than focusing on the point of the story. I had purposefully chosen an editor who would weed those sorts of things out for just that reason.

"True, you are quite...secretive about how you go about getting the information you do," she said slowly, though why she chose her words so carefully was a mystery. "But if you can read between the lines, use your head, and guess what's going on behind the scenes, you get a decent enough picture of things."

"Right," I drew out, watching her warily. "I suppose someone could make a good guess at things if they really wanted to."

"Well, I wanted to," she said bluntly. "Especially a couple of months ago when your name was first mentioned. I wasn't that concerned when Barty mentioned you were sticking your nose in places. At first glance, it seemed like the boy toy of Fairlake's police chief was just getting a little too curious and probably trying to make himself look better."

"Barty?" I wondered and then stiffened. "Please tell me you are not talking about the police chief of Fovel. I'm going to hate myself to the day I die if I missed that."

"Well, isn't *that* funny phrasing?" she asked, giving me that toothy grin again.

"I'm going to go out on a limb here and say you and I have two very different senses of humor," I told her lightly, even as a chill ran down my spine.

"And yes, one and the same," she said, her expression returning to neutral. "He was worried about you, and I wasn't. Well, until I grew curious."

"Yeah, gonna go out on another limb and say you being curious about me is not something I'd have wanted if I had a choice."

"Probably not," she said. "I expected you to lose interest eventually or bumble around and find nothing useful, or you'd get yourself killed at some point. When none of those things happened, I grew curious. It didn't take long to get your name and discover what you'd been up to in your personal time. I can't say screwing around with a cop is really my thing, but at least in terms of looks, you could have done much worse."

"Hey, that's a fine-looking man," I said with a scowl. "And superb in bed, so he's got plenty going for him."

She didn't take the bait like before, which I took as a not-so-great sign of things to come. "And the more I looked into you, the more I found out. Suddenly I didn't have some eager boy scout trying to earn brownie points with his lover, but a man who was more than capable of digging up plenty of unsavory information when his mind was put to it. Now I had a problem and had to consider how to deal with it before things got out of control."

"Wow, you make me sound a lot more competent and dangerous than I would have ever thought of myself," I said, raising a brow.

"Come on," she said, looking almost disappointed. "We both know information is a very handy and dangerous tool in the right hands. If that weren't the case, then spies would be pointless, and governments wouldn't come down so hard on their own people who blow the whistle on what they're doing."

"Valid point, excellent examples," I said, wriggling my wrists to buy myself a little space for comfort's sake.

"Now, the next question floating through my head is...are you really dating Trevor Price? Or was that your flimsy way of disguising what you were doing for a while?"

It was a little unnerving to see just how close to the truth she was. "What? A guy's not allowed to enjoy a little something on the side while also being a good snoop? What the hell else was I supposed to do in Fairlake to occupy my time? Do a little digging, get laid a lot, worked out pretty great for me."

Of course, there was the minor detail of me doing much more than just sleeping with Trevor, but I didn't think that was relevant. Well, and I had zero interest in pouring out my innermost feelings to Ava either. Whether or not I was getting serious about Trevor, more than I had with anyone else in the past was Trevor and my business, and not hers. Of course, I hadn't bothered to mention those feelings to Trevor until the last possible danger-filled moment.

I really needed to work on my timing.

"Ah, so this is where we begin to veer away from being honest, is it?" she asked, tilting her head. "I was wondering when that would start happening."

"Really? You think I'm going to lie about whether or not I'm into the guy when I'm bound, helpless, and unarmed in a chair while you're totally geared up?" I wondered. "That's pretty presumptuous."

"You don't operate in this business as long as I have without knowing when people are lying to you or keeping something from you," Ava said softly, her eyes narrowing. "In fact, if you want to not only live but thrive, you have to learn to pick through everything other people say."

"Wow, that's...paranoid," I quipped and then shrugged. "But hey, I can't talk, now can I?"

"I'm sure you've had to learn when to spot a liar and danger wherever, or however it's hiding."

"That would be a pretty handy skill for me to have."

Her hand came to rest gently on the handle of her knife. "And I hope you understand just what kind of danger you're in."

"Yeah, not to be the smartass that I always am, but the whole being lured into an ambush by armed drug makers and then tied up to a chair in the middle of their operation while their armed and dangerous-looking leader questions me was definitely a strong clue," I told her, dropping any friendly pretense and giving her caustic sarcasm instead.

"Ah, there's a little of the edge I was sure lived in you somewhere," she practically whispered, as if savoring the idea.

"Here's my question," I told her, staring back unflinchingly. "What exactly are you trying to do here? With me, that is."

"Playing with my food," she said without hesitation. "But now, playtime is over. You managed to destroy your phone, which gives us nothing to work out what you've discovered. So instead, you're going to tell me what you know so I know what Trevor Price knows."

"And, uh, why would I do that?" I asked, arching a brow.

"Let's not forget I know all about you, so I know you have a nephew and sister living in town. It wouldn't be all that difficult, middle of the night, get into the house—"

At least I'd had time to warn Trevor and get my family to safety, so the threat had no bite, though she didn't know that. "You threatening my family means fuck all to me, Ava."

"Oh?"

"Yeah, you really think they won't notice when I disappear? Depending on how long it's been, Trevor, at least, will get suspicious. Which means he's going to have the sense to keep my family watched just in case I'm kidnapped instead of dead. He might be a goody two shoes, but he's not stupid, and he's cautious to a fault. You got nothing."

Ava paused, considering that before nodding. "Fair enough. But that doesn't stop my next threat."

"Which is where you...what? Threaten to hurt me?"

"Oh, I very much can and will if I need to," she said, her eyes sliding back and forth over my face. "But honestly, what's the point? You can spare yourself a lot of trouble by just telling me. It's not as if you're threatening other people's lives by telling me. In fact, you're sparing people a lot of trouble. There is zero risk to anyone by telling me."

"You're leaving out the little detail where, whether or not I tell you, I still end up dead and probably thrown into a shallow grave if I'm lucky, just left to rot somewhere if I'm not."

"Quick and easy, or slow and awful. Seems like an easy choice."

"Yeah, except there's one thing you don't seem to understand about me," I told her with a grin.

"And what's that?" she asked warily.

"I'm a difficult ass son of a bitch who does things just to annoy other people," I told her with a smirk. "One of the world's most dedicated, spiteful contrarians that ever graced this planet. I won't tell you anything, not because of some noble dedication to truth and justice, but because I know damn well that not telling you will piss you off."

Her face hardened as she straightened, flexing her fingers. "Fine, then let's put that to the test and see how long you can hold out."

As she prepared herself, I tried to tell myself that being 'interrogated' further meant more time, even though I knew it would hurt like hell.

* * *

I WASN'T ashamed of the weak groan that escaped me as I hung forward, blood trickling down the side of my face. I had to give Ava credit, she certainly hadn't been afraid to work me over. I wasn't sure what it said about me, but this wasn't the first time someone had taken the time to beat the shit out of me, and I recognized she was being careful. Even when the knife had come out, she'd been careful not to nick anything vital or push me over my limit.

"Well," Ava said, the first word she'd spoken since she started. "I have to say, after a couple of hours, I expected a lot more whimpering."

"Ugh," I grunted, picking my head up to stare at her a little drunkenly. "What can I say? I live to disappoint."

"Don't think this magically makes you free of me," she said, wiping her hand with a cloth. "I'm just not going to push you too far. Better yet, I think I'll let you sit here for a few days. Let your stomach get empty, let you piss yourself a few times. See how comfortable that chair is, and then we'll see if you want to share with me."

It was, admittedly, a threat that scared me much more than any physical torture. Psychological torture was so much worse in my assessment. You could only push the body so far before it simply gave out from the stress, but mental torture? That could go on and on, leaving the subject half insane and desperate for even the slightest relief, whatever the cost.

"Your hospitality knows no bounds," I managed to get out. My face was one giant ache, and the lines of fire from the knife marks on my back were a constant reminder of how steady her hand was. Worse was the throbbing under my fingertips, where she'd used the tip of the blade to play around a bit, one of the few times she'd managed to get a cry rather than a grunt of pain out of me.

"We'll see how you feel about it after you've had some time on your own," she said, giving me the grin I now officially knew was a threat.

I didn't have the energy to respond. Our little session had left me drained. I knew it was a problem because my energy levels weren't going to improve if I continued to sit around in this god-awful chair. Pain might have weakened me, and the exhaustion from the torture was heavy, but dehydration and starvation were only going to make me feel worse. The sooner I got my head back in the game, the sooner I could count on saving myself, even if I was weak and graceless.

And hell, maybe if I screwed up badly enough, someone

might get mad or stupid enough to kill me, which would sure beat whatever Ava had in store.

Thankfully, I already had a plan in mind, having managed to scrounge it together in the brief moments of peace while she'd been torturing me. It had all started when she'd been repositioning herself and had kicked one of the screws sticking up from the boards. With what little sense I had, I'd caught it with the bottom of my shoe and held it in place while she walked around me. Strangely, keeping my foot pressed on that screw so it wouldn't rattle and give its presence away was one of the ways I'd managed to endure what I had.

I was thankful I had worn shoes rather than boots as I took a deep breath and forced myself to think clearly. Lifting my shoe, I made sure the screw stayed in place before using the toe of my other shoe to shove at the heel. The shoe slid off, and I carefully let it drop to the floor without a sound. Next came my sock, which I dropped atop the shoe, wiggling and flexing my toes.

"Alright, time to pray for some toe dexterity, and hope I'm still flexible enough to do this," I said in a low voice. It was probably not a good idea to draw attention from my guard, but talking to myself was a way to focus my thoughts, so I just had to hope they thought I was losing my mind.

One more deep breath and I carefully curled my toes around the screw, managing to catch the head on the floor so I could slip it between my toes and hold it in place. Shifting my foot upward, I dug my heel in opposite, leaning my upper body forward. All those times I joked about maintaining my flexibility for fun in the bedroom, and now I was finally using it for more than just fun. Even then, I had to strain to get my foot up to my face and lean forward. My body screamed in protest before I finally gave in, lunging forward to stretch the tension of the cord around my shoulders and chest but managing to catch the screw in my teeth.

Alright, hard part of step one of my escape plan was done. Now for the tedious part.

Tedious was the right word to describe having to use my mouth to scrape at the cord around my chest. Clenched between my teeth, I had to use my tongue to press against the screw head so it stayed in place as I picked and scraped. It was a bungee cord, meaning there wasn't much to get through, but it still took ages. I had to focus on what I was doing until I finally managed to get through enough that I felt confident in shoving my chest forward. When it snapped, there was a moment of victory until the high tension of the cord made a piece of it come up and smack me on the cheek.

"Of corf," I muttered around the screw in annoyance.

Still, that meant my upper body was free, and I could finally lean over and start on one of my wrists. After testing each side, I decided I could best lean to my left and got to work. Now I wasn't working at an odd angle, I could use the sharp tip to work much faster than before. When I'd finally weakened the cord, my wrist came free with a faint snap. I only needed to grab the screw out of my mouth and work on the right wrist.

I had only just begun scraping at the cord when I heard the sound of muffled shouts coming from the distance. My head shot up just in time to hear more shouts and what sounded like gunfire.

"Oh hell," I muttered, scratching at the cord even faster. I couldn't be sure what the source of the noise was, but I knew I didn't want to be still sitting here when they grew closer.

As predicted, the last cord unraveled quickly, falling to the floor as I heard the outer door open. Hopefully, my guard disappearing to discover what was going on.

I stood up, grimacing as my back screeched in pain from

the cuts she'd drawn on my skin, which only burned further when sweat dripped into the wounds. I flexed my fingers, trying to ignore the throbbing as I moved toward the plastic window to peer out. It was nearly night, however, and the scratched surface didn't allow me to see much. There was only the occasional flash followed by a boom telling me that whatever was going on was only getting worse, not better.

Moving to the doorway, I tried the handle as quietly as possible. I wasn't surprised to find it locked and let my hand fall away. In the dim light, I looked over the door, deciding it wasn't all that solid, and I could probably take it down with brute force. The problem with that plan was that doing so would hurt like hell and make a lot of noise. I didn't know how close my wandering guard was, and I didn't consider myself in any state to take a full-grown man on in a straight fight.

Instead, I turned my attention to the window. It appeared to be nailed in place, with only three nails left in three corners. There was a hole where a fourth one would have been, and I could slip my hand into the opening to pull on it, finding the loosest nail close to it and giving a few tugs. I tried to be as quiet as possible, but the nail squealed as it reached the halfway point. I yanked it out with my bare hand, shoving my head through the plastic to look around.

Darkened woods and a couple of buildings in the same dilapidated state were all I could make out in the gloom. I spared a moment to wonder if this was part of the camp's 'residential district' before making sure there was no one around as I squeezed out through the window and dropped to the ground. It was lucky Ava had kept the worst of her abuse to my upper body, meaning my legs were strong enough to catch myself without making too much noise.

Which was good because the sound of fighting was getting closer, and now I could hear people barking orders, some sounding pissed and some authoritative. I could guess which voice belonged to who, but I didn't want to risk finding out I was wrong or get into the middle of a firefight. My expertise had never been in coordinated firefights or tactics. So the best thing I could do for everyone involved was get out of harm's way and ensure I didn't trip up the wrong person.

"Shit," I heard someone hiss from the woods to my right, followed by the unmistakable sound of someone bumbling through the brush. "Shit, shit, shit, shit!"

While I agreed with the sentiment, I wondered who would be stupid enough to run away when Ava was probably leading the fight. It probably wasn't the smartest thing, trying to follow the person making the most noise, but I still veered toward the human-elephant crashing through the woods anyway. At the very least, they were heading away from the fighting, so I was partly achieving my goal.

Careful to make less noise, I slid into the woods just in time to hear a familiar voice call out, "Go and get him! Fucking idiot doesn't know this forest from his ass despite living here his whole life, and you! Go check on our smart ass. Get him somewhere nice and safe in case we need leverage."

Which told me exactly who I was following...and that I needed to follow him faster. I would rather deal with Bartholomew Durkins than whatever goons Ava had just sicced on us.

At least Bart was loud, making my job easier as I trailed him. The guy was freaked out and going as fast as possible, but I'd give him *some* credit, he wasn't panicking so badly he was completely blind. His pace was fast enough to gain distance but not risk falling into a hole or taking himself out on a low branch. I was thankful for that because the woods were dense this far in, which, if I had to guess, meant we were more than a mile away from the two towns or the road.

Considering Bart seemed to be moving steadily in one direction, I decided to speed up, purposefully going wide around the path he was making and being careful not to get caught by the tree limbs. Even though I could sense I was overtaking him, part of me insisted I keep moving forward and not stop until I was safely away. The other part told me the asshole wasn't getting away where he could claim deniability of anything.

Confident I had finally overtaken him, I veered closer to the path I was sure he was following. I had only the growing moonlight to see snatches of forest as I ducked under branches and stepped around low-growing plants. I didn't know what exactly I was going to do. I'd spotted the Fovel chief of police a few times in my investigations. He wasn't exactly a small man. Even if he wasn't that much of a fighter, he had me in weight, and I was still weak from Ava's show of hospitality.

Suddenly realizing I had no plan and terrible odds, I had to catch myself at the last second before I ran face-first into a thick branch. I stared at it and then ahead to the approaching asshole who had a lot to explain, and smirked, wrapping my hand around the branch and pulling.

I wasn't so out of it that I didn't enjoy watching the branch snap through the darkness with an almost deadly-sounding hiss before it caught Fovel's great and respectable police chief dead center. However, when I heard something crack in his chest, I had to wince as he gave a choked grunt and promptly fell on his back with a faint groan. Stopping to grab a thick branch from the ground and checking to make sure it was solid, I approached him slowly.

"The hell?" I heard him groan as I approached from the shadows, prepared for any sudden movements from him.

"That looked like it hurt," I said, keeping my voice light as I rested the thick piece of wood on my shoulder and stared down at him.

His head snapped to me, finally illuminated by moonlight trickling down through the canopy overhead. I'd seen him a few times, but this was the first time I'd seen him up close. Once upon a time, he might have been a good-looking man. It wasn't so much the years that had gotten to him as much as his diet. He wasn't huge yet, but his face had grown thick and heavy with fat, and his god-awful mustache wasn't doing him any favors. This was a man who hadn't worried about taking care of himself, and it showed.

His eyes, which had looked almost beady before, widened when he saw me. "Look, I know what this looks like—"

"Do you?" I asked with a laugh. "Because if you did, you wouldn't bother trying to explain yourself. Your ass is in *so* much trouble, Barty."

"Barty? You're not...one of Ava's men," he said slowly.

It was then I realized I was standing over him, my face cast in shadow. "Well, good thing you're in charge of investigations in the town, Barty, because you're definitely good at figuring things out."

"Who...the fuck are you?" he *tried* to snap at me but only managed to wheeze, unable to hide the wince of pain on his face. "I'm not fucking around today—"

I brought the stick down, not hard enough to do any damage, but enough to sink into his gut and knock the wind out of him. "My friend, I have had a *terrible* day, just terrible. And while I'm sure your day will just get worse, I'm aiming to make mine better. So, you're going to do what I say, or I'm going to take my frustrations out on you and turn you into a human pinata, got me?"

"What the fuck do you want?" he gasped.

"You got your phone on you?" I asked casually.

"My...my what?"

"Your. Phone. Cellular telephone. Electronic device capable of making calls using modern-day spooky magic."

To my amazement, he pulled his phone out, the light almost blinding as it lit up the dark. "Here, just...wait a minute, you're—"

I gave him another whack, this time in the chest with one hand while the other snatched his phone from his fingers. Bart curled up, rolling to one side to escape the next blow that wasn't coming.

"Wow, you really carried a fucking tracking device with you while you cavorted in the woods with drug dealers," I said with a shake of my head. "What's your pin, Barty?"

"You're Price's little fuck boy. I know you."

"And the stupidity continues," I said, this time giving him a hard enough whack I was sure I cracked another rib or two. "That's not a pin, that's just rude. Now try again, or I pick something far more tender to give the stick to. And in case it wasn't obvious what I meant, I'll give you a hint, I'm *really* good at finding a dick in the dark."

His eyes widened, and he spat out the number. I had no illusions that he wasn't pissed, but he was extremely wary of me, too, which was good. I punched in the pin and immediately checked to see if there was service. Apparently, cell towers were either really good in northern Colorado, or I was experiencing my first bit of luck as I began to punch in Trevor's number, ignoring it when it tried to finish typing it out for me. I had made a point to memorize his number just in case I ever needed to call him when I didn't have my cell.

The phone rang several times before going to voice mail, and I tried to ignore the approach of panic creeping its way into my chest. The last thing I needed was to start worrying if Trevor was one of the victims of the gun blasts I'd heard.

Instead, I gave the number another dial, then again, and again.

On the fifth attempt, a voice cut through the ringing in a snarl. "If you had wanted to play nice for once, Bart, you should have answered your phone earlier! I'm busy now, fuck—"

"God," I groaned into the phone. "I've missed the living hell out of the sound of you pissed off."

"E-Ethan?" Trevor stammered, sounding so unlike himself that if he hadn't growled initially, I would have wondered who I was talking to.

"Yeah, it's me. And, uh, please tell me it's you and your cowboys shooting it up with Ava's gang of miscreants."

"Ava?" Trevor muttered. "Wait, are you okay? Where are you? Why are you calling from Bart's phone?"

"So many questions," I chuckled, tensing as I sensed movement and swung hard. This time the crack was cartilage as the attacking Bart fell backward, holding his bleeding nose. "Ah ah ahh, behave yourself, Barty."

"Ethan!"

"Sorry, Ava is the woman in charge of the meth makers. I'm not in any immediate danger, I'm somewhere in the woods away from all the shooting, and Bart is the fucking person helping the manufacturers the whole time."

There was a pause, and I heard Trevor mutter something away from the phone before his voice came back clear. "I'll deal with that last bit of news in a minute. Why do I get the feeling you purposefully didn't answer whether you were okay with a straight answer?"

"Because it's a very relative thing," I told him, smiling when I heard his frustrated growl.

"This is *not* the time, Ethan!"

"Actually, this is the best time because hearing you get

pissed off at me, knowing you're not that far and are here to rescue my dumbass, is the best thing in the world."

His voice grew quiet a moment later. "You're an ass. Please tell me where you are."

"Yeah, can't really do that because I don't know."

"Is Bart going to be a problem?"

"Uhhh, he's probably got a couple of cracked ribs, a broken nose, and a lot more coming to him if he doesn't behave himself, so...maybe?"

There was another pause. "Uh, are *you* going to be a problem?"

I laughed. "Please find a way to get me, Trevor, I want to go home. I want to get yelled at by you and my sister when you guys see what I look like, I wanna hold that weird little creature that's supposed to be my nephew, and I want to fucking go to bed with you, alright?"

"Just...describe what part of the encampment you left from and in what direction if you can."

"Semi-circle of small buildings, smallest one there, I left from the..." I thought about it, remembering where the moon had been rising. "Southwest corner. Kept going in that general direction. I'll light the flashlight on the phone so you guys have an easier time."

"Okay, stay on the line," Trevor warned me. "And don't let Bart—"

"He won't be doing anything but staying right where he is," I said sweetly, looking down. "Isn't that right, Barty?"

"Get *fucked*," he snarled at me, recoiling when I rolled the stick over my shoulder as if to heft it up.

"Oh," I chuckled, hearing Trevor barking orders over the line and counting the minutes until I was out of this stupid forest and back where I needed to be. "You can trust me with that, Barty. I plan on it. After a nice shower and some sleep, but I plan on it."

TREVOR

The news that Ethan had been found eased the weight on my shoulders and the squeeze in my chest. Even then, getting off the phone with him had been one of the hardest things I'd ever had to do. While I waited, keeping everything in order, I told myself that despite how it looked, Ethan was still Ethan. He was a man who knew how to take care of himself and was capable of keeping himself in one piece if it came down to it.

Not that the conversation with him had done much to bolster my confidence. He had been evasive as hell on the phone, and I wasn't going to rest until I saw him with my own eyes and heard him with my own ears.

"How are we looking?" I asked Annie. "We have a number yet?"

"Seems there were about a dozen and a half of them out here," she said, looking around with a furrow in her brow. "Five dead, eight wounded, and of the eight, five of them need medical attention pretty soon."

"Well, they'll have to worry about that when we get someone in here," I said with a grunt. "Try to keep them from bleeding out on the ground if you can. We'll need as many of them as alive as possible. Word on the EMT's ETA?"

"They're right behind us, so five minutes if we give them the all-clear."

That was a tricky call to make. We didn't have an exact number of people at the encampment to know whether we had everyone. My gut told me we didn't. We didn't know if the stragglers on the loose in the woods were a danger. If they were smart, they were hightailing it as far from the encampment as they could to possible safety. There was still the chance someone might come back and decide to start the fight anew.

I went with my gut. "Tell them it's as clear as we can get it, but we've got injured, and I'm not going to lose people if I can help it."

My eyes drifted to her partner, the man holding his side as he staunched the flow of blood. He wasn't the only injured officer, but he was certainly the worst. My people had been solid and well-coordinated, and I'd never been more proud of them. They had done their jobs with the sort of efficiency and dedication I expected. The ambush on the encampment, the spotless sweep as we rounded up or incapacitated the gang, had been a sight to behold.

My thoughts drifted again, and I opened the mic on my shoulder. "Ian, how's things?"

"They're..." he stopped, forcing my heart to stutter before another voice cut across him.

"We're glorious," Ethan quipped. "I'm beat to shit, but I'm making sure he stays miserable with me while I play twenty questions with him about what's going on between him and Kyle...oh right, over."

I rolled my eyes as Ian's weary voice came back. "They're fine, Chief."

"How is he?"

"He's...well, you won't be happy, but he seems to be doing just fine."

"Alright, just don't kill him on the way back. How's our surprise guest?"

"Bitching."

"Sucks for him."

Annie frowned when the conversation stopped. "What does that mean? You won't be happy?"

I grimaced. "I'm going to go out on a limb, and guess it means Ethan isn't...in the best shape."

The whole time we'd been setting up and moving in on the encampment, I'd told myself so long as he was alive, and in one piece, I would take whatever happened. There was no doubt in my mind that they wouldn't be gentle or kind to him while they had him, and I knew they had him stowed somewhere. We'd found his car by the side of the road, but there'd been no sign of him. As terrifying as that had been, I had tried to take it as a sign that they'd taken rather than killed him. Whether or not that was a good thing was something I was going to find out very soon.

"Well," Annie said, clearing her throat. "He sounded like he was doing alright even if he is a little beat up."

"The only way he's going to show he's in terrible shape around everyone here is if he's lost a limb or is on the verge of death," I said with a grimace. "And maybe not even then."

"You know, I met your ex-wife a few times," Annie said.

"I assume there's a point you're trying to make that won't tempt me to retract all goodwill from you," I replied, arching a brow.

She grinned. "I was just going to say, you clearly have a type."

Now my brow shot up. "Excuse me?"

"Stubborn, willful, and the sort of person who'd probably get on your nerves at times," she said with a laugh, patting my elbow. "And while you brood about that, I'm going to get the EMTs here faster."

I scowled after her retreating back. "I don't brood!"

Her laughter did nothing to improve my mood as she walked off, keeping to the lit path we'd established once we were sure the fighting was over. It didn't help that I could see the logic of what she said, even if she hadn't been accurate. Ethan was not like my ex-wife, except for the few things she mentioned. The man really was stubborn, there was no question he was headstrong, and yes, he was pretty good at driving me up a wall. How I had managed to find that both amusing and a little arousing was above my pay grade, but there it was.

More importantly, there *he* was.

Emotions surged inside me as I spotted him coming into the light, his customary smirk on his face as he gazed around. On the one hand, I wanted to dart over to him as quickly as possible, relief and joy at the sight of him almost too much to bear. On the other hand, his face was bruised badly, dried blood coating one side of his jaw and down his neck. His clothes were torn, and I couldn't help but notice how he kept his hands at his side, not clenched but hidden as if he was trying to nurse them without being obvious.

Seeing him made my heart swell and ache in equal measure.

I spotted the exact moment he saw me amidst the crowd of officers. The smirk on his face slipped away in an instant, and his fingers went slack at his side. I stood there, waiting for him to make his way over, only to feel my chest tighten when he took off at a run. I didn't hesitate to step into a clear space, opening my arms before he collided with me, his arms wrapping around my neck and squeezing me hard.

"I knew you'd show up to save the day," he said with a laugh, but I didn't miss the crack in his voice.

"And I knew you were somehow going to find a way to get through this," I told him.

He pulled back, now holding onto my face as he smiled. "Your faith in me is noted and appreciated."

I reached up to take his hands off me, peering down at his fingers. My stomach turned as I saw the marks under his nails, and I felt an ache in my chest as I realized what must have happened. "Jesus, what did they do to you?"

"We can just say they aren't getting a good review from me," he said, closing his hands into gentle fists.

"Ethan," I growled. "Not the time."

He looked away. "Look, I'll give my official report tonight and deal with the emotional bullshit later, okay? I don't...not now, Trevor, please."

"Christ," I muttered, annoyed that Annie had been right. "You're so stubborn."

"Says you," he chuckled, leaning in and kissing me gently. "Have I mentioned how handsome you are when you're cranky?"

"Flattery won't help you," I told him with a scowl.

"Flattery just made some of the lines on your forehead disappear, so it's apparently helping you," he said with a small smile.

"Price, get me out of these cuffs!" I heard an annoyingly familiar voice bark from behind Ethan. "This is outrageous! First, your boyfriend attacks me, then you throw me in cuffs?"

"Is this the part where he pretends he was here on unofficial, official business?" I asked Ethan wryly as Bart was dragged into view.

"Probably," Ethan said, and I could see a glint in his eyes I hadn't seen before. "Where's Ava?"

"Here," a curt voice rose from the group of people we'd

rounded up and sat together in a huddle. "Nice to see you again, Ethan, and not any worse than I left you."

The glint stayed as Ethan turned to face the woman sitting in the middle of the group. It was obvious Ethan didn't share the sentiment, but I watched as his customary smirk slid into place, hiding all but the sharpness of his gaze.

"Shoddy workmanship will do that for you," he told her, cocking his head. "Well, that and guards who take off when they hear trouble instead of securing what could've been a valuable hostage."

"Trust me, if I had a say in the matter, he'd have a bullet in his head rather than zip ties on his wrist," Ava said mildly, glancing at one of the men at the edge of the huddle who ducked his head. "And I see you found Barty for me. Shame I can't put a bullet in his head too."

"So here's a question for you since I get a turn to ask."

"And I should answer?"

"Well, my thought is, you can answer and spite Barty, or you can not answer and spite me."

Somehow I wasn't surprised to see the woman smile at that. "Interesting. Ask your question."

"Was Barty involved in your little manufacturing ring?" Ethan asked with a saccharine smile.

Her eyes darted toward Bart, who glowered at Ethan as though he would have liked nothing more than to wrap his cuffed hands around Ethan's neck and squeeze. "Absolutely. I even kept evidence of his involvement in the entire thing. Call logs, recordings, paper trail of his financial investments and returns. Everything you're going to need to bring him down."

"Lying bitch," Bart snapped, trying to surge forward only to be grabbed and yanked back by a bored-looking Ian.

Ethan smirked again. "And this is the part where you say

you'll only hand over the information if you get to suss things out with your lawyer, right?"

"It is, surprisingly enough," she said, still looking amused. "Kind of a shame, really."

"Yes, well, that's the justice system for you," Ethan said, giving me a sidelong glance.

"No," Ava said, her voice cutting through the noise around us without raising her voice. "I meant it's a shame that someone like you isn't working for me. You could have been a fantastic addition."

"Aww, compliments from the woman who beat the shit out of me and played connect the dots with a knife on my back," Ethan said, his voice unnaturally cold. "Cute."

I turned to face the woman, jaw tightening when she caught my gaze and smiled at me. "She *what*?"

"Right," Ethan grumbled, wrapping a hand around my elbow and pulling. "C'mon, remember you're a respectable police chief who'd find themselves in deep shit if they suddenly decided to beat the hell out of an unarmed, cuffed criminal."

"Trevor!" Bart bellowed over the noise.

I turned on him, gesturing to Ian. "Get him the hell out of here. I want him tossed in a cell as far from the rest of the precinct as possible."

"And hey, if he doesn't shut up, you could always toss him in with Ava," Ethan suggested lightly, and I almost laughed as Bart's red face blanched, turning the color of curdled milk. "I'm sure she would be really good at keeping him quiet."

Just the thought of the threat being followed through stole the wind from Bart's sails, and I saw him deflate as Ian pulled him away without a word, his mismatched eyes not bothering to hide their disgust with the soon-to-be former police chief. "You know, she's right."

"Who, Ava?" Ethan asked, watching everyone secure the area as the medics arrived.

"You would have been good at something like this," I said, now thinking about it. "You're clever, you're quick, you're talented, and from the looks of Barty, not afraid to be a little...direct."

"So, you're saying I should go back and network with her?" Ethan asked, eyeing me.

"I'm not going to answer that," I said with a roll of my eyes.

His arm looped through mine. "Good. Because I vowed only to use my powers for the forces of good, and I don't want to have to change moral stances so late in life."

"How does driving everyone around you crazy count as good?"

"Good for their egos, and makes sure they don't take things too seriously."

"Yeah, I'm not sure that's how that works."

Once we were at the edge of the clearing, he turned to me, expression serious. "Bri, Colin?"

"Completely safe," I said. "Both are being kept under watch by Bennett at the station."

"Good," he said, his shoulders sagging. "I was...well, I was worried as hell when I realized they knew who I was and wanted to get their hands on me."

"*You* were worried?" I asked in disbelief. "Do you have any idea how much the rest of us were worried?"

"Oh, I'm sure I'm going to hear all about how worried you and Bri were for days and days and days," he said, sounding almost delighted at the prospect. "But I'm getting the side eye from Kyle over there, which probably means he wants to check me out."

"Your wounds," Kyle called, clearly having heard him.

"Good," Ethan said with a grin. "Because I'm taken, and

I'm far more interested in taking advantage of your sympathy and professionalism to probe into your private life."

"I have sedatives, and I'm not afraid to use them."

"Oooh, somnophilia, that's kinky. Did Ian get you into that or is this something new?"

"Christ," Kyle muttered as he pointed at a stump. "Sit."

"I'll get someone over to take your statement," I told him. "That way, we can wrap this up as soon as possible for you."

Ethan's eyes lingered on me as he smiled softly. "Sure, just...don't stray too far."

"I'm not letting you out of my sight for a long time," I told him, reluctantly pulling away to do my job. I still had plenty to do, but I knew better than to try to send Ethan away. That was alright, though. We would have plenty of time with each other later.

* * *

I LAY in the comfort of my own bed, watching Ethan's face as he softly snored into the pillow, pressed so hard against it I could already picture the lines his face would have when he finally moved. His steady breathing and peaceful expression helped ease the tension that had been sitting inside me since his kidnapping. Despite the pressure in my bladder, I couldn't bring myself to leave the bed, some part of my mind unable to shake the feeling that he might disappear if I took my eyes off him.

It had been one thing last night not to watch him like a hawk when we were surrounded by officers. At one point, after refusing to go to the hospital and be poked and prodded all night, he had settled by a tree and eventually dozed off. Annie and I made sure there was always someone near him while he slept, though, keeping a close eye on him until dawn when things finally settled enough for me to take him home.

Not that his sister hadn't volunteered to take him, but Ethan had point blank refused, telling his half-panicked sister over the phone that he was safe, he was fine, and he was protected by all the cops. If she thought she'd have better luck convincing me to convince him, she'd been both disappointed and furious. I hadn't even tried to persuade him but simply taken the phone away though I knew he was watching me like a hawk.

"Look," I'd told her, speaking quietly while still keeping an eye on Ethan. "He's not going to come with you. He's not in the best shape."

"What happened?" she hissed.

"He'll have to tell you that...when he's ready."

"Fucking...is this his pride? Or is he worried about me again?"

"Both, I think," I told her. "You won't be happy when you see him. And it's probably best you don't see him right now."

"So, what, he's just going to hide while he heals?"

"No, but he'll probably be in a better mental state to deal with everything after getting some rest and calming down. Look, I'll message you tomorrow and keep you updated. Then you two can decide when you'll see one another."

"I hate this," she said, sounding more miserable than I'd ever heard.

"I'm sorry," I told her.

"Yeah, well, I suppose I should just be glad he has someone he doesn't feel he has to be strong around all the time and someone else who worries about him."

"You can be both upset and happy about that."

"Thanks, I will."

Her last comment left me with a surprised chuckle, but she dropped the call before I could respond. True to my promise, I messaged her when we headed back to my house, then let her know he had stumbled into a shower and crawled into bed. I wasn't surprised when she messaged back both times almost instantly, apparently sleeping as poorly as I did. While Ethan managed to curl up in bed and sleep until almost two in the afternoon, I'd been dipping in and out of sleep from the moment we laid down.

I watched his face scrunch up, fingers curling into a ball against the comforter as he groaned softly. The sound made my stomach clench as he pulled his fist closer, yanking the blanket with him.

"Hey," I said softly, having expected something like this much sooner as I ran a gentle hand down his face. "You're safe now, Ethan. You're at home with me."

A shudder ran through him, and I watched his face slowly relax, his scrunched-up eyes fluttering open. The peace lasted for only a moment before Ethan's body went wire tight, jerking back from my touch and beginning to scramble at the bed.

I didn't move. I simply watched him as he darted his eyes around. "Ethan. It's Trevor."

Everything about him was coiled and ready to strike or spring away, but he stopped moving. There was clear confusion in his eyes, but I didn't see any fogginess to signify he wasn't mentally in the moment, just simply confused between his dream and reality.

His eyes snapped up to mine, and the confusion cleared. "Jesus, Trevor, were you watching me sleep? That's creepy."

I let out the breath I'd been holding. Of course, that was the first thing he'd say. "I guess I can skip the part where I find out if you're still living your nightmare moment."

"I'm subtle like that," he said, now yawning as he stretched and pushed himself upright.

"Do you...want to talk about it?" I asked him gently.

His stretch stopped midway as he winced, clearly reminded of the crisscross marks on his back. A few of them had opened up again in the middle of the night. "I don't need to be babied, Trevor."

"I'm not asking if you need to be babied. I'm asking if you need to get your feelings out and feel taken care of," I told him, pushing myself out of bed to get the first aid kit. "There's a difference."

"Give me a little shake of that bare ass as you leave, and I'll feel plenty taken care of," he called after me.

With any ordinary person, I would have taken the comment as a sign they were feeling better. With Ethan, however, it was probably a sign he was retreating into himself instead.

"You can ogle me later," I told him when I returned with the kit. "For now, you need to show me your back so I can clean it up a bit."

"Kyle said the cuts weren't that deep," he said, and I'd swear he was a moment away from pouting.

"And I'm going to make sure they stay clean," I told him firmly.

His eyes rolled up as if praying for patience. "Fine. Fussy."

I would accept that assessment as I began to fuss over the wounds, wiping them down with the disinfectant wipes. "Better than you finding yourself with a nasty infection."

"That *would* put a crimp in my sense of victory over last night," he muttered, his hands resting on his knees.

"And we can't have that."

"Exactly, you learn fast."

I continued wiping him down in the unusual silence that followed. It wasn't until Ethan stirred restlessly that I realized he was deep in his own thoughts.

"It's not the first time this has happened," he said quietly.

"What's that?"

"Being kidnapped and, uh, interrogated. First time involving knives and fingernails, but yeah."

I couldn't say I was surprised, but hearing it still stung. "How did you get away that time?"

He snorted. "The funny thing about vicious people is that their viciousness isn't reserved for everyone outside the group. There was a fire and a coup on the second night I was locked up. Basically, so much chaos they didn't realize I was gone until a few days later, if they didn't think I was dead."

"Just how many lives do you have?" I asked softly.

"After last night? I'm not sure, two? Or maybe that was the last one," he said with a shrug.

"I know you want this to be a joke, but I was scared shit-less last night," I told him quietly. "All I kept thinking was, 'What if that phone call is the last time I hear from him? What if we never got to say all the things we needed to say?' I've already gone through that once, Ethan."

He didn't move. His head tilted down to stare at his lap. "I-I hadn't thought of it that way. I guess I was always just putting it off, telling myself it was something we could talk about when there was more time, when there wasn't a bunch of shit to distract us."

"Do I really need to point out that someone in your line of work should know better than to think that tomorrow or later is ever guaranteed?" I asked him.

He finally picked his head up, peering over his shoulder at me. "No. You're right. I should know better. I've just...I've never had someone in my life that fits where you do, Trevor. Most people don't bother to look too closely at me, and I know I don't encourage it. But you've stuck around. You've tried to get in, you've tried to figure things out about me. Sure, sometimes you get frustrated, but you've never been fed up with me or just given up, thinking you're the problem. I don't know what to do with that."

I reached out, laying my hand on his bare waist and squeezing gently. "You figure out if that's something you want in your life. All the things in your life that you've faced with minimal fear or hesitation, you don't have to change that just because this is scary."

"It *does* feel weird to find something like this scary," he said with a chuckle, leaning back into my touch. "And all of it went away completely when I was on the phone with you. I remember going through a lot of scary shit, moments where I was almost sure that was the end, and fucked up as it sounds, I always managed to find something in those moments. Some piece of myself, or some truth about my life."

"Sometimes facing your own death ends up with you facing your own life," I said softly, more than familiar with the feeling.

"Okay, so I completely agree, but I want you to know I'm totally stealing that for my next piece of writing," he said with a chuckle.

I snorted. "I see your priorities are straight."

"Nothing about me is straight."

"And I thank God for that every day."

He laughed, finally giving in and scooting forward so he could fall back and rest his head on my lap. There was a softness in his expression I wasn't used to seeing, and I couldn't help but reach down and run my fingers through his hair.

"Do you know what was running through my head as I talked to you on the phone?" he asked me quietly after a few minutes silence.

"What?" I asked, desperate for the answer.

"I realized just how much I wanted to be here, doing what I'm doing now, with you. All the sex, as fantastic as it is, couldn't compare to the feeling of wanting to just lay down in bed with you. Or curl up on the couch and watch crappy shows I don't care about. Hearing you grumble from the other side of the house because I'm giving you shit or watching you smirk at me as I sing while I'm cleaning," he said, his eyes never wavering from my face. "And now that I'm here, I'm not sure if this is what love feels like or if this is just the beginning. Either way, this is what I want from you, from us."

"It's always been here for you," I said, giving his hair a light tug and smiling at him. "And I won't speak for you, but I know I started loving you before you went and got kidnapped."

He groaned. "God, you have the worst taste in men."

"I disagree," I said with a chuckle. "Because now I'm in love with one of the most intelligent, life-loving, capable, frustrating people on the planet. And even if he hasn't quite got there yet, I'm glad I have him here with me...and in one piece."

He closed his eyes. "This is the part where I say I'm sorry for being an idiot and scaring you."

"You can," I said slowly. "But...I also put you on this path with the investigation. We both knew there was danger involved in you doing this, and I can't exactly yell at you for doing your job. I could have taken you off the job at any time, but I didn't. Not just because I knew you could do a lot to solve the problem but because I had faith in your abilities to care for yourself."

"He says to the man who needed rescuing," Ethan chuckled.

"Don't think I didn't read over your statement," I said, giving his hair a sharper tug to make sure he was paying attention. "By all accounts, you wouldn't have needed too much rescuing. You were able to get out of that situation on your own."

"Through a lot of luck."

"Luck wouldn't have mattered for shit if it wasn't for the skills you have."

His eyes searched my face. "Why are you suddenly trying to be my hype man?"

"Why are you suddenly trying to be your biggest critic?" I asked wryly.

"Oh, good, he thinks he's being witty," Ethan muttered, and I had to laugh at his unusual display of grumpiness.

I bent forward, kissing his forehead. "You're a clever, intelligent, capable man, and I'm glad you're alright. And I'm glad to find out that you probably love me in return."

"I'm still working that part out," he told me with a smile.

"I'm in no rush," I told him softly.

"Yeah, neither am I. Except for when we can get to the part where you make me food because, holy shit, I'm starving," he said, eyes going wide.

"Is this supposed to be a pleading face?" I asked, gesturing at his expression.

"This is the face of a man hoping his boyfriend will take pity on him and get some delicious food whipped up so he can stop feeling like he's going to wither away to nothing," Ethan said.

"Fine, but you're going to have to get off me for me to do that."

"Shit, I forgot about that little detail."

"We've got time aplenty for more later," I told him, pleased he was so intent on continuing to lay with me.

"Fine," He sighed heavily, pushing himself upright, "and maybe if you make something really good, I might even sex you up afterward."

"I have this feeling you'd sex me up if I continued to walk around the house naked, even without making you a nice breakfast."

The words had no sooner left my mouth than Ethan

turned, eyes widening. "Oh, you've never done that before. Please tell me you'll do that now."

"Fine, but you aren't getting any bacon," I said.

"Pfft, wear an apron."

"Get out of this bed," I told him with a shove.

His feet hit the ground before he fell, and he got up with a laugh. Despite the ugly lines on his back and the bruises on his face, I couldn't help but admire the sight of him, completely naked and lit by the sunlight leaking through the curtains. I wondered how many of the marks on his back would scar and if, in a couple of years, I'd be able to gently trace the lines and remember the terror but mostly the warmth.

"You know, I can feel you fucking me with your eyes," he said with a snort.

"I'll be using more than my eyes," I growled.

"No!" he yelped, backing up as I leaned forward. I watched him inch around the bed, holding a hand out. "Absolutely not. You get me food first. I haven't eaten since yesterday morning, damn it."

"Oh, suddenly there are rules and stipulations," I said, still watching him closely.

"Yes, empty belly, need food."

"Other things can be filled."

That made him laugh, and he slipped out into the hallway. "Food first!"

I was dead serious about getting a little more hands-on with him in the near future, but more importantly, he had the chance to feel less serious. If there was one thing I'd learned about Ethan, it was that he couldn't maintain a serious emotional conversation for too long without withdrawing for long periods. At the very least, I could say I had him with me now and that, by all accounts, he didn't plan on going anywhere anytime soon.

Which reminded me.

"Ethan?" I called as I stood up.

"What's up?" his voice echoed, signaling he was in the bathroom.

"What exactly are you going to do now?" I asked, waiting until I heard the toilet flush before slipping into the bathroom to take my turn.

"I'm guessing you don't mean right now or today because I plan to become like a cat and find a comfortable place to spread out in the sun after eating," he said as he passed.

"Well, no, I meant in the future. We can officially close our contract, which doesn't leave you much to do."

"I hope you're not about to start wondering if the end of the contract means the end of us."

"No," I chuckled, flushing and washing my hands. "Though I'd be pretty pissed at you if you decided to end things when they're just starting to get good."

"Just?" he asked, peeking into the bathroom to arch a brow at me.

I snorted, sneaking a kiss. "Don't evade the question."

He watched me thoughtfully as I walked past into the kitchen, going through the supplies to pick out what to make. I could practically hear the wheels in his head spinning furiously as he considered my question and mulled it over. By the time I had the batter mixed and the pans heated, I could sense he was nearing a solution.

"I think...honestly, this whole adventure would be a good thing to write about. It's shown up how bad drugs have become, especially meth. It would be something new for me since I normally do international things. Wouldn't hurt to draw attention to a big problem in my own country that doesn't get as much attention as it could," he said while I dropped the sausage patties into one of the pans.

I glanced at him. "Would it be good, talking about something that's so...I don't know, raw?"

"Worried about my feelings again?"

"Concerned about you in general, you'd better get used to it."

My frown immediately became a soft smile when he came up behind me, wrapping his arms around my waist and kissing the back of my neck. "Fine, I'll stop being an asshole for a while."

"He says while intentionally buttering me up."

"Apologizing without words."

I glanced over my shoulder, my smirk disappearing when I saw him staring at me intently, clearly not trying to hide his words behind a joke. After a moment, I nodded to let him know I understood and tried to pour some of the batter into a buttered pan without dislodging him.

"Plus," he said softly after a few minutes, "this wouldn't be the first time I wrote about something so fresh in my mind. It's my way of dealing with things, processing them. Some people talk it out with others, but I prefer to just...write it. Get it all out on the page and let others clean up the mess afterward. There's something purifying about it. Doesn't make the memories or the dreams go away, but at least it doesn't feel like I'm haunted in everyday life anymore."

The explanation made sense, and I could find no fault in it. "That doesn't normally take you long, does it? The writing."

His chuckle was warm on my neck. "Worried I'm going to disappear in a week or two?"

I scooped the patties out and the first few pancakes, adding more batter. "I'm not worried about that. I've known from the start of things growing serious that even if we stayed together, you wouldn't remain in Fairlake forever. You've still got plenty out there to write about, and I'm sure you'll go off on your own to find those things and report on them. And I don't intend to stop you from doing that."

"Okay," he said slowly, and if I was reading his tone right, he was surprised. "Then what are you trying to do?"

"I'm trying to get a feel for your plans," I told him with a shrug. "I don't want to be left in the dark."

"Oh."

"Is that a problem?"

I felt his forehead rest against my neck as he shook his head. "No, not a problem. How about this? I promise I won't leave you in the dark. If I get an idea or inspiration, I'll talk to you about it. You can talk about whatever issues you're having, or we can just...talk. We'll set up, like, times for me to take breaks and come back here to see you while I'm out and about. And I'll make sure to spend plenty of time here between jobs."

I slipped the rest of the food onto plates, turned off the stove, and faced him. "Are you sure? That's a big adjustment for you."

He rolled his eyes. "Trevor. I just got done telling you how much I wished I'd spent more time with you and admitted how I felt, all that crap. Do you really think that doesn't translate to the rest of my life too? I know it's a big adjustment, and I know it means changes galore, some neither of us can anticipate right now, but that doesn't mean I'm not prepared to deal with that. As cheesy as it sounds in my head right now, I got a good idea of how important the things I was putting off were when I saw my life could end with two bullets to the back of the head."

I grimaced at the thought. "That's nice."

"And don't I know it?" he replied grimly. "What I'm trying to say here is I'm prepared to deal with whatever changes need to be made. Being here, in Fairlake, getting to experience what it's like to have family and friends I enjoy being around. To have someone like you in my life, who appreciates what I do, respects what I'm capable of, likes who I am even when I'm a pain, and is a fantastic lay, might I add. Why wouldn't I want this?"

"Of course, your assessment of my bedroom skills came into consideration."

"Hey, you can love a person all you want, but I bet you get real antsy in bed if you're staring at the ceiling and wondering when they're going to get things over with."

"Pretty sure you just described the last few years of my marriage."

"Which is so so tragic, but on the upside, now you have me."

"I'm still waiting on the upside."

Ethan grinned, reaching up to grab my face. "Look, we're officially together now, alright? None of that faking it for the crowd shit. I have officially learned what it's like to love and be loved, to have family, friends, and community. And it's all this town's fault, and yours. So I'm saying I'm in this completely, all the way. It won't always be smooth, as the past twenty-four hours have taught us, but that doesn't mean I don't think it's worth trying."

I wound my arms around his waist, drawing him closer. At that moment, I didn't care that we were completely naked. All that mattered to me were the words he was saying and the earnest, heated look in his eyes to back them up. In some ways, it was easy to love someone you were terrified was dead, but here he was, living and breathing, and I loved him even more than I had when I wondered if I'd find his body in a hole somewhere. This remarkable man who had managed to worm his way into my life and my heart, and to think it all started with me wondering what kind of disaster he would bring to my town.

Instead, he had brought light and vigor to my life that I

hadn't realized was missing. I had quietly resigned myself to losing it one day when he finally went back out into the world to do the one thing he had passion and drive for, and now I got the chance to have it for as long as possible.

It was an easy choice.

"Alright," I said, kissing him gently. "Then let's do this."

"Agreed," he said softly, deepening the kiss. It was just enough that I could feel our bodies stirring in response to our proximity and the heat of passion. And to think, there was no longer a time limit, no longer a desperate need to squeeze what time I could into these little moments. I could have him all to myself, wasting as much time as possible while savoring it as much as possible. Nothing could stop us now. Nothing was in our—

A ferocious set of knocks echoed through the house, startling both of us. Ethan jerked back, his head snapping toward the front of the house where the sound had come from.

"Ethan!" a familiar, angry voice boomed into the house. "Ethan, I swear to *God,* if you don't open this door, I will happily make sure I become an only child!"

"Aww hell," Ethan groaned.

"Shit, I was supposed to keep her updated on your condition," I said with a grimace. "I forgot to text her again."

"And if we don't do something, she's going to break down that door faster than a SWAT team could dream of," Ethan said as Bri continued pounding on the door.

"I'm really sorry about this, Chief Price!" another voice called.

"I'm not," laughed a third. "This is hilarious."

I stared. "Is that Adam and Bennett too?"

"Adam to try to contain Bri as best he can, and Bennett to watch the carnage," Ethan said with a heavy sigh. "Alright, we need to get dressed. Me completely. You in a pair of pants at least. Think you can distract her long enough for me to get covered up?"

"Are you using me as a human shield?"

"Temporarily. Hey, just think of this as part of the price you have to pay to have me in your life."

I gave him a small smile, stealing another kiss. "Fine, but let's be quick before she ruins my door."

"Ethan!"

"Right," he grunted, darting away.

I took a moment to eye his bare ass before following him, hearing Bri get even louder, fueled by frustration and concern. This would probably be one hell of a long afternoon as we tried to talk Bri off the ledge, and I wasn't going to get the private time I was hoping for with Ethan.

But he would be there, and that would be enough.

EPILOGUE

Two Years Later

With a grunt, I heaved the last box onto the pile next to the empty stall. The July sun was beating down on my...everything, and I was drenched in sweat from head to toe. Whatever madness had overtaken me and compelled me to offer to help set up for the Fourth of July celebration had passed, and now I was wondering what was wrong with me to have made the offer in the first place.

The illustrious mayor himself arrived, looking completely clean of any sweat, and clapped me on the shoulder. "Well, that's looking good. Why don't you take yourself a break? You've earned one."

"Yeah," I grunted. "Thanks, Fred."

I watched him go, a little begrudging as he walked over to one of the people setting up another booth, not bothering to help in the slightest except to joke and laugh. Apparently, 'helping' in the mayor's world only involved poking around while others did most of the work. If it wasn't for the fact that he seemed above board and not corrupt, I might have been tempted to add him to the ever-growing list of politicians I despised. But no, he just had to be averse to hard work rather than crooked.

I had checked.

"Thank you," a soft voice from behind the boxes piped up, forcing me to peer around them.

"Oh, hey, Grant," I said, watching as he opened another box, and pulled things out. "This your stall?"

"Yes," he said, giving me a small smile. "I like watching people in town enjoy my work a lot more than the people on the internet."

"This from the man dating the brother of one of the most famous actresses in the country," I noted wryly.

"Yes, but if Tomas wasn't fond of the peace and quiet as well, he probably wouldn't come here as often as he does," Grant said with that same small smile. "And from what I have been told, you aren't all that different."

"You know, once upon a time, I'd have said you were crazy if you tried to tell me I'd end up in some podunk town, trying to live a quiet life," I said, peering up through the trees toward a fluffy cloud that looked like a squished rabbit. "Yet here I am."

"When you're here."

"I could say the same about your man."

"Yes. Both of you leave because you have things outside Fairlake that you love, but you always come back here because it's home."

Startled, I gave a little laugh. "Have you been getting into the beers early?"

For some reason, his cheeks colored as he bent to dig through the box. "I don't drink very often, so no."

"Why do I sense a story?" I asked aloud.

"Because you want there to be a story," he said simply.

It was hard to argue with that, and I decided to leave him be when I saw Devin and Chase approaching, both carrying more boxes. Undoubtedly, they were here to help Grant set up. More accurately, Devin was here to help and had dragged Chase along because the man didn't know the meaning of the word 'no' when it came to Devin. Considering how abrasive the guy could be with everyone around him, I figured it was probably good to have someone who Chase became a giant puddle of pudding around.

"Devin, Chase," I greeted as I passed. "You're looking particularly twinky today, Devin."

"Thanks," Devin said with a chuckle as Chase growled at me. "Hey! I'm officially past the age of being a twink. Let someone call me that."

"I'll call you that then," Chase grumbled, probably unaware I could hear him.

Knowing I'd probably just earned Devin plenty of attention from Chase today, I continued on my way over to where the food for the event was being unloaded. I was alarmed when I saw Bennett in the thick of things but let my shoulders slump in relief when I spotted Isaiah in the crowd as well. I had no idea where their other halves were, but Adam was terrible at keeping Bennett on a leash. In contrast, the friendly but hardheaded Isaiah was perfect for the job...and very enthusiastic about it too.

"Keeping the ship running tight?" I asked Isaiah as I approached. "Or need more help?"

"We're pretty well set here," he said, gesturing someone toward a cooler full of bags of ice. "If you're looking for your sister, she's over with Ira, setting up the stuff for the precinct."

"I've been avoiding going over there, if I'm honest," I said with a chuckle.

"Just because you can't talk your sister out of giving you more work doesn't mean you can avoid her forever."

"More like I know if I go over there, I'm going to end up distracted."

Isaiah rolled his eyes. "Look, if I can manage not to be distracted by Julian, you can manage not to be distracted because Chief Price is hovering around, trying to pretend he knows what he's doing."

"Why, what's Julian doing?" I asked, only for Isaiah to point and force me to follow his directions. "Ah...oh, yes...well, that is—"

Completely unaware of what he looked like, Julian had taken his shirt off while lugging around pieces of what would become the stage. I had no idea how the man managed to get as big as he was, but it was clear he wasn't shy about using his strength when it called for it. His muscles had muscles, and I'd be surprised if there was more than an ounce of fat on his sweat-covered body.

"Exactly," Isaiah said, trying for nonchalance, but I could hear the slight waver in his voice. Apparently, he'd been working hard to keep his attention locked on the work, but I had inadvertently drawn his attention back to his fiancé, who looked like he belonged on a men's fitness cover.

"Well, since you're already distracted, I'm going to go see what kind of distraction I can find," I told him, clapping him on the shoulder and walking away before he could consider what to hit me with. Honestly, it was enough to hear him cursing under his breath as I walked away.

From the looks of things, everything would be ready for the grand celebration tomorrow. It was bound to bring in even more crowds and money for the people running the stalls. Fairlake had seen a boom in revenue and attention in the past couple of years, thanks to the 'commendable and decisive action of Fairlake's police force.' The bust of the meth manufacturers had brought a shit ton of attention down on Fairlake and in the best way possible.

Incidentally, good publicity for the police force and the city meant they got more money from the state. Turns out the great state of Colorado was more than happy to talk about its meth problem so long as it was in a good light. I could still see Trevor's annoyed expression before he'd been pulled in front of the cameras to blather on about the duty of the force and its representative's obligations to its people. Both comments had gone over well with the public, but the second one had ground a few nerves from politicians.

And because of that, Trevor *so* got laid that night.

My mental meandering halted immediately when a small weight jettisoned itself into my thigh with the force of an over-excited goat. I caught myself, instinctively bending down to catch Colin before he slammed into the ground with his enthusiasm.

"Unca Etan! Mommy said calm down!" he piped up at me.

"I'm pretty sure she was talking to you, buddy, not me," I chuckled, ruffling his hair. "What were you doing?"

"I foun' a bug, I showed her, an' then, an' then, I foun' another bug," he babbled, gesturing wildly with his hands. It wasn't like him to be so wound up, he'd grown into a reserved personality like his father, but he still had the odd moments where that almost four-year-old energy came bursting to the surface, ready to sweep the rest of us off our feet. "Daddy said, said it was neat."

"Somehow, I feel Mommy didn't quite agree with that sentiment," I said, picking him up before he could take off again.

"She said calm down," he repeated, now peering into the front pocket of his overalls. "See?"

"That's...a very impressive spider," I told him, grimacing as I took it from him and set it on the nearest tree. Bri had once made the mistake of killing a spider in front of Colin, and it had taken almost twenty minutes to calm the hysterics. We all learned her hard lesson after that. "But we told you not to pick them up. They need to be left alone."

"Look. No touch!"

"Exactly."

"Unca Etan?"

"Yes?"

"Can I get bider?"

I sighed. He had already forgotten the conversation we'd just had. This was typical when he was in one of his tears, unable to be reasoned with, only diverted. "Let's see if your dad has any of those poppers you can throw at the ground."

"Pop, pop, pop!" he shrieked in my ear, forcing me to lean away with a wince.

"Yes, those," I said, jiggling him further up my arm. I had no idea how the kid managed to get so heavy every time I saw him, but like most children, he decided he was going to grow and keep doing it.

Seeing him again after my last stint, this time in South Africa, had been a shock. I'd only been gone four months, the longest I'd been out of the country since I'd first arrived in Fairlake, but I'd sworn Bri had traded out for a different kid. Sure, it looked like him, but Colin had been quieter and grown like a weed. Bri informed me that, yes, children continue to grow even when you go off to another continent to report on a bloody civil war and that Colin's personality had been slowly revealing itself more and more while I was away.

"Daddy!" Colin bellowed in my ear. "Pop, pop!"

Adam peered out from the truck to give me a doubtful look. "This your doing?"

"It was either that or let him stay focused on bothering the local, uh, critter population," I told him with a shrug.

"Alright," he said with a sigh, pushing a crate into view. "Then take this to Bri. She's currently in the middle of an organizational frenzy, and if this doesn't show up in the next minute, she might send out a search party."

"You take this then," I said, shifting Colin around to hold him out.

"Hey there!" Adam said, immediately brightening when Colin faced him. "Poppers, huh?"

"Pop!" Colin replied. "Daddy, I wanna pop pop."

"Then we'll pop pop," Adam said, talking to him as they walked toward the road to throw the paper-wrapped bundles of gunpowder at the ground.

For my part, I grabbed the crate and walked over to where I'd last seen my sister. Her hair was pulled back, and there was a look of intense concentration on her face as she looked over everything. Ira was sitting in a lawn chair beside her with a book, clearly immune to my sister's mood and not bothered by her lack of assistance. Best yet, Trevor stood off to the side, his arms crossed over his chest and waiting patiently for orders.

"My my," I said, dropping the crate near my sister and walking over to Trevor. "Someone's looking devilishly good today."

"You know buttering me up isn't going to save you from your sister, right?" he asked me wryly.

"Stop being a spoilsport," I said with a laugh, leaning closer. "I had to get up bright and early, leaving you alone in bed. Do you have any idea how hard that is to do?"

Bri's annoyed voice interrupted before Trevor could answer. "I'm letting you have a moment together before you get back to work *only* because you've been back for a few days. Don't push it by being dirty around me. I've already had to yell at someone about that once today, and I'm not patient enough to do it nicely a second time."

I raised a questioning brow at Trevor, who chuckled. "Someone found Ian and Kyle making out like teenagers in the trees earlier. She wasn't very happy."

"They're so fucking cute...and horny," I chuckled. "Come on. I want to get something to drink before the taskmaster starts cracking her whip at me again."

"I heard that!" she barked, but I noticed how her eyes lingered on me as I led Trevor away.

"She's still watching to see if anything's wrong with me," I chuckled. "She's as bad as me about showing her emotions sometimes."

"She's not as bad," Trevor said, laughing when I gave him a push. "And you can blame her? And she's not the one who got to see the giant bruise on your back."

"It's a half-healed bruise," I corrected comfortably.

His sigh was quiet, but I sensed the words unspoken, reminding me I couldn't just dismiss his obvious show of concern. He'd been good enough not to press me on it when I'd shown up, so now it was my turn to do right by him.

I gently pulled him into an outcropping. "I need you to know I'm okay."

"I know that," he said, glancing around to be sure we were alone. "Now. But sometimes it's hard to tell the difference between you saying you're okay and you *just* saying you're okay."

"I know," I said softly, reaching to take his hands. "I also realized I was an ass for blowing you off about it. So, I'm sorry about that. I should have been more open. It *really* was worse than it looked. I fell out of a hiding spot. Thankfully, I was safe, but my foot got caught when I was trying to get out, and I tumbled down an incline. I just happened to land on a particularly hard rock, and yes, I made sure to get looked at by professionals while I was down there to make sure it was just bruising."

It was something I might not have done a few years before, but now I had a reason to make sure I didn't accidentally puncture an organ or screw up my back completely. Even if I was dead set on still going to dangerous places to get information, I wanted to do everything I could to ensure I got home healthy and alive, which meant, yes, taking fewer risks, being smarter about the choices I made, and trying not to stay in one place too long even if it was to the detriment of my investigation.

"I didn't want you to worry," I admitted to him with a grimace. "Because you'd have to hear I was hiding, then you'd wanna know what I was hiding from, and then it'd be a whole thing of you worrying."

"As if I'm not worrying the whole time you're gone," he said with a smile, taking hold of my elbow and pulling me in. "I started worrying early on, and I will keep worrying. Worse is not knowing exactly what happened. I can deal if you tell me."

"I know," I said, annoyed with myself. This wasn't the first time we'd had this conversation, and I'd grown better at talking more, but old habits sometimes refused to die. "Can I make up for it by telling you the story at home later?"

"Does it have as good an ending as our first semi-shared adventure?"

"It does not," I admitted with a laugh. "Because it doesn't end with the arrest of a formerly presumed dead heiress."

Because, of course, something I was involved in couldn't have been a simple matter of corruption and greed. Sure, it was interesting enough to see Fovel's police chief get busted on so many charges that his grandchildren would be old by the time his sentence was fulfilled. There had been more than enough evidence to bring him down, and I don't think I'd ever seen Trevor smug until the day we sat in on the sentencing and watched Barty Durkins break down in tears at the multiple guilty verdicts.

But no, it had to be the revelation that 'Ava' was, in fact, Aveline Ender, a cousin of our very own Isaiah Ender. Turned out she'd been 'kidnapped' and presumed dead after years of being missing. When in fact, she'd run off with an old boyfriend and found herself willingly diving into the underbelly of drug manufacturing and selling. I had no idea what the whole story was, but considering she'd agreed to an interview, if I did it, I would get it one of these days and soon.

"That's alright," he said, finally giving in and kissing me. "You can tell me over a couple of beers."

"Or I can tell you while we're in bed, naked," I suggested.

"How have you not tired of being a horn dog with me?" he asked with a laugh, but the twinkle in his eye told me he wasn't complaining.

It was a good question and spoke to one of the worries I'd always had about long-term relationships. It turned out that when you found the right person, sure, the sex dialed back a bit, but you never grew tired of them. I could see him naked a million times and would always find myself staring at him, a twinge of longing in my gut. The gray in his hair was finally winning the war, but honestly, I loved running my hands through it, watching the color shift as it fell back atop his head.

Just like I'd come to love many things I once thought would lose their luster. It was all well and good to let the ache and loneliness of being apart for weeks take over, turning us into teenagers for a week or so afterward. But it was the moments other than the hot and heavy that stuck with me. My head in his lap while he watched TV and I read, drinking beers together on the back porch while we watched the sunset and grumbled about mosquitos, and watching him smile softly at me whenever we went somewhere together, and he let me be my social self.

They were little moments, just specks of time, but they were bright against the backdrop of my life. I had never realized just how much could be added to my life by having someone like Trevor with me. I had always wanted someone who understood and accepted me, and now I had it. Sometimes I forgot that and slipped into old habits, but in the end, he always managed to pull me back down to the earth, where things were warm and safe with him around.

Yeah, I was a sappy bowl of pudding when it came to him.

"Ready to go back and face the dragon lady with me?" I asked, holding out my hand.

"You know I am," he said, squeezing my hand and holding me close as we walked.

I would take being pudding any day.